MOLIÈRE was the stage name of Jean Baptiste Poquelin, the son of a wealthy merchant upholsterer. He was born in Paris in 1622. At the age of twenty-one he resigned the office at Court purchased for him by his father and threw in his lot with a company of actors to found the so-styled 'Illustre Théâtre'. The nucleus of the company was drawn from one family, the Béjarts. Armande, the youngest daughter, was to become his wife.

Failing to establish themselves in Paris, the company took to the provinces for twelve years. When they returned to the capital it was with Molière as their leader and a number of the farces he had devised as their stock in trade. Invited to perform before Louis XIV, Molière secured the King's staunch patronage. In 1659 *Les Précieuses ridicules* achieved a great success, which was confirmed by *L'École des femmes* three years later. With *Tartuffe*, however, Molière encountered trouble; it outraged contemporary religious opinion and was forbidden public performance for several years. *Don Juan* also had a controversial history. *Le Misanthrope*, first played in 1666, is generally considered to be the peak of Molière's achievement. Among the plays that followed were *L'Avare*, *Le Médecin malgré lui*, *Les Femmes savantes*, *Amphitryon* and *Le Bourgeois Gentilhomme*, one of the comedy-ballets to which Lully contributed the music.

By 1665 the company had become 'la troupe du Roi', playing at the Palais Royal. While taking the part of Argan in *Le Malade imaginaire* on 17 February 1673, Molière was taken ill, and he died the same evening. The troupe survived, however, to become one of the forerunners of the Comedie-Française.

JOHN WOOD was born in 1900 and studied at Manchester University. After some years in teaching and adult education he spent his working life in educational administration. Enthusiasm for the arts in education led to his involvement with the theatre and particularly, as a producer and translator, with the work of Molière. He also translated Beaumarchais's *The Barber of Seville* and *The Marriage of Figaro* for Penguin Classics.

DAVID COWARD is Professor of Modern French Literature in the University of Leeds. He has written widely on the literature of France since 1700 and is the translator of tales by Sade and Maupassant, of *La Dame aux Camélias* by Dumas *fils* and of Albert Cohen's *Belle de Seigneur* (Penguin, 1997). A regular contributor to *The Times Literary Supplement*, he is currently writing a history of French literature.

MOLIÈRE

The Misanthrope and Other Plays

Such Foolish Affected Ladies
Tartuffe
The Misanthrope
The Doctor Despite Himself
The Would-Be Gentleman
Those Learned Ladies

Translated by JOHN WOOD *and* DAVID COWARD,
with an introduction and notes by DAVID COWARD

PENGUIN BOOKS

PENGUIN BOOKS

Published by the Penguin Group
Penguin Books Ltd, 80 Strand, London WC2R 0RL, England
Penguin Putnam Inc., 375 Hudson Street, New York, New York 10014, USA
Penguin Books Australia Ltd, 250 Camberwell Road, Camberwell, Victoria 3124, Australia
Penguin Books Canada Ltd, 10 Alcorn Avenue, Toronto, Ontario, Canada M4V 3B2
Penguin Books India (P) Ltd, 11 Community Centre, Panchsheel Park, New Delhi – 110 017, India
Penguin Books (NZ) Ltd, Cnr Rosedale and Airborne Roads, Albany, Auckland, New Zealand
Penguin Books (South Africa) (Pty) Ltd, 24 Sturdee Avenue, Rosebank 2196, South Africa

Penguin Books Ltd, Registered Offices: 80 Strand, London WC2R 0RL, England

www.penguin.com

Published in Penguin Books 2000

8

Tartuffe, *The Misanthrope*, *The Doctor Despite Himself* and *The Would-Be Gentleman*
translation copyright © John Wood, 1959
Introduction and text revisions of the above copyright © David Coward, 2000
Such Foolish Affected Ladies and *Those Learned Ladies* translation
copyright © David Coward, 2000

Set in 10.5/12 pt Monotype Fournier
Typeset by Rowland Phototypesetting Ltd, Bury St Edmunds, Suffolk
Printed in England by Clays Ltd, St Ives plc

The terms for the amateur or professional performance of these plays
may be obtained from the League of Dramatists, 81 Drayton Gardens,
London SW10 9SD, to whom all applications for permission
should be addressed.

CONTENTS

INTRODUCTION

Molière, one of the world's greatest comic playwrights, is a shadowy figure whose physical passage through this life is confirmed by little more than a few receipts and a signature which appears on fifty or so legal documents. No manuscripts of his plays have survived nor is there any extant correspondence. It is said that some time in the nineteenth century a peasant arrived in Paris with a barrowful of Molière's papers which he offered for sale. There were no takers and he was never heard of again. Had there really been such a peasant and such a barrow, there would have been fewer Molières.

For while the Molière of tradition is primarily a public entertainer, scholars and historians, in the absence of firm evidence, have discovered many others lurking in his shadow. Some have suggested that Molière was merely an actor-manager who lent his name to plays written by closet dramatists: Lord Derby, Corneille, even Louis XIV, the Sun-King. He has been identified as the original 'Man in the Iron Mask' who became, by an amazing sequence of events, the forebear of Napoleon. While the eighteenth century thought of him as a comic scourge of men and manners, the Romantics saw a distinctly tragic side to him and played Arnolphe, Alceste and Harpagon as victims of wounded sensibilities. He has been called an embittered satirist, the defender of middle-class values and a champion of the 'golden mean' of moderation in all things. Other admirers, unhappy with Molière simply as a man of sound common-sense, have detected in him dark and dangerous philosophical convictions though, since the 1930s, actors and producers have tended to treat him not as a philosopher but as an essentially theatrical animal, a wizard of stagecraft. His comedies have been found to be indebted to literary borrowings so numerous as to turn him into a shameless plagiarist. Even his acute understanding of human psychology has worked against him: the 'great' comedies turn out not to be plays at all but non-dramatic, abstract studies of character unnecessarily complicated by plot and, regrettably, farce.

In his day Molière had many enemies and they did not mince their words. He alienated a section of the Court, the devout party, doctors, the Faculty of Theology, not to mention rival actors and authors, who called him a 'public poisoner', spread slanderous rumours about his private life and tried to silence him. Against them, however, he could count on literary friends like La Fontaine, and Boileau, the arbiter of classical taste, and the protection of Henrietta of England, the Prince de Condé (who let him perform the controversial *Tartuffe* in his house) and, not least, the king. That he survived at all is an indication of his courage, determination and diplomatic adroitness. But it also suggests a steely determination to succeed which seems at odds with the impression of sturdy optimism given by his plays.

Not that the plays have been allowed to speak for themselves, for they have been made to yield hidden meanings. Working on the assumption that Molière did more than draw 'types' and 'characters' from his observation of people and manners, scholars have unearthed specific 'models' and historical 'originals' on which Don Juan, Alceste, Tartuffe and others were based. Or was he an observer of himself? If so, the plays are coded autobiography. Surely the Molière who married a young woman only months before he staged *L'École des femmes* (*The School for Wives*), must inhabit the skin of Arnolphe who is only prevented from doing the same by a flick of the plot? How much of Molière is there in Alceste, the misanthrope? How close is Argan's hypochondria to his creator's own ill-health? To what extent does Chrysale in *Les Femmes savantes* (*Those Learned Ladies*) articulate Molière's own impatience with pedantry?

The few surviving portraits of Molière are unrevealing, and engravings which show him in costume bury him beneath the roles he played. There is evidence to suggest that he was of medium height, heavily round-shouldered and not handsome. Even those who knew him well left only rare glimpses of his character. They hint that he was an impatient, ambitious man with expensive tastes, perhaps even something of a domestic tyrant. But they also show him to have been generous and honourable and no bearer of grudges. He was a dutiful son and a good husband. Scarron, the burlesque playwright and novelist, thought him rather 'too serious' for a clown, a view confirmed by La Grange, keeper of the register of Molière's activities, who mentions that he was considered rather introspective, even melancholic by disposition. But if Molière seems to fit the classic description of the lugubrious comedian, it is clear that he also possessed considerable personal charm. For while he was far from happy in his relations with women, he earned and kept the loyalty, respect and even affection of the actors he directed.

The historical record is meagre and shows Molière almost exclusively from the outside, in his public and professional life. He was born in Paris in 1622, the first son of Jean Poquelin, a well-to-do tradesman in the rue Saint-Honoré, who in 1631 became one of the suppliers, by royal appointment, of furniture, curtains and carpets to the king's household. His mother died in 1631 and two years later his father remarried. Contact was maintained with his mother's family, however, and his grandfather may have taken the young Jean-Baptiste to see the farces performed by the actors of the Théâtre Italien and the tragedies for which the Hôtel de Bourgogne was famous. He was sent to the Jesuit Collège de Clermont (later the Collège Louis-le-Grand) where his fellow pupils included the sons of the nobility and future free-thinkers like Bernier and Cyrano de Bergerac. Through the father of a school friend, Chapelle, he met the sceptical philosophers Gassendi and La Mothe le Vayer.

In 1637 he became the reversioner of his father's court appointment which, in 1643, he would transfer to his brother, though he remained officially a 'valet de chambre du roi', one of many who held the title. After leaving school, he studied law, possibly at Orléans, but, though he practised for six months, he was not suited to a legal career. He had by then become an honorary member of the Béjart family which was middle class, had literary connections and performed amateur theatricals. In 1642 he informed his father that he proposed to give up law in favour of an acting career, and the following year signed an agreement with Joseph Béjart and his sister Madeleine (1618–72), to set up a drama company to be called the Illustre Théâtre. While premises were being made ready, they played tragedy at Rouen, where Jean-Baptiste met Pierre and Thomas Corneille.

The new company opened its doors on 1 January 1644 and, helped by a fire which closed the theatre at the Hôtel du Marais, made a promising start. A document dated 28 June of that year reveals that Jean-Baptiste Poquelin had taken the stage-name of 'Molière', which he may have borrowed from any one of thirteen hamlets of that name or perhaps from a long-forgotten novelist, Molière d'Essartines. But although the Illustre Théâtre enjoyed the rather distant patronage of

Gaston d'Orléans, brother of the late Louis XIII, it was soon in financial trouble and in the summer of 1645 its creditors sent in the bailiffs. Molière was jailed briefly for debt in August and shortly afterwards left for the provinces where the Béjarts followed him.

They joined a company of strolling players, based at Bordeaux, which was financed by the Duc d'Épernon. For the next thirteen years they toured the towns of Languedoc, few of which had fixed theatres, eventually emerging as the best of the dozen companies then performing in the French provinces. Though no strangers to inconvenience and temporary stages made of trestles, they did not live the hand-to-mouth existence of the struggling touring actors described by Scarron in his novel *Le Roman comique* (1657), nor did they have adventures comparable to those imagined by Gautier in *Le Capitaine Fracasse* (1863), which is set in the 1630 and 1640s. They performed in noble houses to the notables of Languedoc and were well rewarded. Nor did they lose touch with developments in Paris: Molière visited the capital at least once, in 1651.

In 1650 the Duc d'Épernon withdrew his support and in 1653 the company acquired a new patron, the dissolute Prince de Conti, who declared Molière to be 'the cleverest actor in France'. By this time, he had emerged as the leader of the group which, in 1655, performed his first play, *L'Étourdi* (*The Blunderer*), at Lyons and, possibly, his second, *Le Dépit amoureux* (*The Lovers' Quarrel*), the following year, by which time Conti had turned religious and disowned them. But their reputation was growing – Madeleine was said to be the best of the touring actresses – and at last they decided they were ready for Paris, where they arrived in 1658 prepared to do battle.

The Paris stage was at that time dominated by two major companies. The Hôtel de Bourgogne, originally built in 1548 to stage mystery plays, was the home of tragedy, though when faced with competition from Molière its actors responded by adding farce and comedy to their repertoire. After 1670 they reverted to tragedy, and it was in their hands that Racine would score his greatest triumphs. In comparison, the Théâtre du Marais, founded in 1629, had seen better days. Its association with Pierre Corneille in the 1630s and 1640s had made it the rival of the Hôtel de Bourgogne, but in 1660 it was finding difficulty in recruiting and retaining actors and new playwrights. Increasingly it turned to spectacular productions in response to public demand, but closed its doors for good in 1673. A third theatrical presence – if the popular entertainments of the two permanent Paris fairs are discounted – was provided by the Théâtre Italien performing the improvised farces of the *commedia dell'arte* in Italian.

Between them they covered a wide range of theatrical forms, from farce to tragedy by way of intricately plotted comedies. The Hôtel de Bourgogne in particular was increasingly associated with the classical taste which was firmly rooted by the time Louis XIV assumed personal rule of his kingdom in 1661. The doctrine, developed by scholars and theorists over more than half a century, required authors in general to be 'plausible', to respect the niceties of the new, more refined social morality, to avoid extravagant and 'unrealistic' characters and situations, and to adapt to a new purity of language. Dramatic authors were further enjoined to obey the rule of the three unities of time, place and action which were designed to end the confusion of wildly proliferating plots. Originality and imagination were not highly regarded, for the route to excellence lay in the imitation of good models. Tragic authors took their subjects from ancient writers; comic playwrights looked to Spanish and Italian sources for their inspiration.

While the dogma of classicism established a set of standards by which literature should be judged, theatre audiences also responded enthusiastically to less formally constrained entertainments. Thus while the classical ideal set its sights on the universal, they welcomed plays which satirized contemporary French manners and topical events. Farce had been superseded in the capital by the sophisticated requirements of preciosity, but it was kept alive by the rumbustious improvisation of the actors of the Théâtre Italien. Play-goers were intrigued too by the new interest novelists showed in the analysis of sentiment, and took to playwrights who offered a more organized form of the comedy of character. They warmed to the fashion for spectacle which called for lavish productions involving ingenious sets and a liberal use of stage machinery. To Italian opera, they preferred the home-grown comedy-ballet which added music and dance to plays in the form of free-standing interludes and finales normally unconnected with the characters or plot of the main entertainment. Plays with music and song grew in popularity and in 1669 an Académie d'Opéras was opened, a grand theatre which first staged musical extravaganzas before giving birth in 1673 to French opera. Thus, although classical discipline was in the ascendant, public taste was sufficiently flexible to allow authors considerable freedom for manoeuvre. Molière would seize his opportunities with both hands.

In 1658 he found a new patron in Philippe d'Anjou, the king's only brother, leased a theatre and the ten-strong company opened with a season of tragedy which was judged inferior by the standards set by the actors of the Hôtel de Bourgogne. But in October Molière concluded a royal command performance of Corneille's *Nicomède* with a 'modest entertainment', possibly written by himself, *Le Docteur amoureux* (*The Amorous Doctor*). The king laughed and authorized the company to share the Petit-Bourbon, a theatre then used exclusively by the Italian actors. There Molière persisted with tragedy but varied the repertoire by reviving the farces he had written during his touring days. On 18 November 1659 he staged *Les Précieuses ridicules* (*Such Foolish Affected Ladies*) which brought him acclaim both as an author and as an actor. He was said to have only a modest talent for tragedy, but as the Marquis de Mascarille, in a huge wig crowned with a tiny hat, high-heeled shoes and festooned with ribbons, he enjoyed the first of many personal acting triumphs.

He maintained good relations with his Italian co-tenants and improved his own stage technique by observing the body-language they used when miming to audiences who did not understand Italian. When the theatre he shared with them at the Petit-Bourbon was demolished in 1660, Louis XIV, who continued to be amused by Molière, allowed him to move to the Palais Royal which would serve as his base until his death. As manager of the company, he commissioned tragedies and comedies but also staged plays of his own.

At first he persisted with farce, then tried his hand unsuccessfully at a tragi-comedy in verse, *Don Garcie de Navarre* (1661), before discovering a way of combining farce with the more sophisticated comedy of character and manners which pleased his public. His rising popularity was resented by rival authors who did not hide their feelings, and it brought a venomous reaction from the actors of the Hôtel de Bourgogne who felt threatened by his success. But he also brought protests from the religious zealots with *Sganarelle, ou le Cocu imaginaire* (*Sganarelle, or the Imaginary Cuckold*, 1660) which contained the first of his many attacks on those who claimed to direct consciences but often abused their position for their own ends. The bitterness flared into a 'comic war' in 1663 in the aftermath of *The School for Wives* (1662) which pleased theatre audiences but outraged the moral majority who thought it vulgar, tasteless, badly written and an insult to the 'holy mystery' of marriage. Molière was subjected to abuse that was both professional and personal. He was portrayed as a vulgar showman who puffed his plays shamelessly, licked the boots of aristocratic patrons and packed his first nights with his own supporters. But he was also attacked in his private life. Early in 1662 he married Armande Béjart, Madeleine's sister, who was young enough to be her daughter – and his too, as some said openly.

The furore lasted over a year. Molière, assured of the king's support by the award of a royal pension, fought back in 1663 with *La Critique de l'école des femmes* (*The School for Wives Criticized*), a witty rebuttal of the writers who had attacked him, and *L'Impromptu de Versailles* (1663), which was his answer to the charges made by rival actors and the attacks made on his private life. But in May 1664, as the din of battle was fading, he staged for the king at Versailles three acts of a new play 'written against the hypocrites' which the zealots immediately denounced as an attack on religion. Though Louis XIV did not take this view, powerful influences ensured that *Tartuffe* was stopped. Leading the opposition was the Compagnie du Saint Sacrement, a charitable if sinister organization set up in 1627 for the relief of the poor and the promotion of strict religious observance. It used methods so inquisitorial (errant sons were denounced to their families and hardened sinners publicly shamed) that in 1660 Colbert had effectively outlawed it. The effect was to make its operations more secret than ever; backed by persons as important as the Queen Mother and the Prince de Conti, Molière's former patron, it was a force to be reckoned with. Molière was engulfed in a new and much more dangerous controversy, for the penalties for convicted blasphemers were severe: one pamphlet called for him to be burned at the stake. *Tartuffe* was banned, and although he read and staged it in private houses and a toned-down version entitled *L'Imposteur* was given one performance in 1667, the affair grumbled on until 1669 when the play as we know it was finally staged.

Meanwhile, Molière's company continued to perform comedies and tragedies by other hands, though his own plays formed the basis of its repertoire. In 1665 his spectacular version of the life and death of Don Juan who defies God was well received but was withdrawn after its initial run, the victim not of an official ban but of the discreet pressure of the zealots. Molière was reassured, however, when, in August, the king himself became the patron of the company which was henceforth known as 'la troupe du Roi'. A month later, *L'Amour médecin* (*Love's the Best Doctor*), a comedy with ballet and music by Lully, delighted the public with the first of Molière's assaults on the doctors. He offended them further by returning to them in 1666 with a farce, *Le Médecin malgré lui* (*The Doctor Despite Himself*). By then, he had considerable experience of the medical profession. His first child (like the two that would follow) had died in infancy and he himself had been kept off the stage for several weeks at the end of 1666 with a neglected chill which was followed by severe complications. He started to cough, lost weight and by 1667, when he was too ill to appear for two months, he had become, as one contemporary observed, 'a walking skeleton'.

Although he carried a heavy responsibility as author, actor and manager of a company which depended on his talents and management skills, he now entered his most productive period. He maintained his output of farces which proved popular with audiences, and he continued his partnership with Lully who composed the music for a number of his comedy-ballets, notably *Le Bourgeois Gentilhomme* (*The Would-Be Gentleman*, 1670), which were as successful at Court as they were with his Paris public. In 1668 he added *L'Avare* (*The Miser*) to the great comedies of obsession which had begun with *The School for Wives*, *Tartuffe* and *The Misanthrope* (1666).

But as he turned fifty he was dealt a series of body blows. In 1672 Madeleine Béjart died, he lost his third child and the king transferred his favour to Lully who acquired the monopoly of musical plays. Undaunted, he staged *Le Malade imaginaire* (*The Hypochondriac*) on 12 February 1673, casting himself as Argan. The glittering first night audience cheered and the play looked set for success. But the effort had drained Molière who, towards the end of the fourth performance on 17 February, coughed blood, though he remained on stage until the final curtain. La Grange's register records what happened next:

After the play, towards 10 o'clock in the evening, Monsieur de Molière died in his house in the rue de Richelieu, having acted the role of the Hypochondriac while suffering considerably from a cold and an inflammation of the chest which caused him to cough so rackingly that in straining to clear his lungs he burst a vein in his body and did not live above half or three quarters of an hour.

Although Molière had asked for a priest, he died unconfessed and, as an actor, was at first refused a Christian burial. The Archbishop of Paris relented, however, and allowed the body to be interred in the cemetery of his parish, but without ceremony and not during the hours of daylight. His many friends and admirers wrote tributes. His many enemies rejoiced. The Palais Royal gave no performances on the following Sunday and Tuesday but opened again on Friday 24 February, with *The Misanthrope*. The show went on as, doubtless, Molière would have wanted.

In the fourteen years since arriving in Paris, Molière had staged over a hundred plays. Of these, he had written and directed twenty-nine and also acted in twenty-four. He began with what he knew best, farce, which had been the mainstay of his provincial successes. He never abandoned its broad strokes and was not afraid of vulgarity. But for the more discriminating Paris public he rang some sophisticated changes on the staple techniques and themes.

In 1659 audiences were accustomed to two quite distinct types of comedy: farce, unsubtle and often physical, with its traditional comic valets, pedants and boastful soldiers, and the comedy of intrigue with its over-complicated, sometimes incomprehensible plots involving disguises, intercepted letters, pirates and magic spells. The first was largely a French tradition, though the Italian actors had popularized new types, like the Harlequin, while the second drew heavily on Spanish and Italian models. During the 1650s farce had disappeared from the Paris stage, but authors who wished to amuse now began importing it into plays which, for example, might attach a comic valet to a marquis who had embarked on an *amour*. The result was usually a poor fit, with the already wandering plots being unhinged at any moment by an unconnected piece of burlesque business. Molière would bring these disparate comic strands together in plays which drew their unity from a more consistent concern with human behaviour. In his hands, familiar stage types become three-dimensional: comic valets accumulate other functions, pedants are linked to wider social and human foibles, tetchy fathers acquire a new depth of character and young lovers express humane and civilizing values.

Of course, Molière worked within a specific theatrical tradition and, as an experienced actor, had a memory filled with stock jokes and audience-proof stratagems. He recycled familiar ploys and stole old comic routines. He repeated plots, situations and characters from play to play – the father who wishes to give his daughter to a son-in-law who shares his obsession, the valet or maid who conspire against their master, the stagy denouements which restore sanity – because they worked well in theatrical terms. But even his broadest comedy is always used for a purpose: to highlight the folly of his monomaniacs or to show some social failing in an absurd light.

Like his contemporaries he borrowed liberally from a common pool of sources which were mainly French for farce, and Spanish and Italian for comedy of situation, character and manners. But from the start he also drew on his own observation. *Les Précieuses ridicules* is a social comedy which owed less to tradition than to his knowledge of people and their ways. While he remained loyal to farce and continued to recycle theatrical conventions in his plots, the ratio of borrowing to his own experience increases in favour of the latter. He may have taken up the story of Don Juan because the subject was fashionable, but his Don is a much more ambiguous character than any of his predecessors, while the Alceste of *The Misanthrope* has no clear literary precedent at all. Molière may have taken hints and ideas from other writers, but his 'high' comedies – *Tartuffe, The Misanthrope, The Miser, Those Learned Ladies* – are in conception highly original. No two of his *bourgeois* are the same, for although they may be types, they are vividly individualized. Alceste is a fool only in his absurd misanthropy, for many of his strictures about society are well-founded. Monsieur Jourdain we surely know to be gullible only in his longing to be a gentleman and not in other things, rather as Orgon is a man of courage and principle whose weakness is his infatuation with Tartuffe. This depth of characterization prevents Molière's gallery of eccentrics from being caricatures and raises them to the level of enduring types which audiences still recognize.

As much may be said for his social satire which is expressed through characters whose actions contradict what they say. Tartuffe, the conscious hypocrite, cannot overcome the unconscious power of his own appetites, nor can Harpagon sustain his hopes of acquiring an image as a respectable man of business when he is forced to choose between his social ambitions and his money. The same technique is used against philosophers who lose their tempers, poets who trade insults like common lackeys and ladies who pride themselves on their taste and discernment but misread people and situations. It is by drawing these self-incriminating characters of *précieuses*, prudes, zealots, philosophers, doctors, lawyers and well-to-do obsessives that Molière attacks what they represent: preciosity, prudery, zealousness, intellectual pretension, professional dishonesty and obsession. Their discomfiture derives from the mismatch between self-image and reality, and it is through the oldest of comic traditions that Molière shows them to be what they are: when their mask falls, Tartuffe and Trissotin, Célimène and the doctors, poets and *précieuses* stand before us to be judged.

And clearly Molière, who several times stated his belief that theatre has a moral vocation, expected audiences to judge them and learn from their example. Exactly what he wanted his public to learn, however, has been the subject of much debate. There is least disagreement about his social attitudes which are quite clear: he reworked the old jibes about the ignorance and self-interest of doctors and lawyers, the knavery of money-lenders like Harpagon and snobbery in general, not only among the middle classes but among upper-class women and fashionable marquises who were uncritical followers of every passing fad. His literary views also seem clear. While the aim of comedy is to correct manners, the greatest rule of all is to amuse and entertain – even if this meant on occasions courting vulgarity and straying from the path of 'regularity' which the theorists of classicism had clearly signposted. But his own ethical values are much less clear-cut.

At first sight, the 'raisonneur', usually a middle-aged man, seems to put a comprehensive case for moderation and 'le juste milieu'. It is a stance reflected in less rational and more instinctive terms by valets, maids and sometimes wives, who openly mock bourgeois pretension and the follies of monomania. Yet Molière's plots cannot be said to underwrite traditional morality in its entirety, for they require domestics to cheek their masters, and children to defy their parents. They draw attention to the way girls are brought up, for Agnès in *The School for Wives*, who is kept in ignorance, is no better prepared for adulthood than the *précieuses* who are over-educated. Nor is there any support for marriages arranged by parents which are regularly overturned in favour of sentiment. Rather than articulating some mathematically balanced 'golden mean', Molière's plays promote an elastic notion of 'natural' behaviour: tolerance, awareness of other people, spontaneity and the rights of exuberant youth. Molière makes no objection in principle to the social structures and moral assumptions of his society, but rather shows that without love they are oppressive. When imposed without regard to human freedoms, marriage, paternal authority and the hierarchy of established values are empty of human warmth.

Similar reservations must be made about Molière's repeated assault on preciosity, a cultural fashion which was hardly new in 1659. Between 1620 and 1640, what was first known as 'honnêteté' had sought to raise the tone of literature by insisting on only the noblest sentiments, defining love as swoon and anguish, and making a virtue of outlandish similes, metaphors and allegory. By the 1650s the precious taste for bizarre emotion and contorted language had become a butt for satirists. From *Such Foolish Affected Ladies* to *Those Learned Ladies*, Molière repeated jokes which were not only familiar to audiences but even amused the new *précieuses* who laughed at Magdelon and Mascarille – such patent anachronisms – and at the ridiculous Trissotin and his silly poems.

For while Molière mocked the excesses of preciosity, he was not unsympathetic to its call for the improvement of literature and manners. When he allows his young lovers to express their feelings, he puts undeniably precious terms into their mouths. Nor was he at odds with the misgivings expressed by the *précieuses* about female education and the marriage of convenience. Where he parted company with them, however, was in their wish not simply to change literature but to coerce manners. They were all too easily offended and they actively campaigned against what they affectedly regarded as the vulgarity of theatre, poetry, even of certain words, and to physical love preferred platonic relationships and the union of souls. Molière's target is not their call for the refinement of manners and language as such, but the sour chastity of the prudes, which is as much outside 'nature' as Tartuffe's hypocrisy or Harpagon's avarice. Just as it is unnatural for children to be made the victims of their fathers, so it is natural that daughters should wish to marry young men not greybeards. Molière's learned ladies are wrong to despise their home-making role in exactly the same way that Alceste, the misanthrope, errs in rejecting all society: it is natural for people to be sociable. Against them, women like Elmire of *Tartuffe* or Henriette of *Those Learned Ladies* stand out. They are intelligent, unimpressed by fashion and modestly self-assertive. What they want is sane and reasonable, and they know how to set about getting it without offending others, endangering families or making the world march in step with them.

But most controversial of all is Molière's attitude to religion. In his lifetime, he was called an enemy of the Church and an atheist. The eighteenth century regarded him as an early kind of anticlerical deist, rooting moral values in the belief in a creator-god who was neither catholic nor protestant. Since he had some acquaintance with sceptics like Gassendi, some modern scholars have further suggested that he was sympathetic to the current of free-thought, that intellectual *libertinage* which attempted to reconcile a spirit of rational inquiry with Catholicism. His plays reveal that, while he was not a bookish man, he was aware of the scientific and intellectual debate going on around him. He understood the principles of Descartes's solution to the problem of base and sublime matter, followed the debate about the use of antimony as an emetic and was convinced by Harvey's revolutionary thesis of the circulation of the blood. True, his most enigmatic play, *Don Juan*, features a master who believes in nothing except that two and two make four and a servant who is incapable of defending religion. Yet there is nothing to suggest that Molière shared the atheism of his hero. Don Juan, though he has certain admirable traits – not least, his heroic courage in defying the Statue – is portrayed as a hypocrite who behaves callously to his father, Dona Elvira and everyone he encounters, irrespective of social standing. In this, he is no different from Tartuffe who hides behind a façade of religious zeal as a way of serving his own interests.

The modern consensus is that while Molière had little objection to religion in principle (his three children were christened, and on his death-bed he called for a priest), he was probably sceptical in his own beliefs. But in matters of faith, he was as opposed to extremism as he was to any other kind of private or public excess. Indeed, Molière is very even-handed in his approach to religion. He is no more in favour of the laxity of the Jesuits which gave encouragement to Tartuffian directors of conscience, than to the puritanism of the Jansenists which led to intolerance and persecution. Nor does he promote atheism which leads Don Juan to deny all human values. But while Molière invites us to laugh at the gullibility of Orgon in *Tartuffe* or the foolishness of his pedants and learned ladies who talk reason, molecules and 'falling worlds', his message is at times uncompromising. If Don Juan and Tartuffe are stopped in their tracks, it is by means of stagy denouements contrived to please the public, and he leaves us with the uneasy feeling that in real life they would succeed. But whether he is humbling the predators or mocking their prey, Molière never openly attacks religion itself. His targets are the 'impostors' who exploit those foolish enough to be duped by them. Molière attacks the singers, not the song.

He never broke faith with the time-honoured purpose of comedy, which is to correct manners. He had no wish to reform institutional structures in any recognizable modern sense, but aimed at puncturing the pretension and dishonesty of the society in which he lived. His stage is crowded with zealots who do not believe in God, doctors who have a blinkered faith in medicine, lawyers who bend the law, critics who cannot tell good from bad, pedants who use science to acquire honour and reputation, and self-satisfied women whose professed love of literature and ideas is no more than a cover for their endless snobbery. Molière was a moral rather than a philosophical writer, though his morality is not the sum of the exhortations of his raisonneurs to follow custom, discipline desire, and practise honesty because it is not only the best policy but also the safest. His target is rather the generalized mendacity of a society based on hypocrisy, that 'privileged vice' as Don Juan calls it. He challenges intimidation and artifice, and encourages his audience to think clearly, so that they may tell truth from falsehood, honesty from narcissism, self-respect from self-regard, in a word to recognize egoism in others and avoid the promptings of their own baser natures.

He was not, however, a misanthropic social critic like Alceste, nor does he ever raise the spectre of vanity of all human endeavour. Had he been so minded, he would have written tragedies. He judged people and manners sternly, but his plays express his amusement at the follies he castigates. As a moralist, he chose to laugh, and he ensured that audiences laughed with him. In any case, reading moral lessons could not be the principal concern of an actor-manager with a theatre to fill. At a time when thirty performances meant success and playhouses were rowdy even dangerous places, he could not afford to lecture his public. Nor could he ignore changing tastes. He never forgot that farce was the great laughter-maker, but he civilized it, building it into situations which highlighted personal and social folly. Yet he was prepared to experiment and did not allow himself to be governed by the rules of classical theatre which are ignored or bent in at least half his plays. He tried out new genres, staging his first comedy-ballet, Les Fâcheux (The Impertinents), in 1661. He attempted the fashionable 'spectacle play' with

Don Juan, and 'tragi-comedy and ballet' with *Psyché* (1671). In *The Would-Be Gentleman* and *The Hypochondriac* he turned the ballets and interludes into an extension of the plot, devising absurd ceremonies which are comments on the obsessions of Monsieur Jourdain and Argan. Molière blended the various strands of traditional comedy – farce, spectacle, manners, character and situation – into a new kind of integrated comedy of observation. At its heart lies the individualized type, never simple, always three-dimensional, and invariably lightened by an injection of an older, more physical style of comedy: the cuckold as a figure of fun, the misunderstanding which sets characters at cross-purposes or the carefully orchestrated plan which backfires. He allows Orgon to hide under the table, Monsieur Jourdain to take a beating and Argan to speak incessantly of his bodily functions. Farce persists even in his choice of names – if 'Mascarille' and 'Jodelet' are established theatrical fools, 'Trissotin' (which suggests *trois fois sot*, 'thrice a fool') is a barbed coinage and Monsieur Loyal is, as Dorine observes, hardly a good man and true.

During his lifetime the public preferred the farces to the 'great' comedies of monomania which are now most admired. Then, his most performed plays were not *The Misanthrope* or *Those Learned Ladies* but *Sganarelle* (1660) and *L'École des maris* (*The School for Husbands*, 1661), which were essentially farces, and his comedy-ballet *Les Fâcheux*. Changing tastes have long since altered the line-up, and the plays that have worn best are those which, behind the fun, raise questions about human nature and the permanent absurdities of social living. If Tartuffe and Harpagon still wear the face of hypocrisy and avarice, the targets of Molière's satire remain familiar. Preciosity still exists as intellectual snobbery, his zealots represent the perennial forces of intolerance, and his doctors and pedants remain as useful reminders of the limitations of experts.

By giving his archetypes a distinctive personality and by focusing on issues which never lose their topicality, Molière escaped the limitations of the age he lived in. He has travelled effortlessly through space and time. While he was still alive he was performed in England, Holland and Germany, and his plays immediately struck a sympathetic chord with spectators unacquainted with the specific social culture of France. Since then they have continued to hold their universal appeal. They are best taken at speed and rarely leave audiences indifferent. For if Molière the actor wrote fire-proof roles for actors, Molière the director left plenty of space around the dialogue for producers to add stage business of their own. Three and a half centuries on, Molière, the observer of people and manners, remains a magician of the theatre.

CHRONOLOGY

1622　15 January: baptism in the church of Saint-Eustache in Paris of Jean, first of the six children of Jean Poquelin, a well-to-do tradesman, and Marie Cressé. In 1624 a second son, who would die in infancy, is given the same name and the first Jean is known thereafter as Jean-Baptiste.

1631　Jean Poquelin purchases his brother's court appointment as 'tapissier ordinaire de la maison du roi', which meant that he supplied furniture to the Royal Household.

1632　Death of Marie Cressé.

1633　Jean Poquelin remarries.

1636–41　Jean-Baptiste is sent to the Jesuit Collège de Clermont. In 1637 he becomes the reversioner of his father's court appointment. After leaving school he studies law, possibly at Orléans, and is admitted to the Bar in 1641. He practises for six months, and draws close to the Béjart family.

1642　Informs his father that he intends to make a career as an actor.

1643　6 January: transfers his royal appointment to his brother.
February: birth of Armande Béjart, sister of Madeleine (b. 1618).
30 June: Jean-Baptiste signs an agreement with Madeleine and her brother Joseph Béjart and nine actors to create a stage company to be known as the Illustre Théâtre.

1644　1 January: the new company, with Gaston d'Orléans as patron, opens its doors and performs mainly tragedy to a mixed reception.
28 June: first recorded signature of Jean-Baptiste Poquelin as 'Molière'.

1645　2 August: the company having been dunned for debt, Molière is briefly jailed.
Autumn: Molière leaves for the provinces where he is joined by the Béjarts. They enter the touring company of actors supported by the Duc d'Épernon and for the next thirteen years tour the south of France.

1650   The Duc d'Épernon ceases to be their patron.

1653   The company is now 'the troupe of His Grace the Prince de Conti'.

1655   Summer: at Lyons, *L'Étourdi* (*The Blunderer*), the first of Molière's plays to be staged. The Prince de Conti turns to religion and ceases to be his patron.

1656   *Le Dépit amoureux* (*The Lovers' Quarrel*) performed.

1657   Now regarded as the best of the dozen provincial touring companies, Molière and his actors decide to try their fortunes in Paris.

1658   24 October: the company follow a performance of Corneille's tragedy *Nicomède* in the presence of Louis XIV with a farce, *Le Docteur amoureux* (*The Amorous Doctor*) which amuses the king. Molière finds a patron in Philippe d'Anjou who, as the king's younger brother, is known as 'Monsieur'.

        2 November: the 'troupe de Monsieur' receives royal permission to share the theatre of the Petit-Bourbon with the Italian actors. Unable to compete in tragedy with the Hôtel de Bourgogne, Molière stages comedy and farce.

1659   Some of Molière's actors are lured to other troupes and are replaced. He recruits La Grange who, in addition to playing major roles, also keeps an invaluable register of the company's activities.

        18 November: *Les Précieuses ridicules* (*Such Foolish Affected Ladies*) brings Molière success as actor and author.

1660   On the death of his brother, Molière resumes his court appointment. He prosecutes Ribou for publishing *Les Précieuses ridicules* without his consent.

        May: *Sganarelle, ou le Cocu imaginaire* (*Sganarelle, or the Imaginary Cuckold*), a farce.

        October: when the Petit-Bourbon is demolished Louis XIV authorizes the company to move to the Palais Royal.

1661   February: failure of *Don Garcie de Navarre*, a tragi-comedy.

        24 June: *L'École des maris* (*The School for Husbands*), the most performed of Molière's plays during his lifetime.

        August: *Les Fâcheux* (*The Impertinents*), first of the comedy-ballets.

1662   23 January: marries Armande Béjart.

26 December: *L'École des femmes* (*The School for Wives*) which has thirty-one consecutive performances but provokes a controversy that will last for more than a year.

1663   Easter: Molière is awarded a royal pension 'for the fineness of his wit and his excellence as a comic author'.

1 June: *La Critique de l'école des femmes* (*The School for Wives Criticized*).

18 or 19 October: *L'Impromptu de Versailles*.

1664   January: *Le Mariage forcé* (*The Forced Marriage*), a farce with ballet and music by Lully.

19 January: birth of first son, Louis, who dies the following autumn.

May: summoned to provide entertainment at Versailles, Molière stages a comedy-ballet, *La Princesse d'Élide*.

12 May: for the king, Molière performs three acts of a play written 'against the hypocrites': it marks the beginning of the Tartuffe affair which lasts until 1669. The Compagnie du Saint Sacrement uses its influence to have it banned.

1665   15 February: *Don Juan*, with Molière as Sganarelle and La Grange in the title role, is a triumph. But after an initial run, it is never staged again in Molière's lifetime as the result, not of a formal ban, but of discreet pressures.

4 August: birth of Esprit-Madeleine.

14 August: Louis XIV awards Molière a pension of 6000 livres and becomes the company's new patron.

15 September: *L'Amour médecin* (*Love's the Best Doctor*), first of the farces written against doctors.

1666   4 June: *Le Misanthrope*, twenty-one performances.

6 August: *Le Médecin malgré lui* (*The Doctor Despite Himself*), twenty-six performances.

Publication of the first collection of Molière's theatre. His plays are already translated and performed abroad. Continues to be unhappy in his married life. His health begins to suffer. He is unable to appear on stage at the end of the year, and again for two months in 1667.

1667   January–March: as part of the Ballet des Muses, a court entertainment, Molière performs *Mélicerte*, a 'heroic pastoral comedy', and *Le Sicilien*.

5 August: believing he has royal authorization, he performs *L'Imposteur*, a revised version of his play 'against the hypocrites'. It is closed after one performance and, though he writes further in its defence, it is not restaged.

1668 13 January: *Amphitryon*.

18 July: *Georges Dandin*, which is not a success.

9 September: *L'Avare* (*The Miser*), which has a short run. Thereafter, Molière will write no more five-act plays for three years.

Relations with Armande are strained. He rescues his father whose business is in difficulty. His health does not improve and there are rumours that he is dead.

1669 5 February: *Tartuffe* begins a successful run of twenty-eight performances.

25 February: death of Molière's father.

6 October: *Monsieur de Pourceaugnac*, a comedy-ballet with music by Lully, is a triumph.

1670 30 January: *Les Amants magnifiques* (*The Sumptuous Lovers*), a comedy with music and ballet, is staged at Saint-Germain for Louis XIV who dances publicly for the last time.

June: Henrietta of England, on a diplomatic visit to London, sees Molière performed in English.

14 October: exploiting the vogue for 'turqueries' prompted by the visit of Soliman Mustapha in 1669, Molière stages *Le Bourgeois Gentilhomme* (*The Would-Be Gentleman*) with great success.

1671 17 January: *Psyché*, a spectacular comedy-ballet, in part written by Corneille.

24 May: *Les Fourberies de Scapin* (*That Scoundrel Scapin*).

2 December: *La Comtesse d'Escarbagnas*.

1672 17 February: death of Madeleine Béjart.

11 March: *Les Femmes savantes* (*Those Learned Ladies*).

Molière quarrels with Lully who persuades the king to grant him the monopoly of entertainments involving music and dance.

15 September: birth of Jean-Baptiste-Armand, who dies aged eleven days.

1673 10 February: *Le Malade imaginaire* (*The Hypochondriac*).

17 February: Molière is taken ill on stage and dies a few hours later.

21 February: he is buried at night in his parish cemetery of Saint-Joseph.

Lully acquires the Palais Royal as the home of French Opera and Armande relocates the company in the rue Guénégaud.

1680   Louis XIV merges Molière's former company with the Hôtel de Bourgogne and creates the Comédie Française.

1792   During the Revolution the presumed remains of Molière are removed to the convent of the Petits-Augustins and thence in 1817 to the Père Lachaise.

BIBLIOGRAPHY

Of the currently available standard Works of Molière, the *Oeuvres* (1971) edited by Georges Couton for the Pléiade series is the most readily accessible. Helpfully annotated editions of individual plays have been published in a number of French series (Les Classiques Hachette, Les Petits Classiques Bordas, Les Classiques Larousse, etc.) and, in English, *Le Misanthrope* edited by G. Rudler (Oxford, 1947) and *Les Femmes savantes* edited by H. Gaston Hall (Oxford, 1974) provide helpful guidance.

The fullest survey of the literature of the period is Antoine Adam's *Histoire de la littérature française au XVIIe siècle* (5 vols., Paris, 1956); abridged as *Grandeur and Illusion: French Literature and Society, 1600–1715* (Harmondsworth, 1974). In English, H. Carrington Lancaster's *History of French Dramatic Literature in the Seventeenth Century* (9 vols., Baltimore, 1929–42) may still be consulted but more accessible overviews are provided by Martin Turnell, *The Classical Moment* (London, 1947), W. G. Moore, *The Classical Theatre of France* (Oxford, 1971), John Lough, *Seventeenth Century French Drama: the Background* (Oxford, 1979) and Robert McBride, *Aspects of Seventeenth Century French Drama and Thought* (London, 1979). Attitudes to women are analysed by Ian Maclean in *Woman Triumphant* (Oxford, 1977).

Alfred Simon's *Molière, une Vie* (Paris, 1988) is the most recent biography, but highly recommended is Sylvie Chevalley's handsomely illustrated *Molière en son temps* (Paris and Geneva, 1973). Classic studies in French include Jacques Arnavon, *La Morale de Molière* (Neufchâtel, 1945); Antoine Adam's long essay in volume 3 of his general *Histoire*; René Bray, *Molière, homme du théâtre* (Paris, 1954), which views the plays through stage traditions and Molière's role as actor; and Maurice Descotes, *Les Grands rôles du théâtre de Molière* (Paris, 1960). Michel Corvin's *Molière et ses metteurs en scène aujourd'hui* (Lyons, 1985) analyses the way Molière has recently been recycled for modern audiences.

There are many studies of Molière in English of which the following are especially recommended: W. G. Moore, *Molière, a New Criticism*

(Oxford, 1948); Robert McBride, *The Sceptical Vision of Molière* (London, 1977); W. D. Howarth, *Molière, a Playwright and his Audience* (Cambridge, 1982); P. A. Wadsworth, *Molière and the Italian Theatrical Tradition* (Alabama, 1987); and Peter Nurse, *Molière and the Comic Spirit* (Geneva, 1991).

On individual plays included in this volume, see David Shaw, *Molière: Les Précieuses ridicules* (London, 1987), H. Gaston Hall, *Molière's Bourgeois Gentilhomme: Context and Stagecraft* (Durham, 1990) and *Molière: Tartuffe* (London, 1960), J. H. Broome, *Molière: L'École des Femmes and Le Misanthrope* (London, 1980), David Whitton, *Molière: Le Misanthrope* (Glasgow 1991) and Noel Peacock, *Molière: Les Femmes savantes* (London, 1990).

NOTE ON MONEY

1 liard	=	3 deniers
1 sou	=	4 liards
1 livre	=	20 sous
1 écu	=	3 livres
1 louis	=	11 livres

The pistole (a coin minted in Spain and Italy) was worth 10 or 11 livres. The franc was the equivalent of the livre, but was used mainly to designate round sums.

TRANSLATOR'S NOTE

John Wood's alert and readable translations first appeared nearly half a century ago and remain very serviceable. However, given the inevitable changes brought about by passing time in register and vocabulary, they stood in need of some revision and modernization. Moreover, John Wood's original selection omitted plays now judged significant and included others which are considered less so. In this volume, *Les Précieuses ridicules* (*Such Foolish Affected Ladies*) and *Les Femmes savantes* (*Those Learned Ladies*) are newly translated.

My grateful thanks go to my colleague David Shaw for pointing out my errors so patiently and for providing much invaluable advice.

DAC

Such Foolish Affected Ladies
A Comedy

Les Précieuses ridicules
Comédie

First performed on 18 August 1659 at the Théâtre du Petit-Bourbon by the Company of Monsieur

Such Foolish Affected Ladies, the first play Molière wrote after his return to Paris, was staged as an end-piece to an undistinguished royal command performance of Corneille's tragedy, *Cinna*. It was an instant success. Though Molière's enemies succeeded in having it closed twice, it ran for forty-four performances before the Théâtre du Petit-Bourbon was demolished in July 1660 and his 'petite comédie' continued to be performed in a number of aristocratic and princely houses.

He chose not to follow the established practice by which comic authors imitated ancient, Spanish or Italian models – though the name 'Mascarille' is derived from the Italian *maschera*, a mask, and Jodelet appeared with his face whitened in the style of the Italian comedy. Instead, he cast around for a contemporary subject and found it in the 'precious' tone and outlook adopted by an influential, Paris-based élite. 'Preciosity' had begun early in the century as an aristocratic reaction against the tone of a Court dominated by coarse, military men. By the mid-1650s, after the Fronde, it had turned into a refinement of language and taste which in some quarters was judged excessive. In certain salons, affected forms of dress were adopted and love and delicate moral questions were discussed endlessly in an unnecessarily contorted group language characterized by bizarre circumlocutions, complicated conceits and extended metaphors which allowed the making of fine distinctions: thus no fewer than twelve kinds of sighs and nine varieties of 'esteem' were identified.

Molière was not the first to mock Preciosity. But while the cabal was quick to move against him, it was organized not by its devotees but by the actors of rival theatre companies who accused him of plagiarism and sharp practice. No one ever admitted to being 'precious' (the word had long-standing pejorative connotations), and no circle or group felt attacked, so that even those who conversed and wrote in the precious style could believe that his satire was directed not at them but at those who existed on the fringes of their territory. When the text of his play was printed without his permission, Molière, forced by circumstances to become an 'author', published *Les Précieuses ridicules* in January 1660 with a preface which did nothing to disabuse them. He distinguished carefully between 'preciosity' itself and its exponents, observing that 'the most excellent things are liable to be aped by vulgar imitators who deserve to be laughed at', a point of view already implicit in the denouement: Gorgibus may wish all precious talk to the devil, but he is hardly an impartial judge. In any case, it is the 'vulgar imitators' who are pilloried. Mascarille and Jodelet are caricatures of the fashionable marquises and salon poets who prided themselves on their wit, while Magdelon and Cathos are star-struck provincials, who have read the canonical texts but have not understood them.

In one sense, the women are deserving of our sympathy, for they are victims of the authoritarianism of Gorgibus, an early example of Molière's long line of tyrannical fathers. Moreover, Du Croisy and La Grange react in a very masculine way and demand a retribution which hardly reflects their claims to be 'honnêtes hommes'. But although Magdelon and Cathos reject marriage which has been forced on them, they forfeit whatever warmth we might feel for them by deliberately jumping from one frying-pan into another. Dazzled by the glamour of Paris, they lose all sense of reality and remove themselves from the common-sense world.

The quarrels surrounding seventeenth-century preciosity have long been forgotten, but the play still amuses and instructs, as Molière intended. For his strictures are less concerned with the value or otherwise of a particular set of ideas than with human nature. His snobs and their pretentions are still recognizable because they are archetypal. The farcical world into which they are thrust was not new in theatrical terms (masters and valets had changed places before), but here it is given a moral thrust. The comedy centres upon the distance separating his *précieuses'* view of themselves and what the audience knows to be an affectation.

The *Précieuses* was a significant milestone in Molière's career. It brought him success as an actor (his performance as Mascarille was particularly admired) and it turned him into a published author. But more important, he stepped off the well-trodden path of gross farce and complicated love intrigues, and exploited instead the comic possibilities of both monomania and its social equivalent, fashionable fads and fixations.

Characters

LA GRANGE
DU CROISY } spurned lovers

GORGIBUS, an honest burgher

MAGDELON, his daughter

CATHOS, his niece

MAROTTE, servant to Magdelon
    and Cathos

ALMANZOR, a page

THE MARQUIS DE MASCARILLE,
    valet to La Grange

THE VICOMTE DE JODELET, valet
    to Du Croisy

Two chairmen

Neighbours

Violinists

The scene is set in Paris, in the house of Gorgibus

Scene i:

DU CROISY: Monsieur La Grange . . .

LA GRANGE: What?

DU CROISY: Look at me – and no laughing.

LA GRANGE: Well?

DU CROISY: What do you make of the call we've just paid? Are you quite happy about it?

LA GRANGE: Should we be, do you think?

DU CROISY: Not entirely, to be honest.

LA GRANGE: Personally, I confess I am absolutely shocked. Tell me, did anyone ever see two chits of girls fresh from the country put on more airs than those two, or two men treated with more contempt than we were? They could hardly make up their minds to have chairs brought for us to sit on. I never saw as much whispering as went on between them, all that yawning and rubbing their eyes and asking what time it was every two minutes. Did they say anything more than 'yes' and 'no' to all we managed to say to them? So wouldn't you agree that if we'd been the greatest villains on earth, we couldn't have been treated worse than we were?

DU CROISY: It seems to me that you're taking all this very personally.

LA GRANGE: Of course I take it personally, so much so that I am determined to get my own back on them for their rudeness. I know what it is that made them look down their noses at us. The fashion for preciosity has not only infected Paris – it has spread to the provinces too, and these two ridiculous girls have absorbed their share of it. They are, in a nutshell, a mix of affectation and coquetry personified. I know exactly the sort of thing that would go down well with them, and, if you're agreeable, we'll play a little game with them that will make them see how ridiculous they are and teach them to be better judges of people.

DU CROISY: How do you propose to do that?

LA GRANGE: I have a valet, named Mascarille, whom many people reckon is a wit of sorts, for these days nothing comes cheaper than wit. He's quite mad, and has got it into his head that he would like to be a gentleman. He generally prides himself as a gallant and writes poetry, and he looks down on his fellow valets whom he calls 'brutes'.

DU CROISY: And what do you intend to do with him?

LA GRANGE: What do I intend to do with him? We must . . . But first let's get out of here.

Scene ii:

GORGIBUS, DU CROISY, LA GRANGE

GORGIBUS: Well now! You've met my niece and my daughter. Is everything going all right? What was the outcome of your visit?

LA GRANGE: That's something you would do better hearing from them than from us. All we can say is that we are most grateful to you for the honour you have shown us and remain your most humble servants.

DU CROISY: Your most humble servants.

GORGIBUS (*as they leave*): Oh dear! It looks as if they're going away dissatisfied. What could have upset them like that? I must look into this. Hello there!

Scene iii:

MAROTTE, GORGIBUS

MAROTTE: What do you want sir?

GORGIBUS: Where are your mistresses?

MAROTTE: In their room.

GORGIBUS: What are they doing?

MAROTTE: Making salve for their lips.

GORGIBUS: More lip-service, eh? Tell them to come down here (*exit Marotte*). I do believe those hussies intend to ruin me with their lip-salve. All I see everywhere is egg-white, skin-cream and a lot of tomfoolery of the same sort that's quite new to me. Since we've been here they've used up the fat from a dozen pigs at least. Four servants could be fed every day on the sheep's trotters they get through.

Scene iv:
MAGDELON, CATHOS, GORGIBUS

GORGIBUS: Is it really necessary to go to such expense to grease your faces? Tell me what it was you did to those two gentleman I saw leaving who looked so frosty? Didn't I give instructions that you were to receive them like persons I was thinking of giving you as husbands?

MAGDELON: And what view would you have us form, father, of the irregular approach of those two individuals?

CATHOS: And how, uncle, could a girl of any sense be reconciled to their persons?

GORGIBUS: What do you find wrong with them?

MAGDELON: A fine air of gallantry they showed, I must say! I mean, they began immediately with marriage!

GORGIBUS: And where do you expect them to begin? With free love? Isn't that an approach you should both approve of as much as I do? Could anything be more gentlemanly than that? And isn't the sacred tie they hope for evidence that their intentions are honourable?

MAGDELON: Oh father! what you just said is unutterably bourgeois! It makes me feel ashamed to hear you speak like that. You should make a point of getting in tune with the new ways.

GORGIBUS: I'm not interested in new ways nor new tunes neither. I tell you, marriage is a holy and sacred matter and those who start with it are behaving like honourable people should.

MAGDELON: Heavens! If everyone thought like you, novels would be over before they'd begun. A fine thing it would be if Cyrus married Mandane at once and Aronce wed Clélie in chapter one![2]

GORGIBUS (*to Cathos*): What's she talking about?

MAGDELON: Father, my cousin will tell you just as well as I can that marriage must never happen until after the other adventures are over. If a suitor is to be acceptable, he must be able to put noble sentiments into words, express the gentle, the tender, the passionate, and woo his lady according to the rules. First, he must spy the person he is to fall in love with in a church, or while he is out strolling, or at some public ceremony. Or else he must be directed by the hand of fate to her house by a relative or a friend, and leave her presence pensive and sad. For a while he conceals his passion from the object of his love, but nevertheless calls to see her several times when some matter concerning the etiquette of love inevitably crops up to exercise the wits of the assembled company. The day comes when he must make his declaration. This should normally take place in an avenue in some garden while the rest of the party has walked on ahead. This declaration is followed by instant fury which is made visible by our blushes and which for a while banishes the lover from our presence. He then finds a way of placating us, of accustoming us gradually to hear him speak of his passion, of drawing an admission which is so painful for us. Then come the adventures: rivals who step in and thwart an acknowledged affection, the persecution of fathers, jealousies which arise out of misleading appearances, the recriminations, the moments of despair, the elopements and the consequences thereof. That's how these things are managed according to the proper code; these are the rules that cannot be dispensed with in a correctly arranged love campaign. But to come point-blank to a proposal of marriage, to reduce courtship to drawing up a marriage contract and to begin a romance at the end of the story, I'll say it again father, nothing could be more bourgeois than such an approach. I feel quite ill at the mere picture it conjures up!

GORGIBUS: What the devil sort of rubbish talk is that? There's your strutting modern style for you!

CATHOS: Actually, uncle, my cousin's got to the truth of the matter. How is one supposed to receive persons who are abysmally ignorant of the rules of gallantry? I'd wager they've never set eyes on the Map of Love and that Tender Notes, Fond Attentions, Courtly Epistles and Pretty Poems are places they've never even heard of![3] Can't you see how it shows in everything about them and that they have no trace of the manner which immediately gives one a good impression of other people? To come to pay one's court with no pompons at the knee, a hat with no feather in it, with a wig that is positively unkempt and a suit which boasts an almost total absence of ribbons . . . Heavens! What sort of lovers are they? Such impoverishment of dress! Such dryness of conversation! It is not to be endured, it cannot be countenanced! I also observed that their neckbands were not supplied by the right maker and, furthermore, that their breeches were too narrow by a good six inches.

GORGIBUS: I think they're mad, the pair of them. I don't understand a word of this gibberish. Cathos, and you, Magdelon –

MAGDELON: Oh please father, do stop using those barbaric names and call us something else.

GORGIBUS: What do you mean, barbaric names? Aren't they the names you were christened with?

MAGDELON: Heavens! How common you are! Personally, one thing that amazes me is how you ever managed to father such an intelligent daughter as myself. Did anybody ever talk in the elevated style of Cathos and Magdelon? Surely you can see that one of those names alone would be enough to discredit the most beautiful novel ever written?

CATHOS: It's true uncle. An ear with any delicacy could not hear those syllables pronounced without wincing dreadfully. The name Polixène which my cousin has chosen for herself, and Aminte,[4] which I have adopted, have a certain grace, as you will surely agree.

GORGIBUS: Listen, I've only one thing to say: I don't intend that you should have any names other than those which were given to you by your godmothers and godfathers. And as for the two gentlemen in question, I know their families and their fortunes, and I am absolutely determined that you shall make up your minds to receive them as your future husbands. I'm tired of having you on my hands. Looking after two girls is too much of a burden for a man of my age.

CATHOS: For my own part uncle, all I can say is that I consider matrimony to be too too shocking. How can one bear the idea of sleeping next to a man who is quite, but quite, naked?

MAGDELON: Allow us to breathe a whiff of the air of fashionable Paris society. We've only just got here. Do let us alone to weave the fabric of our romance, and don't hurry the denouement on so fast.

GORGIBUS (*aside*): There's no doubt about it, they're completely mad. (*Aloud*:) I repeat, I don't understand a word of all this nonsense. But I intend to be the master here, and I say, to put an end to all this sort of talk, either you will both be married before you're very much older or, by God, you'll go into a nunnery – I take my oath on it.

Scene v:

CATHOS, MAGDELON

CATHOS: Good heavens cousin, how positively steeped your father's spirit is in gross matter![5] How turgid his understanding! How dark it must be in his soul!

MAGDELON: What do you expect, dear coz? I am so ashamed for him. I have difficulty in convincing myself that I am his daughter at all. I believe that one day some event will occur which will show that I was far more nobly born.

CATHOS: I can well believe it. Yes, there is every likelihood that it is so. And in my own case, when I look at myself . . .

Scene vi:

MAROTTE, CATHOS, MAGDELON

MAROTTE: There's a footman at the door asking if you're at home. He says his master would like to see you.

MAGDELON: You must learn, you stupid creature, to express yourself less crudely. Say: 'There's an attendant without who asks if it is a convenience for you to be visible.'

MAROTTE: Look 'ere! I don't understand Latin and I never learned no pie-lossophy from *Syrup the Great* like what you done.

MAGDELON: Stupid creature! I can't bear it! And who is the master of this attendant?

MAROTTE: He told me 'is name was the Marquis de Mascarille.

MAGDELON: Oh coz! A marquis! (*To Marotte:*) Yes, go and say that we are visible. (*To Cathos:*) He's sure to be a wit who's heard about us.

CATHOS: No question of it my dear.

MAGDELON: We'd best receive him here, in the parlour, rather than in our own room. Let's just freshen our hair a touch and live up to our reputation. (*To Marotte:*) Quickly now, come into this room and hold up the counsellor of the Graces for us.

MAROTTE: Merciful heavens! What's that when it's at home? You'll have to talk plain if you want me to understand what you're on about.

CATHOS: Bring us the mirror, you ignoramus! And take care you don't dirty the glass by letting your reflection get in it!

Scene vii:
MASCARILLE (*in a sedan chair*) *and*
TWO CHAIRMEN

MASCARILLE: Hold, bearers, hold it there. Oh, ah, ow, ouch! I do believe the rogues are set on breaking my neck the way they're knocking into walls and bumping me along the ground.

FIRST CHAIRMAN: Couldn't be 'elped, it's the doorway that was narrow. Anyhow, you did say as how we was to bring you all the way in 'ere.

MASCARILLE: Quite so. Did you menials expect me to expose the profusion of my plumage to the inclemency of the rainy season and leave the imprint of my shoes in the mud? Away with you: and get your chair out of here.

SECOND CHAIRMAN: Well pay us then sir, please.

MASCARILLE: Eh?

SECOND CHAIRMAN: Sir, I said you should give us our money, please.

MASCARILLE (*slapping his face*): What do you mean, you rogue, asking a man of my quality for money?

SECOND CHAIRMAN: Is that the way poor people get paid? But is your quality going to give us a bite to eat?

MASCARILLE: Aha! I'll teach you to know your place! You riffraff have got a nerve, trying it on with me!

FIRST CHAIRMAN (*taking one of the poles from his chair*): Come on, pay up, and look sharp.

MASCARILLE: What?

FIRST CHAIRMAN: I said I wants me money and I wants it quick.

MASCARILLE: That's a good argument you have in your head.

FIRST CHAIRMAN: Quickly now.

MASCARILLE: Ah, you speak properly, but your friend is a rogue who can't put two words together correctly. There you are — satisfied now?

FIRST CHAIRMAN: No, I ain't satisfied. You slapped my mate 'ere and . . . (*He raises his pole.*)

MASCARILLE: Just hold on. There, that's for the slap. You can get anything out of me provided you go about it the right way. Now be off with you, but come back for me later and take me to the Louvre, in time for the king's retirement.[6]

Scene viii:
MAROTTE, MASCARILLE

MAROTTE: Sir, my mistresses will be along any minute now.

MASCARILLE: There's no need for them to hurry. I am comfortably ensconced here to await their coming.

MAROTTE: Here they are now.

Scene ix:
MAGDELON, CATHOS, MASCARILLE, ALMANZOR

MASCARILLE (*after bowing to them*): Ladies, you will doubtless be surprised by my boldness in calling like this. But your reputation has brought this distressing visit upon your own heads, for merit holds such potent charms for me that I run after it everywhere.

MAGDELON: If it is merit you pursue, it is not on our domain that you should hunt.

CATHOS: If you find merit under this roof, you must have brought it here yourself.

MASCARILLE: I should apply to the law for redress for your remarks. Fame was right in bruiting your qualities abroad, for you have in your hand kings, aces and trumps which will cap all that is gallant in Paris.

MAGDELON: Your obliging kindness runs on a trifle quickly before the gushing generosity of its praise. My cousin and I shall take good care not to place our entire confidence in the honey of your flattery . . .

CATHOS: Coz, we should have chairs brought.

MAGDELON: Come, Almanzor!

ALMANZOR: Madame called?

MAGDELON: Quickly, convey to us hither the amenities of conversation.

MASCARILLE: But may I take it at least that I am safe here?

(*Having brought the chairs, Almanzor leaves.*)

CATHOS: What is it you fear?

MASCARILLE: That my heart might be stolen away, that its freedom be slain. Here I see eyes that look as though they might be footpads intent on doing violence to a man's liberty, or treating his soul as Turks treat Moorish slaves. Odds bodkins! As soon as a man draws near 'em, they glint and stand murderously on their guard! Upon my soul, I do not trust them, and I shall show them a clean pair of heels, or else I insist upon an iron-clad guarantee that they will do me no harm.

MAGDELON (*to Cathos*): Coz, here is character of the playful lover.

CATHOS (*to Magdelon*): I can see that he's just like Amilcar.[7]

MAGDELON (*to Mascarille*): You have nothing to fear. Our eyes harbour no mischief and your heart can be easy in the certain knowledge of their good behaviour.

CATHOS: But I beg you sir, be not inexorable towards this chair which has been holding its arms out to you for a quarter of an hour. Indulge the wish it has to embrace you.

MASCARILLE (*combs his wig and adjusts the pompons he wears at his knee*): Well now ladies, what have you to say of Paris?

MAGDELON: Alas! What can we say of it? A person would have to exist at the antipodes of reason not to admit that Paris is the great workshop of wonders, the centre of good taste, wit and gallantry.

MASCARILLE: Personally, I hold that outside of Paris there is no salvation for gentlemen of parts and ladies of taste.

CATHOS: That is an incontrovertible truth.

MASCARILLE: It muddies one's boots of course, but we always have the sedan chair.

MAGDELON: It's true: a chair is a marvellous bulwark against the insults of the mud and inclement weather.

MASCARILLE: You have many callers, I imagine? What famous wit is annexed to you?

MAGDELON: Alas! We are as yet little known, but we are becoming more so. For we have a particular friend and she has promised to bring all the gentlemen who contribute to the *Miscellany of Collected Pieces*.[8]

CATHOS: And a number of others who have been pointed out to us as the ultimate arbiters of all things fine.

MASCARILLE: I'm the man who shall see to all that better than anyone else. They all call on me, and I may say that I never get out of bed without being attended by a half-dozen wits.

MAGDELON: Oh heavens! We should be obliged to you to the ultimate degree of obligation if you were to be so kind. For, to be frank, one has to be acquainted with all those gentlemen if one wishes to be part of fashionable society. They it is who make reputations in Paris, and as you know there are some upon whom it is enough to call regularly to set one up with a name as a person of discrimination, even if one has no other claim to be thought so. What I myself consider particularly important is that through meeting with them in feasts of reason and flows of soul, one acquires knowledge of many things which it is vital to know and which are the very essence of wit. That way, a person receives the latest news of fashionable society each day and gets to know what revelations in prose and rhyme are doing the rounds. One is kept up to date, for one is informed that so-and-so has written the prettiest morsel on such-and-such a subject that ever was, that a certain lady has penned new words on such-and-such a tune, that this person has composed a madrigal⁹ on winning his mistress's favour, that another has delivered himself of stanzas on being betrayed in love, that last night Monsieur A wrote a six-line verse to Mademoiselle B and that she sent him her response at eight o'clock this morning, that this author has unveiled the plan of a new book, that another has reached part three of his novel, that a third has just sent his latest to the printer. That is what gets you noticed in society, and if people aren't well up with such things, I wouldn't give a penny for all the wit they might have.

CATHOS: In point of fact, I believe that anyone who claims to be a wit and does not know every little quatrain that's written each day is simply too ridiculous for words. I personally would die of shame if someone came up to me and asked if I'd seen something new and I hadn't.

MASCARILLE: You're quite right. It is too shaming not to be the first to have sight of everything that's being written. But you mustn't worry. I intend to set up an Academy of Wits here, in your house, and I promise you that not a line of poetry will be written in the whole of Paris that you will not know by heart before anyone else does. Why, I who stand before you now have been known to scribble the odd

verse when the mood takes me, and you will find doing the rounds
of the most exclusive circles in Paris two hundred lyrics of mine, the
same number of sonnets, four hundred epigrams and over a thousand
madrigals, not counting riddles and character sketches.

MAGDELON: I will confess to you that I am mad about character sketches.
I don't think there's anything quite so smart.

MASCARILLE: Character sketches are difficult to pull off, for they require
depth of wit. You shall see some samples of my manner and you will
not find them displeasing.

CATHOS: Personally speaking, I positively dote on riddles.

MASCARILLE: Riddles exercise the brain – I dashed off another four this
morning, which I'll let you hear to see if you can guess their meaning.

MAGDELON: Madrigals are agreeable if they're well done.

MASCARILLE: They're my speciality. I am currently turning the whole
of Roman history into madrigals.

MAGDELON: Indeed! But that would be passing fine! I shall insist on
having at least one copy if you have it printed.

MASCARILLE: I promise you shall have one each, in the very best
binding. Of course, publication is beneath my rank.[10] I only do it to
put a little money in the pockets of the booksellers who are forever
pestering me.

MAGDELON: I imagine it must be very gratifying to see oneself in print.

MASCARILLE: I should say so! But now that I think of it, I must recite
you an impromptu I concocted yesterday at the house of a friend of
mine, a duchess, upon whom I had called. I am devilish good at
improvising.

CATHOS: The impromptu is undeniably the touchstone of wit!

MASCARILLE: Then listen.

MAGDELON: We are all ears.

MASCARILLE: 'Ah! I was lightsome and all unsuspecting:
   But while I gazed on your charms so affecting
   Your felonious eye stole my heart on the sly.
   Stop thief! Stop thief! Stop thief! Stop thief! I cry!'

CATHOS: Oh my goodness! That is surely the last word in the gallant
mode!

MASCARILLE: Everything I write has a certain dash. There's never
anything pedantic in it.

MAGDELON: It's a million miles from pedantry.

MASCARILLE: Did you note the beginning? 'Ah!' It's extraordinary: 'Ah!' Like a man who is suddenly struck by something: 'Ah!' The surprise of it: 'Ah!'

MAGDELON: Yes, I think that 'Ah!' is a master-stroke.

MASCARILLE: Yet there doesn't seem much to it.

CATHOS: Gracious me! Whatever are you saying? Why, it's exactly the sort of thing to which it is impossible to attach too high a value.

MAGDELON: That's undeniable. I would rather have written that 'Ah!' than a whole epic poem.

MASCARILLE: By Jove! You have good taste.

MAGDELON: Well, it's not entirely bad.

MASCARILLE: But were you not also taken with 'I was lightsome and all unsuspecting'? 'Lightsome and all unsuspecting', that is, I was off my guard, it's a perfectly natural turn of phrase: 'I was lightsome and all unsuspecting.' 'But while I gazed on your charms so affecting', while innocently, intending no harm, like a fond little sheep, 'I gazed on your charms', that is, I was enjoying looking at you, observing you, contemplating you. 'Your eye . . . my heart . . . on the sly' – what do you think of 'on the sly'? Isn't it well chosen?

CATHOS: It's splendid.

MASCARILLE: 'On the sly'. It conjures up the image of a cat that's just caught a mouse. 'On the sly'!

MAGDELON: It couldn't be bettered.

MASCARILLE: 'Stole my heart', you made off it with it, snatched it from me. 'Stop thief! Stop thief! Stop thief! Stop thief! I cry!' Wouldn't you say it was a man shouting and running after a thief to catch him? 'Stop thief! Stop thief! Stop thief! Stop thief! I cry!'

MAGDELON: There's no denying that it has a witty, gallant ring.

MASCARILLE: I'll sing you the tune I've set it to.

CATHOS: You have learned music?

MASCARILLE: I? Not at all.

CATHOS: So how can you –

MASCARILLE: Persons of quality know everything without ever having learned anything.

MAGDELON: That's so, coz.

MASCARILLE: Listen and see if you like the tune. (*Clearing his throat*) Ahem! La la la. La la la. The rudeness of the season has played utter havoc with the timbre of my voice. But no matter, this is not a command performance. (*He sings:*) 'Ah! I was lightsome and all unsuspecting . . .'

CATHOS: Oh, there is passion in that tune! One could die of the pleasure of it!

MAGDELON: There is definitely something chromatic about it.

MASCARILLE: Didn't you think the thought was well expressed musically? 'Stop thief!' And then, just as if one were shouting very loud: 'Sto-o-o-p THIEF!!' And then a dying fall, like a person out of breath: 'I cry'.

MAGDELON: You show a fine understanding of the subtleties, the subtler subtleties, the subtlest of the subtleties. It is all quite wonderful, I do assure you. Both the words and music send me into ecstasies!

CATHOS: I never heard anything so forceful!

MASCARILLE: Everything I compose comes to me naturally – it's all quite untutored.

MAGDELON: Then Nature has treated you like a truly loving mother and you are her favoured son.

MASCARILLE: And how do you ladies spend your time?

CATHOS: We don't do anything.

MAGDELON: Until now we have been frightfully starved of amusements.

MASCARILLE: I should be glad to take you to the theatre one of these days, if you wish. As a matter of fact, a new play is about to be put on and I'd be delighted if we were to see it together.

MAGDELON: We wouldn't say no.

MASCARILLE: But I must ask you to applaud in the proper manner when we're there. For I've given my promise to make sure the play is a success – the author called on me again this morning to beg for my support. It's the custom here that authors come and read their new plays to us persons of quality, to persuade us to give them puffs and thus enhance their reputations. And as you can well imagine, when we have pronounced, the spectators in the pit would not dare go against us. I myself always keep my word strictly. When I have given an author my promise, I always shout 'Bravo, wonderful!' even before they've lit the footlights.

MAGDELON: There's no need to say any more. Paris is a wonderful place. So many things happen here each day of which one knows nothing in the provinces, however clever one may be.

CATHOS: Enough said! Now that we've been told how things are, we shall make a point of cheering every word that's spoken in the approved manner.

MASCARILLE: I could be mistaken, but you look to me as though you might have written a play yourself.

MAGDELON: Oh, there might be something in what you say.

MASCARILLE: Then, by God, we'll have to take a look at it. Just between ourselves, I've written one which I intend to have performed.

CATHOS: Really? And to which stage company do you intend to give it?

MASCARILLE: Good question! To the actors of the Hôtel de Bourgogne.[11] They're the only ones capable of making the most of good lines – all the rest are ignorant mummers who speak their parts naturally, the way people talk. They have no idea how to rant nor do they know how to pause when there's a particularly fine line – and how is one to know when there is a fine line if the actors don't pause and thus indicate when one is supposed to applaud and show one's appreciation?

CATHOS: That's right. There are ways of making the spectator alive to the beauties of a play. A text is only as good as it is made to seem.

MASCARILLE: How do you like my trimmings? Do you think they go with my suit?

CATHOS: Perfectly.

MASCARILLE: And would you say the ribbon was well chosen?

MAGDELON: Furiously well. It's got Perdrigeon[12] written all over it.

MASCARILLE: What do you think of my knee-lace?

MAGDELON: It's everything knee-lace should be.

MASCARILLE: I think I can boast at least that it's a good foot longer than what is commonly made.

MAGDELON: I don't mind admitting that I have never seen vestimentary style carried to such a pitch of elegance.

MASCARILLE: Subject these gloves for a moment to your olfactory judgement.

MAGDELON: They smell thrillingly good.

CATHOS: I never ever inhaled a more perfectly blended fragrance.

MASCARILLE: And what about this? (*He leans forward so that they can smell his powdered wig.*)

MAGDELON: That is supreme quality – it impinges deliciously on the seat of the senses.

MASCARILLE: You've not said anything about my plumes. How do you like them?

CATHOS: Frighteningly lovely.

MASCARILLE: The top one cost me a gold louis, you know. It's a fad of mine – I always insist on having the very best.

MAGDELON: I assure you that you and I are of one mind. I am most awfully fussy about what I wear. I cannot abide anything, not even stockings, which hasn't been bought at the right shop.

MASCARILLE (*crying out suddenly*): Oh! Aaah! stop! Dammit, ladies, this is no way to treat me! I have every reason to complain of your behaviour. It's deucedly unfair!

CATHOS: What's wrong? What's the matter?

MASCARILLE: What's the matter? When you both lay siege to my heart at once, and attack me from right and left? Oh! it's against international treaty! It's not an equal contest. I'm going to scream 'murder!'.

CATHOS (*to Magdelon*): You must admit, he has a special way of putting things.

MAGDELON (*to Cathos*): His mind has a marvellously witty turn to it.

CATHOS (*to Mascarille*): Tish! You are more alarmed than hurt and your heart cries out before it is wounded.

MASCARILLE: The devil it does! Why, it's quite cut to ribbons, from top to bottom!

Scene x:

MAROTTE, MASCARILLE, CATHOS, MAGDELON

MAROTTE: Madame, there's someone asking to see you.

MAGDELON: Who is it?

MAROTTE: Vicomte Jodelet.[13]

MASCARILLE: Vicomte Jodelet?

MAROTTE: Yes sir.

CATHOS: Do you know him?

MASCARILLE: He is my closest friend.

MAGDELON: Show him in at once.

MASCARILLE: We haven't seen each other for some time and I'm delighted by this happy conjuncture.

CATHOS: Here he is.

Scene xi:

JODELET, MASCARILLE, CATHOS, MAGDELON,
MAROTTE, ALMANZOR

MASCARILLE: Ah! Vicomte!

JODELET (*as they embrace*): Ah! Marquis!

MASCARILLE: I'm so glad to meet you again!

JODELET: I'm overjoyed to see you here!

MASCARILLE: Come, embrace me again, if you will.

MAGDELON (*to Cathos*): My dear coz, I do believe we are beginning to be known. All that is best in society is beating a path to our door.

MASCARILLE: Ladies, allow me to introduce this gentleman to you. You have my word that he is worthy of your acquaintance.

JODELET: It is only right that one should come to offer the respect to which you are entitled. Your manifold charms exact seigneurial dues right royally from your vassals of every rank and station.

MAGDELON: This is carrying politeness to the outermost limits of flattery.

CATHOS: Today must go down in our diary as a red-letter day.

MAGDELON (*to Almanzor*): Look alive boy, do you always have to be told everything twice? Can't you to see that an addendum of one chair is required?

MASCARILLE: You mustn't be put out by the way the vicomte looks. He has only just got over an illness which has left him with a very pale face,[14] as you see.

JODELET: Such is the reward of staying late at Court and undergoing the ardours of war.

MASCARILLE: Are you ladies aware that the vicomte here is one of the bravest men of the age? He is an eighteen-carat hero.

JODELET: You have as many carats as I, marquis. We know what you are capable of too.

MASCARILLE: It's true, we've both been observed in the thick of the occasional fray.

JODELET: And in some decidedly hot spots at that.

MASCARILLE (*looking at both Cathos and Magdelon*): That's right — though none were as hot as the spot we are in here! Ha ha ha!

JODELET: We became acquainted in the army, and when we first met, he was in command of a cavalry regiment aboard the galleys of the Knights Templar.[15]

MASCARILLE: Quite right. But you were in the service before I was, and, as I recall, I was only a junior officer when you were already in command of two thousand horse.

JODELET: War's a fine thing, but by God these days the Court is very stingy in rewarding serving men such as us.

MASCARILLE: That's why I'm going to hang up my sword.

CATHOS: Oooh! I have the most stupendous weakness for warriors!

MAGDELON: Mm! I'm fond of them too, but for me courage must be seasoned with wit.

MASCARILLE: Do you recall, vicomte, that half-moon we took from the enemy at the siege of Arras?[16]

JODELET: What are you talking about, half moon? It was a full moon, by God!

MASCARILLE: I do believe you're right.

JODELET: I mean, I should remember it – I was wounded in the leg there by a burst from a grenade. I've still got the scars. Have a feel of it, if you would be so good, and you'll get an idea what sort of wound it was. Just there.

CATHOS (*after touching the place*): You're right. There's a great big bump.

MASCARILLE: Give me your hand a moment and feel that one, there, just on the back of my head. Got it?

MAGDELON: Yes, I can feel something.

MASCARILLE: That was done by a bullet from a musket during my last campaign.

JODELET (*bearing his chest*): This is another thrust that went clean through me and out the other side at the attack on Gravelines.[17]

MASCARILLE (*reaching for the top button of his breeches*): I'll show you a stupendous wound –

MAGDELON (*hastily*): That won't be necessary. We don't need to see to believe.

MASCARILLE: They're badges of honour. They show what sort of stuff a man is made of.

CATHOS: We don't doubt for a moment what you are.

MASCARILLE: Vicomte, have you got your carriage here?

JODELET: Why?

MASCARILLE: We could take these ladies for a drive beyond the city walls and offer them refreshment.

MAGDELON: We can't go out today.

MASCARILLE: Then let's call for fiddles and dance.

JODELET: By God! That's a capital notion!

MAGDELON: We can agree to that. But we shall need an extension to our circle.

MASCARILLE: Hey! Champagne, Picard, Bourguignon, Casquaret, Basque, La Verdure, Lorrain, Provençal, La Violette! Damme, where have all my lackeys got to? I don't think there can be another gentleman in the whole of France who is as badly served as I am. The rogues are forever going off and leaving me unattended.

MASCARILLE: Almanzor, go and tell the marquis's servants that they're to find fiddlers and ask the neighbours to come in — gentlemen and ladies — to people the solitude of our dancing party. (*Exit Almanzor.*)

MASCARILLE: Vicomte, what do you reckon to those eyes?

JODELET: And what do you reckon to them, marquis?

MASCARILLE: Me? I reckon both my liberty and yours will have the devil's own job to get out of here unscathed. I at least, speaking for myself, feel strangely buffeted and my heart hangs by a single thread.

MAGDELON: How natural everything he says sounds! He has the most charming way of putting things.

CATHOS: Quite. He does not stint on the wit.

MASCARILLE: To show you I am perfectly sincere, I shall compose an impromptu on the subject. (*He concentrates.*)

CATHOS: Oh do! I beseech you with all that my soul holds sacred: let us hear something that's been specially written for us!

JODELET: I'd dearly like to do likewise, but I find that my poetic vein is still recuperating after the number of times I've bled it these last few days.

MASCARILLE: What the devil's the matter with me? I can come up with the first line all right, but I can't seem to manage the others. Zounds! I'm being rushed. It'll take me a while longer to dash off an example of improvisation which will thrill you.

JODELET: He's got the wit of the devil.

MAGDELON: And it's so gallant and cleverly put.

MASCARILLE: Vicomte, tell me, is it long since you saw the countess?

JODELET: I haven't been to call on her for more than three weeks.

MASCARILLE: Did you know the duke came to see me this morning and wanted to whisk me off to the country to hunt stag with him?

MAGDELON: Here are the ladies now.

Scene xii:
JODELET, MASCARILLE, CATHOS, MAGDELON,
MAROTTE, LUCILE, CÉLIMÈNE, ALMANZOR,
VIOLINISTS

MAGDELON: Heavens, my dears, you really must forgive us! These gentlemen took a fancy to setting the souls of our feet a-tripping and we sent for you to fill the vacuum in our little gathering.

LUCILE: But it is we who are only too infinitely obliged to you.

MASCARILLE: It's only a spur-of-the-moment affair. One of these days we shall arrange a proper ball for you. Are the fiddlers here?

ALMANZOR: Yes sir, they've come.

CATHOS: Well come along dear friends, and take your places.

MASCARILLE (*dancing alone to start them off*): La la la, tum te to, la la la, tum tum . . .

MAGDELON (*to Cathos*): He cuts an elegant figure.

CATHOS (*to Magdelon*): He certainly looks as if he can dance.

MASCARILLE (*taking Magdelon by the arm to dance with her*): I fear this *coranto*[18] may run off with my heart as it runs away with my legs! Keep time there fiddles, hold the time. Ignorant rogues! There's no way anyone can dance to that. Damn your eyes! Can't you keep the time? La la la, tum te to. Keep it steady, you village scrapers!

JODELET (*dancing*): Hold on, don't take it so fast. I've been ill you know.

Scene xiii:

DU CROISY, LA GRANGE, MASCARILLE, JODELET,
CATHOS, MAGDELON, LUCILE, CÉLIMÉNE,
MAROTTE, VIOLINISTS

LA GRANGE (*carrying a stick*): Aha! You good-for-nothings! What are you doing here? We've been looking for you these last three hours.

MASCARILLE (*feeling the stick on his shoulders*): Ow! Ow! Ow! You didn't say sticks were to be part of the arrangement!

JODELET: Ow! Ow! Ow!

LA GRANGE (*to Mascarille*): It's typical of you, wretched oaf that you are, to want to cut a dash as a man of consequence.

DU CROISY (*to Jodelet*): That'll teach you to know your place.

(*Exit La Grange and Du Croisy.*)

Scene xiv:

MASCARILLE, JODELET, CATHOS, MAGDELON,
LUCILE, CÉLIMÈNE, MAROTTE, VIOLINISTS

MAGDELON: What's the meaning of this?

JODELET: It was a bet.

CATHOS: What! To let yourself be thrashed like that?

MASCARILLE: By God! I decided I'd just ignore them. I can get violent and I'd have lost my temper.

MAGDELON: But how could you put up with such insulting behaviour in our presence!

MASCARILLE: It's nothing. Let's not leave off dancing. We've known each other for ages, and with old friends you don't fall out over little things like that.

Scene xv:

DU CROISY, LA GRANGE, MASCARILLE, JODELET,
MAGDELON, CATHOS, LUCILE, CÉLIMÈNE,
MAROTTE, VIOLINISTS

LA GRANGE: By God, you villains! You'll not make fools of us, I promise you. Right men, in here.

(*Enter three or four hired ruffians.*)

MAGDELON: What effrontery is this? How dare you come here and disturb us like this in our own house!

DU CROISY: What? Ladies, are we supposed to stand by while our servants get a warmer welcome than we did, pay you their addresses at our expense and arrange dances for you?

MAGDELON: Your servants!!

LA GRANGE: Yes, our servants. And it's neither decent nor honest to turn their heads as you're doing.

MAGDELON: Great heavens! The impertinence of it!

LA GRANGE: But they shan't have the advantage of using our clothes to blind you with their elegance. If you still want to fall in love with them, it'll have to be for their natural good looks. Come, strip them and be quick about it.

JODELET (*as he is stripped*): So it's goodbye to our glad rags!

MASCARILLE (*as his finery is removed*): Behold, the marquisate and the viscountcy bite the dust!

DU CROISY: Ha! You damned rogues, so you had the impudence to think you could fill our boots! Well, you can go and look elsewhere for outfits to dazzle your conquests with, believe me!

LA GRANGE: It really is too much, trying to take our place – and with our own clothes too!

MASCARILLE: O fickle Fate!

DU CROISY (*to the ruffians*): Quickly, remove all their finery.

LA GRANGE: Take all these things away with you, and hurry. (*Exit ruffians.*) Now ladies, you can carry on with your amours with them in their present state to your heart's content. We shall leave you completely free to do so and you have our solemn word that neither I nor my friend will be the least jealous.

(*Exit Du Croisy, La Grange, Lucile, Célimène and Marotte.*)

CATHOS: Oh! How too embarrassing!

MAGDELON: I could die of shame!

VIOLINIST (*to Mascarille*): What's going on here? Who's going to pay us?

MASCARILLE: Ask his excellence the vicomte.

VIOLINISTS (*to Jodelet*): Who's going to give us our money?

JODELET: Ask his honour the marquis.

Scene xvi:
GORGIBUS, MASCARILLE, JODELET, MAGDELON, CATHOS, VIOLINISTS

GORGIBUS: Why, you little hussies, here's a pretty pickle you've landed us in from what I can see. I've just heard about your fine goings-on from those gentlemen and ladies as they were on their way out.

MAGDELON: Oh father! It was all a cruel game they've played with us.

GORGIBUS: Yes, it was a cruel game, but it was the result of your own rudeness, you wicked girls! They took exception to the way you treated them and now, to my misfortune, I have no choice but to swallow the insult.

MAGDELON: Oh! I vow that we shall be avenged, or that I shall die in the attempt. (*To Mascarille and Jodelet:*) And as for you two wretches, how dare you linger here after your insolent behaviour!

MASCARILLE: That's no way to speak to a marquis! But that's the way of the world – the first hint of disgrace and you're shunned by those who were your dearest friends. Come on comrade, let's go and seek our fortunes somewhere else. I can see that hereabouts what people value is appearance without substance. They have no regard whatsoever for virtue unadorned.

(*Exit Mascarille and Jodelet.*)

Scene xvii:

GORGIBUS, MAGDELON, CATHOS, VIOLINISTS

VIOLINISTS: Sir, we look to you to pay us, since they've gone, for the music we played here.

GORGIBUS (*taking a stick to them*): Oh yes, of course I'll foot the bill, and this is the coin I'll pay it with! (*To Magdelon and Cathos:*) And as for you, you damned good-for-nothings, I don't know what's stopping me doing the same to you! We're going to be the talk of the town, a laughing-stock – that's what you've brought on yourselves with all your silly notions. Go and hide your faces, you bumpkins, and keep them hidden. (*Magdelon and Cathos leave.*) And as for you, the cause of their folly, you nonsensical notions, you pernicious amusements of idle minds, all you novels, verses, songs, sonnets, tomes and pomes, the devil take the whole lot of you!

Tartuffe
A comedy

Le Tartuffe:
Comédie

First performed in five acts on 5 February 1669 at the Théâtre du Petit-Bourbon in Paris by the King's Players

The controversy surrounding *L'École des femmes* (*The School for Wives*), which had begun a successful run on 26 December 1662, had not entirely subsided when, on 12 May 1664, by royal command, Molière staged a new play at Versailles. It was in three acts, was called *Tartuffe* (from 'Tartufo', the mountebank of Italian comedy) and was written 'against the hypocrites'. Though it amused the king it was seen as an attack on the mysteries of religion by the Compagnie du Saint Sacrement (see introduction) which, backed by the Queen Mother, the Archbishop of Paris and Lamoignon, First President of the Paris Parlement, succeeded in stopping any further public performances. It was, however, staged several times in private houses in the autumn by which time, according to La Grange's register, it had acquired a fourth act. On 5 August 1667, believing he had received royal authorization to play it, Molière presented a revised version, in five acts, now called *L'Imposteur*, with Tartuffe renamed 'Panulphe' and stripped of his clerical garb. But although Molière's hypocrite has ceased to be a devout believer and appeared as a secular 'man of the world', and while the Compagnie was not the force it had been in 1664, Lamoignon intervened. The play was again stopped and the archbishop threatened its author with excommunication. The ban was not lifted until 5 February 1669 when *Tartuffe*, in the only version that has survived, began a highly successful run of twenty-eight consecutive performances and proved subsequently to be one of the most enduring of all Molière's comedies.

In the preface to the published text he denied any intention to mock 'those things which should be revered'. He also expressed surprise that the 'hypocrites' should have reacted so violently whereas the fashionable wits, *précieuses*, cuckolds and doctors he had satirized in other plays had not complained unduly and had even pretended to be amused. He also rejected the view held by the Compagnie du Saint Sacrement that the theatre was what the early Church Fathers had said it was, a 'school for vice' which gave comfort to immorality. He repeated that his sole intention was to serve the public good by exposing those unscrupulous men who, for their own self-serving reasons, abused the confidence of God-fearing people whose consciences they claimed to direct.

Though *Tartuffe* raises no metaphysical or theological issues in the way that *Don Juan* came close to doing in 1665, it does challenge the narrow view of religion promoted by the puritans and fundamentalists in general and by the Compagnie du Saint Sacrement in particular. All Molière's plays champion tolerance, moderation and openness, which were the antithesis of the intolerance, extremism and secrecy of the cabal of which Tartuffe is a clear echo. To this extent, religiosity, rather than religion, is central to the play, and when free to revert to his original conception, Molière abandoned the secular Panulphe of 1667 and revived the religious hypocrite of the play as we know it. For Tartuffe as a crooked lawyer, say, or a sharp accountant, would have been a figure of melodrama, a sticky-fingered villain, rather than the sinister figure who exploits the beliefs of others.

But Molière's theatre also mounts a consistent attack on anything which threatens to disrupt or ruin the family: his Would-Be Gentleman, his Miser and his Hypochondriac are all prepared to sacrifice their children's happiness to their obsessions. It is from this standpoint and not for reasons of doctrine that Molière exposes the hypocrisy of Tartuffe and mocks the credulity of Orgon and Madame Pernelle. Neither the bland common-sense of Cléante nor the gamy resistance of Elmire are enough to halt the villain, and it takes a *deus ex machina* to humble him. The fifth act has often been criticized for its implausibility and sometimes excused as perhaps a survival from the 1664 version, or as a prudent genuflection to the authority of Louis XIV from a grateful playwright. Yet it works well in theatrical terms and is perfectly consistent with the general sense of the play. It can be seen as an ironic warning: only in plays are the Tartuffes so easily halted.

Characters

MADAME PERNELLE, Orgon's
    mother
ORGON
ELMIRE, his wife
DAMIS, his son
MARIANE, his daughter, in love
    with Valère
VALÈRE, in love with Mariane
CLÉANTE, brother-in-law of
    Orgon
TARTUFFE, a religious hypocrite
DORINE, maid to Mariane
MONSIEUR LOYAL, a bailiff of
    the court
AN OFFICER
FLIPOTE, maid to Madame
    Pernelle

The scene is set in Paris

Act I

Scene i:

MADAME PERNELLE: Come Flipote, I'll not stay under the same roof as them a minute longer.

ELMIRE: You're walking so fast we can hardly keep up.

MADAME PERNELLE: Then don't try, daughter-in-law, don't come another step. All this fussing is exactly what I can do without.

ELMIRE: We're only showing you the consideration you deserve. But mother-in-law, why are you rushing away like this?

MADAME PERNELLE: Because I can't stand the way you carry on here and because no one pays any attention to my wishes. Oh yes, I shall leave this house singularly unedified. My views have been opposed at every turn. You have no respect for anything, everyone here says exactly what they think, it's a madhouse.

DORINE: But —

MADAME PERNELLE: You, miss, are a servant, too ready with your tongue and most impertinent. You are far too free with your opinions.

DAMIS: But —

MADAME PERNELLE: And you, my lad, are, in a word, a fool, you can take that from me. And if your grandmother can't say it, who can? Many's the time I've warned my son, I mean your father, told him you were going to the bad and would cause him nothing but trouble and grief.

MARIANE: I think —

MADAME PERNELLE: As for you my girl, you're his sister, but you seem sensible enough. You behave very sweetly and you don't make tongues wag. But you know what they say: still waters run deep. You carry on behind our backs and I don't like it.

ELMIRE: But —

MADAME PERNELLE: As a daughter-in-law, and you won't mind my saying this, your behaviour is thoroughly unsatisfactory. You should be setting them a good example — their poor dead mother did her duty far better. You have expensive tastes and I am shocked to see you going about dressed like a princess. A wife who wishes to please only her husband has no business to be so concerned with her appearance.

CLÉANTE: On the other hand –

MADAME PERNELLE: For you, as Elmire's brother, I have great respect, affection and the highest regard. But really, if I were in my son's place, which is to say her husband, I would strongly advise you not to set foot in my house. You persist in preaching rules of conduct no respectable person should follow. I do not mince my words, I'm not the sort who does: I don't beat about the bush when I've got something to say.

DAMIS: Your Tartuffe must be quite exceptional then.

MADAME PERNELLE: He is a good man who deserves to be listened to. It makes me extremely angry when I hear him abused by imbeciles like you.

DAMIS: But why should I allow some carping, sanctimonious bigot to come here and behave like a bully to the point where we can't enjoy ourselves unless His Mightiness first grants his gracious permission?

DORINE: If you listened to him and believed everything he says, nobody could do anything that wasn't a sin. He's a pious busybody and he rules the roost.

MADAME PERNELLE: Any roost he rules is well ruled. All he wants is to set you on the road to salvation, and my son should do everything he can to make you love him.

DAMIS: Never! Grandmother, neither my father nor anyone else can force me to like the man. I would be a hypocrite if I said otherwise. I find the way he behaves absolutely infuriating. I can see only one outcome. I and this yokel are going to have it out in a big way.

DORINE: Yes, it's an absolute scandal that a nobody like him should just walk in and take over. When he first came here he was poverty-stricken. No shoes on his feet and clothes you couldn't have given away. Now he's got so above himself that he pokes his nose into everything and orders everybody about.

MADAME PERNELLE: Mercy be! We would all be better off if you obeyed his saintly commandments.

DORINE: You only imagine he's a saint, but you can take it from me, everything he does is hypocrisy.

MADAME PERNELLE: Listen to the girl talk!

DORINE: I wouldn't trust him an inch without a written guarantee, nor his man Laurent neither.

MADAME PERNELLE: I can't say I know what the servant is like, but I will vouch for the master who is a good man. The reason you resent him and will not listen is that he tells each one of you unpleasant truths. His whole being is offended by sin, and doing God's work is his only purpose.

DORINE: Very well. But why in that case, why is it, and especially just recently, that he won't have visitors coming to the house? What is there so sinful about a straightforward visit to justify him making such a terrific fuss? Do you want me to tell you what I think the reason is, just between ourselves? I think that he is in love with the mistress. So there!

MADAME PERNELLE: Be quiet and mind what you say. He is not the only one who disapproves of all these visits. All these people you know make a terrible nuisance of themselves. They have carriages forever waiting in the street outside and their footmen make a dreadful noise: it creates a very bad impression on the whole neighbourhood. I am prepared to accept that it's all quite harmless. But the fact is that people are gossiping, and that is not a good thing.

CLÉANTE: But surely, Madame Pernelle, you are not suggesting that we should do away with conversation? Life would be very much the poorer if we had to stop seeing our best friends just because silly people were saying unpleasant things about us. And even if we wanted to, do you really think you could make everybody stop talking? There is no defence against malicious rumour-mongering. So let's pay no attention to the wagging tongues. Let's try to live good lives and let the gossips say whatever they like.

DORINE: I don't suppose by any chance it's Daphne next door and that little husband of hers who have been saying nasty things about us? People who live in glass houses are always the first to throw mud. They never miss a turn. They pounce eagerly on the dimmest flicker of what might be an affair, and spread the news with great glee, giving it the slant they want other people to believe. By painting other people's behaviour in their own colours, they hope to justify what they do themselves. They believe the comparison will make their own sordid intrigues look blameless, though it never works out like that, or they think they can deflect on to others some of the criticisms which rightly land at their door.

MADAME PERNELLE: All this discussing is quite beside the point. It is common knowledge that Orante is an example to us all. Everything she does she does for God. Now, it has come to my attention through certain of my acquaintance that she condemns the way you carry on in this house in no uncertain terms.

DORINE: And a fine example she is! A really good woman! It's quite true that she lives a her life according to strict principles. But it was age that lit the pious fire in her soul, for it's also common knowledge that she is only such an awful prude because she has no choice. As long as men went on finding her attractive, she made the most of her advantages. But when she saw her eye lose its sparkle, she decided to turn her back on the world which had in fact turned its back on her, and cloaked her faded beauty beneath a noble veil of virtue. That's how all coquettes finish up nowadays. It's not easy for them when they see their admirers desert them. Left to themselves, they become bitter and fret and they can see no other alternative than to turn into stuffy old harridans. These self-righteous ladies are very strict: they damn everybody and show no mercy. They point accusing fingers at the way other people live, not out of Christian charity but from envy, because they simple cannot bear to see other people enjoying pleasures which the passing years have put beyond their reach.

MADAME PERNELLE: So this is the kind of ridiculous nonsense you must have to keep you happy. I see, daughter-in-law, that I am not allowed to get a word in edgeways in your house, for this hussy never stops talking all day. But I intend to have my say in my turn. I tell you it was the most sensible thing my son ever did to welcome this saintly man under his roof. The Lord sent him here, where he was needed, to direct you back to the path from which you have strayed. You should all listen to him for the good of your souls, for he finds fault only in those things which need mending. All these visits, dances and idle talk are the inventions of Lucifer. Pious words are never heard in your get-togethers, only tittle-tattle and singing and silly nonsense. Friends and acquaintances always come in for their fair share of sniping and no one is spared. Even sensible people get carried away by the confusion in such gatherings, tongues start wagging in next to no time and, as a man of the cloth remarked only recently, these occasions are a Tower of Babylon, with everyone jabbering nineteen to the dozen. And having made this point, he went on to say ... (*Pointing to Cléante*) Do I see this gentleman beginning to snigger? Why don't you find somebody else to laugh at, and if ... Daughter-in-law, goodbye. I'll not say another word. But I'll have you know that this house has gone down a long way in my estimation and it will be a long time before I ever set foot in it again. (*Giving Flipote a slap*) Come along, you! You've got your head in the clouds! What are you gawping at? God give me patience, I'll warm your ears for you! Shift yourself, you lazy good-for-nothing, let's be off!

Scene ii:
CLÉANTE, DORINE

CLÉANTE: I'm not going after her in case she turns on me again. How that old girl –

DORINE: It's a pity she can't hear you talking like that. She'd tell you what she thinks of you in no uncertain terms and point out that she's far too young to be called an old woman.

CLÉANTE: But to let fly at us for so little! She seems absolutely smitten with this Tartuffe of hers!

DORINE: But that's nothing compared to the way her son is. If you'd seen the master recently, you'd say he was much, much worse. During the late troubles,[1] he made himself a name for shrewdness and was very brave in the king's service. But ever since he's been besotted with Tartuffe; it's as if he's completely lost his grip. He calls him brother and loves him far more than his mother, son, wife or daughter. He tells him all his secrets and regards him as a prudent adviser. He spoils and pampers him, and I don't think he could be fonder of a mistress. He insists on putting him at the head of the table and looks on delightedly while he eats enough for six. He sees to it that the others let him have the pick of everything and if he belches,[2] he just says: 'God bless you'. All of which means that the master's mad about Tartuffe. He's his ideal, his hero. He admires everything he does and repeats everything he says. The most insignificant thing he does is a miracle and all his pronouncements are oracles. On the other hand, Tartuffe, who knows a fool when he sees one and has made up his mind to make the most of it, has all sorts of subtle ways of pulling the wool over the master's eyes. He is forever getting money out of him with his sanctimonious humbug and he's taken it upon himself to pass judgement on as many of us as catch his eye. Even that half-wit he has for a servant thinks he can put us right on everything. When Tartuffe preaches at us, his eyes blaze and he throws our ribbons, rouge and beauty patches away. The other day the snake in the grass found a modesty kerchief in a book of saints' lives and tore it to pieces with his bare hands. He said we'd committed a horrible sin by putting holiness and the devil's allurements together.

Scene iii:

ELMIRE, MARIANE, DAMIS, CLÉANTE, DORINE

ELMIRE: It was a good thing you weren't there to hear the oration she gave us at the door. But I caught a glimpse of my husband. He didn't see me, so I'm going upstairs. I'll wait for him there.

CLÉANTE: And I'll wait for him here, it'll save time. I just want to say hello. (*Elmire and Mariane leave.*)

DAMIS: Do have a word with him about my sister's marriage. I suspect Tartuffe is against it and that it's he who is making my father drag his heels. For you are aware that I have an interest in this business. If my sister and my friend Valère are in love, I, as you know, am no less attached to Valère's sister, and if I had to –

DORINE: He's coming!

Scene iv:

ORGON, CLÉANTE, DORINE

ORGON: Ah, good morning brother-in-law.

CLÉANTE: I was just leaving. I'm glad to see you home again. The countryside is looking very dead at this time of year.

ORGON: Dorine ... (*To Cléante:*) One moment please brother. Would you allow me, to put my mind at rest, to make a few inquires about how things are here? (*To Dorine*:) Has everything gone off well these last two days? What's everyone been up to? Are they all well?

DORINE: The day before yesterday the mistress had a touch of fever which lasted till evening. And an awful headache, rather worrying.

ORGON: And Tartuffe?

DORINE: Tartuffe? In fine fettle. Hale and hearty. The picture of health. Roses in his cheeks.

ORGON: Poor man!

DORINE: By the evening she was feeling sick and couldn't touch her dinner because her headache was still very bad.

ORGON: And Tartuffe?

DORINE: He dined alone with the mistress and made devout work of a couple of partridge and half a leg of mutton cut up small.

ORGON: Poor man!

DORINE: She never closed her eyes the whole night long. Her temperature was up and it stopped her sleeping. We had to sit up with her all night.

ORGON: And Tartuffe?

DORINE: Feeling pleasantly tired, he went straight from dinner to his room, jumped into a nice warm bed and slept like a log until the following morning.

ORGON: Poor man!

DORINE: In the end she listened to what we'd been saying and agreed to be bled. Afterwards she felt easier almost at once.

ORGON: And Tartuffe?

DORINE: He picked himself up manfully and, arming his soul to face adversity, downed four large glasses of wine with his breakfast to make up for the blood the mistress had lost.

ORGON: Poor man!

DORINE: So both of them are better again. I'll run along and tell the mistress how anxious you are to know how she's coming on.

Scene v:

ORGON, CLÉANTE

CLÉANTE: She was mocking you to your face brother. And without wishing to anger you. I'd say in all honesty she was quite right. Did anyone ever speak so unthinkingly? Can it be possible that this man should now cast such a spell that he has made you put everything second to him? That having saved him from poverty under your roof, you should be prepared to –

ORGON: Not another word brother. You talk about him but you don't know what he's like.

CLÉANTE: As you say, I don't know him. But to have an idea of what kind of man he is –

ORGON: Brother, you would be delighted to meet him, and would go on endlessly being delighted. He is a man . . . who . . . er . . . a man . . . in a word, a man. Anyone who follows his teaching strictly will find perfect peace and come to look upon everyone else as scum. Yes, I've become a different person since I've been under instruction. He teaches me to be emotionally detached and is trying to free me from all ties of love, to the point where now I'd happily watch my brother, my children, my mother and my wife all die and not care tuppence.

CLÉANTE: These are very human sentiments brother, I must say!

ORGON: Oh if you'd seen how I got to know him, you'd feel exactly the way I do. He used to appear in church every day, so meek and mild, and come and get down on both knees right next to me. He attracted the attention of the whole congregation by the fervour with which he prayed to heaven. He'd sigh and cry out and humbly kiss the ground at every conceivable opportunity. And as I left he would hurry on ahead and stand by the door so he could offer me the holy water. Having learnt though his servant, who behaved exactly as he did, about his poverty and about what sort of man he was, I gave him money. But being modest he always insisted on giving some of it back, saying: 'It's too much, too much by half. I am not worth your pity.' And if I refused to take it back from him, he would distribute it among the poor while I watched. In the end, heaven directed me to welcome him into my house and from that moment

on everything has seemed to prosper here. I observe that he finds
fault with everything and that he takes a close interest in my wife,
to protect my honour: he tells me about anyone who tries to flirt
with her and is ten times more jealous than I am. But you'd never
believe how exalted he is in the faith. The least of his own shortcomings
he counts a sin and his slightest failing is enough to offend him to
the point where he came to me the other day full of remorse because
he'd caught a flea while he was saying his prayers and had killed it
in a fit of anger.

CLÉANTE: God, you're crazy brother, that's how it strikes me! You're
having me on, surely, by talking like this. What do you hope to gain
by spinning such foolish tales –

ORGON: Your words have a ring of unbelief to them. There is an
atheistical streak in your heart and, as I've warned you a score of
times, you will bring serious trouble on yourself one of these days.

CLÉANTE: That's how people like you talk, always wanting everyone
else to be as blind as they are. Anyone who has eyes to see is an
atheist, and whoever does not fall for your psalm-singing tomfoolery
has neither respect nor reverence for what is sacred. Oh no, all your
talk doesn't scare me! I know what I'm saying and God sees what is
in my heart. Not all of us are taken in by your self-righteous bigots.
There are bogus men of God just as there are bogus men of courage.
And in the same way as we see that when their honour is put to the
test the men of courage are not the ones who make the most noise,
so the truly pious men of God, in whose footsteps we should follow,
are not those who put on the biggest show. Surely you make a
distinction between hypocrisy and true belief? Yet you insist on
dealing with them in the same terms and respect the mask as you
would the face, putting deceit on the same level as sincerity, confusing
appearance and truth, persona and person, false coin and legal tender.
People, for the most part, are oddly made! You won't find them very
strong on moderation. They think that reason imposes constraints
which are too strict. Whatever kind of person they are, they invariably
overstep the mark and frequently ruin the noblest causes because
they overdo things and take them too far. But all this was by way
of saying that –

ORGON: Ah! I see you are a man of learning, the kind people look up
to, the sole repository of all the knowledge in the world. No one is

as enlightened or wise as you. In this age of ours, you are an oracle, a new Cato, and compared to you all men are fools.

CLÉANTE: I am no learned man, nor am I the repository of all knowledge. But I will say this: one thing I do know, and that is how to tell the difference between true and false. And just as I believe that if there are still heroes none should be more respected than those who sincerely believe in God, and that nothing on earth is finer or more noble than the sacred fervour of true faith. I also think that there is nothing more odious than a brazen show of spurious piety by shameless hypocrites and self-advertising Pharisees who strike sacrilegious, two-faced attitudes and unrestrainedly exploit and freely mock everything humankind holds most holy and most sacred; people who, putting their own interest first, turn faith into a profession and a commodity and set out to buy credit and public honours by rolling their hypocritical eyes and faking zeal. I mean the ones you see displaying spectacular fervour and turning the path to heavenly salvation into the road to earthly fortune. Ablaze with faith and praying like publicans, they always have their hands held out and preach withdrawal from the world to others while they themselves go on enjoying life at Court. They trim their zeal to suit their vices and are quick to judge and vindictive, have no faith, use underhand methods and, when they decide someone should be brought down, have the effrontery to use the interests of religion as a cover for their self-serving malice. In their unforgiving wrath, they are all the more dangerous because they turn against us weapons we all respect and because their eager purpose, for which they are much thanked, is to cut us down with the sword of God. There are all too many instances of such sham and fraud. But true believers are easy to recognize. Brother, there are in our own times many such people who can stand as glorious examples to us. Take Ariston, Periandre, Oronte, Alcidamas, Polydore or Clitandre; no one doubts their claims. They do not trumpet their virtue abroad nor will you see them wallowing insufferably in holy ecstasy. Their piety is humane and tolerant. They do not criticize everything people do – they see the arrogance behind carping of that kind. They leave such proud talk to others and correct our failings by the way they behave. They are not fooled by what appears to be wickedness, for their hearts ensure they judge other people fairly. No factions for them nor plots to hatch: all they are seen to do, the only thing that matters to them, is to try to live good lives. They never turn venomously on sinners but direct their hatred towards sin itself and never defend the cause of heaven with greater zeal than heaven itself requires. Those are the people for me, that is the way we should behave and theirs is the example we should try to follow. To be blunt, your man is not like that. You are obviously sincere in making so much of his zeal, but I believe you have been misled by false appearances.

ORGON: Is that all you wanted to say?

CLÉANTE: Yes.

ORGON (*makes as if to leave*): I am obliged to you.

CLÉANTE: Just a moment, one more word. Let's leave this subject. You do remember you have given Valère your word that he shall marry your daughter?

ORGON: I do.

CLÉANTE: And that you named the day?

ORGON: Correct.

CLÉANTE: Then why have you put the wedding off?

ORGON: Couldn't say.

CLÉANTE: Do you have something else in mind?

ORGON: Perhaps.

CLÉANTE: You're not planning to go back on your word?

ORGON: I'm not saying that.

CLÉANTE: I can't see any obstacle that would prevent you keeping your promise.

ORGON: That's as maybe.

CLÉANTE: Why must you prevaricate instead of giving a straight answer? Valère asked me to speak to you.

ORGON: Heaven be praised!

CLÉANTE: So what am I to tell him?

ORGON: Whatever you like.

CLÉANTE: But I must know your intentions. What do you mean to do?

ORGON: Whatever God wills.

CLÉANTE: Let's not beat about the bush. Valère has your word. Do you intend to keep it, yes or no?

ORGON: Goodbye. (*Exit.*)

CLÉANTE: I'm afraid Valère is going to be disappointed in love. I must let him know how things stand.

Act II

Scene i:

ORGON, MARIANE

ORGON: Mariane.

MARIANE: Father?

ORGON: Come here. I've something to tell you in private.

MARIANE: What are you looking for?

ORGON (*peering into a small side-room*): I'm looking to see if there's anyone about who might hear us. This little room is ideal for eavesdroppers. It's all right, we're safe. I've always found you to be a sweet-natured girl Mariane. You've always been very close to my heart.

MARIANE: I am thankful to know I have a father's love.

ORGON: Well spoken my girl, and to deserve it you should have no other thought than to do what pleases me.

MARIANE: I take the greatest pride in doing so.

ORGON: Excellent. Now, what do you think of our guest, Tartuffe?

MARIANE: What do I think?

ORGON: Yes, you. And be careful how you answer.

MARIANE: Ah! Then I'll say anything you want about him.

ORGON: Very sensible. So tell me, my dear, that his many qualities shine out of him, that you love him and that you would be pleased if I were to choose him to be your husband. What do you say to that?

MARIANE (*starting with surprise*): Oh!

ORGON: What's the matter?

MARIANE: I beg your pardon!

ORGON: What?

MARIANE: Did I hear you correctly?

ORGON: What do you mean?

MARIANE: Who is this person, father, I'm supposed to say I love and would be pleased to have if you were to choose as my husband?

ORGON: Tartuffe.

MARIANE: That's not the way things are at all father I swear. Why do you want me to say something that isn't true?

ORGON: But I want it to be true, and all you need to know is that my mind's made up.

MARIANE: But father, you can't mean –

ORGON: Yes, my girl. It's my intention to make Tartuffe a member of my family by giving you to him in marriage. He will be your husband. I've decided. And as for your wishes . . .

Scene ii:
DORINE, ORGON, MARIANE

ORGON: What are you doing here? Your curiosity, miss, must be working overtime for you to come creeping up on us like this.

DORINE: I couldn't really say how the news got around, whether it was idle speculation or just guesswork, but when I heard about this marriage I thought it was a joke.

ORGON: Joke? Is it unbelievable?

DORINE: So unbelievable that I wouldn't believe it if I heard it from your own lips.

ORGON: I can make you believe it.

DORINE: Get away with you. You're spinning us some silly story.

ORGON: I'm telling you exactly what will happen, and soon.

DORINE: Don't talk rubbish!

ORGON (*to Mariane*): What I'm telling you, my girl, is no joke.

DORINE: Oh, don't listen to your father. He's having you on.

ORGON: I'm telling you –

DORINE: It's no good, we shan't believe you.

ORGON: If you go on like this I'll get so angry that –

DORINE: All right, all right, we believe you, and on your own head be it. But how can you! Is it possible that you, sir, who seem to be a sensible man, especially with that venerable beard on your chin, should be crazy enough to want to –

ORGON: Now listen here. You have got into a habit of familiarity, my girl, and I'm telling you I don't care for it.

DORINE: Oh please, can't we discuss this without losing our tempers sir? Did you come up with this idea of yours as some sort of joke? Your daughter isn't the right sort to wed a bigot who, in any case, ought to have other things on his mind. Besides, what's in this marriage for you? With all the money you've got, why on earth would you choose a son-in-law who hasn't got a penny to his name?

ORGON: Be quiet! If he has nothing, then that is precisely why we should respect him. His poverty is unquestionably honest poverty and it raises him above all material honours, for he has left himself without support by his neglect of temporal things and his unswerving attachment to things eternal. But a little help from me will give him the means to rise out of his financial embarrassment and enter once more into full possession of his property. He has estates which are highly thought of in his part of the country. You only have to look at him as he is now to realize that he is very much a gentleman.

DORINE: Yes, as he's always reminding us. It's vanity sir, and it doesn't square very well with piety. A man who accepts the simple goodness that goes with a devout life shouldn't boast so much of his name and family connections, for the humility of true faith is hardly helped by ambition of this sort. Why take pride in such things? . . . But you find the subject offensive, so let's forget his noble birth and talk about the man. Do you really think you can give someone of his sort a girl like your daughter and not expect trouble? Shouldn't you consider the proprieties and give some thought to what the results of such a union might be? Take it from me, when a girl is forced to marry against her choice, her virtue is put under serious stress. Her intention to be a good wife will depend on the qualities of the husband she's been given, and men whose cuckold's horns attract attention are often the ones who've made their wives the way they are. It's very hard to be faithful to a certain kind of husband, and any father who gives his daughter to a man she hates is responsible to God for the sins she commits. Think of what dangers this plan of yours could expose you to.

ORGON (*to Mariane*): Well I declare! Am I supposed to let her teach me how to manage my life?

DORINE: You could do worse than take my advice.

ORGON: Daughter, let's not waste any more time on all this nonsense. I'm your father and I know what's best for you. True, I did give my word to Valère. But apart from the fact that they say he likes gambling, I also suspect he's something of a free-thinker. I haven't noticed that he's much of a church-goer.

DORINE: Do you expect him to trot along to church at the times you fix, like those who only turn up to be seen?

ORGON: I didn't ask for your opinion (*To Mariane*:) Now Tartuffe on the other hand is on the very best terms with God, which is an asset that surpasseth all other earthly riches. Marrying him will give you everything you could wish for. It will be wedded bliss, all sweetness and joy. You'll live together as loving and faithful as a couple of children or a pair of turtle-doves. There'll be never a cross word between you and you'll be able to do whatever you like with him.

DORINE: Will she? She'll turn him into a cuckold, that's what she'll do, take it from me.

ORGON: Hush! That's no way to talk!

DORINE: I tell you, he looks the type. It's in his stars sir, and all your daughter's virtue won't prevent it.

ORGON: Stop interrupting. Try keeping your mouth shut and stop poking your nose into matters which are none of your business.

DORINE (*interrupting him again just as he turns to speak to his daughter*): I'm only telling you for your own good.

ORGON: There's no need to go to such trouble. Please, just be quiet.

DORINE: If I weren't so fond of you –

ORGON: I don't want people to be fond of me!

DORINE: But I insist on being fond of you sir, whether you like it or not.

ORGON: Bah!

DORINE: I worry about your reputation. I won't let you become a laughing-stock, a butt of everybody's sneers.

ORGON: Won't you ever be quiet?

DORINE: I'd never forgive myself if I stood by and allowed you to go ahead with this marriage.

ORGON: Silence, you serpent, you insolent –

DORINE: Temper, temper. And you a man of God!

ORGON: Yes, all your silly chatter is making my blood boil. I'm telling you one last time: hold your tongue.

DORINE: As you wish. But not saying anything doesn't mean I've stopped thinking.

ORGON: Think away, if you must. But do your very best not to tell me about it, or else . . . But that's enough. (*Turning to his daughter*:) Being a wise parent, I've weighed it all up carefully.

DORINE: It's infuriating not being allowed to speak. (*She stops when he looks round.*)

ORGON: Tartuffe may be no Adonis, but his looks . . .

DORINE: A pretty face, I don't think!

ORGON: . . . his looks are the kind that even if you don't see any other qualities in him . . . (*He turns to face her and stares with his arms folded.*)

DORINE: That's her fixed up! I tell you, if I were in her shoes, no man would marry me against my will and hope to get away with it! The wedding would hardly be over before I showed him that a woman can always find ways of getting her own back.

ORGON: So you refuse to do what I said?

DORINE: What are you complaining about? I'm not talking to you.

ORGON: What are you doing, then?

DORINE: Talking to myself.

ORGON: Good. (*Aside*) To punish her for being downright insolent, I'm going to have to let her feel the back of my hand. (*He positions himself to administer the blow; but every time he looks in her direction Dorine snaps to attention and says nothing.*) Mariane, you must approve my plan . . . and believe that the husband . . . I've selected for you . . . (*To Dorine:*) Why is it you're not talking to yourself now?

DORINE: I haven't got anything to tell me.

ORGON: Say just one more little word.

DORINE: Don't want to.

ORGON: But I was waiting for you to –

DORINE: Look, I'm not that stupid!

ORGON: So Mariane, you must show what an obedient daughter you are by accepting my choice without question.

DORINE (*running out of reach*): I'd despise myself if I agreed to take someone like him as a husband. (*He tries to hit her and misses.*)

ORGON (*to Mariane*): This maid of yours is a damned pest. I won't stay in the same room with her any longer. If I did, I might do something I'd be sorry for. I'm in no fit state to go on with this business now. Her insolent talk has made me far too angry to think straight. I'm going outside for a breath of air to calm me down.

Scene iii:

DORINE, MARIANE

DORINE: Tell me, has the cat got your tongue? Do I have to be your understudy? You let him put the craziest scheme to you and you don't say a single word against it!

MARIANE: What do you expect me to do against a tyrant of a father?

DORINE: Whatever it takes to stand up to his threats.

MARIANE: Like what?

DORINE: Tell him that no one can love another person to order. Say that you'll get married to please yourself not to suit him, that since you are the one all this marrying business is about, it's you the husband has to please, not him, and that if he thinks Tartuffe is so wonderful there's nothing to stop him marrying him himself.

MARIANE: I admit that fathers have such power over their children that I've never felt brave enough to tell him what I think.

DORINE: Well, let's work it out. Valère has made a move for you. Tell me, do you love him or don't you?

MARIANE: Dorine, how can you be so unfair to my feelings! How can you ask such a question? Haven't I opened my heart to you any number of times? Surely you know how madly I love him?

DORINE: How am I supposed to know if what your tongue says is what your heart thinks and that you really are in love with this young man of yours?

MARIANE: It is very wrong of you, Dorine, to doubt it. I've made my feelings all too clear.

DORINE: So you *do* love him?

MARIANE: Yes, madly.

DORINE: And as far as you can tell he loves you too?

MARIANE: I believe he does.

DORINE: And the pair of you really want to get married?

MARIANE: Oh yes!

DORINE: What are you going to do about this other marriage?

MARIANE: I'll kill myself if they make me.

DORINE: Wonderful! That's one solution I hadn't thought of: ending it all as a way of getting yourself out of a mess. Obviously a miracle cure. Oh I get very angry when I hear that sort of talk!

MARIANE: Gracious Dorine, how callous you can be! You have no sympathy for other people's misfortunes.

DORINE: I have no sympathy for people who talk rubbish and give up in a crisis, as you are doing now.

MARIANE: But what do you want from me? If I'm not very brave . . .

DORINE: But you have to be strong when you're in love.

MARIANE: I've never weakened in my love for Valère. Anyway, isn't it up to him to ask my father for his permission?

DORINE: What! So even though your father is a hardened old curmudgeon who drools over his precious Tartuffe and cancels the wedding he said could go ahead, it's Valère who has to take all the blame?

MARIANE: But won't a flat refusal, a scathing no, be tantamount to admitting how much I love the man I've set my heart on? However wonderful he is, would it be right for me to deny my maidenly modesty and my duty as a daughter on his account? Do you want me to display my feelings for all to see and –

DORINE: No, I don't want anything. But it's obvious to me you want to marry Monsieur Tartuffe and, come to think of it, I'd be wrong to try to talk you out of such an advantageous step. Why should I want to oppose your wishes? As suitors go, he's an excellent prospect. Monsieur Tartuffe! Ah! You're being offered a real catch there. When you think about it, Monsieur Tartuffe is not a man, absolutely not, without considerable merit and it would be thought no small honour to be his better half. Everyone already treats him with the greatest respect. He's known as a gentleman wherever it is he comes from, and he's ever so handsome with his red ears and that blotchy face. You'd be happy ever after with a husband like that.

MARIANE: Oh God!

DORINE: You'd have a song in your heart if you were the wife of such a good-looking husband.

MARIANE: Oh please stop talking like that and show me how I can get out of this wedding. I'm convinced. I surrender. I'm ready to do anything.

DORINE: No, a daughter must do her father's bidding, even if he wants to make her marry an ape. It's a pretty good outlook, so what are you complaining for? You'll take the public coach to the little town he comes from and you'll find it oozing with uncles and cousins.

You'll enjoy talking to them. You'll walk straight into high society, go calling and be welcomed by the wives of the town clerk and the local justice of the peace who do you the honour of letting you sit down with them as their equal. When carnival time comes round, you can expect a ball and full orchestra – that is a couple of bagpipes – and sometimes a performing monkey and puppets. But if your husband –

MARIANE: Stop! It's more than flesh and blood can bear! Can't you give me any advice that would help me?

DORINE: It's not for me –

MARIANE: Oh please Dorine.

DORINE: This wedding will have to go through. It'll teach you a lesson.

MARIANE: Dorine!

DORINE: No.

MARIANE: I've told you how I feel –

DORINE: I said no. Tartuffe's the man for you and Tartuffe you shall have.

MARIANE: You know I've never had any secrets from you. Won't you –

DORINE: No. Believe me, you're going to be thoroughly Tartuffed!

MARIANE: All right. Since my predicament won't move you, just leave me to my despair, for in despairing I shall find relief: I know a certain cure for all my unhappiness. (*She starts to leave.*)

DORINE: Hey, come back, I won't get angry again. I can't help feeling sorry for you, in spite of everything.

MARIANE: If they force me to go through with this terrible ordeal, I tell you Dorine, it will kill me.

DORINE: Don't take on so. If we play our cards right, we'll soon put a stop . . . But here's your Valère.

Scene iv:

VALÈRE, MARIANE, DORINE

VALÈRE: Mariane, there's a story going round, and not a very nice one. It was news to me.

MARIANE: What is it?

VALÈRE: That you're to marry Tartuffe.

MARIANE: It's certainly what my father plans.

VALÈRE: Your father . . .

MARIANE: . . . has changed his mind. He himself has just this minute put it to me.

VALÈRE: What, seriously?

MARIANE: Yes, seriously. He has his mind set on the match.

VALÈRE: And which of these marriages is your heart set on?

MARIANE: I don't know.

VALÈRE: That's a fine answer! You don't know?

MARIANE: No.

VALÈRE: No?

MARIANE: What would you advise?

VALÈRE: I'd advise you to marry him.

MARIANE: Is that your advice?

VALÈRE: Yes.

MARIANE: You mean it?

VALÈRE: Of course. It's an honour to have been asked and you should think about it very seriously.

MARIANE: Well, if that's your advice, I'll take it.

VALÈRE: I don't expect you'll find it very hard to follow.

MARIANE: No harder than it was for you to offer it.

VALÈRE: Oh, I only offered it to please you.

MARIANE: And I'll take it – to please you.

DORINE (*aside*): Let's see where all this leads.

VALÈRE: It that what you call love? You were deceiving me when you –

MARIANE: Let's not go into all that, please. You told me straight out that I should agree to have the husband I've been offered. I tell you in return that's precisely what I intend to do, since your very sensible advice is that I should.

VALÈRE: Don't use what I said as an excuse. You'd already made up your mind and you're just seizing on a piffling pretext to justify going back on your word.

MARIANE: Quite true, you put it very well.

VALÈRE: Of course it's true. You never really loved me at all.

MARIANE: Ah! You're perfectly entitled to think so.

VALÈRE: Of course I'm entitled! But the sting of rejection might well prompt me to get my retaliation in first. I know where I can take my affections and find myself another wife.

MARIANE: I don't doubt it for a moment. And the love that your excellent qualities will inspire –

VALÈRE: Oh God, let's leave my qualities out of it. I probably don't have many, as your behaviour shows. But I have reason to hope I shall be treated better elsewhere, for I know someone who will have no qualms about consoling me in my loss once she knows I am free.

MARIANE: It's not much of a loss and the change will help you get over it very quickly.

VALÈRE: I'll do my best, believe me. When someone throws your love back at you, there's the matter of self-respect: you've got to try your hardest to forget the other person too, and if you can't manage it, then at least you have to pretend to. You can never forgive yourself if you are weak enough go on loving someone who has stopped loving you.

MARIANE: What noble, what lofty sentiments!

VALÈRE: Indeed they are, and they should commend themselves to everyone. Surely you don't expect me to pine for you eternally and stand idly by while you give yourself to somebody else, without wanting to find another home for the affections you no longer want?

MARIANE: On the contrary, that's exactly what I'd like. I wish it had happened already.

VALÈRE: Is that what you want?

MARIANE: Yes.

VALÈRE: That's the final insult. I shall go and see to it that you get your wish forthwith . . . (*He starts to leave and then comes back again.*)

MARIANE: Good.

VALÈRE: At least remember that it was you who drove me to this extremity.

MARIANE: I shall.

VALÈRE: And that in doing what I am about to do I shall simply be following the example you set.

MARIANE: My example. So be it.

VALÈRE: There's no more to say. In the fullness of time you shall get what you want.

MARIANE: So much the better.

VALÈRE: You'll never see me again as long as I live.

MARIANE: Wonderful!

VALÈRE (*departs and when he has almost reached the door, turns*): Pardon?

MARIANE: What?

VALÈRE: Did you call?

MARIANE: Me? You're imagining things.

VALÈRE: Oh. Well in that case I shall be on my way. Goodbye, Madame.

MARIANE: Goodbye, sir.

DORINE: I think the pair of you have taken leave of your senses behaving
in this absurd way. I let you go on squabbling to see just how far
you would go. Hey, Valère! (*She grabs his arm to stop Valère who
puts up a show of resisting.*)

VALÈRE: What do you want Dorine?

DORINE: Come here.

VALÈRE: No, I'm much too cross. Don't try to prevent me doing what
she wants.

DORINE: Stop it.

VALÈRE: I won't. You see, there's nothing more to say.

DORINE: Is that so?

MARIANE: He can't stand the sight of me, he can't bear to be near me
and the best thing for me would be to leave him to it.

DORINE (*abandoning Valère and running after Mariane*): Now the other
one's at it! Where are you going?

MARIANE: Leave me alone!

DORINE: You mustn't go!

MARIANE: Out of the question Dorine. It's no good trying to make me
stay.

VALÈRE: I can see she hates the very sight of me. I'd best go and spare
her further pain.

DORINE (*abandoning Mariane and running after Valère*): Not again! Damn
you, I won't let you go! Now stop your silly bickering and come
here both of you. (*She drags them both together.*)

VALÈRE: What's the idea?

MARIANE: What are you trying to do?

DORINE: To get you two back together and help you out of this pickle
(*To Valère:*) Where's your common-sense, quarrelling like this?

VALÈRE: Didn't you hear how she spoke to me?

DORINE (*to Mariane*): And are you out of your mind, letting yourself
get so cross?

MARIANE: Didn't you see for yourself how he treated me?

DORINE (*to Valère*): You are one as silly as the other. All she wants is to go on being yours, as I can testify. (*To Mariane:*) You're the only one he loves, and all he wants is to be your husband, I'd stake my life on it.

MARIANE: Then why did he give me such advice?

VALÈRE: Why did you ask my advice about such a matter?

DORINE: You're both off your heads. Put your hands here, the pair of you. (*To Valère:*) Come on, you.

VALÈRE (*giving Dorine his hand*): What good will my hand do?

DORINE (*to Mariane*): Right, now yours.

MARIANE (*also giving her hand*): What's the point of all this?

DORINE: Lord give me strength! Get a move on! Best foot forward! You're both much more in love with each other than you think.

VALÈRE (*to Mariane*): Do it without looking so pained. Try not to stare at a fellow as if you loathed him. (*Mariane looks at Valère and gives a little smile.*)

DORINE: The truth is that people in love are all mad!

VALÈRE: Hold on! Didn't I have good reason to complain? And if you are honest wouldn't you say you were very mean to enjoy breaking such terrible news to me?

MARIANE: Ooh! And aren't you the most ungrateful man who ever –

DORINE: You can argue about that some other time. Let's think how we can stop this gruesome marriage.

MARIANE: Do tell us what steps we should take.

DORINE: We'll be taking all sorts of steps. Your father can't mean it, it's all so ridiculous. But as a first move, it would be a good idea if you were to act very sweetly and pretend to go along with this mad scheme of his. Then if things start to go wrong it will be easier to postpone the wedding. If we can gain time, we'll set everything to rights. You can say you've come down suddenly with some illness which means putting it off. Or you can talk about premonitions: you're upset because you've seen a corpse, you broke a mirror or had a dream about muddy water. Remember, the best part is that no one can make you marry anyone except Valère unless you say 'I do'. But to increase our chances I think it would be wisest if you weren't seen talking together. (*To Valère:*) Away you go. Quickly now, get your friends to intervene so that her father keeps his word. We'll go and persuade his brother-in-law to try again, and see if we can get Mariane's stepmother on our side. Goodbye.

VALÈRE (*to Mariane*): Whatever plans we might all have, my best hope really is you.

MARIANE (*to Valère*): I can't answer for what my father wants. But I shall never marry anyone else but you Valère.

VALÈRE: You make me so happy! Whatever others might plot –

DORINE: Oh! why is it that young love never stops talking! Be off with you, I say.

VALÈRE (*starts to go then turns*): But . . .

DORINE: My, how you do go on. (*Holding each by the shoulder*) Now you go this way and you go that.

Act III

Scene i:
DAMIS, DORINE

DAMIS: Strike me dead on the spot, call me the greatest villain alive, I don't care: there's no duty or power that can hold me back, nothing that will stop me taking matters into my own hands!

DORINE: For heaven's sake, calm down! Your father has only talked about it, that's all. People never do everything they say they're going to. There's many a step between the thought and the deed.

DAMIS: I've got to put a stop to the swine's little game. I think I'll have a quiet word with him, in private . . .

DORINE: Ah! easy now! Leave it to your stepmother to handle both him and your father. She has some influence over Tartuffe. He listens to what she says and may very well have more than just a soft spot for her. I hope to God he does! That would be a bonus! Actually, she's on your side, which is why she's sent for him. She wants to know how he stands on this wedding you're so anxious about, to find out how he feels about it and make him see what unpleasantness there'll be if he decides to go along with the idea. His man told me he was saying his prayers so I couldn't see him. But his man also said he'd be down soon. So please go and leave me to wait for him.

DAMIS: I could be there while they talked.

DORINE: Out of the question. They must be alone.

DAMIS: I won't say anything to him.

DORINE: Don't fool yourself! We all know how inflammable you are. It would be the best way of ruining everything. Just go away!

DAMIS: No. I want to see it. I shan't lose my temper.

DORINE: What a nuisance you are! He's coming. Be off with you.

Scene ii:

TARTUFFE, LAURENT, DORINE

TARTUFFE (*noticing Dorine*): Laurent, you may put away my hair-shirt and my scourge and pray that Heaven may light your every step. If anyone asks for me, say I have gone visiting the prisoners where I shall be giving away the meagre sums which I myself receive in charity.

DORINE: What a brass-faced, hypocritical . . .

TARTUFFE: What do you want?

DORINE: To tell you —

TARTUFFE (*he takes a handkerchief from his pocket*): For the love of God! I beg you! Before you say another word, take my handkerchief.

DORINE: What for?

TARTUFFE: Cover your bosom which I cannot bear to see. Such sights offend the purest soul, for they prompt sinful thoughts.

DORINE: You must be very susceptible to temptation if a glimpse of flesh has that much effect on you! I can't possibly think why you should get so excited but, speaking for myself, I don't get worked up so easily. I dare say you could stand before me without a stitch on and your whole carcass wouldn't tempt me.

TARTUFFE: Temper your speech with a degree of modesty, or I shall be forced to leave the room.

DORINE: No, I'm the one who will go and leave you in peace. All I had to say was that Madame will be down directly and asks if you would be good enough to give her a few moments.

TARTUFFE: Ah! Most gladly.

DORINE (*to herself*): That's sweetened his temper. Yes, I still think what I said is true.

TARTUFFE: Will she be long?

DORINE: I think I hear her now. Yes, here she is. I'll leave you together.

Scene iii:
ELMIRE, TARTUFFE

TARTUFFE: May Heaven, in its infinite goodness, ever grant you health of mind and body and shower you with as many blessings as the most humble of men whom divine love inspires could wish.

ELMIRE: I thank you for the pious thought. But let's sit down. We'll be more comfortable.

TARTUFFE: How do you feel now? Are you better?

ELMIRE: Much better. I had a temperature but it did not last long.

TARTUFFE: My prayers are not worthy enough to have secured this blessing from on high. Yet of all the devout petitions which I offered up to Heaven, there was not one in which your recovery was not remembered.

ELMIRE: Your zeal on my behalf need not have gone to such lengths.

TARTUFFE: There are no lengths too extreme where your precious health is concerned, and to preserve yours, I would have willingly given my own.

ELMIRE: That's taking Christian charity rather far, but I am most grateful for all your kind thoughts.

TARTUFFE: Anything I can do for you is less than you deserve.

ELMIRE: I wanted to talk to you about a certain matter in private. No one will overhear us here, I'm glad to say.

TARTUFFE: I'm glad too and very delighted, Madame, to be alone with you. Such a moment is something I have beseeched Heaven to grant me, though my prayer has not been answered until now.

ELMIRE: All I ask is a word with you, and that you will be absolutely open with me and keep nothing back.

TARTUFFE: And all I ask too, as a special favour, is that I might open my heart completely to you and give you my word that any remarks I may have made about the way your beauty attracts so much company were not the effect of personal malice but rather of a passionate and pure zeal which –

ELMIRE: That's exactly how I took it, for I believe that you were prompted by a concern for the good of my soul.

TARTUFFE (*squeezing her fingertips*): Oh yes Madame, absolutely, and my devotion is such that –

ELMIRE: Ouch! You're hurting me!

TARTUFFE: I was carried away by my devotion. I didn't mean to hurt
you in any way. I would rather have . . . (*He puts his hand on her
knee.*)

ELMIRE: What is your hand doing there?

TARTUFFE: Feeling your dress. The material is so soft!

ELMIRE: Please don't. I'm dreadfully ticklish. (*She moves her chair back.
Tartuffe brings his closer.*)

TARTUFFE: My word! How fine this lace is. They're wonderfully clever
with their hands these days. Was there ever such workmanship?

ELMIRE: Very true. But to return to the business in hand. They're saying
my husband intends to go back on his word and wants you to marry
Mariane. Tell me, is this true?

TARTUFFE: He did mention something of the sort. But if I may speak
frankly Madame, that is not the happiness to which I aspire, for the
wondrous beauty in which I place all my hope of felicity is located
elsewhere.

ELMIRE: You mean because you are above all earthly concerns.

TARTUFFE: The heart that lies within this breast is not made of stone.

ELMIRE: I'm sure that all your thoughts are fixed on Heaven and that
there's nothing on this earth that you desire.

TARTUFFE: The love which binds us to beauty eternal does not drive
from human hearts a love of the beauties of this world. Our senses
are easily moved by the spectacle of Heaven's perfect handiwork.
Such shining perfection is reflected in women such as yourself, but
in your case Heaven has displayed its rarest wonders. Upon your
face it scattered beauties which dazzle the eyes and delight the heart.
I have never been able to look at you, perfect specimen that you are,
without worshipping through you the Creator of the world, without
feeling my heart gripped by an all-consuming love as I contemplate
the fairest image through which He has revealed Himself. At first, I
feared my secret passion might be an artful snare set by the devil,
and even made up my mind to avoid seeing you, for I believed you
were an obstacle to my salvation. But in time, O comeliest of women,
I saw that my passion need not be sinful, that I could reconcile it
with the purest sentiments, that I could submit to it heart and soul.
I confess I presume greatly in daring to make you an offering of my
love. But to obtain my dearest wishes, I look more to your goodness

than to the vain efforts of my own unworthy self. In you are my hope, my welfare and my peace of mind. On you depend my torment or my bliss. For by your decree alone shall I at last be happy, if such is your wish, or wretched, if it so please you.

ELMIRE: A very pretty declaration but one, I must admit, that I find somewhat surprising. It seems to me you ought to arm your breast more stoutly and think seriously about what you have in mind. A man of faith such as yourself, a pious man whom everyone says is —

TARTUFFE: Pious I may be, but I am also a man, and when a man is confronted with beauty as divine as yours, his heart will have its way and does not stop to think. I know that such words must sound strange on the lips of one such as myself, but when all is said and done, Madame, I am no angel and if you are offended by the declaration I have made to you, then you must lay the blame on your own bewitching loveliness. The moment I first saw its barely mortal radiance, my soul was yours to command. Your glance, angelic and sweeter than words can say, overcame my stubbornly resisting heart. It conquered all — fasts, prayers, tears — and redirected my every wish towards your beauty. A thousand times my eyes, my sighs, have given expression to my feelings for you but now, to say it more clearly, I resort to words. If you were to look with kindness upon the anguish of your unworthy slave, if your indulgence should give me comfort and condescend to gaze down at my insignificance, I would feel for you, miracle of loveliness, a devotion unlike any other. Your honour is safe with me, nor need you fear that I shall bring disgrace upon you. The strutting peacocks of the Court that women go mad for, flaunt their deeds and speak words of vanity. They are seen on all occasions boasting of their conquests. If a lady favours them, they immediately blurt it out, and their indiscreet tongues, in which so much trust is placed, profane the altar on which they offer up their hearts. But men such as I smoulder with less incandescent flames, and secrets are always safe with us. The care we take in preserving our good name makes us answerable for the reputation of the one we love, and it is with us that the woman who receives our affections will find love without scandal, pleasure without fear.

ELMIRE: I have heard you out and the meaning of your eloquent words is all too plain to me. Aren't you afraid that I might take it into my head to tell my husband all about your ardent protestations and that by declaring your love in this way you might well change the friendly feelings he has for you?

TARTUFFE: I know you are far too charitable to do any such thing, that you will forgive my boldness and attribute to human weakness the violence of a love which offends you. And when you look into your mirror, you will reflect that I am not blind and that a man is made of flesh and blood.

ELMIRE: Other women might perhaps take a different view of this matter, but I prefer to use discretion. I will say nothing of all this to my husband, but I shall want something from you in return: you will do all you can, candidly and unstintingly, to expedite the marriage of Valère and Mariane. You will give up, of your own accord, the improper influence which allows your hopes to prosper at the expense of these young people. Moreover –

Scene iv:

ELMIRE, DAMIS, TARTUFFE

DAMIS (*emerging from the closet where he has been hiding*): No, no! All this must be made public. I was in that closet and heard everything. I feel I was brought here by Heaven in its wisdom to humble the pride of a brute who wrongs me, to show me a way of being revenged for all his insolence and hypocrisy, of undeceiving my father and of exposing once and for all the soul of this swine who speaks to you of love.

ELMIRE: No Damis, it will be enough for him to mend his ways and try to deserve the forgiveness I have said I grant him. I gave my word. Do not make me break it. It's not my nature to make a fuss. A wife pays no attention to silliness of this sort and doesn't bother her husband with such things.

DAMIS: You have your reasons for wanting it that way, but I've also got my reasons for having it otherwise. You don't seriously intend to let him off the hook? His insolence, his pride, his canting humbug have got the better of my legitimate resentment too often and caused too much trouble in this house. The scoundrel has ruled my father for too long and he has frustrated the course both of my love and

Valère's. My father must be made to see what a two-faced swine he is and the Good Lord has sent me an easy way of doing it. I am indebted to Providence for giving me this opportunity. It's too good a chance to miss. I'd deserve to have it taken away from me if, having it within my grasp, I failed to make the most of it.

ELMIRE: Damis —

DAMIS: No, if you don't mind, I must do it my way. I feel elated, euphoric. And it's no good you telling me I should deny myself the pleasure of having my revenge. I'm going to settle this business before I do another thing — and here comes my means of obtaining satisfaction.

Scene v:
ORGON, DAMIS, TARTUFFE, ELMIRE

DAMIS: Father, we've got something entertaining to mark your arrival, something that's just happened which will amaze you. All your kindness has been repaid in full and this gentleman has acknowledged your concern for him in the handsomest terms. He has just shown how zealous he has been in your cause. He proposes nothing less than to dishonour you. Here, in this very room, I have just overheard heard him make the most unseemly declaration of his guilty passion for Madame. She has the kindest nature and, being discreet to a fault, was all for keeping it quiet. But I cannot stand by and condone the man's nerve. I consider that to say nothing would be to do you a gross injustice.

ELMIRE: Well, I don't believe a wife should ever trouble her husband's peace of mind with such foolish nonsense. The honour of wives does not hang on such things and we can be safely left to take care of ourselves. That's how I feel, and if I'd had my way, Damis, you'd have kept all this to yourself. (*Exit Elmire.*)

Scene vi:

ORGON, DAMIS, TARTUFFE

ORGON: Merciful heaven! Am I to believe what I have just heard?

TARTUFFE: Oh yes, dear brother! I am guilty, a knave, a miserable sinner steeped in iniquity, the most wicked villain who ever lived. Every moment of my existence is rank with wickedness – it is nothing but a heap of crimes and the foulest deeds. And I see that Heaven, to punish me, is bent on seizing this opportunity for my mortification. Whatever this great wrong I am accused of may be, I shall not give way to pride and try to defend myself. Believe what they say, stoke up your anger and send me from your house like a common criminal. Whatever shame is heaped on me, I shall have deserved it – much, much more.

ORGON (*to his son*): Oh, you snake in the grass! How dare you try to smear his virtue with such lies!

DAMIS: You don't mean that the hypocrite's bogus claptrap is all it takes for you to refuse to –

ORGON: Silence! A plague on you!

TARTUFFE: Oh let him speak. You are wrong to take him to task. It would be far better if you just listened to what he says. How is it that you still think so well of me after what has happened? After all, do you know what I am really capable of? Do you take me, brother, for what I seem to be? And if you go by what you see, why do you think me the better for it? No, no, you are letting yourself be taken in by appearances, for I am, alas, exactly what I am thought to be. People believe I am a good man. But the truth is that there is no health in me. (*Turning to Damis:*) That's right dear boy, speak out, say I am two-faced and vile, a reprobate, a thief and a murderer! Go on, heap names far worse than these on me! I shall not deny any of them. I deserve them all and I shall suffer the shame of them on bended knee as a penance for a lifetime of crimes!

ORGON (*to Tartuffe*): Dear brother, this is too much. (*To his son:*) Doesn't your heart feel differently now, you reptile?

DAMIS: You don't mean to say his fine words have taken you in to the point where –

ORGON: Silence, you ungrateful wretch! (*To Tartuffe:*) Oh brother, please get up. (*To his son:*) You are despicable!

DAMIS: He can —

ORGON: Be quiet!

DAMIS: This is more than I can take! Why, must I —

ORGON: If you say another word, I'll break every bone in your body!

TARTUFFE: Dear brother, for the love of God, do not let anger get the better of you! I would rather suffer any punishment than have the smallest harm come to him on my account.

ORGON (*to Damis*): Ungrateful wretch!

TARTUFFE: Let him be. If necessary, I shall get down on my knees and beg you to forgive him . . .

ORGON (*to Tartuffe*): You will do no such thing! (*To his son:*) Now do you see how good he is, you cur!

DAMIS: So —

ORGON: Silence!

DAMIS: What! Am I —

ORGON: I told you to hold your tongue! Oh, I know the reason why you've turned on him. You all hate him, and at this moment I see everybody — my wife, my children, the servants — baying for his blood. There are no lengths you won't go to to get this saintly man out of my house. But the harder you try to get rid of him, the more determined I am to do all I can to keep him here. And I shall waste no more time in arranging for him to marry my daughter to confound the pride of the whole family.

DAMIS: You don't mean you're going to force her to marry him?

ORGON: Oh yes, you snake, and it shall be done this very evening, to spite the whole lot of you. Oh, I defy you all! I'm going to show you that I must be obeyed, that I am master here. Come, you will take everything back and you will get down on your knees this instant, wretch, and ask to be forgiven.

DAMIS: What, me? Ask to be forgiven by this swine whose hypocrisy —

ORGON: Oh, so you refuse, you blackguard, and add insult to injury? Fetch me a stick, I want a stick! (*To Tartuffe:*) Don't try to stop me! (*To his son:*) Get out of my house this instant and don't ever dare show your face here again!

DAMIS: Very well, I'll go. But —

ORGON: I said get out. I hereby disinherit you, you wretch, and moreover I lay a father's curse upon you.

Scene vii:
ORGON, TARTUFFE

ORGON: How dare he insult a saintly man like that!

TARTUFFE: Oh Heaven, forgive him the pain he has caused me! (*To Orgon:*) If you only knew how sad it makes me to know that other people are so intent on blackening my good name to my brother.

ORGON: Alas!

TARTUFFE: The very thought of such ingratitude is a sharp dagger in my breast . . . I feel the full horror of it . . . My heart is so full that I cannot speak. I do believe all this will be the death of me.

ORGON (*runs with tears in his eyes to the door through which he sent his son packing*): You wretch! I'm sorry now I let you off so lightly. I should have let you feel the full weight of my hand there and then. (*To Tartuffe:*) Don't take on so brother. Don't upset yourself.

TARTUFFE: An end, let's have an end to all this distressing talk. I see I have brought great trouble upon you and your house. I conclude that it would be best, brother, if I were to leave.

ORGON: Leave! You aren't serious?

TARTUFFE: Everyone here hates me and it is quite obvious that they are all determined to make you doubt my sincerity.

ORGON: What of it? You don't think I pay any attention to them?

TARTUFFE: Obviously they're not going to leave matters as they are. And the kind of tales they've been telling, which you now dismiss, may prove more believable next time round.

ORGON: Never brother, never.

TARTUFFE: Oh, dear brother, a wife can twist a husband round her little finger with no trouble at all.

ORGON: No, no.

TARTUFFE: By turning me out, you will enable me to deprive them of any grounds for renewing such attacks on me.

ORGON: No. You shall stay. It's a matter of life and death to me.

TARTUFFE: Very well, I see I have no choice but to sacrifice my own wishes. Still, if you wanted to . . .

ORGON: Yes?

TARTUFFE: No, no, let's not pursue it. But I know how I must conduct myself. Honour bruises easily. As a friend, I am bound to give no comfort to idle rumour and damaging innuendo. I shall avoid your wife and you will never observe me –

ORGON: No, you shall see her, and they can think what they like. There's nothing I like better than making them furious. I shall insist that you are seen with her all the time. And there's more: I shall defy them all by choosing you as my sole heir. I'll go now, this very minute, and arrange for a proper deed to be drawn up making you the recipient of all my worldly goods. A good and faithful friend, chosen by me for a son-in-law, is far dearer to me than son or wife or any of my family. Do you accept the offer?

TARTUFFE: May His will be done in all things!

ORGON: Poor man! Let's go and have the papers drawn up. And may the hearts of the envious stew in their own resentment!

Act IV

Scene i:

CLÉANTE, TARTUFFE

CLÉANTE: Yes, everyone's talking about it and, take it from me, the scandal this news has caused has done your reputation no good. Meeting you like this gives me a timely opportunity to tell you bluntly what I think. I won't go into details about what people are saying. Taking all that as read and assuming the worst, let's suppose that Damis did behave badly and you've been wrongly accused. Now shouldn't it be your duty as a Christian man to turn the other cheek and forget any thought of revenge? How can you stand by and see a son turned out of his father's house, just because you've fallen out with him? I repeat, and I'll make no bones about it, there is no one, high or low, who is not thoroughly shocked. And if you want my opinion, you should calm the situation and not take matters to extremes. Sacrifice your anger to God and reconcile the son with his father.

TARTUFFE: Alas, if there were only myself to consider, I would willingly do so. I feel no bitterness towards him. I forgive him completely, I have absolutely nothing against him and would be glad to help him in whatever way I could. But Heaven has an interest in this and Heaven could never agree to it: if he returns to this house, then I must go. After what he's done, which is quite unheard of, any further contact between us would be a scandal: God knows what people would think! It would be put down to clever manoeuvring on my part. People everywhere would say that I felt guilty and was putting on a display of charity towards my accuser, that in my heart I was afraid of him and was being nice to him to persuade him in secret to keep his mouth shut.

CLÉANTE: Don't try to fool me with spurious excuses. All your arguments are far too convoluted. Why do you take it on yourself to defend the interests of Heaven? Does God need our help to punish sinners? Just leave it to Him to take care of divine vengeance. Keep your mind on the forgiveness which He would have us show to those who trespass against us, and forget human justice when you try to follow God's supreme commandments. Surely silly fears of what people might think cannot dull the brightness of doing a good deed? Of course not. So let us just do what Heaven bids us and not allow any other consideration to cloud our judgement.

TARTUFFE: I've already told you I've forgiven him in my heart, which is precisely what Heaven commands. But after this scandal and his insulting behaviour today, Heaven does not require me to live in the same house as him.

CLÉANTE: And does Heaven command you to pay any heed to his father's silly whims and accept as a gift property to which you have no legal claim?

TARTUFFE: People who know me will not think that my actions are those of a self-interested man. Worldly possessions hold few attractions for me. I am not dazzled by their false glitter. If I decide to accept the benefaction which the father is kind enough to offer, it is only because I honestly fear that otherwise the property will fall into the wrong hands and end up being left to people who will put it to sinful use rather than employ it, as I plan to, for the greater glory of God and the good of my fellow men.

CLÉANTE: Come sir, forget your fine scruples. They could give the rightful heir grounds for legal action. Allow him to have what is his, let him take the risk and don't give it another thought. Think how much better it would be for him to squander the money than for you to be accused of trying to cheat him out of his inheritance. I'm only surprised that you could entertain such an offer without being highly embarrassed. Does true piety lay down any dogma which states that rightful heirs should be deprived of their inheritance? And, assuming Heaven has indeed given you this irresistible aversion to living under the same roof as Damis, wouldn't it be better to do the decent thing and leave quietly rather than allow the son of the house to be turned out on your account against all reason? Believe me, it would show you to be a fair-minded and —

TARTUFFE: It is now half past three and a requirement of religious observance calls me upstairs. You will forgive me for leaving you so soon.

CLÉANTE: Oh! (*Exit Tartuffe.*)

Scene ii:
ELMIRE, MARIANE, DORINE, CLÉANTE

DORINE: Please, won't you help us and use your influence on her behalf sir? She's in a dreadful state. The betrothal ceremony her father has arranged for tonight is making her desperate. Here he comes. I beg you — join forces with us and let's try by hook or by crook to put a stop to this awful plan which is very worrying to us all.

Scene iii:
ORGON, ELMIRE, MARIANE, CLÉANTE, DORINE

ORGON: Ah! I'm glad to see you all together. (*To Mariane:*) I've got something here in this contract that will put a smile on your face — and you already know what it is.

MARIANE (*kneeling*): Father, in the name of Heaven which knows how miserable I am, and by all that can touch your tenderest feelings, waive your rights as a father and release my heart from its obligation to obey you in this matter. Don't drive me to complain to Heaven that I am your daughter by insisting strictly on your rights. Don't make the life you gave me a misery father. If, contrary to the dearest hopes I have nurtured, you now forbid me to marry the man I have dared to love, at least save me – and on my knees I implore you – from the torment of belonging to a man I loathe! Don't force me to take some desperate step by pushing your authority over me to its limits.

ORGON (*feeling himself touched by compassion*): Come, steel yourself man! No human weakness!

MARIANE: Your affection for him doesn't upset me. Don't be afraid to show it, give him all your money and, if that isn't enough, let him have mine too. I consent with all my heart and freely give it to you – but at least don't include me with it. Instead, let me spend such unhappy days as Heaven shall grant me within the austere walls of a convent.

ORGON: Aha! That's right, girls always start going on about convents the moment their fathers try to put a stop to their romantic notions! Get up! The harder you find it to accept him, the better it will be for your eternal soul. Mortify the flesh by marrying him and stop making my head ache with all this bawling!

DORINE: But what –

ORGON: You be quiet! Mind your own business! I absolutely forbid you to say another word!

CLÉANTE: If you will allow me to reply with a piece of advice . . .

ORGON: Brother, your advice is always excellent, most thoughtful and I value it highly, but be so good as to let me get by without it.

ELMIRE (*to her husband*): Watching all this, I am at a loss to know what to say. I can only marvel at your blindness. You must be bewitched by the man – infatuated – to doubt our word after what has happened today.

ORGON: With respect, I go by appearances. I know you have a weak spot for that worthless son of mine. You were afraid to say it was wrong of him to try to do the dirty on the poor man. You took it much too calmly for me to believe you. You would have reacted very differently if the allegation had been true.

ELMIRE: Why should a woman behave as if her honour were threatened by a mere declaration of love? Is there no other reaction to whatever threatens it except blazing eyes and a raging tongue? Personally, I just laugh off such advances. I hate all the fuss that's made of these things. I'd much prefer it if we women behaved quietly, with decorum. I have no use for virtuous harridans who defend their honour with tooth and claw, and scratch out a man's eyes at the first suggestive word. Heaven preserve me from such prudery! The kind of virtue I want to see is not so prickly. A snub coolly and discreetly administered is, I think, sufficiently effective in rebuffing unwanted attentions.

ORGON: All the same, I know where I stand and won't be led up the garden path.

ELMIRE: I marvel more and more at this peculiar infatuation. You don't believe us – but what would you say if I were to show you that we're telling the truth?

ORGON: Show me?

ELMIRE: Yes.

ORGON: Rubbish!

ELMIRE: Not so hasty! Suppose I could find a way of letting you see with your own eyes?

ORGON: Stuff and nonsense!

ELMIRE: What a man you are! At least give me an answer. I'm not asking you to take my word for it. But supposing I arranged for you to see and hear everything from a place we'd choose, what would you say then about that excellent man?

ORGON: In that case, I'd say ... I wouldn't say anything because it can't be done.

ELMIRE: This delusion of yours has been going on for too long. I've had enough of being accused of deceiving you. The time has come when, for my own satisfaction, I'm going to have to make you a witness to the truth of what we've been telling you.

ORGON: Very well, I'll take you at your word. We'll see how clever you are. Let's find out how you can keep your promise.

ELMIRE (*to Dorine*): Ask him to come here.

DORINE: He's cunning. He may be difficult to catch.

ELMIRE: Not at all. People are easily taken in when they covet something and their vanity leads them to deceive themselves. Send word that he's to come down to me. (*To Cléante and Mariane:*) And you, make yourselves scarce.

Scene iv:
ELMIRE, ORGON

ELMIRE: Give me a hand with this table. Now get under it.

ORGON: What?

ELMIRE: It's vital you should be hidden.

ORGON: But why under the table?

ELMIRE: Oh, for heaven's sake, leave this to me. I know what I'm doing. You'll see why in due course. Just get under and when you're there, mind no one can see or hear you.

ORGON: I don't know why I'm going along with this, but I must see how you bring your little scheme to a conclusion.

ELMIRE: I don't think you'll have any cause for complaint. (*Orgon gets under the table.*) Now, I'm going to say some rather strange things. Don't be shocked. I must have a free hand in whatever I say – it's to convince you, as I promised. Since you leave me no choice, I intend by gentle persuasion to force the hypocrite to drop his mask, to flatter his impertinent desires and give his effrontery all the encouragement necessary. If I pretend to respond to his advances, I shall be doing it for your sake, to show him up for what he is. I can stop as soon as you admit defeat: things will go only so far as you want them to. It will be up to you to call a halt to his outrageous passion when you think it's all gone far enough. You can spare a wife's blushes by exposing me to no more than is necessary to make the scales drop for your eyes. That will be your business, and it will be for you to decide . . . But here he comes. Stay where you are – and make sure you're not seen.

Scene v:
TARTUFFE, ELMIRE

TARTUFFE: I was informed you wished to speak to me here.

ELMIRE: Yes, I have something to say to you in confidence – but shut the door before I begin and take a good look round in case anyone's listening. We don't want another business like this morning's. I was never so taken aback in all my life. Damis made me terribly afraid for you. You must have seen what efforts I made to stop him and calm his anger. The truth is I was so disconcerted that it never entered my head to deny his accusations. But thank Heaven it all turned out for the best and we are much more secure now as a result. The high regard people have for you deflected the storm and my husband won't be suspicious of you now. He insists on our being seen together as often as possible to show what he thinks of idle talk. Which means I can be alone with you here in this room, and not be afraid of being criticized for it. It also means I can reveal the feelings of my heart which is perhaps only too ready to acknowledge your love.

TARTUFFE: I find it difficult to follow your drift, Madame. Only a little while ago you spoke very differently.

ELMIRE: How little you know about a woman's heart if such a rebuff has offended you! How little you understand what we mean to convey when we put up such weak defences! In such moments our modesty still does battle with the tender sentiments you start in us. However compelling the arguments in favour of the love which subdues us, we are still too diffident to admit it. At first we resist, but soon our manner of resisting sufficiently reveals that in our heart of hearts we have surrendered, that though our lips are honour bound to deny our feelings, our resistance in fact promises everything. I realize that I am being very frank in admitting all this and that I show scant regard for womanly modesty. But since I am speaking so freely, should I have been so anxious to restrain Damis, should I have heard you out so indulgently, do you think, when you declared you loved me, should I have reacted as I did, if the offer had not been entirely unwelcome to me? Moreover, when I tried to force you to say no to the marriage which had just been announced, what was that intended to convey to you if not that I was attracted to you and regretted the tying of a knot which would leave me to share an affection which I wanted entirely to myself?

TARTUFFE: Ah, Madame! it is delightful indeed to hear such words from the lips of the woman one loves! Their honey sets coursing through my whole being sensations sweeter than any I have ever know before. To find favour in your eyes is my principal care and all my hope of paradise lies in your love. Yet forgive this heart of mine if it dares to doubt of its own felicity. I might interpret what you say as a

virtuous stratagem to induce me to give up my impending marriage.
And if I may put the matter to you frankly, I shall place no faith in
your sweet words unless I am first vouchsafed some small foretaste
of the favours for which I yearn – that alone will reassure me that
what they say is true and plant in my heart an unshakeable belief in
the delectable affection you express for me.

ELMIRE (*coughing to attract her husband's attention*): Why must you go
so fast? Would you have me reveal everything I feel for you all at
once? It has cost me dear to confess my tenderest regard for you
and it's still not enough! Is there no way of satisfying you except by
taking matters to ultimate lengths?

TARTUFFE: The less deserving we are, the less we dare to hope. Our
dearest wishes take little comfort in words and we place little faith
in the prospect of felicity: we must enjoy it before we can believe in
it. Knowing myself how little I deserve your favours, I doubt the
outcome of my boldness. I shall not believe it, Madame, until you
give me proofs strong enough to satisfy my passion.

ELMIRE: Heavens! How masterful you are when passion speaks! I'm left
not knowing where I am! Your love has a power over other people
which is quite irresistible: how imperiously it insists on having what
it wants! Gracious! is there no way of escaping your attentions?
Won't you even allow me a moment to catch my breath? Is it decent
to be quite so peremptory and give no quarter in demanding to have
what you have asked for? How can you press a person so hard and
take advantage of the fondness she has for you?

TARTUFFE: But if you look upon my advances with a favourable eye,
why refuse me convincing proof?

ELMIRE: How can I consent to what you ask without offending Him
whose name is ever on your lips?

TARTUFFE: If fear of Heaven is the only barrier to my passion, that is
an obstacle I can easily remove. It is not something that should hold
you back.

ELMIRE: But are we not told to fear the wrath of Heaven?

TARTUFFE: I can dispel these foolish fears for you Madame. I know the
art of removing such scruples. It is true that Heaven forbids certain
forms of self-indulgence[3] but one can reach accommodations with
Heaven. According to the circumstances of the case, there is a method
of easing the constraints of conscience, of rectifying the evil we have

done by pointing to the purity of our intentions.⁴ I can instruct you in these secret matters Madame. All you need do is allow yourself to be led by me. Satisfy my desires and have no fear. I shall be answerable for everything and will take the sin upon myself. That's a nasty cough you have.

ELMIRE: Yes, I feel as though I am on the rack.

TARTUFFE: Would you care for a little of this liquorice water?

ELMIRE: It's a most obstinate cold, really, and I fear that all the liquorice water in the world won't help me now.

TARTUFFE: It's obviously a trial for you.

ELMIRE: Yes, more than I can say.

TARTUFFE: As I was saying then, your scruples can be overcome easily. You can be sure that all this will remain absolutely secret. The harm of an action lies only in its being known. The public scandal is what constitutes the offence: sins committed in private are not sins at all.

ELMIRE (*coughs again*): Very well, I see that I must make up my mind to submit and agree to give you everything you want. It's no use hoping that anything less will satisfy you or that just saying I surrender will do. Obviously, it is hard that things should come to such a pass and it is very much against my will that I should take such a step. But since you insist on leaving me no choice, since you refuse to believe all I've been saying and since you require more convincing proofs, I must agree to do what will give satisfaction. But if in consenting I offend, then so much the worse for the man who forces me to such extremes. The fault can surely not be accounted mine.

TARTUFFE: Yes Madame, on my head be it, and –

ELMIRE: Open the door a moment and please look and make sure if my husband isn't in the gallery.

TARTUFFE: Why are you so worried about him? Between ourselves, he's the sort of man who's easily led by the nose. He takes immense pride in our little talks together, and I've got him to the stage where he could see anything with his own eyes and not believe it.

ELMIRE: All the same, please step outside a moment and take a good look round.

Scene vi:

ORGON, ELMIRE

ORGON (*emerging from beneath the table*): There goes – I admit it – an abominable scoundrel! I can't get over it! It's all too much for me!

ELMIRE: Why have you come out from under there so soon? You'll spoil everything. Get under that table again, it's not time yet. Wait till the very end and make quite sure. Don't just trust to guessing.

ORGON: No! No! Hell itself never produced anything more wicked.

ELMIRE: Good Lord! you shouldn't jump to conclusions so quickly. Wait until you're absolutely convinced before admitting you were wrong. Don't be so hasty – you might be making a mistake. (*She hides her husband behind her.*)

Scene vii:

TARTUFFE, ELMIRE, ORGON

TARTUFFE: All things conspire to favour my happiness Madame. I've looked in all the rooms. There's no one about and my rapture –

ORGON (*stopping him*): Hold it there! You're letting your lustful feelings run away with you. You shouldn't get so excited. So, my good and saintly man, you've a mind to go behind my back. You give in to temptations pretty easily, I must say! You were set on marrying my daughter and all the while were lusting after my wife! For a long time I couldn't bring myself to believe that this was how things really were and went on thinking I'd hear you change your tune. But now the evidence has gone far enough. I'll settle for it and, for my part, require no further proof.

ELMIRE (*to Tartuffe*): It was against my better feelings that I did all this, but I was put under pressure to treat you in this way.

TARTUFFE: Surely you can't believe . . .

ORGON: Oh come now! let's have no more of it, please. Get out of this house, and quick about it.

TARTUFFE: My intention –

ORGON: That sort of talk won't wash any more. You must leave my house at once!

TARTUFFE: You're the one who is going to have to leave – you who talk as though you were the master here. The house belongs to me and I intend to let you know it. I'll show you that it's no use resorting to petty stratagems like this to start an argument with me. You're not on such sure ground as you think when you insult me. I have ways of exposing and punishing your hypocrisy, of avenging this affront to Heaven and of making those who talk of making me leave regret it.

Scene viii:
ELMIRE, ORGON

ELMIRE: What's he talking about? What does he mean?

ORGON: Oh God, this is awkward. It's no laughing matter.

ELMIRE: What do you mean?

ORGON: What he said makes me realize my mistake. My deed of gift is beginning to worry me.

ELMIRE: Deed of gift?

ORGON: It's all signed and sealed. But there's something else that disturbs me.

ELMIRE: What?

ORGON: I'll tell you everything. But first I must go at once and see whether a certain casket is still upstairs.

Act V

Scene i:
ORGON, CLÉANTE

CLÉANTE: Where are you rushing off to?

ORGON: Lord, how do I know?

CLÉANTE: It seems to me that we should start by putting our heads together and think of what needs to be done in the circumstances.

ORGON: It's the casket that worries me most. I'm more concerned about that than anything else.

CLÉANTE: Is there some important secret attaching to the casket?

ORGON: Argas, a friend I miss greatly, left it with me for safe-keeping. He gave it into my charge, swearing me to total secrecy. He chose me for this purpose when he fled the country. It contains documents, so he said, on which his life and property depended.

CLÉANTE: Then why did you entrust them to someone else?

ORGON: Because of a scruple of conscience. I went straight to that scoundrel and took him into my confidence. What he said convinced me it was better to let him have the casket to keep, so that if anyone asked I could deny that I had it. That way I would have a ready-made answer which would safeguard my conscience against bearing false witness against what I knew to be true.

CLÉANTE: You're in an extremely difficult position, judging by how things look. Both the deed of gift and your decision to confide the casket to him were, if I may say so, steps you took all too lightly. Now he has them, he can get you into very serious trouble. It was also very unwise of you to provoke him once he'd got such a hold over you. You ought to have been less hasty in dealing with him.

ORGON: What? Go easy on a man who could hide such double-dealing, such wickedness under the outward appearance of fervent piety? Someone I took under my roof as a down-and-out, a penniless beggar? That's all finished, I'll have no more to do with men of God. From now on, I shall regard them with the most utter loathing and behave as if no treatment is too good for them!

CLÉANTE: Ah! there you go, flying off the handle again. You're incapable of being moderate and sensible. You have no conception of plain common-sense. You always rush from one extreme to another. You can see your error now; you've discovered how you were taken in by a pretence of piety. But where's the sense in trying to correct one mistake by committing an even bigger one and failing to make any distinction between a deceitful rogue and people who are genuinely good? Just because one scoundrel has had the nerve to pull the wool over your eyes with a convincing imitation of righteous morality, you mustn't think that everybody is like him and that there aren't any sincerely devout men left nowadays. Leave such foolish inferences to the free-thinkers,[5] separate real virtue from its outward appearance, don't be so quick to give your respect and keep a sense of proportion.

Take care if you can not to defer to impostors but neither should you say anything against true faith. If you must go to extremes, better to err on the same side as you did before.

Scene ii:
DAMIS, ORGON, CLÉANTE

DAMIS: Father! Is it true that the swine is threatening you, that he has forgotten all the kindness you showed him and that with an effrontery which is enough to make anyone see red, the coward is turning your own generosity against you?

ORGON: Yes my boy, and very painful it is to me too.

DAMIS: Leave this to me! I'll cut his ears off! It's no good taking half-measures with such damned impertinence. I'll take care of him, I'll get rid of him for you! If we're going to get out of this, I'm going to have to give him a good seeing to!

CLÉANTE: That's young man's talk. For goodness' sake, calm down and don't get so excited. We live under a king in an age when those who resort to violence come off worst.

Scene iii:
MADAME PERNELLE, MARIANE, ELMIRE, DORINE,
DAMIS, ORGON, CLÉANTE

MADAME PERNELLE: What's all this? What are these strange and terrible things I hear are going on in this house?

ORGON: It's all only just happened, I saw it all with my own eyes. So that's the reward I get for all my pains! Out of Christian charity I help a man who has fallen on hard times, I give him a room in my house and treat him as I would my own brother. I heap kindness on him daily. I give him my daughter and every penny I possess. And meanwhile, this deceitful, ignoble man embarks on a foul intrigue to seduce my wife. And not content with such underhand schemes, he now has the audacity to threaten me with my own benevolence and intends to ruin me by using as weapons the advantages my own unwise generosity has placed in his hand, to evict me from the house which I made over to him and reduce me to the gutter from which I rescued him.

DORINE: Poor man!

MADAME PERNELLE: My son, I simply cannot believe that he intended to do such a wicked thing.

ORGON: I beg your pardon?

MADAME PERNELLE: People always envy those who walk in righteousness.

ORGON: What on earth do you mean, mother?

MADAME PERNELLE: I mean that there are queer goings-on in this house and I'm quite aware of how much he is hated here.

ORGON: What has his being hated to do with what I'm telling you?

MADAME PERNELLE: When you were a little boy, I used to tell you over and over: 'Virtue on earth is persecuted ever; the envious die, but envy never.'

ORGON: But what has that to do with what's going on now?

MADAME PERNELLE: They'll have been making up endless idle stories about him for your benefit.

ORGON: I've already told you, I saw it for myself.

MADAME PERNELLE: There's no end to the malice of slandering tongues.

ORGON: You'll drive me to perdition, mother. I told you: I saw his wickedness with my very own eyes.

MADAME PERNELLE: Malicious tongues always have plenty of poison to spread and there's nothing in the here below that can be done to prevent them.

ORGON: Now you're talking nonsense. I saw him, I tell you, saw him with my very own eyes, in the fullest sense of the word 'saw'. How many times must I go on telling you? Do I have to shout it at the top of my voice?

MADAME PERNELLE: Good gracious, appearances are deceptive more often than not. You shouldn't always judge by what you see.

ORGON: I can't stand this!

MADAME PERNELLE: It's human nature to think badly of people. Goodness is often misinterpreted.

ORGON: Am I to interpret it as an act of kindness when someone tries to seduce my wife?

MADAME PERNELLE: You shouldn't make accusations unless you have good cause. You should have waited until you were quite sure of your ground.

ORGON: The devil take it, how could I have been surer? I should have waited, should I, waited and watched until he . . . You'll make me say something I shouldn't.

MADAME PERNELLE: All I see is a man moved by the purest faith. I simply cannot imagine he meant to do what you are saying he did.

ORGON: Oh God! If you weren't my mother, I don't know what I'd say to you, I'm that angry!

DORINE: Serves you right sir. That's how things go in this world. You wouldn't believe us and now she won't believe you.

CLÉANTE: We are wasting time with this nonsense when we ought to be making plans. We can't afford to go to sleep in the face of the villain's threats.

DAMIS: Why! Do you think he'd really have the nerve to carry them out?

ELMIRE: Personally, I don't think he'd have much of a case. His ingratitude is too glaring.

CLÉANTE: Don't count on it. He'll find ways of justifying whatever action he takes against you. Intrigues and cabals have landed people in serious trouble on less evidence than this before now.[6] I repeat what I said a while ago: since he's in such a strong position, you ought never to have pushed him so far.

ORGON: True. But what could I do? The villain had such colossal nerve that I lost control of myself.

CLÉANTE: I only wish we could patch together some sort of reconciliation between the two of you.

ELMIRE: If I'd known what a strong position he was in, I'd never have been a party to creating such unpleasantness, and my . . .

ORGON (*to Dorine*): Whoever's this? What's he want? Quick, go and find out. I'm in no fit state to receive visitors.

Scene iv:

MONSIEUR LOYAL, MADAME PERNELLE, ORGON,
DAMIS, MARIANE, DORINE, ELMIRE, CLÉANTE

MONSIEUR LOYAL (*to Dorine*): Good day, dear sister in the Lord. Please inform your master that I wish to speak to him.

DORINE: He's got company. I shouldn't think he can see anyone at the moment.

MONSIEUR LOYAL: I haven't come here to cause trouble. I don't think my visit will upset him in any way. In fact he'll be very pleased with what I've come about.

DORINE: Your name?

MONSIEUR LOYAL: Just tell him I've come here on behalf of Monsieur Tartuffe, for his own good.

DORINE (*to Orgon*): It's someone sent by Monsieur Tartuffe. He seems very civil. He says you'll be pleased to hear what he's come about.

CLÉANTE: You'll have to see the man and find out what he wants.

ORGON: Perhaps he's come here to patch things up between us. How should I behave to him?

CLÉANTE: You mustn't show how resentful you are. If he talks of reconciliation, you must listen to him.

MONSIEUR LOYAL: My respects to you sir. May Heaven confound all those who would do you harm, and look upon you with as favourable an eye as I could wish.

ORGON (*to Cléante*): This civil beginning confirms my impression and already points to some kind of reconciliation.

MONSIEUR LOYAL: I have always been devoted to all your family. I was once in your father's service.

ORGON: Sir, I am most embarrassed and ask your pardon for not recognizing or even knowing your name.

MONSIEUR LOYAL: The name's Loyal, a native of Normandy and, though there's some would have had it otherwise, I am a court bailiff. For forty years, Heaven be praised, I've been fortunate enough to discharge my duty with honour and now I'm here, sir, to serve this writ upon you, excusing the liberty.

ORGON: What! You've come to . . .

MONSIEUR LOYAL: Now, easy does it sir. It's nothing, just a writ, an order for you and yours to get out of this house, remove your possessions and make room for another party, without delay or postponement, as herein provided.

ORGON: What me? Leave this house?

MONSIEUR LOYAL: Yes sir, if you don't mind. This house now belongs, as you are duly aware, to good Monsieur Tartuffe, no question about it. From this day forth, he is lord and master of everything you own by virtue of a deed I have about my person. It's perfectly legal and it'll do no good disputing it.

DAMIS: You've got to admire the man's nerve!

MONSIEUR LOYAL (*to Damis*): Sir, my business is not with you but with this gentleman. He's reasonable and amenable and he's far too aware of what an upright man's duty is to want to interfere with the course of justice.

ORGON: But . . .

MONSIEUR LOYAL: Oh yes. I know you'd never resist the law, no, not for a million. You'll allow me to carry out the orders I've been given as a decent gentleman should.

DAMIS: At this rate, brother bailiff, you could end up feeling the weight not of the law but of my arm, black gown or no black gown.

MONSIEUR LOYAL: Ask your son to hold his tongue, sir, or go away. I'd be very sorry to be obliged to make a note of this and put you in my report.

DORINE (*aside*): By the way he carries on, he should be called not Loyal but Disloyal.

MONSIEUR LOYAL: I have a soft spot for God-fearing folk and I only took service of this writ out of consideration for you sir, to be helpful, and stop the job going to somebody who mightn't have my kindly sentiments for you and wouldn't have gone about things as tactfully as what I have.

ORGON: And what could be worse than ordering a man out of his own house?

MONSIEUR LOYAL: You're being given time. I'll grant you a stay of execution until tomorrow. I'll just come and stay the night here with ten of my men, with no fuss or scandal. For form's sake, I shall have to ask you, if you don't mind, to hand over the keys before you go to bed. I'll take good care not to disturb your rest and I'll see that nothing isn't as it should be. But tomorrow morning, first thing, you'll have to look sharp and clear everything out of the place, down to the last cup and saucer. My men will give you a hand. I picked a strong set of lads so that they'll be of real use in helping you get everything out. I don't think anybody could treat you fairer than that, and, seeing as how I'm going so easy on you, I ask you to treat me the same way sir, by which I mean you won't do anything to get in the way of me discharging my duty.

ORGON (*aside*): I'd willingly give the last hundred louis I've got left if for the pleasure of landing this oaf the hardest punch in the history of fists!

CLÉANTE (*whispers to Orgon*): Don't. Let's not make matters worse.

DAMIS: I can hardly restrain myself! The bare-faced cheek of the man! I'm itching to get my hands on him!

DORINE: Gracious, Monsieur Loyal, that broad back of yours could do with a good dusting with a broom-handle.

MONSIEUR LOYAL: I could get you into trouble for talking like that, my girl. The law applies to women as well, you know.

CLÉANTE: Let's have no more of this sir. That'll do. Please hand over the document and go.

MONSIEUR LOYAL: Until we meet again then. May the Lord make the sun to shine upon you!

Scene v:

ORGON, CLÉANTE, MARIANE, ELMIRE,
MADAME PERNELLE, DORINE, DAMIS

ORGON (*as Monsieur Loyal goes*): Ay, and may He confound you and the man who sent you! (*To Madame Pernelle:*) Well mother, you can see now if I was right or not, and you can judge the rest of it by what's just happened. Do you now realize what a treacherous rogue he is?

MADAME PERNELLE: I don't know what to say. I'm flabbergasted!

DORINE: You've no cause to complain and mustn't blame him. All this merely confirms his pious intentions – it's the ultimate expression of his love for his neighbour. He knows that earthly possessions can

corrupt a man and it's selfless charity on his part to remove anything
that might stand in the way of your salvation.

ORGON: Be quiet! I'm always having to tell you.

CLÉANTE: Let's see what advice we can get as to the course of action
we should follow.

ELMIRE: Go to the authorities and expose the ungrateful scoundrel. This
latest outrage surely invalidates the deed of gift. His utter lack of
scruple will appear too vile to allow him to succeed as he thinks he
will.

Scene vi:
VALÈRE, ORGON, CLÉANTE, ELMIRE, MARIANE

VALÈRE: I'm very sorry to be the bringer of bad news sir, but I had no
choice. You are in great danger. I have a friend who loves me dearly
and knows what interest I have such good cause to take in your
welfare. Now, at my request and in the strictest confidence, he has
violated the secrecy due to affairs of state, and has just sent me
information the gist of which is that you must get away at once. The
villain who has so long imposed upon you went to the king an hour
ago and denounced you. Among the various accusations he made,
he handed over a substantial casket belonging to a political agitator
which, he claims, you are guilty of concealing in breach of your duty
as a subject. I don't know the particulars of the crime you are charged
with, but a warrant has been issued for your arrest, and to ensure
that it is properly carried out Tartuffe himself has been ordered to
accompany the officer who is to apprehend you.

CLÉANTE: Ah, he's strengthened his hand! This is how the villain intends
to back his claim on your possessions and make himself master of
everything you own!

ORGON: I'll say this: the man is an absolute brute.

VALÈRE: The slightest delay could be fatal to you. I have my carriage
waiting outside to take you away, and a thousand louis which I have
here. There's not a moment to lose: this is a shattering blow – there's
no way out except by making a run for it. I offer my services to lead
you to a place of safety. I'll stay with you until you're out of danger.

ORGON: Oh, I am deeply indebted to your kindness! But I must leave
my thanks to another time. All I ask is that some day Heaven will
give me a chance to repay your kindness.

CLÉANTE: Go quickly brother. We'll see to it that everything necessary
is done.

Scene vii:
OFFICER, TARTUFFE, VALÈRE, ORGON, ELMIRE,
MARIANE, *etc.*

TARTUFFE: Not so fast sir, hold it just there. Don't rush off like that.
You won't have to travel very far to get where you're going. You
are a prisoner in the name of His Majesty.

ORGON: Villain! You've kept this piece of knavery for last! With this
stroke you complete my ruination you scoundrel, it's the culmination
of all your double-dealing!

TARTUFFE: Your insults are powerless to provoke me. I am schooled
to suffer everything for the Lord's sake.

CLÉANTE: I never saw such meekness!

DAMIS: Why, the impudent villain makes mock of Heaven!

TARTUFFE: Such outbursts leave me unmoved. I have no thought other
than to do my duty.

MARIANE: What credit do you expect to get out of this? How can you
believe that what you are doing is honourable?

TARTUFFE: Whatever we do can only be honourable if it proceeds from
that authority which has directed my steps to this place.

ORGON: And have you forgotten, you ungrateful wretch, that it was
my charitable hand which rescued you from the gutter?

TARTUFFE: Yes, I am mindful of the help I received from you, but my
first duty is to the interests of the king, and that sacred obligation is
so strong as to extinguish in me all sense of gratitude. To such a
powerful allegiance, I am ready to sacrifice friends, wife, family and
myself with them.

ELMIRE: Hypocrite!

DORINE: How cunningly he covers his villainy with the mantle of
everything we hold most dear!

CLÉANTE: But if this consuming zeal you lay claim to, and make so much of, is as great as you say, then why did it wait to manifest itself until he caught you making advances to his wife? Why did it never occur to you to denounce him until he was in honour bound to turn you out? If I raise the matter of the gift of all his property which he has made over to you, it's not to deflect you from your duty. But if you now insist on treating him like a criminal, why did you agree to accept anything from him in the first place?

TARTUFFE (*to the Officer*): Deliver me from this shouting match sir, and be good enough to proceed to the execution of your orders.

OFFICER: Yes, I suppose I've taken too long about it already and you do well to remind me of my duty: So, to carry out my instructions, I order you to follow me forthwith to the prison where you are to be held.

TARTUFFE: Who, me?

OFFICER: Yes, you.

TARTUFFE: But why prison?

OFFICER: I am not obliged to explain anything to you. (*To Orgon:*) Calm yourself sir, you've had a serious fright. We live under a prince who does not tolerate fraud, a monarch who can read the hearts of men, and who is not taken in by the wiles of hypocrites. The keen discernment of that lofty mind at all times sees things in their true perspective; nothing can get past the firm constancy of his judgement nor lead him into error. On men of worth, he confers everlasting glory but he never distributes his favour blindly: his love for good men and true does not exclude hatred of those who are false. This man could never have deceived him – he has avoided far more cunning traps than this. From the outset, his quick mind saw the full baseness of the villain's heart. In coming to denounce you, he gave himself away and by a stroke of supreme justice revealed himself as a notorious scoundrel of whose activities under another name His Majesty was informed. The long list of the details of his dark crimes would fill volumes. In short, the king, filled with horror for his base ingratitude and treachery towards you, added this to his other terrible crimes, and only put me under orders to see to what lengths his effrontery would go and to make him give you full satisfaction. All the documents of yours he says are his I am to take from him and return to you. His Majesty, by an act of sovereign prerogative, annuls the deed which gives him title to all your possessions. Furthermore, he pardons you that clandestine offence in which the flight of a friend involved you. This clemency he bestows upon you in recognition of your loyal service which he saw you show in former times in maintaining his rights, to let it be known he can reward a good action when it's least expected, and that he is never closed to true merit and chooses rather to remember good than evil.

DORINE: Heaven be praised!

MADAME PERNELLE: Now I can breathe again!

ELMIRE: It's all turned out well!

MARIANE: Who would have predicted this?

ORGON (*to Tartuffe*): There! You see, you villain, you –

CLÉANTE: Oh, enough brother! Don't descend to such indignity. Leave the wretched man to his fate and don't crow over the remorse which must now be overtaking him. Rather hope that he may henceforth return to the paths of virtue, reform his life by learning to hate his vices and so earn some mitigation of the king's justice. Meanwhile, you must go down on bended knee and give thanks for the kindness His Majesty has shown you.

ORGON: Yes, that's well said. Let us go rejoicing and offer him thanks for the leniency he has shown us. Then, that first duty done, we have in all justice another to perform – to crown the happiness of Valére, a constant lover and sincere friend.

The Misanthrope
A Comedy

Le Misanthrope
Comédie

First performed on 4 June 1666 at the Théâtre du Palais Royal in Paris by the King's Players

Although Molière gave a private reading in 1664 of the first act of what would become his most sophisticated play, *The Misanthrope* was not staged until June 1666. It was well received in the literary press but it disappointed his following which was accustomed to broader theatrical strokes. Audiences did not warm to Molière as Alceste. Abandoning the costume (and the trademark moustache) of his popular comic roles, he appeared elegantly dressed as a *grand seigneur*. Nor did they find farce to amuse them or a love *imbroglio* to catch their interest: the aristocratic setting which Molière, for the only time, chose for his play was the home of talk not action and called for subtler dramatic and psychological registers. In one sense, Molière's public was right. There is no structured plot, and events – like the quarrel with Oronte – are not exploited to raise the temperature. The denouement resolves nothing. Célimène refuses to change, and Alceste, though seemingly brought to the point of implementing his plan to flee the world, may yet be dissuaded to give up his 'foolish plan'. Yet even if Philinte's closing lines are intended as an unconvincing nod in the direction of the conventional happy ending (will there be reconciliation after all?), they leave us with a distinct sense of unfinished business.

The Misanthrope was at most a *succès d'estime*. It was played thirty-four times before the end of the year but thereafter received only twenty-five performances before Molière's death in 1673. Its fortunes did not revive until the nineteenth century, but since then only *Tartuffe* and *The Miser*, of the 'great' comedies, have been staged more often. While Molière's contemporaries regarded the play as primarily a satire of the Court and the nobility based on recognizable figures (numerous candidates were proposed as models for Alceste and Célimène), it has subsequently been made to yield other meanings. In the eighteenth century Rousseau saw Alceste as a hero, a man who has the courage not to compromise with a society which values cleverness and success more than honesty and plain dealing. In 1790 Fabre d'Églantine turned him into a revolutionary symbol: he was to be congratulated for being out of step with the hated ancien régime. For the Romantics he was a tragic figure who rebelled against philistine conformity. Subsequently, critics have made Alceste a self-portrait of an anxious, socially awkward Molière who despised worldly values, and have further argued that Alceste's unrequited love for Célimène was a clear echo of Molière's own marital difficulties with Armande Béjart who played her.

Yet when set against the rest of his plays, it is clear that Molière thought of *The Misanthrope* as a comedy. If the plot is low-keyed, it has the mechanics of farce: Alceste is a man who tries to talk seriously to a woman and is constantly prevented from doing so. But he is also an obsessive. When Molière registered the play it was subtitled 'ou l'Atrabilaire amoureux', which suggests that Alceste is closely related to Orgon, Monsieur Jourdain, or Argan, the 'imaginary invalid', who are all obsessed by a self-view that does not withstand scrutiny or reality. That Alceste should be both atrabilious (that is, his dominant humour is the 'black bile' of melancholy) and in love is contradiction enough. But that he should be in love with a coquette who represents everything he loathes is a very superior kind of comic paradox.

But Alceste is drawn in much subtler colours than Molière's other 'imaginary' obsessives. He has a very large ego and considers himself a cut above other people, for they are prepared to lie, cheat and compromise. He is unsociable, impatient and intolerant, and his combustibility is his comic flaw. And yet he has qualities which makes it impossible to laugh at him outright as we laugh at Monsieur Jourdain or Harpagon the miser. While they are clearly misguided, Alceste is in many ways right. Moreover, he is sincere, sensitive to a fault and idealistic enough to hear the voice of true love, not in contrived sonnets but in an old, popular song. If his psychology and actions are sometimes hard to read, it is because he enshrines the two strands of Molière's presentation of human nature, which are elsewhere kept apart and identified with distinct groups of characters. He is a monomaniac of frankness, an unconscious hypocrite blind to faults in himself that he berates in others, and as much a moral fundamentalist as the worst of the religious bigots. Yet at the same time he represents the honesty, naturalness and unpretentiousness which Molière defends in all his plays.

This explains why he appears most sympathetic not when stating his extreme views to Philinte (whose defence of tact and a 'more flexible kind of virtue' has a reasonableness to which he is closed) but when he is confronted by living examples of the deceit, pretence and generalized mendacity of which he complains. For if *The Misanthrope* is a complex and delicate character study, it is also a portrait of society which raises its status from chamber theatre to a play which fills the whole stage. Oronte is the courtly wit, and Acaste and Clitandre represent the vacuousness of courtly ambition. Arsinoé is a sly, prudish hypocrite and Célimène is rescued from her failings only by her youth and beauty and our suspicion that she is probably the victim of an arranged marriage. She is intelligent but vain and is prepared to be unkind if malice will add to her reputation for cleverness. Against them Molière sets the 'sincere' Éliante and Philinte, Alceste's loyal friend, a well-balanced couple who, without undervaluing themselves, are patient and tolerant and settle reluctantly for an amused acceptance of the way of the world. If Molière leaves us wondering how Alceste and Célimène will fare, it is at least clear that Éliante and Philinte will fare better.

Characters

ALCESTE, in love with Célimène
PHILINTE, his friend
ORONTE, in love with Célimène
CÉLIMÈNE, in love with Alceste
ÉLIANTE, cousin to Célimène
ARSINOÉ, friend of Célimène
ACASTE, a marquis
CLITANDRE, a marquis
BASQUE, Célimène's manservant
DU BOIS, Alceste's manservant
OFFICER of the court of the
Marshals of France

The play is set in Paris, in the house of Célimène

Act I

Scene i:

PHILINTE, ALCESTE

PHILINTE: What is it? What's the matter?

ALCESTE: Oh, leave me alone, please.

PHILINTE: But I ask you once again what bizarre idea —

ALCESTE: Let me be, I say, and get out of my sight.

PHILINTE: You might at least hear what people have to say without getting annoyed.

ALCESTE: I will get annoyed and I won't listen.

PHILINTE: I don't understand you when you get these sudden fits of temper. Friends though we are, I'm one of the first —

ALCESTE: Me, your friend? You can get that out of your head! Until now I have professed myself such, but after what I've just seen of you I declare I can do so no longer. I'll have no share in a corrupted affection.

PHILINTE: You consider I'm really at fault then Alceste?

ALCESTE: You should be mortally ashamed of yourself. What you did was absolutely inexcusable, and utterly shocking to any honourable man. I see you loading a man with every mark of affection, professing the tenderest concern for his welfare, overwhelming him with assurances, protestations and offers of service. And then, when he's gone and I ask who he is, you can scarcely tell me his name! Your enthusiasm dies with your parting and to me you speak of him as though he mattered nothing to you. God! What a base, degrading, infamous thing it is to stoop to betraying one's integrity like that! If ever I had had the misfortune to do such a thing I'd go and hang myself on the spot out of sheer self-disgust.

PHILINTE: Well, personally, I don't see that it's a hanging matter, so I'll ask you to be good enough to allow me to reduce your sentence and not hang myself this time, if you don't mind.

ALCESTE: Oh! This is no laughing matter.

PHILINTE: Seriously then, what do you expect me to do?

ALCESTE: I expect you to be sincere and as an honourable man never to utter a single word that you don't really mean.

PHILINTE: But when someone comes along and shows such pleasure in seeing you, surely you must repay him in kind, respond to his enthusiasm as far as you can, return offer for offer, exchange vow for vow?

ALCESTE: No! I can't bear these despicable mannerisms that so many of your men of fashion affect. There's nothing I hate more than the contortions of your protestation-mongers, the affable exchangers of fatuous greetings, polite mouthers of meaningless words, who bandy civilities with all comers and treat everyone, blockhead and man of sense, alike. What satisfaction can there be in having a man express his consideration for you, profess friendship, faith, zeal, esteem and affection, and praise you to the skies when he'll hasten to do as much for the first worthless scoundrel he runs into? No, no! No man with any self-respect wants that sort of debased and worthless esteem. There's precious little satisfaction in the most glorious of reputations if you find you have to share it with the whole universe. Esteem must be founded on some sort of preference. Bestow it on everybody and it ceases to have any meaning at all. Surrender to the foolish manners of the age and, by God, you're no friend of mine! I despise the all-embracing, undiscriminating affection which makes no distinction of merit. I want to be singled out and, to put it bluntly, the friend of the whole human race is not my line at all.

PHILINTE: But surely, if you live in the world you must observe such outward forms of civility as use and custom demand.

ALCESTE: No, I tell you! We should have no mercy whatever on the shameful trade in simulated friendship. I want us to be men and say what we really mean in all circumstances. Let what we have in our hearts be apparent in our words; let it be our hearts that speak, and let us not allow our feelings to be concealed under a mask of empty compliments.

PHILINTE: But surely there are many circumstances in which complete frankness would be ridiculous or intolerable. With all due respect to these austere standards of yours, there are times when it's as well to hide what we really feel. Would it be right and proper to go round telling people exactly what we think of them? Suppose there's someone you loathe or find disagreeable, should you tell him so?

ALCESTE: Yes!

PHILINTE: So you would tell old Émilie how badly it suits her to pass

herself off as a beauty at her time of life? How shocking it is to see
her painting and powdering the way she does?

ALCESTE: Undoubtedly!

PHILINTE: And Dorilas, that he's a dreadful bore, that there's not a
single person at Court who isn't tired of hearing him droning on
about his military exploits and the glorious feats of his ancestors?

ALCESTE: Unquestionably!

PHILINTE: You're not serious?

ALCESTE: I most certainly am! This is an issue on which I'll spare no
one. I've seen and suffered too much of it. Court and town furnish
me with nothing but occasions to stoke my fury. It fills me with
black depression and reduces me to utter despair to see men living
as they do. I meet with nothing but base flattery, injustice, selfishness,
treachery, villainy everywhere. I can't stand it any more. It infuriates
me. I mean to fling my gauntlet in the face of the whole human race!

PHILINTE: Your philosophical rage is a rather overdone. It makes me
laugh to see you in these gloomy fits of yours. I always think that –
brought up together as we were – we are like the brothers in *The
School for Husbands*[1] whose –

ALCESTE: Oh! For goodness' sake spare me your futile comparisons!

PHILINTE: No, seriously, give up these violent outbursts. The world
won't change its ways on account of anything you may do. But since
you're so fond of frankness, let me tell you plainly that this foible
of yours makes you a laughing stock wherever you go. You just
make yourself look ridiculous to everyone by getting so incensed
against the manners of the age.

ALCESTE: By God! So much the better! So much the better! That's all
I ask. It's a good sign and I welcome it. I find mankind so odious
that I should hate to have it approve of me.

PHILINTE: You are very hard on human nature!

ALCESTE: Yes, I'm coming to loathe it.

PHILINTE: And are all poor mortals without exception to be included
in this aversion? Isn't there a living creature in the age we live in –

ALCESTE: No. It's universal. I hate all mankind, some men because they
are wicked and perverse, others because they tolerate wickedness –
because they show no sign of the intense loathing that vice should
inspire in all virtuous hearts. Look what inexcusable indulgence
people extend to the arrant scoundrel I'm at law with! The rogue is

plain to see beneath the mask! Everyone knows what he is! He may roll his eyes and speak in accents of humility, but he only fools people who are strangers here. We know that the despicable cur, who fully deserves to be stopped in his tracks, has got on in the world by dirty tricks and that the dazzling success which his methods have brought him undermines honest striving and makes virtue blush. Whatever shameful honours are heaped on him on all sides, no one really respects him as an honourable man. Call him an infamous rogue, a damnable scoundrel, and everybody agrees! No one will contradict you – and yet his cringing hypocrisy gains him acceptance everywhere. People receive him into their homes, they smile on him as he worms his way in everywhere. If there's a job to be had by lobbying, you'll see him triumph and better men passed over. God! It breaks my heart to see how men connive with vice! There are times when the urge suddenly takes me to find some solitary place and avoid all contact with humankind.

PHILINTE: Good Lord! Let's not worry so much about the manners of the age and make more allowance for human nature. Let's judge it less severely and look more kindly on its faults. What's needed in society is a flexible kind of virtue. It's wrong to be too high principled. True reason lies in avoiding extremes and requires us to be wise in moderation. This stiff-backed passion for the virtues of ancient days is out of step with our age and accepted practice. It requires too much perfection of mere mortals. We need to move with the times and not be too rigid, and it's the height of folly for anyone to take upon himself the task of setting the world to rights. Like you, I observe many times each day things which could be better if they were done differently. But whatever I happen to see, I don't show my irritation openly as you do. I don't get hot and bothered, but take men as they are, school myself to put up with what they do and firmly believe that both at Court and in town, my self-possession is no less philosophical than your intemperate spleen.

ALCESTE: And can nothing ruffle this self-possession of yours, most rational of philosophers? Suppose a friend betrayed you, suppose someone plotted to get his hands on everything you own, or did his damnedest to spread scandalous rumours about you, could you sit back and watch it happen and not be angry?

PHILINTE: Of course. I look upon these faults which you are so concerned about as defects inseparable from human nature: it disturbs me no more to find men base, unjust or selfish than to see apes up to no good, wolves snarling or vultures ravenous for carrion.

ALCESTE: So I am to see myself betrayed, torn to pieces, robbed with never a . . . God! That argument is so full of impertinent nonsense that I'll say no more.

PHILINTE: Indeed, it would be best if you did keep quiet. Rail less against your adversary and give some thought to your lawsuit.

ALCESTE: I'll do no such thing. On that my mind's made up.

PHILINTE: Then who do you think will use their influence in the right quarters on your behalf?

ALCESTE: I'll tell you: reason, justice, the rightness of my cause.

PHILINTE: Won't you be calling on any of the judges then?

ALCESTE: No! Is my cause doubtful or unjust?

PHILINTE: It is not, I grant you. But your opponent will lobby and that can do you harm, so –

ALCESTE: No. I'm determined not to take a single step. Either I'm in the right or in the wrong.

PHILINTE: I wouldn't count on it.

ALCESTE: I won't lift a finger.

PHILINTE: You have a powerful adversary. He can bring considerable influence to bear . . .

ALCESTE: No matter.

PHILINTE: You may find you've made a mistake.

ALCESTE: So be it. I'll await the outcome.

PHILINTE: But . . .

ALCESTE: I shall have the pleasure of losing my case.

PHILINTE: But surely . . .

ALCESTE: This case will show me whether people can really have the effrontery, be so wicked, so villainous, so corrupt, as to do me injustice openly before the eyes of all the world.

PHILINTE: What a man!

ALCESTE: I'd be happy to lose my case, whatever it cost me, to have the satisfaction of putting that to the test.

PHILINTE: Really, Alceste, people would laugh if they heard you talk like that.

ALCESTE: So much the worse for them.

PHILINTE: But do you find this rectitude that you're always insisting on, this absolute integrity you set such store by, in the lady you're in love with? I'm surprised that while you seem to be at daggers drawn with the whole human race, you have found, in spite of everything that makes it odious to you, one member of it who has power to charm you. What amazes me even more is the strange choice on which your affections have settled. Éliante is a model of sincerity and she likes you; the prudish Arsinoé makes sheep's eyes at you, but you refuse your heart to them while Célimène binds it fast and toys with it – Célimène, whose coquettishness and love of scandal seem to chime so well with the manners of the age. How does it come about that, hating these characteristics as you do, you can tolerate their embodiment in her? Do they stop being faults when they appear in such an attractive shape? Is it that you don't you see them, or do you find excuses for them?

ALCESTE: No. My love for this young widow does not blind me to the faults I find in her. Despite the passion she inspires in me, I am the first to see them as I am to condemn them. And yet for all that, do what I may, I have to confess my weakness. I am captivated by her. I see her faults, but it makes no difference: I condemn them in vain. She makes me love her in spite of myself. Her charm is irresistible and I'm sure my love will rescue her from the follies of our times.

PHILINTE: If you do that it will be no small achievement! You think she loves you then?

ALCESTE: Heavens, yes! I shouldn't love her if I didn't think so.

PHILINTE: But if she has made it clear that she loves you, why is it that you are so concerned about your rivals?

ALCESTE: Because true love demands undivided affection in return. That's my sole purpose in coming here now – to open my heart to her on that very matter.

PHILINTE: Well, if it was me and I was going to fall in love, I'd be looking in the direction of her cousin Éliante. She loves you and her affection is constant and sincere. She'd be a far better and more suitable choice for you.

ALCESTE: That's true. And so the voice of reason tells me every day. But then love's not ruled by reason.

PHILINTE: I fear greatly for your love. Your hopes may well prove . . .

Scene ii:

ORONTE, ALCESTE, PHILINTE

ORONTE: I was informed downstairs that Éliante had gone out on an errand and Célimène too, but as they told me that you were here I came up to assure you sir, in all sincerity, of the extraordinarily high opinion I have of you, and to express the ardent ambition I have long had to be numbered among your friends. Yes, there's nothing I love more than giving merit its due sir, and I long to be united with you by the bond of friendship. I assume that the sincere friendship of a man of my rank and quality is not to be rejected. (*At this point Alceste's mind seems elsewhere and he appears not to hear what Oronte is saying to him.*) It is to you sir, if you please, that my remarks are addressed.

ALCESTE: To me sir?

ORONTE: To you sir. Have you any objection?

ALCESTE: Not in the least but I'm very much surprised. I wasn't expecting such an honour.

ORONTE: The fact, sir, that I hold you in such esteem should not surprise you. Your claims to it are universally acknowledged.

ALCESTE: Sir —

ORONTE: You enjoy an immense reputation without parallel in this country.

ALCESTE: Sir —

ORONTE: Yes, in my opinion you are a man of quite outstanding distinction.

ALCESTE: Sir —

ORONTE: May I be struck down by heaven above if I do not speak the unvarnished truth! And now permit me sir, in confirmation of my sentiments, to embrace you most heartily and solicit a place in your affection. Your hand on it, if you will! You promise me your friendship?

ALCESTE: Sir —

ORONTE: What! You decline?

ALCESTE: Sir, you do me too much honour, but friendship is not quite so simple a matter. Indeed it is a profanation of the word to use it on every occasion. It is a relationship which should spring from discerning and deliberate choice. We should be better acquainted before we commit ourselves. It might turn out that our characters may well be such that we should repent of the bargain.

ORONTE: By Jove! Spoken like a man of sense! I admire you all the more for it. Let us then leave it to time to establish this happy relationship between us. Meanwhile I am entirely at your service. If there is anything I can do for you at Court, I am known to cut some figure with His Majesty. I have his ear and he treats me, by God, with the greatest possible consideration. Once again then – count on me entirely. And now, since you are a man of taste and discrimination, may I venture to show you, by way of placing our relationship on a sound footing, a sonnet I have only recently composed? I would like your opinion as to whether it's fit to be published.

ALCESTE: Sir, I'm quite the wrong person to pronounce on such matters. Pray be good enough to excuse me.

ORONTE: But why?

ALCESTE: It's a failing of mine that I tend to be a little more frank in these things than I should.

ORONTE: But that's what I want! I should have cause to be aggrieved if, when I had gone so far as to ask you to give me your honest opinion, you failed to do so or kept anything back from me.

ALCESTE: Well then, I agree, since you insist.

ORONTE (*reading*): 'Sonnet' . . . it's a sonnet. 'Hope' . . . the lady in question has deigned to give some encouragement to my hopes . . . 'Hope' . . . It's not lofty or elaborate – just a few simple lines . . . tender and full of feeling. (*He looks at Alceste at each pause.*)

ALCESTE: We shall see.

ORONTE: 'Hope' . . . I don't know if you'll think the style sufficiently easy and flowing or if the choice of words will please you.

ALCESTE: We shall see sir.

ORONTE: Another thing – I should mention that I didn't spend more than a quarter of an hour on it.

ALCESTE: Let's hear it sir. The time spent on it is quite immaterial.

ORONTE (*reads*): 'Hope doth assuage, 'tis true, one's pain,
            And for a while breeds consolation.
            But, Phyllis, wherein lies the gain
            If on Hope's heels comes cold Frustration?'

PHILINTE: I am quite smitten with this beginning!

ALCESTE (*aside*): What! You have the audacity to admire that?

ORONTE:　　　'Once you showed me some munificence:

　　　　　　Less had been better, take my word;

　　　　　　Why did you go to such expense

　　　　　　If Hope was all you could afford?'

PHILINTE: Oh! Very nicely turned indeed!

ALCESTE (*aside to Philinte*): Damn you, you vile flatterer! How can you praise such rubbish?

ORONTE:　　　'Since on Eternity I needs must wait

　　　　　　And fruitless passion be my fate,

　　　　　　Death must be my last resort.

　　　　　　Your fond regrets afford me no comfort

　　　　　　For, fair Phyllis, we know despair

　　　　　　When to Hope is all that we may dare.'

PHILINTE: It has a dying fall. Quite lovely. Admirable!

ALCESTE (*aside*): Damn you and your fall, you lying toad. I wish you'd take a fall – and break your neck!

PHILINTE: I never heard lines more gracefully phrased.

ALCESTE (*aside*): Good God!

ORONTE (*to Philinte*): You flatter me, sir. Perhaps you think –

PHILINTE: No, I'm not flattering you in the least.

ALCESTE (*aside to Philinte*): Then what are you doing, you two-faced –

ORONTE (*to Alceste*): And now sir, you remember what we agreed. Please give me your candid opinion.

ALCESTE: Well sir – it's always a delicate business, for when it comes to questions of taste we all like to be flattered. But as I was saying only the other day to a person whose name I won't mention, on looking over some lines he had composed, a gentleman should always be careful to control that itch for scribbling to which we are so prone. We should keep a tight rein on any desire we might have to create a stir with such diversions or else, in our eagerness to show our work, we run a risk of cutting a pretty poor sort of figure.

ORONTE: Are you trying to tell me that I was wrong in wanting to . . .

ALCESTE: No, I'm not saying that. But what I went on to tell him was how deadly the effect of a dull piece of writing can be, how it only needs a foible of that sort to ruin a man's reputation, and though one might have countless fine qualities, people only notice the weaknesses.

ORONTE: Are you saying there's something wrong with my sonnet?

ALCESTE: No, I'm not saying that. But to put him off writing, I did point out the harm this sort of craving has done to some very worthy people in our own times.

ORONTE: Do I write badly? Am I to assume I resemble them?

ALCESTE: No, I'm not saying that. But what I did say to him finally was this: do you really need to write poetry and if so, why the deuce do you insist on being published? The only people who can be excused for unleashing a bad book on the world are the poor devils who have to write for a living. Take my word for it, resist the temptation, hide what you do from the public, and don't go and prejudice the honourable reputation you enjoy at Court — however much people may urge you to do so — for the sake having conferred on you by the hand of some grasping printer the wretched and ridiculous title of author. That's what I tried to impress on him.

ORONTE: That's all very well. I think I understand what you mean, but may I not be told what there is in my sonnet that —

ALCESTE: Frankly, the only thing to do with it is to put it away and forget it. You have formed your style on bad models. The expressions you use aren't natural. What's the meaning of 'and for a while breeds consolation'? or 'on Hope's heels comes cold Frustration'? What did you mean by 'Why did you go to such expense If Hope was all you could afford?' or: 'For, fair Phyllis, we know despair When to Hope is all that we may dare'? This figurative style people pride themselves so much on is false and untrue. It's just playing with words — sheer affectation! It isn't a natural way of speaking at all. I find contemporary taste appalling in this respect. Our ancestors, crude and unpolished as they were, did very much better. I prefer to any of the stuff people admire so much nowadays an old ballad such as:

> If good King Henry said to me
> 'Here's Paris town, so grand, so fair:
> All this and more I'll give to thee
> If you'll forsake your own true dear,'
> I'd up and say to good Henry
> 'Keep your Paris grand and fair:
> I love my sweetheart more, truly,
> Much more I love my dear.'

The rhymes may be clumsy and the style out-dated, but don't you see how much better it is than all the trumpery that offends one's common-sense? Don't you feel that this is the voice of true love speaking?

> If good King Henry said to me
> 'Here's Paris town, so grand, so fair:
> All this and more I'll give to thee
> If you'll forsake your own true dear,'
> I'd up and say to good Henry
> 'Keep your Paris grand and fair:
> I love my sweetheart more, truly,
> Much more I love my dear.'

That's just what a man who was really in love would say. (*To Philinte*:) Yes sir, you may laugh, but whatever your wits and your critics may say, I prefer that to the overblown, flowery tinsel that people make such a fuss about.

ORONTE: And I, sir, maintain that my lines are excellent.

ALCESTE: You have your reasons for thinking so. Permit me to have mine which allow me to think otherwise.

ORONTE: It is enough for me to know that other people think well of them.

ALCESTE: That is because they possess the art of dissimulation. I do not.

ORONTE: So you think you have a pretty good share of wit?

ALCESTE: I should, if I could see anything in your verse!

ORONTE: I shall manage very well without your approval.

ALCESTE: I'm afraid you'll have to.

ORONTE: I should like to see you try to compose something of your own on the same theme.

ALCESTE: I might well have the misfortune to do equally badly, but I'd take good care not to show other people the result.

ORONTE: You speak with a good deal of assurance, sir. Such self-opinionated –

ALCESTE: I suggest, sir, that you pursue your search for flattery elsewhere.

ORONTE: Come little man, adopt a less lofty tone.

ALCESTE: Upon my word, Sir High and Mighty, I shall adopt whatever tone I like . . .

PHILINTE (*coming between them*): Now gentlemen! That's enough! Please leave it at that!

ORONTE: Ah! I'm at fault – I admit it. I'll take my leave. (*To Alceste, ironically*:) I am, sir, your most devoted.

ALCESTE (*ironically*): And I, sir, your most obedient.

Scene iii:

PHILINTE, ALCESTE

PHILINTE: Well, you see? That's where your precious sincerity has landed you, with a damned awkward business on your hands! I saw perfectly well that Oronte wanted to be flattered and –

ALCESTE: Don t talk to me!

PHILINTE: But –

ALCESTE: Leave me alone!

PHILINTE: It's too –

ALCESTE: Go away!

PHILINTE: If I –

ALCESTE: Not another word!

PHILINTE: But what –

ALCESTE: I won't listen.

PHILINTE: But –

ALCESTE: Still there?

PHILINTE: You insult –

ALCESTE: Oh God! That's enough! Stop following me about (*He goes out*).

PHILINTE: Oh! Don't be absurd. I'm not going to leave you. (*He follows.*)

Act II

Scene i:

ALCESTE, CÉLIMÈNE:

ALCESTE: May I speak frankly Madame? I'm far from pleased with the way you behave. I'm beginning to find it intolerable. I can see that we shall have to go our separate ways. Yes, it would be deceiving you to tell you anything else. We shall undoubtedly reach breaking-point sooner or later. Even if I gave you my word to the contrary a thousand times over I should be unable to stand by it.

CÉLIMÈNE: So from what I see, you only insisted on seeing me home so that you could scold me.

ALCESTE: I'm not scolding you. But, Madame, you have a way of according your affections too freely to anyone who happens to come along. You have too many admirers forever hanging round you and I just cannot bear it.

CÉLIMÈNE: So you blame me for having admirers? Can I prevent people from finding me attractive? When they are kind enough to go to the trouble of coming to see me, am I supposed to reach for a stick and drive them from my door?

ALCESTE: No Madame, it's not a stick you want. But you need to be less tolerant, less accessible to their advances. I know you can't help being attractive wherever you are, but your attitude encourages those who fall under the spell of your glances. Your indulgence to those who surrender completes the conquest begun by your beauty. The alluring hopes you hold out keep them dancing attendance upon you. If you were less free with your favours, you would thin the ranks of those who languish and sigh for you. You might at least tell me how it is that your friend Clitandre has the good fortune to find such favour with you. On what qualities, on what sublime virtue is your regard for him founded? Is it the length of his little finger-nail that has acquired your esteem? Have you, like the rest of fashionable society, succumbed to the ostentatious merits of his blond periwig? Is it perhaps the wide frills at his knees that have captured your heart or his accumulation of ribbons that you find so enchanting? Has he endeared himself by the charms of his billowing breeches while he protests that he is your slave? Or is it his laugh or that falsetto voice of his that have found the secret of pleasing you?

CÉLIMÈNE: It's most unfair of you to take umbrage on his account. You know perfectly well why I keep in with him. Don't you see that he can interest all his friends in my lawsuit — as he has in fact promised to do?

ALCESTE: Resign yourself to losing your case, Madame, with a firm mind. Don't try to ingratiate yourself with a man whose rivalry is so offensive to me.

CÉLIMÈNE: You're becoming jealous of the whole universe.

ALCESTE: That's because the whole universe enjoys your favour.

CÉLIMÈNE: But shouldn't the very fact that I distribute my favour so widely afford some reassurance to your unquiet heart? Wouldn't you have more reason for being offended if you saw me bestowing it on one person?

ALCESTE: But I ask you, Madame, what advantage do I – whom you reproach for being so jealous – have over any of them?

CÉLIMÈNE: The satisfaction of knowing that you are loved.

ALCESTE: And what reason have I to cherish any such belief?

CÉLIMÈNE: I think when I have gone so far as to tell you so, such an admission should be quite sufficient.

ALCESTE: But what assurance do I have that you aren't perhaps saying as much to others at the same time?

CÉLIMÈNE: A pretty compliment from a lover, I must say! And a nice opinion you have of me! Very well! To relieve you of any such concern, I here and now unsay all that I have said in the past. Now no one can deceive you but yourself. Perhaps you're happy now.

ALCESTE: By God! Why do I have to be in love with you? If I could only take back my heart from out of your hands, how thankful I should be for the blessing! I make no secret of it – I have done everything I possibly can to break this cruel infatuation, but so far all to no purpose. It must be for my sins that I love you as I do.

CÉLIMÈNE: Love such as yours is unprecedented.

ALCESTE: Yes. On that count I can challenge the whole world! My love is beyond all imagining. No man, Madame, has ever loved as I do.

CÉLIMÈNE: And you certainly have a novel way of showing it! You love people so that you can quarrel with them. The only words you can find to express your passion are offensive and ungracious. I've never heard of a lover who grumbled and scolded the way you do.

ALCESTE: But it is entirely within your power to put an end to my black moods. Let's be done with all these arguments, I beseech you. Let us be entirely open with each other and see if we can stop . . .

Scene ii:
CÉLIMÈNE, ALCESTE, BASQUE

CÉLIMÈNE: What is it?

BASQUE: Acaste is downstairs.

CÉLIMÈNE: Very well. Show him up. (*Exit Basque.*)

ALCESTE: What! Am I never to have a word with you alone? Must you always be willing to receive callers? Can you never bring yourself to say, not even for one single moment, that you are not at home?

CÉLIMÈNE: Would you have me offend him?

ALCESTE: You consider people's feelings too much for my liking.

CÉLIMÈNE: He's the sort of man who would never forgive me if he knew that his presence was unwelcome.

ALCESTE: And why should that bother you?

CÉLIMÈNE: Heavens! The goodwill of people like him is important. He's one of those men who have acquired, goodness knows how, the privilege of making their opinions heard in Court circles. You find them butting in to every conversation. Though they can do you no good, they may do you harm. Whatever support you may have elsewhere, you should never get embroiled with that braying crowd.

ALCESTE: In other words, you'll always find reasons for remaining on good terms with everyone – whoever they may be and whatever they may do. You are so cautious in your judgements that . . .

Scene iii:
BASQUE, ALCESTE, CÉLIMÈNE

BASQUE: Clitandre is here as well, Madame.

ALCESTE: Oh, of course, he would be! (*Makes as if to leave.*)

CÉLIMÈNE: Where are you running off to?

ALCESTE: I'm going.

CÉLIMÈNE: Stay.

ALCESTE: What for?

CÉLIMÈNE: Do stay.

ALCESTE: I can't.

CÉLIMÈNE: I want you to.

ALCESTE: It's no use. These conversations only bore me. It's asking too much to want me to put up with them.

CÉLIMÈNE: But I want you to, I want you to!

ALCESTE: No. I can't do it.

CÉLIMÈNE: Very well then. Go! Be off. Do as you please!

Scene iv:

ÉLIANTE, PHILINTE, ACASTE, CLITANDRE, ALCESTE, CÉLIMÈNE, BASQUE

ÉLIANTE: The two marquises are coming up with us. Did no one come to tell you?

CÉLIMÈNE: Yes. (*To Basque*:) Chairs for the company. (*To Alceste*:) Haven't you gone?

ALCESTE: No Madame. I intend to make you explain your mind – to their satisfaction or mine.

CÉLIMÈNE: Hush!

ALCESTE: You shall explain yourself here and now.

CÉLIMÈNE: Have you lost your senses?

ALCESTE: Not at all! You shall say where you stand.

CÉLIMÈNE: Oh!

ALCESTE: You must take one side or the other.

CÉLIMÈNE: I suppose this is a joke?

ALCESTE: No, but choose you shall. I've been patient for too long.

CLITANDRE: Egad! I'have come straight from the Louvre. Cléonte has been making a perfect fool of himself there at the king's levée.[2] Has he no friends who could in charity advise him how to behave?

CÉLIMÈNE: He certainly has a habit of making himself look ridiculous in company. His manner is always very conspicuous and when one sees him again after an interval, it seems even odder.

ACASTE: Egad, talking of odd fellows I have just had a dose of one of the most tiresome of them all – I mean that garrulous bore, Damon! He kept me out of my sedan chair for an hour, if you please, and in the blazing sun too!

CÉLIMÈNE: How he does talk! He contrives to say nothing at the most inordinate length and I can never make any sense of what he is talking about. It's like listening to so much noise.

ÉLIANTE (*to Philinte*): Not a bad start at all. The conversation's already taking a lively turn at pulling one's acquaintances to pieces!

CLITANDRE: Now what about Timante? Don't you think he's an admirable character?

CÉLIMÈNE: The complete mystery man, from head to foot! He throws you an absent-minded glance as he bustles by, for he's always so busy though he has nothing to do! Anything he has to tell you is conveyed with signs and grimaces – it's quite a performance and utterly overwhelming! He's forever interrupting the conversation because he has some secret or other to confide to you, but there's never anything in it. He converts the merest trifle into a major scandal and everything, even his 'good morning', has to be whispered in your ear.

ACASTE: And Géralde, Madame?

CÉLIMÈNE: Oh! That pretentious gossip! He can never throw off his lordly manner. He only moves in the highest circles and never mentions anybody below the rank of duke, prince or princess. He's obsessed with the quality and can talk of nothing but horses, carriages and dogs. He speaks most familiarly to people of the highest rank, so much so that he has forgotten how to use plain 'Monsieur'.

CLITANDRE: They say he's on very good terms with Bélise.

CÉLIMÈNE: That empty-headed creature – she's dreary company I must say. I suffer agonies when she comes to call on me. It's one continual struggle to find something to say to her. She's so utterly unresponsive that she just kills all conversation stone dead. You clutch at all the usual banal topics to try to break down her stupid silence, but it's not the least use – the fine weather or the rain, how cold it is or how hot it has been – before long you've exhausted them all and her visit, unbearable enough anyway, becomes more and more awful as it drags out its hideous length. You may ask the time and yawn as much as you like, but she'll no more stir than a block of wood.

ACASTE: And what do you make of Adraste?

CÉLIMÈNE: Too conceited for words! The man's blown up with his own importance. He's forever sounding off about the Court because he thinks he's not appreciated there. There's never an appointment made or a place or preferment offered that isn't an injustice to his own idea of himself.

CLITANDRE: And young Cléon? Everyone who is anybody gathers at his house nowadays. What do you say about him?

CÉLIMÈNE: That he owes his reputation to his cook. People don't go to see him, they go to visit his table.

ÉLIANTE: He does go to the trouble of providing good food.

CÉLIMÈNE: Yes, if only he didn't serve up his own company with it! His stupidity takes a good deal of stomaching. To my mind, it completely ruins the dinners he gives.

PHILINTE: His uncle, Damis, is highly thought of. What do you say about him Madame?

CÉLIMÈNE: He's a friend of mine.

PHILINTE: I think he's sound, a man who looks sensible enough.

CÉLIMÈNE: Yes, but what annoys me is that he's always trying to be clever. He's so high and mighty and always so obviously trying to be witty in everything he says. Since he's taken it into his head to show how smart he is, there's just no suiting his taste — he's so difficult to please. He insists on finding fault with everything anyone writes, and he thinks that to praise is beneath the dignity of a man of taste, that to find something to criticize is the sign of a scholarly mind, that only fools allow themselves to admire things or be amused, and that he demonstrates his superiority to everyone else by disapproving of all contemporary works. Even in ordinary conversation either he'll find something to cavil at or else the subject will be so far beneath his notice that he'll just fold his arms and look down in pity from the height of his own wisdom on everything that anyone says.

ACASTE: Dammit! That's got him to a T!

CLITANDRE: You have a wonderful gift for capturing people to the life!

ALCESTE: Aye! Stick to it, gentlemen, like the true courtiers that you are! You spare no one. Everyone suffers in turn. But let any one of them appear on the scene and you would all rush to meet him, shake his hand warmly, and in the most flattering terms protest your eternal devotion.

CLITANDRE: But why get cross with us? If what's been said offends you, it's the lady here you should address your reproaches to.

ALCESTE: No, dammit! I blame you. It's your toadying laughter that encourages her to these slanderous outbursts. Her satirical humour is fed and watered by your wicked flattery. She would find less satisfaction in her mockery if she saw that you did not applaud her.

Flatterers are always to blame for the vices which prevail among mankind.

PHILINTE: Why are you so ready to show such concern for people you yourself would condemn for the very same reasons?

CÉLIMÈNE: But surely the gentleman must be allowed to contradict! Would you have him reduced to sharing the common view of things? Is he to be prevented from taking any opportunity of displaying the contrary spirit heaven bestowed on him? He can never go along with other people's opinions. He must always take the opposite view. He'd think he was cutting a very ordinary figure if he found himself agreeing with anyone else. He's so fond of contradicting that he often takes up an argument against himself and opposes his own sentiments as soon as he hears other people expressing them.

ALCESTE: The laugh's on your side Madame, there's no doubt about that! You may safely indulge your satire against me.

PHILINTE: But it is true none the less that you're always up in arms against everything people say. You yourself admit to being equally intolerant, whether they're praising or blaming.

ALCESTE: Dammit, it's because other people are never right, because there's always a good reason for being angry with them, because I observe that in all matters they are invariably as misguided in their praise as they are rash in their condemnation.

CÉLIMÈNE: But —

ALCESTE: No Madame, no. I'll say it if it kills me. You take a delight in things I find intolerable, and it's downright wrong of these people here to be encouraging you to adopt the very habits they criticize you for.

CLITANDRE: Well, I don't know about that. But I don't mind admitting freely that I've always thought the lady perfection itself.

ACASTE: To me she's everything that's charming and gracious. If she has any faults, I haven't noticed them.

ALCESTE: But I notice them and, far from shutting my eyes to them, she knows I make a point of reproaching her on their account. The more you love someone, the less you should flatter them. The proof of true love is to be unsparing in fault-finding. I personally would banish any lover so faint-hearted as to agree with all my opinions and feebly and obsequiously pander to my extravagances.

CÉLIMÈNE: Then if you had your way as to how lovers behaved, we would have to show our feelings by avoiding all tenderness and define the supreme testimony of perfect love as being rude to whoever it is we're in love with.

ÉLIANTE: That isn't really how love works at all for most people. You find that a man in love always justifies his own choice. His passion makes him blind to all faults and in his eyes everything in the woman he loves is lovable. He counts her defects as perfections or finds flattering names for them. If she's pale, it's the pale beauty of the jasmine flower. She may be swarthy enough to frighten the horses, but for him she's an adorable brunette. If she's thin, she's slender and graceful; if fat, she has a queenly dignity; if she neglects her appearance, slight though her attractions may be, she is said to have a 'careless beauty'; if she's tall, she'll have the majesty of a goddess; if she's short, she's an abridged version of all the virtues under heaven! If she's proud, her nature is regal. If she's sly, she's clever. If she's stupid, she's all heart. If she talks all the time, she's cheerful. If she never talks at all, she's proper and modest. And so it is that the true and passionate lover worships the very faults of the woman he loves.[3]

ALCESTE: Well for my part I maintain —

CÉLIMÈNE: Suppose we drop the subject now and take a turn in the gallery. What? Are you going gentlemen?

CLITANDRE *and* ACASTE (*together*): By no means, Madam.

ALCESTE (*to Célimène*): You seem very much concerned lest they should go. (*To Clitandre and Acaste:*) Leave whenever you please, gentlemen, but I warn you I shall stay until you go.

ACASTE: Unless I thought the lady would be inconvenienced, I could stay all day.

CLITANDRE: Provided I return for the hour of His Majesty's retiring, I have no business that need call me away.

CÉLIMÈNE (*to Alceste*): You think this amusing, I suppose?

ALCESTE: Not in the least; but we'll see whether I'm the one you want to go.

Scene v:

BASQUE, ALCESTE, CÉLIMÈNE, ÉLIANTE, ACASTE,
PHILINTE, CLITANDRE

BASQUE (*to Alceste*): Sir, there's a man outside who'd like to speak to
you on business which he says won't wait.

ALCESTE: Tell him I have no business of such urgency.

BASQUE: He has a long pleated coat with gold braid all over it.

CÉLIMÈNE (*to Alceste*): Go and see what it is, or else have him come
up.

ALCESTE (*to the Officer as he enters*): Come in sir. What is it you want?

Scene vi:

OFFICER, ALCESTE, CÉLIMÈNE, ÉLIANTE, ACASTE,
PHILINTE, CLITANDRE

OFFICER: I needs a word with you sir.

ALCESTE: You may say your piece here. Tell me what this is about.

OFFICER: The Marshals of France,[4] whose warrant I bear, require you
to appear before them, sir, immediately.

ALCESTE: Who? Me sir?

OFFICER: You sir. In person.

ALCESTE: For what purpose?

PHILINTE: It's that absurd squabble with Oronte.

CÉLIMÈNE (*to Philinte*): What's this?

PHILINTE: Oronte and he had words about some trifling verses which
he didn't think much of. They want to nip the quarrel in the bud.

ALCESTE: I won't stand for any miserable compromise.

PHILINTE: But you must obey the summons. Come, get ready.

ALCESTE: What sort of compromise do they intend to force on us? Will
those gentlemen sentence me to approve the lines we quarrelled
about? I won't go back on what I said. I still think they're dreadful.

PHILINTE: If you would only be a little more –

ALCESTE: I won't budge an inch. The poem is execrable!

PHILINTE: You must try to be reasonable. Come along.

ALCESTE: I'll go – but there's no power on earth that will make me retract.

PHILINTE: Let us go and put in an appearance.

ALCESTE: Short of His Majesty's express command to approve the verses all this fuss is about, I shall never cease to maintain, by God, that they are bad and that the man who wrote them deserves to be hanged. (*To Clitandre and Acaste who are laughing:*) Confound it gentlemen! I was not aware I was so amusing.

CÉLIMÈNE: Go quickly and obey the summons.

ALCESTE: I'm going Madame, but I shall come straight back to finish our discussion.

Act III

Scene i:

CLITANDRE, ACASTE

CLITANDRE: You look remarkably pleased with yourself, my dear Marquis. Everything amuses you and you haven't a care in the world. Tell me frankly, and looking at the matter squarely: do you really believe that you have good reason for looking so cheerful?

ACASTE: Egad! When I examine myself closely I can't see any reason for dissatisfaction. I'm rich, I'm young, I come of a house which can with some reason account itself noble. By virtue of my birth and the precedence it gives me, I believe there are very few posts which are beyond my reach. As to valour, which we should, of course, put before everything else, I think I may say in all modesty that I'm known not to be wanting in that respect. I have shown that I can pursue an affair of honour with sufficient vigour and boldness. Brains I have beyond question, with good taste sufficient to pass judgement and give an opinion on everything without benefit of study, to sit on the stage and perform as a critic at first nights (occasions I dote on) and give a rousing lead to the audience at all the fine passages that deserve applause. I'm pretty adroit, have a good manner and good looks, particularly fine teeth, and a very lithe figure. As for knowing how to dress, well, not to flatter myself unduly, I defy anyone to compete with me in that department. I'm as popular as any man can be, attractive to women, and stand well with His Majesty. I think that with such advantages, my dear Marquis, a man might rightly feel pleased with himself anywhere.

CLITANDRE: Yes, but finding easy conquests elsewhere as you do, why is it that you sigh in vain here?

ACASTE: Me? Sigh in vain? Damn me! I'm not the sort of man to put up with any woman's indifference, nor am I inclined to. It's all very well for fellows who are wanting in any sort of grace or distinction whatever to burn for unyielding beauties, languish at their feet, and submit to their rigours with undying constancy. They may resort to sighing and tears in an attempt to obtain by assiduous courtship the favours they don't get and don't deserve. But men of my stamp, Marquis, men of my stamp are not in the habit of giving their hearts on credit and doing all the paying themselves. No, no! Rare though the merits of the fair sex may be, I contend that we, heaven be praised, have our value as they have theirs, and that it's unreasonable that any of them should enjoy the honour of a love such as mine without it costing her anything. At least, to keep the scales even, there should be some give and take on both sides.

CLITANDRE: You think then, Marquis, that you stand pretty well here?

ACASTE: I have some grounds for thinking so, Marquis.

CLITANDRE: Believe me, you should rid yourself of any such illusion. You are flattering yourself, my dear fellow – it's sheer self-deception!

ACASTE: Oh! Of course I'm flattering myself and being blind!

CLITANDRE: But what reason have you for thinking you are so fortunate?

ACASTE: I flatter myself!

CLITANDRE: On what basis are your hopes founded?

ACASTE: Self-deception!

CLITANDRE: Have you any positive proof?

ACASTE: I tell you, I deceive myself.

CLITANDRE: Has Célimène given you some secret assurance of her feelings?

ACASTE: No, I am cruelly used!

CLITANDRE: Give me a straight answer, please!

ACASTE: I meet with nothing but rebuffs.

CLITANDRE: Oh! Just stop joking for a moment and tell me: what reason has she given you to hope?

ACASTE: I am a spurned wretch and you are the lucky one. She detests me. One of these days I shall have to go and hang myself.

CLITANDRE: Well now Marquis, couldn't we both come to an understanding as to how we conduct our courtship in future? If one of us can show some proof of the preference Célimène has for him, let the other give way to him as the successful suitor and so rid him of a troublesome rival.

ACASTE: By God! Now that's the sort of talk I like! I'll be glad to agree to this arrangement. But hush! Here she . . .

Scene ii:
CÉLIMÈNE, ACASTE, CLITANDRE

CÉLIMÈNE: Still here?

CLITANDRE: It's love that detains us Madame.

CÉLIMÈNE: I heard a carriage below. Do you know who it is?

CLITANDRE. No.

Scene iii:
BASQUE, CÉLIMÈNE, ACASTE, CLITANDRE

BASQUE: Arsinoé is coming up to see you Madame.

CÉLIMÈNE: What does that woman want with me?

BASQUE: Éliante is talking to her downstairs.

CÉLIMÈNE: What can she be thinking of? Who on earth asked her to come here?

ACASTE: She has a reputation everywhere of being the most complete prude. She's so pious that —

CÉLIMÈNE: Yes, she's all hypocrisy! She's completely worldly at heart. Her only interest is in catching a man — so far without any success — and she can't restrain her envy when she sees anyone else with admirers. Because her own sorry charms are ignored by everybody, she's forever up in arms against the blindness of the age, trying to conceal the awful emptiness of her existence beneath a pretence of virtue and modesty and consoling herself for her waning attractions by branding as sinful the pleasures she has no chance of enjoying herself. But a lover would be very acceptable to the lady. She even has a fancy for Alceste and regards the attentions he pays me as an insult to her beauty. According to her I am stealing something that's hers! So her barely concealed spite and jealousy find outlets in underhand attacks on me at every opportunity. It all seems utterly stupid to me. She's really the silliest, most tiresome . . .

Scene iv:
ARSINOÉ, CÉLIMÈNE

CÉLIMÈNE: Ah! What happy chance brings you here? Madame, in all honesty, I have been so worried about you.

ARSINOÉ: I came about something I thought it was my duty to tell you.

CÉLIMÈNE: Heaven be praised! I'm so pleased to see you.

(*Clitandre and Acaste leave, laughing.*)

ARSINOÉ: They couldn't have chosen a better moment to go.

CÉLIMÈNE: Shall we sit down?

ARSINOÉ: No, there's no need for that Madame. Since friends have a particular duty to each other in matters which may concern them most directly, and because nothing is more important than honour and propriety, I have come to demonstrate my friendship for you by telling you of something which touches your own reputation. Yesterday I was with some extremely God-fearing people when, the conversation turning upon you, your behaviour and the sensation it causes, were, unhappily, not considered commendable. The crowds of men you permit to come calling, your flirtatiousness, and the talk there is about it, found all too many critics and were more severely judged than I would have wished. You may imagine which side I tried to take! I did all I could to defend you. I made every excuse for you on the ground that you meant no harm by such things. I offered to go bail for your goodness of heart, but, as you know, there are things in life which, with the best will in the world, one cannot defend. I was obliged to agree that your behaviour did bring a measure of discredit upon you, that it created an unfortunate impression in many quarters, that all sorts of unpleasant stories are going the rounds, and that, if you were so minded, your whole manner of life could well be made less open to criticism. Not that I really believe your virtue to be compromised. Heaven preserve me from thinking any such thing! But people are ready to seize upon the slightest hint of misconduct and it is not enough to live sufficient unto oneself. You are, I believe Madame, much too sensible not to take this useful advice in good part or to believe that I have any motive other than concern for your own best interests.

CÉLIMÈNE: Madame, I really am most deeply grateful to you. Your advice places me in your debt and, far from taking it ill, I propose to return the favour immediately by giving you information which equally concerns your own reputation. Just as you have demonstrated your friendship by telling me what people were saying about me, so I in turn will follow your well-meant example and tell you what they are saying about you. At a house where I was paying a call the other day, I met some exceptionally good people who were discussing what constituted a virtuous life, and the conversation turning on you Madame; your severe principles and excessive piety were not accounted good models: the affected gravity with which you behave, your everlasting sermons on morals and propriety, your habit of exclaiming and frowning at the least hint of indecency to which an innocently ambiguous word may give rise, your high opinion of yourself and your pitying condescension for everyone else, your perpetual moralizing and the sourness with which you condemn things which are in reality innocent and pure – all this, if I may speak frankly, was quite unanimously condemned. 'What is the use', they said, 'of her modest bearing and her outward appearance of virtue, if everything else contradicts it? She's meticulous about saying her prayers, and yet she beats her servants and never pays them. She makes great parade of her piety in devout circles and yet she paints her face and tries to make herself look attractive. She covers up the nudity in paintings but she's not averse to the real thing!' Of course I took your part against the whole company and roundly charged them with slandering you. But they were all united against me and their conclusion was that you would be well advised to concern yourself less with other people's behaviour and more with your own, that we should examine ourselves thoroughly before condemning others, that strictures on our neighbours carry more weight if our own lives are exemplary, and that when it comes to the point it's far better to leave such matters to the men of the cloth whom Heaven has made responsible for them. You are, I believe Madame, much too sensible not to take this useful advice in good part or to believe that I have any motive other than concern for your own best interests.

ARSINOÉ: One inevitably lays oneself open by offering any word of reproof, but I did not expect such a reply. I perceive, Madame, from the bitterness of your tone that my warning, though given in all sincerity, has wounded you deeply.

CÉLIMÈNE: On the contrary Madame, if people were wiser, these mutual exchanges would become the norm. If we were prepared to be honest, we might put an end to our great blindness about ourselves. It rests entirely with you to say whether we should continue these friendly offices with the same enthusiasm as we have begun and make a point of repeating to each other everything that we hear – you of me and I, Madame, of you.

ARSINOÉ: Oh! I could never hear anything said against you Madame. I'm the one who has all the faults.

CÉLIMÈNE: Madame, I don't believe there's anything that can't be praised or criticized, and everyone is right in what they say, according to their age and tastes. There's a season for love and another for prudishness, and we may consciously choose the latter when the hey-day of our youth has passed – it may serve to conceal some of life's disappointments! I don't say I shan't follow your example one day – there's no saying what age will bring us to – but you must agree, Madame, that twenty is not the age for being prim.

ARSINOÉ: Really! You pride yourself on a very small advantage! You make far too much of your youth. Whatever the difference in our ages may be it is not so great that it warrants making such a fuss about. Moreover I don't know why you are getting so cross Madame, nor what reason you have for turning on me like this.

CÉLIMÈNE: Nor do I know why it is that wherever you are, you go out of your way to attack me. Must you forever be taking your resentment out on me? Can I help it if men take no notice of you? If they find me attractive and insist on paying me every day those same attentions you would like to see me deprived? What of, what can I do about it? It's not my fault. You have a clear field. It's not me who's preventing you being attractive enough to bring them running.

ARSINOÉ: Dear me! Do you think I worry about the number of admirers you so pride yourself on? Or that one can't perfectly well guess the price that's set nowadays on their attentions? Would you have us believe, things being the way they are, that they come flocking round you simply for your good qualities, and that they are happy to burn with pure love and court you for your virtues alone? People can easily see through your subterfuges: no one's taken in by them! I know women endowed with every quality to inspire love, but they don't encourage men to come to their houses. It follows that we can draw the conclusion that men's affections aren't gained without making considerable concessions, that they don't love us just for our looks, and that all their attentiveness has to be bought. So don't be so puffed up with pride in your petty triumphs! Moderate the arrogant opinion you have of your own beauty which makes you so contemptuous of others! If one envied your conquests, I think one could do as other people do – abandon all restaint and let you see that lovers can be had when we've a mind to have them.

CÉLIMÈNE, Have them then, by all means Madame! Let's see how you do it. Show us the secret, try to make yourself attractive and –

ARSINOÉ: Let us drop this discussion Madame, or it may try both our tempers too far. I should have taken my leave already had my carriage not kept me waiting.

CÉLIMÈNE: You may stay as long as you please Madame. There's no occasion for hurry. I won't weary you with the customary civilities but shall leave you to better company. (*Enter Alceste.*) The gentleman who has just arrived most opportunely will take my place and entertain you better than I can. Alceste, I must go and write a note which I can't very well postpone without being thought remiss. Stay with this lady and she'll the more easily excuse my rudeness. (*Exit.*)

Scene v:

ALCESTE, ARSINOÉ

ARSINOÉ: You see, she wishes me to speak with you for a moment while I'm waiting for my carriage to come. She could have offered me no greater pleasure than this opportunity to have a conversation with you. Of course, we all love and admire men of outstanding abilities, but there is something about you, some mysterious power, which makes me deeply concerned for your interests. I only wish the Court would turn a more propitious eye on your merits and treat you more justly. You have every reason to complain. It makes me very angry to see the days pass and nothing at all is done for you.

ALCESTE: For me Madame? On what grounds could I make any claim? What services am I supposed to have rendered the State? What have I done, may I ask, that is so outstanding that I have reason to complain that the Court does nothing for me?

ARSINOÉ: Not all those on whom the Court looks with favour have rendered the kind of distinguished service you mean. Opportunity is needed as well as ability, and in fact the talents and abilities which you display ought to be –

ALCESTE: Good Lord! Let us say no more about my abilities, I beseech you! Why do you think the Court should be bothered about them? The Court would have enough to do, more than enough, if it had to go round unearthing people's abilities!

ARSINOÉ: Outstanding abilities unearth themselves. Yours are very highly spoken of in many quarters. I may say that only yesterday I twice heard you praised in the most influential circles by people of great consequence.

ALCESTE. Why Madame! They praise everyone nowadays. This is an age which shows no discrimination whatever in that respect. Brilliant gifts are attributed to everybody in equal degree. It's no longer an honour to be praised: we have praises coming out of our ears. Praise is thrown around wholesale. Why! My valet has had a mention in the newspapers!

ARSINOÉ: Nevertheless, I really wish a post at Court had more appeal for you, so that you were more in the public eye. If you showed the slightest inclination that way, I could pull a few strings. I have good friends whom I could ask to use their influence on your behalf and smooth the way for you.

ALCESTE: And what would you have me do in such a post Madame? My character is such that I should stay well away from such things. I'm not suited by nature to the atmosphere of the Court. I don't feel I have the qualities necessary for success there or to make my fortune in it. My main gift is for frankness and sincerity. I have no talent for deceiving people with words. A man who can't hide what he thinks shouldn't stay too long in such places. Away from the Court one no doubt misses the influence and the honours it dispenses these days. But in forgoing those advantages one at least avoids the humiliation of making a fool of oneself and suffering many a cruel rebuff, or having to praise Monsieur So-and-So's poems, dance attendance on Lady Such-and-Such, or put up with the inanities of our inimitable marquises.

ARSINOÉ: Well, since you prefer it, suppose we leave the subject of the Court. But I can't help observing how much I deplore your love affair. If I may tell you frankly how I see it, I could have wished your affections had been more wisely bestowed. You deserve a much happier fate. The lady you are so smitten with is not worthy of you.

ALCESTE: Kindly remember when you say such things, Madame, that the lady in question is your friend.

ARSINOÉ: Yes, but it really does go against my conscience to let her continue to wrong you any further. It distresses me too much when I see what position you're in. I warn you. She's deceiving you.

ALCESTE: That's very kind and considerate of you Madame. Information of that kind is most gratifying to a man in love.

ARSINOÉ: Yes, although she's my friend, she is, and I am not afraid to say so, unworthy of the love of an honourable man. Her affection for you is mere pretence.

ALCESTE: That may well be Madame. We cannot see into other people's hearts, but you might in charity have refrained from putting such thoughts into my head.

ARSINOÉ: If you prefer not to be undeceived I need say no more. That's easy enough.

ALCESTE: No. In a case like this, whatever we are told can't be as bad as remaining in doubt, but I myself would rather be told nothing except what can be plainly demonstrated.

ARSINOÉ: Very well. I'll say no more. You shall have all the demonstration you want. Yes, I won't ask you to believe anything but your own eyes. Give me your hand as far as my house and there I'll give you incontrovertible proof of the lady's unfaithfulness. Should you then have eyes for the charms of another, it might be possible to offer you something by way of consolation.

Act IV

Scene i:
ÉLIANTE, PHILINTE

PHILINTE: No, I never came across a more pig-headed man nor a lawsuit where it was so hard to reach an understanding. They tried every way to shift him but it was no use. There was simply no getting him to change his mind. I don't suppose their Lordships' wisdom was ever exercised by such a bizarre case before. 'No, your Honours,' he said, 'I will not withdraw. I'll agree to anything you like except that . . . What is he offended at? What does he say I've done? Suppose he doesn't write well, is that a blot on his honour? What does my opinion matter that he should have taken it so much amiss? One can be a worthy man and still write wretched verse. Honour is not involved in these things. I consider him an accomplished gentleman in every way, a man of quality, courage, ability, anything you like, but a very poor poet indeed. If you wish I'll praise his retinue and the style he keeps up, his horsemanship, his skill in arms or in dancing, but as for his verse – no! There he must excuse me. If people can't manage to do better than that, they should let poetry well alone – unless they're forced to take it up on pain of death!' In the end the most he could be persuaded to bring himself to say by way of concession or amends – and he thought he was being very conciliatory – was 'I regret, sir, to be so difficult to please and I do most heartily wish, out of respect for you, that I could have thought better of your sonnet.' Whereupon to bring the matter to a conclusion they made them shake hands and left it at that.

ÉLIANTE: Yes, his behaviour is most peculiar, but I must say I admire him for it. There's something in its way quite noble and heroic in this sincerity he so prides himself on. It's a rare virtue nowadays. I only wish there were more people like him.

PHILINTE: Well, the more I see of him, the more amazed I am by this passion for Célimène in which he is so deeply involved. I can't imagine what he thinks he's doing, given the sort of fellow he is, to go falling in love at all, still less how your cousin comes to be the one to take his fancy.

ÉLIANTE: It just shows that love isn't always a matter of temperamental affinities. All the usual ideas of hidden compatibility are proved quite wrong in this case.

PHILINTE: And do you believe, from what you can see, that she loves him?

ÉLIANTE: It's hard to say. How is one to judge whether she's really in love with him? She's not entirely sure of her feelings herself. Sometimes she's in love without knowing it and at other times she fancies she's in love when she isn't at all.

PHILINTE: I'm afraid our friend will have more trouble with this cousin of yours than he imagines. To be honest, if he felt as I do he'd turn his attentions in quite a different direction. He'd be far better advised, Madame, if he took advantage of the feelings *you* have for him.

ÉLIANTE: Well, I make no bones about it – I think we should be open and honest in such matters. I don't oppose his love for Célimène; on the contrary I encourage it. If it was up to me, he would marry the lady of his choice with my blessing. But if, as may well happen in this case, his love were to encounter some obstacle and Célimène gives her heart to someone else, I might bring myself to accept his addresses without being offended by the fact someone else had already rejected them.

PHILINTE: And I for my part, Madame, do nothing to oppose his high regard for your beauty. He could tell you himself, were he so minded, what I have gone out of my way to say to him on this matter. If, however, they were indeed to marry and you in consequence were not in a position to receive his addresses, then I should do all I could to win for myself those signal favours you now so generously accord him. I should count myself happy if, he having renounced them, you transferred them to me.

ÉLIANTE: You're joking, Philinte.

PHILINTE: Not at all Madame, I say it in all sincerity. I await the opportunity of offering you my entire devotion. All my hopes are directed towards that happy moment.

Scene ii:

ALCESTE, ÉLIANTE, PHILINTE

ALCESTE: Ah Madame, avenge me! Avenge an injury which is more
than my constancy can bear!

ÉLIANTE: What is it? Whatever can have upset you so?

ALCESTE: Something beyond mortal experience! A calamity more overwhelming than anything within the realms of nature! It's all over!
... My love ... I don't know how to say it!

ÉLIANTE: Try to calm down a little.

ALCESTE: Merciful heaven! Why should such graces go with such odious,
such criminal baseness?

ÉLIANTE: But what can have –

ALCESTE: It's the end of everything. I'm ... I'm betrayed, and utterly
undone! Célimène ... who would have believed such a thing ...
Célimène has deceived me! She's faithless after all!

ÉLIANTE: Have you some good reason for believing this?

PHILINTE: Maybe it's some hasty misconception? Your jealous temper
sometimes makes you imagine things.

ALCESTE: Confound it! Mind your own business, sir! What more certain
proof of her treachery could there be than to have, here in my pocket,
a letter written in her own hand? Yes Madame, a letter written to
Oronte, that's the evidence of my betrayal and her shame ... Oronte,
whose advances I thought she shunned ... of all my rivals the one
I feared least!

PHILINTE: A letter may well give the wrong impression. Sometimes it's
not as compromising as it seems.

ALCESTE: You again sir! Be so good as to let me alone and just mind
your own business!

ÉLIANTE: You should try to control yourself. The trouble –

ALCESTE: Madame, the remedy lies with you. It's to you I turn now to
heal me of this intolerable hurt. Avenge me against this ungrateful
and faithless relative of yours who has betrayed my constant love so
despicably. Avenge an action which must surely fill you with horror.

ÉLIANTE: I avenge you? How?

ALCESTE: By accepting my love. Take it Madame! Take the heart she
has betrayed. That's how I shall be avenged! I shall punish her by

dedicating to you in ardent sacrifice my sincerest vows, my profoundest love, my devotion, my respect, and my unfailing duty.

ÉLIANTE: You may be sure I feel for you in your distress. I don't in
the least undervalue the love you offer me. But it may be there's less
harm done than you think and you may get over this urge for
vengeance. When we suffer at the hands of the person we love, we
make many a plan that we never carry out. However strong the
reasons for breaking off relations may seem, they are often not strong
enough. Guilt in the one we love soon turns to innocence again,
resentment quickly vanishes: we all know what lovers' quarrels
are!

ALCESTE: No, no Madame, no! The injury's too deep. There's no going
back. I'm breaking with her. Nothing can alter the decision I have
made. I couldn't forgive myself if I ever loved her again. Here she
is! My rage redoubles at the sight of her. I'll confront her in no
uncertain terms with her villainy, confound her utterly, and then
bring to you a heart entirely freed from her perfidious charms.
(*Exit Philinte and Éliante.*)

Scene iii:
CÉLIMÈNE, ALCESTE

ALCESTE (*aside*): Oh, heavens! Can I keep a grip on my feelings now?

CÉLIMÈNE: What's this? Whatever's the matter with you? Why the
sighs? What do these black looks mean?

ALCESTE: They mean that all the horrors of which the soul is capable
are nothing in comparison with your disloyalty! That fate, hell,
heaven in its wrath never produced a thing so vile as you!

CÉLIMÈNE: These are novel compliments, I must say!

ALCESTE: Ah! Don't make light of it! This is no time for laughter. Far
better blush, for you have good cause to! I have positive proof of
your treachery. This is what was meant by my premonitions and it
was not for nothing that I was alarmed. My frequent suspicions,
which you found so odious, have brought me to the very misfortune
that my eyes have now seen. Despite all your precautions and your
cunning in deceit, my guiding star revealed to me what I had cause
to fear! But don't assume that I shall suffer the humiliation of being

deceived and not seek my revenge! I know that our feelings are not ours to control, that love strikes where it will, that hearts cannot be won by force and that every soul is free to choose to its conqueror. Nor should I have had any reason for complaint if you had spoken frankly: if you had rejected my addresses from the start, I should have had no quarrel save with fate. But to flatter my hopes with a false assurance that you returned my feelings was an act of betrayal and perfidiousness for which no punishment could be too severe, and it justifies my giving free rein to my resentment. Yes, yes, after such behaviour you may fear the worst! I am no longer myself: I am consumed by anger! Under the impact of this deadly blow, my passion is no longer subject to the constraints of reason! I yield to the impulse of my righteous wrath. I am not answerable for what I may do!

CÉLIMÈNE: Why are you raving like this? Tell me, have you taken leave of your senses?

ALCESTE: Yes, yes indeed! I took leave of them the moment I first set eyes on you and had the misfortune to drink the poison that now destroys me, when I thought to find sincerity in those treacherous charms which cast their spell upon me!

CÉLIMÈNE: What treachery have you to complain of?

ALCESTE: Ah! The duplicity! How skilled her heart is in pretence! But I have the means at hand to bring it to the test. Cast your eyes on this and admit to your own writing! This letter coming to light is all that is needed to expose your deceit. And against this evidence, there is no reply.

CÉLIMÈNE: So this is what's troubling you?

ALCESTE: Don't you blush at the sight of this document?

CÉLIMÈNE: Why should I blush?

ALCESTE: What! You have the audacity to persist in your deceit? Do you intend to disown it because it is not signed?

CÉLIMÈNE: Why should I disown a letter in my own handwriting?

ALCESTE: Can you look upon it and not blush for the wrong it does me? The whole tone of the letter convicts you!

CÉLIMÈNE: You are, truly, a strange and foolish man!

ALCESTE: What! You still persist in the face of this overwhelming evidence? Isn't this revelation of your feelings for Oronte sufficient reason for my anger and your shame?

CÉLIMÈNE: Oronte? Who said the letter was meant for him?

ALCESTE: The people who placed it in my hands today. But supposing I were willing to grant it might have been meant for someone else, should I have any less reason to complain? Would it genuinely make you less guilty towards me?

CÉLIMÈNE: But if the letter were addressed to a woman, what harm would it do you? What would there be wrong in that?

ALCESTE: Ah! That's a clever ploy! An admirable excuse! I confess, I was not expecting it! And naturally, I'm totally convinced! How dare you resort to such a shabby trick! Do you think people have no sense at all? But do go on! Let's see what other wiles and stratagems you'll use to sustain so palpable a lie, how you'll manage to make out that so passionate a letter could be from one woman to another. Reconcile – if you are to cover up your faithlessness – what I am about to read with –

CÉLIMÈNE: No, indeed I won't. I consider it ridiculous of you to presume to such authority and to dare say such things to my face!

ALCESTE: Now now. Don't fly into a temper! Just take a moment to try and explain what these words mean.

CÉLIMÈNE: No, I'll do no such thing. You can think what you like about it. It matters little to me.

ALCESTE: Show me, I beg you, that such a letter could really be intended for a woman and I'll be satisfied.

CÉLIMÈNE: No, it was written to Oronte. I'd rather you thought that. I delight in his attentions, enjoy his conversation, admire his qualities – I'll agree to say anything you want. Go on, carry on with this quarrel, don't let anything stop you . . . as long as you don't pester me with it any more.

ALCESTE (*aside*): Heavens! Could there ever be anything so cruel? Was any man in love ever treated like this? Why! Here am I with every justification for being furious with her – I'm the one making the complaint and yet it's me who's getting the blame! She drives me to the limits of despair and suspicion, leaves me to believe the worst – and glories in it! And yet I still haven't the strength of mind to bring myself to break the chains that bind me to her, to steel my heart to show my proud contempt for this unworthy object of my too fond desires! (*To Célimène:*) Perfidious creature! How well you know how to turn my weaknesses against me and exploit to your own advantage the fatal and excessive love those faithless eyes inspire! At least deny a crime which is more than I can bear! Stop pretending that you are guilty! Prove to me, if you can, that the letter is innocent! My love will lend a helping hand. Try to seem true to me in this and I in turn shall try to believe that you are.

CÉLIMÈNE: No, no! You are mad when you are in these jealous fits and don't deserve the love I have for you. What, I should like to know, what could make me stoop to the baseness of deceiving you? Why, if my affections were indeed given to another, should I not tell you so frankly? Doesn't the fact that I choose to reassure you of what I feel for you protect me against your suspicions? How can those suspicions carry any force at all after you have been given such assurances? Is it not an insult to me that you still give credence to them? And when a woman's heart goes to the extreme of admitting that she's in love, and when the honour of our sex, ever at war with our passions, is so strongly opposed to such admissions, how can a lover, who sees us clamber over this obstacle for his sake, doubt so solemn an assurance with impunity? Isn't he to blame if he's not satisfied with what a woman can only express at all after a great inward struggle? No! Such suspicions warrant my anger! You aren't worthy of the consideration I have shown you! I'm a fool! I'm cross with myself for being so naïve as to go on being fond of you. I ought to bestow my affections elsewhere and give you proper grounds for complaining.

ALCESTE: Ah, the duplicity of it! Strange indeed is my weakness for you! You are certainly deceiving me with your honeyed words but no matter, I must accept my destiny! My very soul is committed to your love. I must see to the very end what that love is made of and whether you will really be so base as to betray me.

CÉLIMÈNE: Oh no, you don't love me as you should.

ALCESTE: Ah! My love is extreme and beyond all comparison! Such is my desire to make it manifest to all the world that I could even wish misfortune might befall you – yes, I would wish that no man should find you attractive, I would have you reduced to misery or born with nothing, without rank or birth or fortune so that I might in one resounding act of loving sacrifice repair the injustice of your fate and experience the joy and satisfaction of knowing that today you owed everything to my love.

CÉLIMÈNE: A strange way of showing how much you care for me!

Heaven grant you may have no such opportunity! But here comes your man, Du Bois — and most oddly dressed.

Scene iv:
DU BOIS, CÉLIMÈNE, ALCESTE

ALCESTE: What's the meaning of that get-up? Why are you looking so alarmed? What's the matter?

DU BOIS: Sir . . .

ALCESTE: Well?

DU BOIS: A lot of strange goings-on.

ALCESTE: What is it?

DU BOIS: Our affairs are in a sorry state sir.

ALCESTE: What do you mean?

DU BOIS: Can I say it out loud?

ALCESTE: Yes, and get on with it.

DU BOIS: Is there anybody about who —

ALCESTE: Stop beating about the bush! Spit it out man.

DU BOIS: Sir, we've got to beat a retreat.

ALCESTE: What?

DU BOIS: We must decamp — and no one must know.

ALCESTE: Why?

DU BOIS: I tell you we must get out of here.

ALCESTE: What for?

DU BOIS: We've got to go sir, and no time for farewells.

ALCESTE: Why are you talking like this?

DU BOIS: Why sir? Because we must pack up and be off.

ALCESTE: Ah! Explain what you mean you oaf, or I'll warm your ears for you.

DU BOIS: Sir, a man with a face as black as his coat walked right into the kitchen and left us this paper — a paper so scrawled over that you'd have to be as fly as the devil himself to read it. It's to do with your lawsuit, I shouldn't doubt, but Old Nick himself couldn't make head nor tail of it.

ALCESTE: Very well then you clod, what has the paper to do with what you were saying about going away?

DU BOIS: That's what I'm here to tell you sir. An hour later a gentleman that often comes to see you arrives and asks for you urgent like, and not finding you at home, orders me, on the quiet, to tell you . . . knowing as how that I am your faithful servant, to tell you that . . . now wait a minute, what was his name?

ALCESTE: Never mind his name you dog, just tell me what he said.

DU BOIS: He's a friend of yours, anyway sir, we'll leave it at that. He told me that you are in danger here and like to be arrested if you hang around.

ALCESTE: But why? Did he give no reason?

DU BOIS: No, he just asks me for ink and paper and writes you a letter. I don't doubt it'll tell you all you're wanting to know.

ALCESTE: Hand it over, then!

CÉLIMÈNE: What's behind all this?

ALCESTE: I don't know but I mean to find out. (*To Du Bois:*) Have you got it yet, you blundering oaf?

DU BOIS (*after a long search*): Blow me sir, I've left it on your desk.

ALCESTE: I don't know what's stopping me from –

CÉLIMÈNE: Don't lose your temper. Go and find out what all this means.

ALCESTE (*going*): Try as I may, it seems the fates conspire to prevent me from having a conversation with you. But to ensure that they will not prevail, Madame, will you allow me to see you again before the day is out?

Act V

Scene i:

ALCESTE, PHILINTE

ALCESTE: I tell you, my mind's made up.

PHILINTE: But however serious this blow may be, do you really need to . . .

ALCESTE: No, you can talk and argue as much as you like, nothing will make me go back on what I have said. There's too much baseness in the world today. I'm determined to have nothing more to do with mankind. Why! Honour, integrity, decency, the law itself were all against my opponent, the justice of my cause was acknowledged on all sides, I was confident I was in the right, and yet I have been wronged by the verdict. Justice was on my side, but I lost my case! Thanks to the blackest of lies, a rogue, whose scandalous past is notorious, emerges triumphant! Honesty is made to yield to his duplicity. He cuts my throat and yet he ends up by being fully vindicated! He puts on a front of sheer hypocrisy through which shines the most palpable fraud, right is overthrown and justice perverted! Then to crown his villainy, he obtains a writ against me, and, not content with the wrong thus done me, there's an abominable book in circulation, a work it's criminal even to read, one for which no punishment could be too severe, and the scoundrel has the audacity to attribute the authorship to me! And on top of all that, I hear that Oronte has been going round whispering against me and spitefully lending support to the rumour – yes, Oronte, who has a reputation at Court for being an honourable man, whom I've always treated with frankness and sincerity. Yet he must come all eager and insistent and pester me against my will for an opinion on his verses, and because I treat him honestly and will neither lie to him nor betray the truth, he joins in accusing me of a crime I haven't committed! Now he's become my bitterest enemy! He'll never forgive me in his heart for not liking his sonnet. That's human nature for you, by God! That's what vanity leads men to! That's the measure of their good faith, their love of virtue, the sort of honour and justice that you find among them! No, no! The trouble they're making for me is more than I can stand. Let's flee this jungle, this cut-throat world! Since you live together like wolves, you shall never include me among your number as long as I live!

PHILINTE: I think the course of action you propose rather too hasty. Things aren't as bad as you make out. The accusations your opponent has made against you haven't gained sufficient credence to lead to your arrest. The falsity of his story is self-evident and his actions may yet rebound on him.

ALCESTE: On him? He's not afraid of any scandal his duplicity might bring! He's a licensed scoundrel. Far from his reputation suffering from this affair, you'll see that tomorrow it will stand higher than before.

PHILINTE: Nevertheless, the fact remains that people have attached little importance to the malicious rumours he's been spreading about you. So far you have nothing to fear on that score. As for your lawsuit of which you have good cause for complaint, you can easily appeal against the outcome and –

ALCESTE: No, I intend to abide by it. The verdict may have done me a glaring wrong, but I have no intention of wanting to have it quashed. It shows all too plainly how right may be abused. I want it to go down to posterity as a notorious instance, a notable testimony, of the wickedness of our generation. It may cost me twenty thousand francs, but those twenty thousand francs will give me the right to denounce the iniquity of human nature and cherish an undying hatred for it.

PHILINTE: Come now . . .

ALCESTE: Come now, your concern is not needed! What can you possibly find to say to me on this subject? Will you even have the audacity to justify to my face the dreadful things that have happened?

PHILINTE: On the contrary, I'll agree to anything you like. The world is governed by intrigue and self-interest, and it's sharp practice these days that wins every time. Men ought to be different from what they are. But is their disregard for justice a reason for withdrawing from their society? The failings of human nature in this life give us opportunities for exercising our philosophy, which is the best use we can put our virtues to. If all men were righteous, all hearts true and frank and loyal, what purpose would most of our virtues serve? Their usefulness lies in enabling us to stay calm and bear the injustices others inflict upon us when we are in the right. And in the same way that a noble mind –

ALCESTE: Sir, I know that you are a fine talker and never at a loss for an argument. But your eloquent words are a waste of breath. Reason requires me to retire from the world for my own good. I do not have sufficient control of my tongue. I can't answer for what I may say. I might make no end of trouble for myself. Don't say any more, just leave me to wait for Célimène: I need her to agree to what I intend to do. Now I shall see if she really loves me. This is the moment that will put my doubts to the test.

PHILINTE: Let us go up to Éliante's room and wait for her there.

ALCESTE: No. I've got too much on my mind. You go and see her and leave me to this dark corner and my gloomy thoughts.

PHILINTE: That's strange company for you! I'll go and persuade Éliante to come down here. (*He leaves.*)

Scene ii:

ORONTE, CÉLIMÈNE, ALCESTE

ORONTE: Yes Madame, it's for you to decide now whether you wish to tie the knot that will make me entirely yours. I must have absolute assurance of your love. This is not an issue on which a lover can bear to be kept in uncertainty. If the ardour of my passion has moved you, you should not hesitate to tell me. After all, the proof I now ask is no more than that you permit Alceste's attentions no longer, that you sacrifice him to my love, and, in short Madame, that you banish him from your house this very day.

CÉLIMÈNE: But what terrible thing is it that has turned you so much against him? I have often heard you speak highly of his qualities.

ORONTE: There's no need to go into that Madame. The question is: what are your feelings? Please, make your choice. Take one or other of us. I am in your hands.

ALCESTE (*emerging from his corner*): Yes Madame, this gentleman is right. You must make your choice. His request accords with my own wishes. I am moved by the same impatience and the same concern. My passion also requires an unequivocal sign from yours. Things can't go on any longer as they are. The time has come for you to say what you have decided.

ORONTE: I have no wish to ruffle your happiness in any way, sir, by allowing my own passion to intrude . . .

ALCESTE: Nor have I the least desire, sir, call it jealousy or what you will, to share her affections with you.

ORONTE: If she feels that your love is preferable to mine . . .

ALCESTE: If she's capable of the slightest regard for you . . .

ORONTE: I renounce any further claim to her hand.

ALCESTE: I swear I'll never see her again.

ORONTE: Madame, it's for you to speak freely.

ALCESTE: Madame, you need not fear to say where you stand.

ORONTE: All you need do is to tell us where your affections lie.

ALCESTE: All you need do is to make up your mind and choose between us.

ORONTE: What! Can you really find it difficult to make a choice between the alternatives?

ALCESTE: What! Are you wavering? Can you be in any doubt?

CÉLIMÈNE: Heavens! Your insistence is quite inappropriate! How unreasonable you both are! I'm quite capable of making up my mind. It's not my heart that hesitates: I'm in no doubt – there's nothing simpler than making a choice. But what I do find very awkward, I must admit, is having to state my preference to you personally. I feel that one should not have to say such disagreeable things in the presence of the people concerned. One can give sufficient indication of one's preference without being forced to throw it in a person's face. Some gentler form of intimation should be enough to convey to a lover the failure of his attentions.

ORONTE: No, no! I have nothing to fear from a frank statement. There's no objection on my part.

ALCESTE: And I demand it! I insist on its being made openly, here and now. I have no wish to see you soften the blow. You are always anxious to keep in with everybody. No more delay! No more uncertainty! You shall explain exactly where you stand. If you won't, then I shall take that to be your decision. I shall know, for my part, what interpretation to put upon your silence: I'll assume the worst.

ORONTE: I'm most grateful to you for putting it so strongly sir. I say to the lady the same thing that you have.

CÉLIMÈNE: How tiresome you are with these unreasonable demands! I ask you, is it fair to put such a question? Haven't I already explained the reason why I hold back? But here comes Éliante. I'll ask her to be the judge.

Scene iii:

ÉLIANTE, PHILINTE, CÉLIMÈNE, ORONTE, ALCESTE

CÉLIMÈNE: Cousin, I'm being persecuted by these two gentlemen who seem to have joined forces against me. They both demand, with equal insistence, that I declare which of them has the prior place in my affections, and that I make an open pronouncement in their presence forbidding one or the other to pay his addresses to me in future. Tell me, did you ever hear of such a thing in all your life?

ÉLIANTE: Don't ask me about it! You may find you've come to the wrong person. I'm for people who speak their minds.

ORONTE: It's no use your refusing, Madame.

ALCESTE: Your evasions will get no support from her.

ORONTE: You really must say and come down on one side or the other.

ALCESTE: You need only continue to keep silent.

ORONTE: One single word will end the argument for me.

ALCESTE: And I shall understand if you say nothing at all.

Scene iv:

ACASTE, CLITANDRE, ARSINOÉ, PHILINTE, ÉLIANTE, ORONTE, CÉLIMÈNE, ALCESTE

ACASTE: Madame, we've both come here to clear up a small matter with you, if you don't mind.

CLITANDRE (*to Oronte and Alceste*): It's most fortunate, gentlemen, that you should be here, since you are also involved in this business.

ARSINOÉ: You are surprised to see me Madame, but it's these gentlemen who are responsible for my being here. They came and complained to me about something I couldn't bring myself to credit. I have too high an opinion of your character to believe you could ever be guilty of such an appalling action. Refusing to believe the evidence they showed me, strong though it appeared to be, and overlooking our little disagreement in the interests of friendship, I agreed to accompany them here and see you clear yourself of this slander.

ACASTE: Yes Madame, let us see, coolly and calmly, how you will set

about defending yourself on this point. Did you write this letter to
Clitandre?

CLITANDRE: Did you address this tender missive to Acaste?

ACASTE (*Oronte and Alceste*): This writing is not unknown to you
gentlemen. The civilities she has extended to you have no doubt
made the hand familiar. But this is worth the trouble of reading.
(*Reads:*) 'What a strange man you are to condemn me for my high
spirits and accuse me of never being so happy as when I am not with
you. Nothing could be more unfair, and unless you come soon and
beg my pardon for your offence, I shall never forgive you so long
as I live. That great booby, the viscount . . .' It's a pity he's not
here! 'That great booby, the viscount, with whom you begin your
complaints, isn't at all the sort of man to appeal to me. I have never
thought much of him since the day I saw him spitting into a well,
making rings in the water, for fully three-quarters of an hour. As
for the little marquis . . .' That's me, gentlemen, not to flatter myself
unduly . . . 'As for the little marquis who held my hand yesterday
for an age, he's a person of no significance whatsoever, and as
poor as younger sons usually are. As far the man with the green
ribbons . . .'[5]

(*To Alceste:*) It's your turn now sir. 'As for the man with the green
ribbons, he does sometimes amuse me with his bluntness and his
churlish bad temper but there are many occasions when I find him
the most tiresome man on earth. Then there's the man with the
waistcoat . . .'

(*To Oronte:*) This is where you get it. 'Then there's the man with
the waistcoat who has got the idea that he's a wit and is determined
to be an author despite what anyone says. I just can't bring myself
to listen to what he says. I find his prose as tedious as his verse, so
do please get it into your head that I don't always enjoy myself as
much as you think, that I miss you most dreadfully at all the functions
I'm obliged to attend, and that being with someone we are fond of
adds a wonderful relish to the pleasures we enjoy.'

CLITANDRE: And now for me. (*Reads:*) 'You mention your friend
Clitandre who gets so mawkish, but he's the last man in the world
I'd ever take a fancy to. He's quite mad to believe I'm in love with
him; and you are as bad to believe that I don't love you. Be sensible,
exchange opinions with him, come and see me as often as you can

and help me to put up with the misery of being pestered by him.'
(*To Célimène*:) A very fine pattern of virtue we have before us here,
Madame. No doubt you know the name normally given to such
persons. But enough! We'll all now go our various ways and hold
up for all to see this splendid picture of you as you really are.

ACASTE: There's a great deal I could say to you – it's a subject rich in
possibilities. But I don't think you're worth getting angry about.
Instead I'll show you that little marquises can find consolations
superior to anything you have to offer. (*Acaste and Clitandre leave.*)

ORONTE: To think that you could tear me to pieces like that after all
you've written to me! And you offer the same specious promises of
love to everyone in turn! Ah! I was fooled too easily, but it shan't
happen again. You have done me a useful service in letting me see
you as you really are. I am better off to the tune of one heart which
you have now returned to me, and I have the satisfaction of knowing
that the loss is entirely yours. (*To Alceste*:) Sir, I shall stand in the
way of your love no longer. You may come to terms with the lady.
(*He leaves.*)

ARSINOÉ: This really is the most disgraceful business I ever heard of!
I just cannot remain silent, I am very shocked. Was there ever such
behaviour as yours! I'm not concerned about the others, but did this
gentleman whom you were fortunate enough to attract, a most
honourable and worthy man who worshipped the very ground that
you trod on, deserve to be –

ALCESTE: Madame, kindly leave me to look after my own affairs and
don't meddle with what does not concern you. No purpose would
be served by your taking up my quarrel. I'm in no position to repay
your zeal on my behalf. You aren't the person my thoughts would
turn to if I wanted to avenge myself by transferring my affections
elsewhere.

ARSINOÉ: Oh! Do you imagine, sir, that I harboured any such idea?
Why should I be so anxious to have you? You have too much vanity
in your character, I think, if you entertain any such impression! This
lady's cast-offs are a commodity which it would be wrong for any
woman to want! Open your eyes, I beg you, and don't be so high
and mighty! Women like me are not for the likes of you. Better go
on pining for her. I should love to see so suitable a match. (*She
leaves.*)

ALCESTE (*to Célimène*): Well. I have held my peace in spite of everything I've seen. I let them all have their say before me. Have I contained myself long enough? May I now . . .

CÉLIMÈNE: Yes, you may say anything. You have a right to complain and reproach me with anything you care to name. I'm in the wrong and I admit it. I'm too ashamed to put you off with lame excuses. The anger of the others I despised, but you I agree I have wronged. Your resentment is entirely justified. I know how guilty I must seem in your eyes, how everything points to my having betrayed you. You have indeed good reason to hate me. Well then, hate me. I consent.

ALCESTE: Ah! But can I, when you have deceived me so? Can I overcome all my feelings for you? Try as I may to hate you, can I find it in my heart to do so? (*To Éliante and Philinte:*) You see the power of abject love! I call you both to witness my weakness. Yet to confess the truth, I do not intend to stop there: you shall observe me push my weakness to its furthest limit and show how wrong it is to call any of us wise and demonstrate that there's some touch of human frailty in every one of us. (*To Célimène:*) Yes, you betrayed me, yet I am prepared to forget what you did and shall find it in my heart to excuse your behaviour by attributing it to the waywardness into which the wickedness of the age has led you because you're young – provided you will agree to join me in my plan to flee all humankind and undertake to accompany me forthwith into the rustic solitude in which I have sworn to live. Thus, and only thus, can you make amends in people's minds for the harm done by your letters, and, after this scandal so abhorrent to a noble mind like mine, may I be allowed to go on loving you.

CÉLIMÈNE: What? Renounce the world before I'm old and bury myself in some rural wilderness!

ALCESTE: Ah! If only your love matched mine, what would the rest of the world matter? Can I not give you everything you want?

CÉLIMÈNE: Solitude is a frightening prospect when you are twenty. I don't feel I have the necessary fortitude or strength to bring myself to take such a decision. But if the offer of my hand would satisfy you, I could agree to tie the knot, and marriage –

ALCESTE: No! At this moment I hate you! Your refusal is far worse than the rest of what you have done. Since you can't bring yourself to accept marriage and within it make me your everything as you are everything to me, I reject your proposition. This bitter insult releases me from your ignoble fetters for ever. (*Exit Célimène. Alceste turns to Éliante*:) Madame, your beauty is graced by countless virtues. I have never known you to be anything but sincere. I have long held you in the greatest esteem. Permit me to continue to do so, but forgive me if, beset as I am with troubles, I do not aspire to the honour of your hand. I feel myself unworthy of it and I begin to realize that heaven did not intend me for marriage, and that a heart which another has refused would be too poor a tribute to offer you . . . and in fact –

ÉLIANTE: Please, go on thinking that if you wish. I have no worries about where I might bestow my hand, and without needing to trouble myself unduly, I think your friend here might contrive to accept it if I asked him to.

PHILINTE: Ah, Madame! I could ask no greater honour. For that I would sacrifice my life itself.

ALCESTE: May you ever continue to cherish such feelings for each other and so come to know true contentment. Betrayed on all sides, with injustice heaped upon me, I mean to escape from this abyss where vice reigns triumphant and scour the world for some place so remote that there a man might be free to live as honour bids. (*Exit.*)

PHILINTE: Come Madame, we must do all we can, to make him give up this foolish plan.

The Doctor Despite Himself
A Comedy

Le Médecin malgré lui
Comédie

First performed on 6 August 1666 at the Théâtre du Palais Royal by the King's Players

If *The Misanthrope* had been given a mixed reception, *The Doctor Despite Himself*, staged two months later, was an immediate success. It was also another acting triumph for Molière who played Sganarelle in a drooping moustache, black beard, wide ruff and a suit which made him look 'like a parrot'. It was performed fifty-nine times in his lifetime and since his death has remained one of his most frequently revived plays.

Compared with his great comedies of obsession, it seems slight and unambitious and, since it absorbed the relative failure of *The Misanthrope*, it has sometimes been thought of as an shameless attempt to recapture his audience and mend the finances of his company. But it appears far more likely that Molière, who regularly varied his output, had simply moved on.

But moving on meant returning to the broader comedy he had learned as a strolling player in the provinces. While *The Misanthrope* was based on observation rather than on literary precedents, his new farce drew on traditional comic types – incompetent, mercenary doctors, domineering wives, impudent peasants and resourceful lovers – and stock situations. The medieval story of the peasant who mascarades as a doctor had been retold several times, while a century earlier Rabelais (*Gargantua and Pantagruel*, Book II, Ch. 35) had pitted a wife who pretends to be dumb against the husband she deceives. In Molière's new doctor play the second plot is grafted on to the first, and while the resulting structure, in terms of motivation and logic, is not entirely satisfactory, it has a firm narrative and especially psychological unity. Martine's determination to get her own back is the thread which connects the two situations, but it is Sganarelle who holds the play together. He begins as a liar, a drunk and a wife-beater, but once he becomes a doctor he takes control of events and even acquires a personality. Without ceasing to be believable, the woodcutter who is not quite under his wife's thumb turns into a bogus doctor before becoming a comic valet who uses his wits to serve young love, and is very much a better man for his experience.

The rest of the cast are given functional roles, though Martine is not entirely two-dimensional (she springs to the defence of her husband against outsiders). Yet they are very much part of the pace and energy which makes the play work so well as comic theatre. The comedy is physical, but it also emerges from situations which hinge on disguises of different kinds: Sganarelle is not the doctor Géronte believes him to be, Léandre dresses as an apothecary and Lucinde pretends to be dumb. Much of the humour is verbal, from Sganarelle's jumbled Latin to the one-liners about men not wanting speech restored to their womenfolk or patients not being allowed to die without a doctor's prescription. Molière's satire is directed not against Medicine itself, but against those who hide behind obfuscation. He puts a case for empirical good sense against the entrenched attitudes of tradition which echoes his non-conforming views on religion and current social and intellectual fashions. That he should vary a well-tried formula so inventively and, above all, give such depth of character to a buffoon, is a measure of the distance he had travelled from his French and Italian sources and the slapstick of the *commedia dell'arte*.

Characters

SGANARELLE
MARTINE, his wife
MONSIEUR ROBERT, his
    neighbour
VALÈRE, steward to Géronte
LUCAS, husband of Jacqueline
GÉRONTE
LUCINDE, his daughter
LÉANDRE, in love with Lucinde
JACQUELINE, a wet-nurse
    employed by Géronte, wife to
    Lucas
THIBAUT, a peasant
PERRIN, his son

The scene is set in the country

Act I

A forest near Sganarelle's house

Scene i:
SGANARELLE: *and* MARTINE *enter quarrelling*

SGANARELLE: No! I tell you I'll have nothing to do with it and it's my word that goes. I'm the master here.

MARTINE: And I'm telling you that you'll do exactly what I say. I didn't marry you to put up with all your nonsensical goings on.

SGANARELLE: Oh! The misery of married life! How right Aristotle was when he said wives were the very devil!

MARTINE: Just listen to the clever clogs – him and his stupid Aristotle!

SGANARELLE: Oh, I'm clever all right! Show me a woodcutter who can argue and hold forth like me, a man who's served a famous doctor for six years and has had his Latin grammar by heart since he was a boy!

MARTINE: A plague on the fool!

SGANARELLE: A plague on you, you shrew!

MARTINE: A curse on the day and hour when I took it into my head to say 'I will'!

SGANARELLE: And a curse on the cuckold of a notary who made me sign my name to own ruin.

MARTINE: A fat lot of reason you have to complain about in this business, I must say! You ought to thank Heaven every day of your life that you have me for your wife. Do you think you deserved to marry a woman like me?

SGANARELLE: It's true you did me a great honour and I had good cause to be satisfied with my wedding night. But dammit, don't start me talking about that – I might say things . . .

MARTINE: Such as?

SGANARELLE: No, let's leave it at that. We know what we know. That's enough. You were very lucky to find me.

MARTINE: You call finding you lucky – a man who's brought me to the workhouse, a lying, dissolute rogue who eats me out of house and home?

SGANARELLE: That's a lie. I drink as well as eat!

MARTINE: Who's sold every stick of furniture in the house, one by one –

SGANARELLE: That's called living on your means!

MARTINE: Who's even taken the bed I sleep on –

SGANARELLE: You'll get up all the earlier!

MARTINE: Who hasn't left a single thing in the whole place –

SGANARELLE: It simplifies moving house.

MARTINE: And does nothing but gamble and drink from morning to night!

SGANARELLE: It's only so I don't get bored.

MARTINE: And what am I supposed to do with the family in the meantime?

SGANARELLE: Whatever you like.

MARTINE: I've got four small children on my hands

SGANARELLE: Then put them down on the floor.

MARTINE: They're always crying for something to eat.

SGANARELLE: Give them a taste of the whip. When I've had a skinful and eaten all I can, I like everybody in my house to be full up too.

MARTINE: And do you think, you drunken sot, that things can go on like this?

SGANARELLE: Now wife, just take it easy, if you don't mind.

MARTINE: That I'll go on putting up with your bullying and debauchery for ever?

SGANARELLE: Now let's not get carried away my dear.

MARTINE: That I don't know how to make you face up to your responsibilities?

SGANARELLE: What you do know, my sweet, is that I'm not very long-suffering and that I've got a hefty right arm.

MARTINE: Your threats don't scare me.

SGANARELLE: My sweet, my dear, you're itching for trouble, as usual.

MARTINE: I'll show you I'm not afraid of you.

SGANARELLE: Dearest, you really are asking for it . . .

MARTINE: Do you think that anything you say frightens me?

SGANARELLE: Delight of my soul, I'm going to have to warm your ears for you.

MARTINE: Boozy sot that you are!

SGANARELLE: I'll thump you!

MARTINE: You old soak!

SGANARELLE: I'll give you a walloping!

MARTINE: You horrible man!

SGANARELLE: I'll tan your hide!

MARTINE: Liar! Beast! Twister! Coward! Wretch! Villain! Cheap-jack!
You beggarly, scoundrelly, rascally thief . . .

SGANARELLE (*picking up a cudgel and beating her*): Oh! Since you
wanted it, you shall have it.

MARTINE: Ow! Ow! Ow!

SGANARELLE: That's the right way to quieten you down!

Scene ii:

MONSIEUR ROBERT, SGANARELLE, MARTINE

MONSIEUR ROBERT: Hallo! Hallo! Hallo! Come come! What's all this
about? Disgraceful behaviour! Confound you, you wretch, beating
your wife like that!

MARTINE (*confronting Monsieur Robert, arms akimbo, forcing him to retreat
and in the end slapping his face*): I want him to beat me.

MONSIEUR ROBERT: Ah! Then I heartily agree —

MARTINE: What are you butting in for?

MONSIEUR ROBERT: It was wrong of me.

MARTINE: Is it any business of yours?

MONSIEUR ROBERT: You're right.

MARTINE: Just fancy! What cheek! Wanting to stop husbands beating
their wives!

MONSIEUR ROBERT: I take it back.

MARTINE: What's it got to do with you?

MONSIEUR ROBERT: Nothing.

MARTINE: What right have you got to stick your oar in?

MONSIEUR ROBERT: None at all.

MARTINE: Then mind your own business.

MONSIEUR ROBERT: I won't say another word.

MARTINE: I like being beaten.

MONSIEUR ROBERT: All right.

MARTINE: It's no skin off your nose!

MONSIEUR ROBERT: That's true.

MARTINE: You're a fool to come meddling in what's got nothing to do with you. (*When she slaps him, he goes towards Sganarelle who speaks to him in the same way, forcing him to retreat, beating him with the same cudgel and making him run away.*)

MONSIEUR ROBERT: I beg your pardon friend, most sincerely. Carry on, beat your wife, knock the living daylights out of her. I'll give you a hand if you like.

SGANARELLE: No, I don't want to.

MONSIEUR ROBERT: Ah! That's different then.

SGANARELLE: I'll beat her if I want to. I won't beat her if I don't want to.

MONSIEUR ROBERT: Very well.

SGANARELLE: She's my wife, not yours.

MONSIEUR ROBERT: Unquestionably.

SGANARELLE: You can't go about giving me orders.

MONSIEUR ROBERT: Of course not.

SGANARELLE: I don't need your help.

MONSIEUR ROBERT: That's fine by me.

SGANARELLE: You've got a nerve, thinking you can interfere in other people's business. Remember what Cicero said: don't put the bark of a tree between the trunk and your finger.[1] (*He thwacks Monsieur Robert and drives him off, then returns to his wife and takes her hand.*) Well now, suppose we make peace. Your hand on it.

MARTINE: Oh yes! After you beat me like that!

SGANARELLE: That was nothing. Your hand.

MARTINE: Don't want to.

SGANARELLE: Come on . . .

MARTINE: No.

SGANARELLE: My helpmeet!

MARTINE: Shan't!

SGANARELLE: Come on now I say.

MARTINE: No, I won't.

SGANARELLE: Come, come, come!

MARTINE: No! I'm cross and I mean it!

SGANARELLE: Bah! It was nothing! Oh come on!

MARTINE: Let me be.

SGANARELLE: Shake hands, I tell you.

MARTINE: You went too far.

SGANARELLE: Oh, go on then: I'm sorry. Shake hands on it!

MARTINE: I forgive you. (*Aside*) But you'll pay for it.

SGANARELLE: You're silly to pay any attention. These little things have to be now and then – they're a necessary part of a loving relationship and a few thwacks with a stick, between man and wife, only serve to put the zest back into their affection. Right then, I'm off to the woods and I promise you shall have a hundred bundles of sticks and more before the day's out. (*Exit.*)

Scene iii:
MARTINE

MARTINE: Yes, go. I shan't forget my resentment whatever face I put on it. I can't wait to come up with some way of paying you out for all the times you've beaten me. I know very well that a wife always has ways and means of getting her own back on her husband, but that sort of punishment is too good for my good-for-nothing layabout. What I want is the kind of revenge that'll hit him much harder or else it will be no satisfaction for what I've had to put up with.

Scene iv:
LUCAS, VALÈRE, MARTINE

LUCAS: Oh Lordy! A right ticklish errand we've gone and took on the pair of us. I can't see what we stand to get out of it neither.

VALÈRE: That's the way things ar,e Lucas. We have to obey our master. Besides, we both have an interest in the health of his daughter who's our mistress. Moreover, her marriage, which has been put off because of her illness, ought to be worth something to us. Horace is free with his money and out of those who have asked for her hand he stands a good chance. She may have shown a fancy for this Léandre, but you know very well that her father has never been keen to have him for a son-in-law.

MARTINE (*aside to herself*): Can't I think of any way at all of getting my own back?

LUCAS: But what sort of daft idea has he gone and got into his noddle now that them doctors have run out of Latin words?

VALÈRE: If you try hard enough you sometimes find what you couldn't find when you started looking, and often in the most obvious place . . .

MARTINE (*aside*): Yes, I must get my own back whatever it costs. I can't get over that walloping he gave me. I'm not going to take it lying down and . . . (*Still talking to herself and not noticing the two men, she bumps into them as she turns and says:*) Oh, I'm sorry. I didn't see you there. I was miles away, trying to find an answer to something that's worrying me.

VALÈRE: We all have our troubles in this world. We're also looking for something we'd very much like to find.

MARTINE: Is it something I could help you with?

VALÈRE: Possibly. We're trying to find a learned man, more particularly a doctor, who can help our master's daughter. She's been struck down by a sickness which suddenly deprived her of the use of her tongue. A number of doctors have tried all they know on her, but sometimes you can find people with remarkable secret knowledge, special remedies of their own, who can succeed where others have failed. That's what we are looking for.

MARTINE (*aside*): Here's a heaven-sent way of getting my own back on my swine of a husband. (*Aloud*) You couldn't have asked anyone better able to put you in the way of what you are looking for. We've got somebody here who's the most marvellous man in the world for hopeless diseases.

VALÈRE: And where, if you'll be so good, might we find him?

MARTINE: You'll find him now somewhere over there, busy cutting wood.

LUCAS: A doctor chopping wood!

VALÈRE: Perhaps you mean he's busy gathering herbs?

MARTINE: No. He's peculiar. He likes chopping. He's an odd, eccentric, crotchety sort of man. You'd never take him for what he is. He goes about dressed in the strangest clothes, sometimes pretending he doesn't know anything and keeping his knowledge to himself. There's nothing he hates more each day than using the wonderful gift for medicine that heaven has given him.

VALÈRE: It's a remarkable thing, but great men usually have some kind of kink, some little grain of foolishness mixed in with their learning.

MARTINE: This man's foolishness is beyond all belief. It goes to the length sometimes of preferring a thrashing to admitting what he's capable of. I warn you, you'll never get anything out of him, he'll never confess to being a doctor, if that's how the fancy takes him, unless you each take a stick and thrash him into admitting in the end what he'll begin by denying. That's what we do when we need him.

VALÈRE: What a strange carry on!

MARTINE: True. But once you've done that you'll find he works wonders.

VALÈRE: What is his name?

MARTINE: He's called Sganarelle. You'll have no difficulty recognizing him. He's got a big black beard and wears a ruff and a yellow and green coat.

LUCAS: Yellow and green coat! He's a parrot doctor then?

VALÈRE: And is he really as clever as you say?

MARTINE: Clever? He's a man who can work miracles. Six months ago there was this woman who'd been given up on by all the doctors. Everybody thought she'd been dead for six hours and they were making arrangements for the funeral when they forced the man we're talking about to come. He took one look at her, put a little drop of something-or-other into her mouth, and immediately she got out of bed and started walking round the room as if nothing had happened.

LUCAS: Ah!

VALÈRE: It must have been a drop of gold elixir.

MARTINE: Maybe! Then again, not three weeks since, a young lad of twelve fell off the top of the church tower and smashed his head, arms and legs on the pavement below. No sooner had they sent for this man than he rubbed him all over with a special ointment he makes himself and the boy immediately got to his feet and ran off to play marbles.

LUCAS: Ah!

VALÈRE: He must have the secret of the Universal Remedy.

MARTINE: No doubt about it!

LUCAS: Lordy! He's the very man we're after. We gotter go quick and look for 'im.

VALÈRE: Thank you very much for the help you've given us.

MARTINE: Mind you don't forget what I told you.

LUCAS. Cor' lumme! Leave it to us. If it's no more'n a matter of a thrashin', the job's as good as done already.

VALÈRE (*to Lucas*): We were very lucky to meet her. I'm feeling very hopeful indeed.

Scene v:

SGANARELLE, VALÈRE, LUCAS

SGANARELLE (*enters singing, with a bottle in his hand*): Tum te to, tum te to . . .

VALÈRE: I can hear someone singing and cutting wood.

SGANARELLE. Tum te to! By God! That's enough work done to deserve a drink. Let's take a breather. (*He drinks.*) This wood must be very salty, it makes a man as thirsty as the very devil. (*He sings:*)

> See me lift my little bottle
> Hear the gurgle in my throttle!
> Ah! How folk would envy me,
> Think how happy I should be
> If every time I took a pull
> I still found my bottle full.
> Ah! How happy I should be!
> Alas! Why can't it really be?

Well, there we are. It's no good getting glum about it.

VALÈRE (*to Lucas*): It's the very man!

LUCAS: I reckon you're right. We've bumped right into 'im!

VALÈRE: Let's take a closer look.

SGANARELLE (*noticing them, turns and looks first at one and then the other, lowers his voice and kisses his bottle*): Ah! you little rogue. How fond I am of thee, little bottle of mine. (*Sings:*) 'How folk would envy me, Think how . . .' Now what the devil do these two want?

VALÈRE: It's him all right.

LUCAS: He's the spittin' image of him what she was tellin' us about.

SGANARELLE: They're talking together and staring at me. What are they up to? (*He puts the bottle down. As Valère bends forward to bow, Sganarelle thinks he means to take it and puts it on the other side of him. When Lucas does likewise, Sganarelle picks up the bottle again and clutches it to his stomach, with a great deal of further stage business.*)

VALÈRE: Sir, is your name not Sganarelle?

SGANARELLE: What's that?

VALÈRE: I asked is your name not Sganarelle?

SGANARELLE (*turning first to Valère then to Lucas*): Yes and no, according to what you want with him.

VALÈRE: We only want to show him every possible courtesy.

SGANARELLE: In that case I'm Sganarelle.

VALÈRE: We're delighted to meet you sir. We have been recommended to you as a person who can help us find what we're looking for. We've come to beg you to give us the assistance we need.

SGANARELLE: If it's anything in my line of business, gentlemen, I'm entirely at your service.

VALÈRE: Sir, you are too kind. But do be good enough to put your hat on sir. You might find the sun troublesome.

LUCAS: Aye, get that 'at on sir.

SGANARELLE (*aside*): They're very polite, these two.

VALÈRE: Don't think it strange, sir, that we should come to you. Clever men are always in demand and we have been informed of your abilities.

SGANARELLE: True enough gentlemen. There's not a man alive can cut firewood like me.

VALÈRE: Ah! Sir . . .

SGANARELLE: I give it all I got. Nobody complains about the way I do the job.

VALÈRE: That's not what I have in mind.

SGANARELLE: And what's more, I sell 'em at a hundred and ten sous for a bundle of a hundred.

VALÈRE: Please, let's not talk about that.

SGANARELLE: I assure you I couldn't take less.

VALÈRE: We know how things stand sir.

SGANARELLE: If you know how things stand, then you know that's my price.

VALÈRE: This is all very well as a joke, but . . .

SGANARELLE: It's no joke to me. I can't take any less.

VALÈRE: Please, don't let's go on like this.

SGANARELLE: You may get it for less somewhere else. There's firewood and firewood. But mine —

VALÈRE: Suppose we leave the topic, sir, and —

SGANARELLE: I swear you shan't have any for a penny less.

VALÈRE: Really —

SGANARELLE: No, upon my conscience, that's the price you'll have to pay. I mean what I say. I'm not the sort who overcharges.

VALÈRE: Does a gentleman like you, sir, seriously need to indulge in these clumsy pretences and descend to talking in this manner? Can a man of such learning, a famous doctor like you, really want to hide his identity from people and keep his great talents concealed?

SGANARELLE (*aside*): He's mad!

VALÈRE: Please sir, don't try to deceive us.

SGANARELLE: How do you mean?

LUCAS: All this taradiddle won't do you no good. We knows what we knows.

SGANARELLE: What do you know? What are you getting at? Who do you take me for?

VALÈRE: For what you are — a great doctor.

SGANARELLE: Doctor yourself. I'm not one and never have been.

VALÈRE (*aside*): This is how the fit takes him. (*To Sganarelle:*) Sir, please don't go on denying it any further. Don't let us have to resort to regrettable extremes.

SGANARELLE: To what?

VALÈRE: To do something we'd be sorry for.

SGANARELLE: By God, you can resort to anything you like but I'm not a doctor. I don't know what you're talking about.

VALÈRE (*aside*): I can see we shall have to give him the treatment. (*To Sganarelle:*) Once again sir, I ask you to admit to being what you are.

LUCAS: Hell's teeth! Don't mess about no more. Just come out with it straight and say as how you're a doctor.

SGANARELLE (*aside*): I'm losing my temper!

VALÈRE: Why deny what we know?

LUCAS: Why all this 'ere rigmarole? What's the use of it?

SGANARELLE: Gentlemen! I can say it in one word as well as in a thousand: I am not a doctor.

VALÈRE: You're not a doctor?

SGANARELLE: No.

LUCAS: You ain't no doctor?

SGANARELLE: No, I tell you.

VALÈRE: Since that's the way you want it, there's no choice. (*They each take a cudgel and beat him.*)

SGANARELLE: Ow! Ow! Ow! Gentlemen. I'm anything you please!

VALÈRE: Why do you drive us to this violence sir?

LUCAS: Why make us go to all the bother of giving you a thrashin'?

VALÈRE: I assure you, there's nothing I regret more.

LUCAS: Dammit, I'm heartily sorry, that I am.

SGANARELLE: What the devil is all this about? For goodness' sake gentlemen, is it a joke or are you both out of your minds, insisting that I'm a doctor?

VALÈRE: What? Haven't you given in yet? Do you still deny you are a doctor?

SGANARELLE: Devil take me if I am!

LUCAS: So it ain't true as how you're a doctor?

SGANARELLE: No. May the plague choke me. (*They begin to beat him again.*) Ow! Ow! Ow! All right then, yes gentlemen, I agree, since you insist. I'm a doctor. I'm a doctor. Apothecary as well if you like. I'll agree to anything rather than get myself beaten to a pulp.

VALÈRE: Ah! That's better then. I'm pleased to find you coming to your senses sir.

LUCAS: I'm delighted I'm sure to hear you talkin' that way.

VALÈRE: I do most heartily beg your pardon.

LUCAS: Beg pardon for the liberty we went an' took.

SGANARELLE (*aside*): Ah! I suppose I can't be mistaken? Can I have become a doctor without noticing?

VALÈRE: You won't regret admitting what you are sir. Rest assured, you'll be well rewarded.

SGANARELLE: But gentlemen tell me, aren't you making some mistake here? Is it quite certain I'm a doctor?

LUCAS: Aye, by God!

SGANARELLE: Honestly?

VALÈRE: Beyond question.

SGANARELLE: I'm damned if I knew.

VALÈRE: Why, you're the cleverest doctor in the world.

SGANARELLE: Ha ha ha!

LUCAS: A doctor what's cured more disease than I can count.

SGANARELLE: Good Lord!

VALÈRE: A woman had been pronounced dead for six hours or more. She was about to be buried when you brought her round with a drop of something-or-other and she started walking about the room.

SGANARELLE: Fancy!

LUCAS: This lad of twelve fell off the top of the church tower, broke his head and his legs and his arms he did, and you put some sort of ointment on him, I dunno what it was, and then up he gets to his feet and off he goes to play marbles.

SGANARELLE: The devil he did!

VALÈRE: There you are sir, you'll have good cause to be satisfied with us. You shall have any fee you ask for if you'll come along with us.

SGANARELLE: I'll get any fee I ask for?

VALÈRE: Yes.

SGANARELLE: Ah! Then I am a doctor. No doubt about it. I'd forgotten but I remember now. What's the problem? Where do we go?

VALÈRE: We'll take you. It's a case of a young lady who has lost her voice.

SGANARELLE: Well, I haven't got it.

VALÈRE (*aside to Lucas*): He will have his little joke. (*To Sganarelle:*) Come along sir.

SGANARELLE: What, without my doctor's gown?

VALÈRE: We'll get you one.

SGANARELLE (*handing Valère his bottle*): Carry that, you. I keep my cordials in there. (*Turning to Lucas and spitting on the ground:*) You, stand on that. Doctor's orders.

LUCAS: By all the saints, here's the doctor for me. I reckon he'll do the job – he's a real card.

Act II

A room in Géronte's house

Scene i:

GÉRONTE, VALÈRE, LUCAS, JACQUELINE

VALÈRE: Yes sir, I think you'll be satisfied. We've brought you the greatest doctor in the world.

LUCAS: Aye, that we have! There ain't nobody to touch 'im. The rest of 'em, they ain't fit to clean his boots.

VALÈRE: He's a man who has performed the most miraculous cures.

LUCAS: Cured them as was dead and done for, he has.

VALÈRE: As I mentioned, he's rather eccentric. His mind wanders at times and then he doesn't appear to be at all what he is.

LUCAS: Aye, he likes playing the fool. Folk do say – excuse me mentioning it – as how he's a bit touched, like.

VALÈRE: But in reality he's a deeply learned man, and he often says most remarkable things.

LUCAS: When he puts his mind to it, he talks straight off like he was readin' from a book.

VALÈRE: His fame is already spreading hereabouts and people are coming in droves to consult him.

GÉRONTE: I can't wait to meet him. Show him in at once.

VALÈRE: I'll go and get him. (*Exit.*)

JACQUELINE: Mark my word sir, this 'un will do just what the others have done. I reckon it'll be the same old story. The best medicine you could give your daughter, to my way of thinking, would be a strapping young man for a husband, one as she could take a fancy to.

GÉRONTE: Now now, Nurse dear, you're always interfering!

LUCAS: Hold your tongue, our Jacqueline. It ain't none of your business, so don't go stickin' your nose in.

JACQUELINE: I'm telling you, aye, and a dozen times over, that all these 'ere doctors won't do any earthly good. It ain't rhubarb or senna your daughter needs. A husband's the best poultice for curing a young woman's ailments.

GÉRONTE: Would any man want to burden himself with her in her present state of infirmity? When I decided she should be married, didn't she set herself against my wishes?

JACQUELINE: I should think so too. You wanted to hand her over to a man she's not in love with. Why couldn't you give her to this Monsieur Léandre that she's taken a fancy to? She'd have obeyed you quick enough then. I reckon he'd have her just as she is if you was minded to give him the chance.

GÉRONTE: Léandre isn't what she needs. He hasn't the money the other one's got.

JACQUELINE: He's got a rich uncle and he's his only heir.

GÉRONTE: All that talk of money to come seems very dubious to me. There's nothing like having it in hand. It's a chancy business counting on money someone else is keeping warm for you. Death doesn't always pay much attention to the wishes and prayers of the noble company of heirs. You can have plenty of time to get long in the tooth if you wait in hopes of dead men's shoes.

JACQUELINE: Well, I've always heard tell that in marriage, like in everything else, peace of mind is more important than money. Fathers and mothers always have this nasty habit of asking: 'How much is he worth?' or 'How much has she got?' Old Pierre gave his daughter Simonette to fat Thomas because he had a few more square yards of vineyard than young Robin whom she'd taken a shine to, and look how the poor girl's gone all yellow, like a quince she is, and she's never been herself since. It should be an example to you sir. We only have our fun once in this life and I'd rather give a girl of mine a good husband that she liked than have all the tea in China.

GÉRONTE: Dammit all nurse, how you do go on! Do be quiet. Go on worrying yourself like that and you'll spoil your milk.

LUCAS (*poking Géronte in the chest*): By God, hold your tongue, you're too forward by half! The master 'ere knows what he's about and he don't want none of your lip. Just get on with feeding the baby and don't do so much argufying. The master's his daughter's father and he's a good sensible man what knows what she needs.

GÉRONTE: Steady on, now, go easy!

LUCAS (*poking Géronte in the chest again*): I want to put her in her place a bit, sir. Jest learnin' her to show the proper respect that's due to you.

GÉRONTE: Yes, but you don't need to be so physical about it.

Scene ii:

VALÈRE, SGANARELLE, GÉRONTE, LUCAS, JACQUELINE

VALÈRE: Get ready sir. Here comes our doctor.

GÉRONTE (*to Sganarelle*): Sir, I'm delighted to see you in my house. We're in great need of your help.

SGANARELLE (*in doctor's gown and steeple hat*): Hippocrates says . . . that we should both keep our hats on.

GÉRONTE: Hippocrates says that?

SGANARELLE: Yes.

GÉRONTE: In what chapter please?

SGANARELLE: In his chapter . . . er . . . on hats.

GÉRONTE: If Hippocrates says so, we must do it.

SGANARELLE: My dear doctor, having heard of the remarkable things –

GÉRONTE: May I ask whom are you talking to?

SGANARELLE: You.

GÉRONTE: But I'm not a doctor.

SGANARELLE: You aren't a doctor?

GÉRONTE: No.

SGANARELLE (*picks up a cudgel and beats him as he was beaten*): Honestly?

GÉRONTE: Honestly. Ow! Ow! Ow!

SGANARELLE: You are now. That's all the qualifications I ever had.

GÉRONTE (*to Valère*): What the devil sort of man have you brought here?

VALÈRE: I told you he was a droll sort of doctor.

GÉRONTE: I'll send him packing, him and his drollery.

VALÈRE: Pay no attention sir. It's only his joke.

GÉRONTE: I don't like that sort of joke.

SGANARELLE: Sir, I ask your pardon for the liberty I took.

GÉRONTE: Don't mention it.

SGANARELLE: I'm sorry . . .

GÉRONTE: It's nothing.

SGANARELLE: . . . about the cudgelling . . .

GÉRONTE: There's no harm done.

SGANARELLE: . . . which I had the honour of giving you . . .

GÉRONTE: We'll say no more about it. I have a daughter who has fallen victim to a very strange malady.

SGANARELLE: I'm delighted, sir, that your daughter should be in need of my good offices. I heartily wish you needed them too – you and your whole family, so that I could have shown how eager I am to be of service to you.

GÉRONTE: I'm obliged to you for your sentiments.

SGANARELLE: I assure you I mean it most sincerely.

GÉRONTE: You do me too much honour.

SGANARELLE: What's your daughter's name?

GÉRONTE: Lucinde.

SGANARELLE: Lucinde! A beautiful name for a patient! Lucinde!

GÉRONTE: I'll just go and see what she's doing.

SGANARELLE: Who's this fine upstanding woman here?

GÉRONTE: She s the wet-nurse to a young child I have.

SGANARELLE (*aside*): By God! She's a handsome piece of goods. (*To Jacqueline:*) Ah Nurse, delightful Nurse, my medicine is the very humble servant of your nurseryship! I only wish I was the fortunate little nursling who (*he lays his hand on her bosom*) imbibes the milk of your kindness. All my remedies, all my knowledge, all my abilities are yours to command, and –

LUCAS: Beggin' your pardon Doctor, just you let my wife alone, if you don't mind.

SGANARELLE: What!! Is she your wife?

LUCAS: Aye.

SGANARELLE (*making as if to embrace Lucas, he turns to the Nurse and kisses her*): Really. I didn't know. I'm very glad of it on account of the affection I feel for both of you.

LUCAS (*pulling him to one side*): Go easy, if you don't mind.

SGANARELLE: I assure you I'm delighted that you are man and wife. I congratulate her on having such a husband as you (*again he makes as if to embrace Lucas but, ducking under his hands, throws his arms around his wife's neck*), and I congratulate you on your part, on having so handsome, so sensible and so shapely a wife.

LUCAS (*pulling him away again*): By God, let's have less of the compliments, if you don't mind.

SGANARELLE: Don't you want me to share your appreciation of such a lovely conjunction of parts?

LUCAS: With me, as much as you like. But with my wife, that's enough ceremonials.

SGANARELLE: I have the happiness of both of you at heart (*same by-play as before*) and if I embrace you to show how very pleased I am – I embrace her for the same reason.

LUCAS (*pulling him away again*): By God Doctor, you've got a way of carrying-on with you!

Scene iii:
SGANARELLE, GÉRONTE, LUCAS, JACQUELINE

GÉRONTE: Sir, they're bringing my daughter to you now.

SGANARELLE: I await her coming, backed by all the panoply of medical science, sir.

GÉRONTE: Where is it?

SGANARELLE (*tapping his forehead*): In here.

GÉRONTE: Excellent.

SGANARELLE (*who attempts to fondle the Nurse's bosom*): But since I take an interest in all members of your household, I must make a little test of your nurse's milk and examine her breasts.

LUCAS (*pulling him away and making him spin round*): 'Ere! I'm not having none of that.

SGANARELLE: It's the doctor's duty to examine the breasts of all wet-nurses.

LUCAS: Duty or no duty, I'm not standin' for it!

SGANARELLE: You have the audacity to oppose the doctor's orders? Get out!

LUCAS: I don't care tuppence!

SGANARELLE (*giving him a sinister look*): I'll give you a fever.

JACQUELINE (*taking Lucas by the arm and spinning him round*): Get out of the road. Ain't I old enough to take care of meself if he tries anythin' he didn't ought to?

LUCAS: I don't want him touching you.

SGANARELLE: Fancy that, a miserable clod who's jealous of his own wife!

GÉRONTE: Here's my daughter.

Scene iv:

LUCINDE, GÉRONTE, SGANARELLE, VALÈRE,
LUCAS, JACQUELINE

SGANARELLE: Is this the patient?

GÉRONTE: Yes, she's my only daughter. It would break my heart if she were to die.

SGANARELLE: She mustn't do anything of the kind. She can't die without a doctor's prescription.

GÉRONTE: Come, a chair.

SGANARELLE (*seated between Géronte and Lucinde*): She's not a bad-looking patient. (*To Lucinde:*) I should think a strong healthy man might make something of her.

GÉRONTE: You made her laugh sir.

SGANARELLE: Good. It's an excellent sign when the doctor makes his patient laugh. (*To Lucinde:*) Now then, what seems to be the trouble? What's wrong with you? Where does it hurt?

LUCINDE (*replies with signs, touching her mouth, head and chin with her finger*): Haw he ho haw ho!

SGANARELLE: Eh? What are you saying?

LUCINDE (*gesturing as before*): Haw he haw haw he ho!

SGANARELLE: What?

LUCINDE: Haw he ho.

SGANARELLE (*imitating her*): Haw he ho haw ha. I don't understand you. What the devil sort of language is that?

GÉRONTE: That's exactly her trouble sir. She's lost the power of speech and so far no one has been able to find the reason for it. It just happened and has caused her marriage to be postponed.

SGANARELLE: But why?

GÉRONTE: The man she's to marry wants to wait until she's better.

SGANARELLE: What sort of imbecile is he, not wanting his wife to be dumb? I wish to God mine had the same trouble! I wouldn't want her cured.

GÉRONTE: Nevertheless sir, I beg you to do everything you can to cure her affliction.

SGANARELLE: Oh! Don't you worry yourself. Tell me now, does she have much pain?

GÉRONTE: Yes sir.

SGANARELLE. Good. Are the pains very severe?

GÉRONTE: Very severe.

SGANARELLE: Splendid. Does she go . . . you know . . . go?

GÉRONTE: Yes.

SGANARELLE: Freely?

GÉRONTE: I really couldn't say.

SGANARELLE: And is it the normal sort of . . .

GÉRONTE: I don't know anything about that.

SGANARELLE (*turning to his patient*): Give me your hand. (*To Géronte:*) A pulse like that tells me that your daughter is dumb.

GÉRONTE: Ah yes sir, that's exactly her trouble. You've got it straight away!

SGANARELLE: Aha!

JACQUELINE: See, he guessed what her trouble was!

SGANARELLE: We eminent doctors can tell these things at a glance. An ignorant physician would have puzzled his brains and said 'It's either this or that', but of course I put my finger on the trouble first time and I inform you that your daughter is dumb.

GÉRONTE: Yes, but I'd very much like you to tell me how it came about.

SGANARELLE: Nothing simpler. It came about because she lost the power of speech.

GÉRONTE: Very good. But why has she lost the power of speech?

SGANARELLE: All the best authorities would tell you that it's due to an impediment in the use of her tongue.

GÉRONTE: Yes, but what do you think is the cause of the impediment in the use of her tongue?

SGANARELLE: What Aristotle said about this was . . . very interesting.

GÉRONTE: I well believe it.

SGANARELLE: Ah! He was a great man!

GÉRONTE: Undoubtedly.

SGANARELLE: A very great man indeed. A greater man than I am . . . by . . . that much! (*He raises his arm from the elbow.*) But to come back to what we were talking about. I consider that the impediment in the use of her tongue is caused by certain humours which we learned physicians call morbid – morbid, that is to say morbid humours – so that the vapours formed by the exhalations of influences which arise in the diseased region coming – so to speak . . . do you understand Latin?

GÉRONTE: Not at all.

SGANARELLE (*drawing himself up in astonishment*): You don't understand Latin?

GÉRONTE: No.

SGANARELLE (*accompanying his speech with various comic gestures*): *Cabricias arci thuram, catalamus, singulariter, nominativo haec musa*, the Muse, *Bonus, bona, bonum, Deus Sanctus, estne oratio Latinas? Etiam.* Yes. *Quare?* Why? *Quia substantivo et adjectivum, concordat in generi, numerum et casus.*[2]

GÉRONTE: Ah. If only I had been a scholar!

JACQUELINE: There's a clever man for you!

LUCAS: Aye, it's that clever I don't understand a word of it.

SGANARELLE: But these vapours I referred to, passing from the left side where the liver is to the right side where the heart is, it happens that the lungs which we call in Latin *Armyan* having communication with the brain which in Greek we call *Nasmus* by means of the hollow vein which we call in Hebrew the *Cubile*, encounter on the way the vapours aforesaid which fill the ventricles of the omoplate, and because the said vapours – note this particularly please – and because the aforesaid vapours have a malignant quality – listen very carefully . . .

GÉRONTE: Yes.

SGANARELLE: . . . have a certain malignant quality – give me your full attention please . . .

GÉRONTE: I'm doing so.

SGANARELLE: . . . caused by the acidity of the humours engendered in the concavity of the diaphragm, it so happens that these vapours – *Ossabandus, nequeis, nequer, potarium, quipsa milus.* And that's precisely what's made your daughter dumb.

JACQUELINE: Ah! don't he talk lovely Lucas!

LUCAS: I wish I had a tongue on me like 'im!

GÉRONTE: It was very clearly explained, of course, but there was just one thing which surprised me – that was the positions of the liver and the heart. It seemed to me that you got them wrong way round, that the heart should be on the left side, and the liver on the right.

SGANARELLE: Yes, that was the way they used to be, but we've changed all that. Everything's quite different in medicine nowadays.

GÉRONTE: I didn't realize that. Forgive my ignorance.

SGANARELLE: That's quite all right, you can't be expected to know as much as we doctor's do.

GÉRONTE: Of course not. But what do you think ought to be done about this trouble of hers sir?

SGANARELLE: What do I think ought to be done?

GÉRONTE: That's it.

SGANARELLE: My advice is to put her back to bed and make her take some bread dipped in wine.

GÉRONTE: Why that sir?

SGANARELLE: Because bread and wine mixed together have a certain sympathetic virtue that's conducive to talking. They give parrots nothing else you know. That's how they learn to talk.

GÉRONTE: That's true. What a great man! Quick! Some bread and wine.

SGANARELLE: I'll come back and see how she is this evening. (*To the Nurse:*) Wait a minute, you. (*To Géronte:*) I must now administer a few little remedies to your nurse sir.

JACQUELINE: Me? I'm as fit as a fiddle.

SGANARELLE: That's bad Nurse, very bad. A state of rude good health gives great cause for concern. It would do you no harm to bleed you a little or administer you a nice emollient purge.

GÉRONTE: But this is an approach I don't understand sir. Why start bleeding someone when they're not ill?

SGANARELLE: That's neither here nor there, the approach is a salutary one. Just as you drink as precaution against future thirst, so one should be bled in preparation for illnesses to come.

JACQUELINE (*going*): Gracious me! I don't reckon anything to that. I don't want myself turned into a chemist's shop.

SGANARELLE: You're an awkward patient, but we'll find a way of making you toe the line. (*To Géronte:*) I give you good day sir.

GÉRONTE: Wait a moment please.

SGANARELLE: What do you want?

GÉRONTE: I want to give you some money sir.

SGANARELLE (*holding his hand out behind him, underneath his gown while Géronte is opening his purse*): I won't take it sir.

GÉRONTE: But sir . . .

SGANARELLE: I couldn't.

GÉRONTE: Just a minute.

SGANARELLE. No, no, no!

GÉRONTE: Please.

SGANARELLE: You're joking.

GÉRONTE: Here, take it.

SGANARELLE: I will not.

GÉRONTE: But . . .

SGANARELLE: I don't work for money.

GÉRONTE: I quite understand.

SGANARELLE (*after taking the money*): Is it full weight?[3]

GÉRONTE: Of course sir.

SGANARELLE: I'm not a mercenary man.

GÉRONTE: I'm sure you aren't.

SGANARELLE: I'm entirely disinterested.

GÉRONTE: I never thought otherwise.

Scene v:
SGANARELLE, LÉANDRE

SGANARELLE (*looking at the money*): By heaven, that's not bad at all, and provided . . .

LÉANDRE: Sir, I've been waiting ages for you. I've come to beg you to help me.

SGANARELLE (*grabbing his wrist*): Your pulse is very weak.

LÉANDRE: I'm not ill sir. That's not why I've come to you.

SGANARELLE: If you aren't ill, why the devil didn't you say so?

LÉANDRE: Please! To put the whole thing in a nutshell, my name's Léandre and I'm in love with Lucinde whom you've just examined. I'm forbidden all access to her by her curmudgeon of a father, so I've taken the risk of asking you to help me to carry out a plan I've thought up for having a word or two with her. My whole life and happiness depend on it.

SGANARELLE (*pretending to be angry*): What do you take me for? How

dare you presume to ask me to serve your amours and debase the
dignity of a doctor by lending myself to that sort of business!

LÉANDRE: Sir, not so loud.

SGANARELLE (*pushing him away*): I'll do as I choose. You've got some
nerve!

LÉANDRE: Go easy sir.

SGANARELLE: An ill-mannered good for nothing!

LÉANDRE: Please!

SGANARELLE: I'll show you I'm not that sort of man and that it's the
height of insolence to . . .

LÉANDRE (*pulling out a purse and giving it to Sganarelle*): Sir . . .

SGANARELLE (*taking the purse*): . . . think of employing me. I'm not
talking about you. You're a respectable gentleman and I'd be delighted
to help you out. But there are impertinent folk around who come
and take the wrong attitude to people and I admit that makes me
angry.

LÉANDRE: I beg your pardon sir, for taking the liberty of . . .

SGANARELLE: Don't mention it. What do you want?

LÉANDRE: I wanted to tell you that this illness which you are here to
cure is all faked. The doctors have done the usual diagnosis and
they've not hesitated to say how it arose. According to some, from
the brain or the bowels, according to others from the spleen or the
liver, but the fact is that the real cause is love. Lucinde only pretended
to have the symptoms in order to avoid being forced into a marriage
which she hated. But let's get out of here in case we're seen together.
I'll tell you what I want you to do as we go along.

SGANARELLE: Come along sir. You've made me more interested in this
affair of yours than you could possibly imagine. Either I'm no sort
of doctor or the patient shall snuff it or be yours.

Act III

A place near Géronte's house

Scene i:
LÉANDRE, SGANARELLE

LÉANDRE: I don't think I look too bad got up like this as an apothecary. The old man has hardly ever seen me, so the change of coat and wig should be enough of a disguise.

SGANARELLE: No doubt about it.

LÉANDRE: All I need now is to know five or six long medical words to spice my talk with and make me sound like a man of learning.

SGANARELLE: Oh no, that isn't necessary. The clothes are quite enough. Besides, I don't know any more than you do.

LÉANDRE: How do you mean?

SGANARELLE: I'm damned if I know the first thing about medicine! You're a decent sort and I'm willing to confide in you just as you confided in me.

LÉANDRE: What! You're not actually . . .

SGANARELLE: No, I tell you. They made me a doctor in the teeth of my objections. I never set up to be as learned as all that. I didn't get beyond the bottom class at school. I can't think where they got the idea, but when I saw that they were absolutely set on wanting me to be a doctor, I decided to be one and let other people take the consequences. But you wouldn't believe how the mistake has got around and how crazy everybody is about taking me for a man of learning. They come to see me from all over. If things keep on as they are, I reckon I'll stick to medicine for good. I find it's the best of all trades because whether you do good or harm you still get your money. We never get blamed for doing a bad job. We just hack away at the stuff we are working on, and whereas a cobbler making shoes can't spoil a piece of leather without having to foot the bill himself, in our trade we can make a mess of a man without it costing us a penny. If we make a mistake, it isn't our look out: it's always the fault of the fellow who's dead. And the best part of it is that there's a sort of decency about dead people, remarkably tactful they are: you never find them making complaints about the doctor who killed them!

LÉANDRE: Yes, the dead are certainly very considerate in that respect.

SGANARELLE (*seeing people approaching*): These people look as if they are coming to consult me. Go and wait for me outside your young lady's house.

Scene ii:

THIBAUT, PERRIN, SGANARELLE

THIBAUT: Sir, we've come lookin' for you, my lad Perrin and me.

SGANARELLE: What's the matter?

THIBAUT: His poor ole mother, Pierrette they call her, she been ill, bedfast, this past six month.

SGANARELLE (*holding out his hand for money*): And what do you expect me to do about it?

THIBAUT: We want you to give us a bit of some druggery or other to cure her.

SGANARELLE: But I need to know what's wrong with her.

THIBAUT: She's sick with the hypocrisy sir.

SGANARELLE: Hypocrisy?

THIBAUT: Aye. That's to say she's swole up all over. They do tell it's on account of a lot of seriosities wot she've got inside of her. Her liver, her belly or her spleen, as you might call 'em, instead of making blood send out nothing but water. Then, every other day, she do get the quotigian fever with aches and pains in the muscules of her legs. You can hear the phlegm in her throat fit to choke her. And sometimes she's that taken with syncups and conversions we think she's a goner. We've got a hapothecary in our village, all due respect to him, that have given her I don't know how many prescriptories and have cost me more than a dozen good crowns in enemas – excuse me mentioning it – and apistumes he's made her take, infections of hyancinth and cordial portions, but it was all, as you might say, summat an' nothin'. He was minded to give her some sort of drug called emetical wine but I took fright I did, honest, that it would send her to join her forefathers, for they do say as how these great doctors have killed I don't know how many folk with that there discovery.

SGANARELLE (*still holding out his hand and waving it about to show he's asking for money*): Come to the point my man, come to the point.

THIBAUT: The point is, sir, we come 'ere to ask you to tell us what to do.

SGANARELLE: I don't understand you at all.

PERRIN: Me ma's sick sir, and here's a couple of crowns we brought you so as you can give us some medicine for her.

SGANARELLE: Ah! I get you. Here's a lad who speaks up and explains what he means properly. You say your mother is ill with the dropsy, that her body is greatly distended, that she is feverish, has pains in her legs, and at times is liable to syncope and convulsions – that is to say fainting fits?

PERRIN: Aye sir, that's exackly how she is.

SGANARELLE: I understood you immediately. Your father here doesn't know what he's talking about. Now, you are asking me for medicine?

PERRIN: Yes sir.

SGANARELLE: Something to cure her?

PERRIN: That's what I mean.

SGANARELLE: Right. Then here's a piece of cheese. You must see that she eats it.

PERRIN: Cheese sir?

SGANARELLE: Yes, it's a special cheese containing gold, coral and pearls, with various other precious ingredients.

PERRIN: We're terrible obliged to you sir. We'll go and make her have a mouthful straight away.

SGANARELLE: Go, and if she dies make sure you give her the best funeral you can.

Scene iii:

JACQUELINE, SGANARELLE *and* LUCAS, *upstage*

A room in Géronte's house

SGANARELLE: Here's my beautiful nurse. Ah! Nurse of my heart, I'm delighted to see you. The sight of you is as good as rhubarb, cassia and senna for purging my soul of melancholy!

JACQUELINE: Lawks a'mercy Doctor, talk like that's too fancy for me. I don't understand all that there Latin of yours.

SGANARELLE: Be ill Nurse, be ill, I beseech you. Fall ill for my sake. It would give me all the pleasure in the world to make you better.

JACQUELINE: Thank you kindly sir, but I'd rather not have to be cured.

SGANARELLE: How I pity you, fair Nurse, for having such a tiresome, jealous husband as you have.

JACQUELINE: What would you have me do sir? 'Tis a punishment for my sins, and as we make our beds so we must we lie on 'em.

SGANARELLE: What! A clod like that! A man who watches you all the time and won't let anybody speak to you!

JACQUELINE: Alas! You ain't seen the half of it: that was only a small sample of his nasty nature.

SGANARELLE: Is it possible? How can a man have the heart to mistreat a person like you? Ah! I know people Nurse, and not so far away either, who would think themselves happy only to kiss your little tootsies! How does a fine-looking woman like you come to have fallen into the hands of a beastly, dull, stupid creature like . . . Forgive me for talking like that about your husband, Nurse.

JACQUELINE: Oh sir, I know very well that he deserves every word of it.

SGANARELLE: Yes, he certainly does, Nurse, and what he deserves even more is that you should make certain horny items sprout on his forehead to punish him for his suspicions.

JACQUELINE: 'Tis true enough that if I only thought of what he deserved, it might make me do some very strange things.

SGANARELLE: My word! You'd do well to get your own back on him with somebody else. I tell you, it would serve him right. And if I were lucky enough, fair Nurse, to be chosen . . . (*At this moment they both notice Lucas behind them listening to all that they say. They make off in opposite directions, the doctor with comic business*[4].)

Scene iv:
GÉRONTE, LUCAS

GÉRONTE: Hello there Lucas. Have you seen our doctor anywhere about?

LUCAS: Aye, the devil I have! And my wife with him as well.

GÉRONTE: Then where can he have got to?

LUCAS: I dunno. But I wish he was with the devil in hell!

GÉRONTE: Be off and see what my daughter is doing.

Scene v: ·
SGANARELLE, LÉANDRE, GÉRONTE

GÉRONTE: Ah! I was just asking where you were sir.

SGANARELLE: I was in your courtyard busy relieving myself of a little superfluous liquid imbibed earlier in the form of drink. How is the patient?

GÉRONTE: Rather worse since she took your prescription.

SGANARELLE: Excellent. That means it's working.

GÉRONTE: Yes, but I'm afraid that it may choke her in the process.

SGANARELLE: Don't you worry. I have remedies that scoff at all illness. I'm just waiting until she's at death's door.

GÉRONTE (*pointing to Léandre*): Who's this you've brought with you?

SGANARELLE (*making signs with his hands to indicate that he is an apothecary*): He's . . . a . . .

GÉRONTE: A what?

SGANARELLE: . . . He's the man . . .

GÉRONTE: Eh?

SGANARELLE: . . . who . . .

GÉRONTE: I understand you.

SGANARELLE: Your daughter will need him.

Scene vi:
LUCINDE, GÉRONTE, LÉANDRE, JACQUELINE,
SGANARELLE

JACQUELINE: Sir, here's your daughter. She felt like a bit of a stroll.

SGANARELLE: That'll be good for her. (*To Léandre:*) You, Mr Apothecary, go with her and take her pulse now and again while I discuss her symptoms with her father. (*He takes Géronte aside and putting one hand on his shoulder holds him under the chin with the other so that he has to look at him and can't turn round to see what his daughter and the apothecary are doing, and saying the following to distract him:*) It's a very important and debatable point among learned doctors, sir, whether women are easier to cure than men. I'd like you to listen carefully to this if you please. Some say yes, others say no. I myself say both yes and no. Inasmuch as the incongruity of the opaque humours which arise from the natural temperament of women is the reason for the usual dominance of the physical over the intellectual, we observe that the instability of these opinions depends on an oblique movement of the lunar cycle: and as the sun launching its rays on the concavity of the earth finds . . .

LUCINDE (*to Léandre*): No. I am utterly incapable of any change in my affections.

GÉRONTE: That's my daughter's voice! She's talking! Oh, it's the wonderful remedy! Oh most admirable of doctors! How grateful I am to you sir for this miraculous cure! What can I do for you in return for such a service?

SGANARELLE (*walking up and down the stage wiping his brow*): It's been a very troublesome case!

LUCINDE: Yes father, I have recovered my speech, but I've recovered it to tell you that I'll never have any husband but Léandre and that it's no use your wanting to make me marry Horace.

GÉRONTE: But –

LUCINDE: My mind's made up and nothing can make me change it.

GÉRONTE: What!

LUCINDE: It's useless to argue against it.

GÉRONTE: If –

LUCINDE: Nothing you say will do any good.

GÉRONTE: I —

LUCINDE: It's something I have decided.

GÉRONTE: But —

LUCINDE: No paternal authority can make me marry against my will.

GÉRONTE: I have —

LUCINDE: You can do your utmost.

GÉRONTE: He —

LUCINDE: I'll never submit to such tyranny.

GÉRONTE: The —

LUCINDE. I'll shut myself up in a convent rather than marry a man I don't love.

GÉRONTE: But —

LUCINDE (*in a deafening voice*): No! It's no use! Nothing doing! You're wasting your time! I won't do it. That's final!

GÉRONTE: Oh, what a torrent of words! There's no doing anything with her. (*To Sganarelle*:) I beg you sir — make her dumb again.

SGANARELLE. That's something I can't do. All I could do to help you would be to make you deaf, if you like.

GÉRONTE: No thank you very much! (*To Lucinde*:) So you think —

LUCINDE: No. Nothing you say will make the slightest impression on me.

GÉRONTE: You'll marry Horace this very evening.

LUCINDE: I'd sooner marry death itself!

SGANARELLE (*to Géronte*): For goodness' sake stop. Let me deal with this business. It's her illness that's still affecting her, but I know what remedy to apply.

GÉRONTE. Is it possible, sir, that you can also cure a malady of the mind such as this?

SGANARELLE: Yes. Leave it to me. I've got cures for everything. Our apothecary is the man to apply this one. (*He beckons to the apothecary and says to him*:) One word. You see that her ardent affection for Léandre is entirely contrary to her father's wishes. There's no time to lose; the humours are fermenting and an immediate remedy for the trouble must be found — delay may make things worse. I see only one thing for it — a dose of run-away purgative which you will mix with two drachms of matrimonium in pills as necessary. She may make some difficulty about taking it, but you know your job. You must persuade her and get her to swallow it as best you can. Go and take her for a little turn round the garden to put the humours into condition while I stay here and talk to her father. Above all, waste no time. Get to work with the remedy, and quick about it. The one and only remedy for the case!

Scene vii:
GÉRONTE, SGANARELLE

GÉRONTE: What were those drugs you were referring to sir? I don't seem to have heard of them.

SGANARELLE: Drugs that are used in emergencies.

GÉRONTE: Did you ever see such insolence?

SGANARELLE: Daughters can sometimes be headstrong.

GÉRONTE: You wouldn't believe how she dotes on this Léandre.

SGANARELLE: It's the heat of the blood makes young people like that.

GÉRONTE: Ever since I discovered how madly in love she was, I've kept her shut up in the house.

SGANARELLE: You were quite right.

GÉRONTE: I even prevented them from communicating with each other.

SGANARELLE: Excellent.

GÉRONTE: They would have got up to some folly if I had let them see each other.

SGANARELLE: Unquestionably.

GÉRONTE: I think she might even have run away with him.

SGANARELLE: Very prudently thought of.

GÉRONTE: I've been warned that he's been making all sorts of efforts to speak to her.

SGANARELLE: The fool!

GÉRONTE: But he'll be wasting his time.

SGANARELLE: Ha ha!

GÉRONTE: I'll stop him seeing her all right!

SGANARELLE: He's not dealing with an idiot: you know the rules of the game better than he does. He'll have to get up early in the morning to get the better of you!

Scene viii:

LUCAS, GÉRONTE, SGANARELLE

LUCAS: Oh lumme! ! Here's a fine ole how d'you do sir. Your daughter's run off with that Léandre. 'Twas him that was the apothecary and it's the doctor what done this 'ere fine operation.

GÉRONTE: What! How could you stab me in the back like that? Here! Fetch a magistrate! Stop him from leaving. Ah! You blackguard! I'll have the law on you!

LUCAS: By stars Doctor, you'll be hanged! Don't you stir from there.

Scene ix:

MARTINE, SGANARELLE, LUCAS

MARTINE (*to Lucas*): Oh my goodness! What a time I've had finding this house. Tell me, have you any news of the doctor I found for you?

LUCAS: There he is and he's going to be hanged!

MARTINE: What! My husband going to be hanged! Oh dear! What did he do to deserve that?

LUCAS: He fixed it for the master's daughter to be run away with.

MARTINE: Oh no! Dear husband, is it really true they're to hang you?

SGANARELLE: As you see. Oh!

MARTINE: Must you die with all those people watching?

SGANARELLE: What d'you want me to do about it?

MARTINE. If you'd only finished cutting the wood, I wouldn't have felt so bad about it.

SGANARELLE: Go away. You're breaking my heart.

MARTINE: No. I'd prefer to stay and help you keep up your courage as you die. I'll not leave you till I've seen you hanged.

SGANARELLE: Oh!

Scene x:

GÉRONTE, SGANARELLE, MARTINE, LUCAS

GÉRONTE (*to Sganarelle*): The magistrate will be along shortly and he'll put you in a place where he'll be answerable for you.

SGANARELLE (*cap in hand*): Aiee! Couldn't this be settled with a few thwacks with a cudgel?

GÉRONTE: No, the law will decide – but what's this I see?

Scene xi:

LÉANDRE, LUCINDE, JACQUELINE, LUCAS,
GÉRONTE, SGANARELLE, MARTINE

LÉANDRE: Sir, I come to produce Léandre for you and restore Lucinde to your keeping. We did intend to run away and get married, but that plan has given way to a more honourable intention. I have no wish to rob you of your daughter. I prefer to receive her from your own hands. I have to inform you sir that I have just received letters from which I learn that my uncle is dead and that I have inherited all his possessions.

GÉRONTE: Sir, I have the utmost consideration for your virtues. I give you my daughter with all the pleasure in the world.

SGANARELLE (*aside*): A close shave for the medical profession.

MARTINE: Since you aren't going to be hanged, you can thank me for having become a doctor: I was the one who procured you the honour.

SGANARELLE: Aye, and you who got me the most terrible thrashing.

LÉANDRE (*to Sganarelle*): It's done you too much good for you to harbour any resentment.

SGANARELLE: Oh, very well. (*To Martine:*) I forgive you for the thrashing in consideration of the dignity you have raised me to. But from this day forth be prepared to show proper respect to a man of my consequence. And remember that a doctor's wrath is more to be feared than you could possibly imagine.

The Would-Be Gentleman
A Comedy-Ballet

Le Bourgeois Gentilhomme
Comédie-Ballet

First performed on 14 October 1670 at the Château de Chambord for the entertainment of the King

Half of Molière's plays were written as entertainments for the king. *Le Bourgeois Gentilhomme* was one of them. It was first staged in the royal palaces of Chambord and Saint-Germain in October 1670 before being transferred to Paris on 23 November. There it was performed twenty times before the annual Easter closure of the capital's theatres. After Molière's death it was relatively neglected, for it was expensive to stage. It was not until Monsieur Jourdain was brought to life, first by Jules Raimu in 1941 and then by Louis Seignier in 1951, that it re-emerged as one of his most good-natured and best-loved plays.

It was devised as a topical entertainment. The vogue for 'Turkeries' had been relaunched after the visit to Paris of the Sultan's ambassador at the end of 1669. The Chevalier d'Arvieux, recently returned from the Levant, supervised the design of the costumes and Lully (who played the Muphti in a mask) was invited to compose music in the vein of his *Récit turquesque* of 1660. But Molière also exploited the taste for spectacle which had grown during the 1660s, and the result was viewed by his contemporaries less as the play it has become than as a 'divertissement' consisting of music and dance accompanied by a comedy.

It was the ninth of Molière's 'comedy-ballets' and it reveals him not merely as a comic writer but as a complete showman. Dance, music and words are all contained within the framework of the entertainment Monsieur Jourdain has promised Dorimène. He listens to the music he has had specially composed, and learns how to bow and express himself in the 'gallant' style. But Madame Jourdain's interference in Act II raises the question of a suitable husband for their daughter, and her opposition is continued by Covielle who devises a scheme which tricks Monsieur Jourdain into allowing Lucile to marry Cléonte. And so the entertainment planned for Dorimène duly takes place, with, in the end, only Monsieur Jourdain unaware of what is really happening. While other authors kept 'ballet' and 'comédie' separate, Molière fused them into an integrated spectacle.

It is not surprising, therefore, if the comedy element hardly respects the classical rules of theatre. The first two acts may establish Monsieur Jourdain's folly, but they are essentially a collection of linked sketches. The action proper does not begin until Act III, but thereafter Molière rings the changes on the triumph of ruse over foolishness. It is a staple theme of farce and is pursued in farcical terms. The pace is fast and physical (the beatings, disguises, rages), the jokes are verbal (Monsieur Jourdain is as impressed by the jargon of his teachers as by the nonsense spoken by the 'Turks') and the cast is familiar − a greybeard with peculiar ideas, an impertinent maid, a comic valet, a nagging wife and a collection of pedants. But the comedy grows more sophisticated as the love intrigue develops, with misunderstandings and manipulations creating situations which mock personal obsession and satirize social pretentiousness.

The Would-Be Gentleman is more than an anthology of comic techniques, however, for all the characters rise above their farcical roles and acquire a personality. Madame Jourdain is too kind-hearted to be a gorgon. Nicole and Covielle escape their traditional function as agents of Cupid by falling in love. Even the pedants have distinctive characters: the fencing master is all bluster and the philosopher is unphilosophically combustible, the music master is pretentious and the dancing master visibly self-interested. Monsieur Jourdain may be obsessed but he is never a threat to his family, like Orgon or Harpagon the miser. His 'passion' for Dorimène is no threat, for only he, lusting more after her title than her person, believes she can be his. He remains to the end a good-humoured innocent whom we know will appreciate the joke played on him and probably turn into a doting grandfather.

Even so, he has sometimes been taken more seriously and portrayed as a victim cruelly abused and duped by his family and society. Such a reading runs contrary to the movement of the play which sets Monsieur Jourdain, the pedants and (at least to begin with) Dorante and Dorimène against Madame Jourdain, Nicole, Lucile, Cléonte and Covielle − a division which makes vanity, private and public, Molière's subject. Monsieur Jourdain's snobbery (less a vice than a brainstorm in his case) is mildly punished and Cléonte is left to define true nobility. The family remains intact, young love is never endangered and the denouement − which leaves Monsieur Jourdain with his illusions for a moment longer − breathes a spirit of reconciliation.

Characters

MONSIEUR JOURDAIN, a
    merchant
MADAME JOURDAIN, his wife
LUCILE, his daughter
NICOLE, a servant
CLÉONTE, in love with Lucile
COVIELLE, Cléonte's valet
DORANTE, a count, in love with
    Dorimène
DORIMÈNE, a marquise
MUSIC MASTER

MUSIC MASTER'S PUPIL
DANCING MASTER
FENCING MASTER
PHILOSOPHY MASTER
MASTER TAILOR
Master Tailor's assistants
Two footmen
Singers, musicians, dancers,
    cooks and other characters
    who feature in the interludes
    and ballets

The play is set in Paris

Act I

*The overture is played by the full orchestra. At the
centre of the stage is discovered a pupil of the music
master, sitting at a table, where he is composing a
tune which Monsieur Jourdain has commissioned
for his concert.*

Scene i:

MUSIC MASTER, DANCING MASTER, *three singers,
two violinists and four dancers*

MUSIC MASTER (*to the singers*): This way, come in here and rest while
you're waiting for him.

DANCING MASTER (*to the dancers*): And you likewise, on this side.

MUSIC MASTER (*to his pupil*): Is it finished?

PUPIL: Yes.

MUSIC MASTER: Let me see . . . Yes, very good!

DANCING MASTER: Is it something new?

MUSIC MASTER: Yes, it's a piece for a concert I set him to compose
while we were waiting for our friend to get up.

DANCING MASTER: May I see what it is?

MUSIC MASTER: You'll hear it when he comes, with counterpoint and
harmonies. He can't be much longer now.

DANCING MASTER: We're both being kept pretty busy these days.

MUSIC MASTER: True enough. We've found the very man we both
needed. We're on to a good thing with this Monsieur Jourdain and
all the fantastic notions of gentility and gallantry he's got into his
head. I only wish, both for my music and your dancing, that everybody
was like him.

DANCING MASTER: I can't altogether agree. For his own sake I'd like
him to have a little more understanding of what we lay on for him.

MUSIC MASTER: True, he doesn't understand very much. But he pays
well and these days that's what your art and mine both need more
than anything else.

DANCING MASTER: Yes, but I don't mind admitting I thrive on applause:
I lap it up. To my mind it's sheer agony for any artist to perform in

front of fools and see his work criticized by some uncultured imbecile. Say what you like, it is a real joy to work for people who have a feeling for the finer points of one's art, who can appreciate the beauties of a work and repay all one's labours by making flattering comments. Yes, the most delightful reward one can receive for what one has done is to see one's work known and acclaimed by those whose applause brings honour. In my view, there's nothing which repays all our efforts better. To be praised by discerning minds is delightful, exquisite.

MUSIC MASTER: I couldn't agree more. I love it too. There's absolutely nothing more flattering than the recognition you speak of. But you can't live on applause. Praise alone doesn't pay the bills. You need something more substantial. The best sort of praise to have is the kind you can put in your pocket. Now it's true that this man of ours has no great share of enlightenment. He usually gets hold of the wrong end of the stick and claps in all the wrong places. But his money makes up for the weakness of his judgement. His taste is located in his wallet. His applause has cash value. Ignorant and middle class he might be, but he's worth more to us, you know, than the cultured nobleman who put us in touch with him.

DANCING MASTER: There's certainly something in what you say, but I think you place too strong an emphasis on money. Financial considerations are so sordid that no cultivated person should be serious about such matters.

MUSIC MASTER: All the same, you don't refuse to take our man's money.

DANCING MASTER: Of course not. But to me money isn't everything. I still wish that in addition to all the wealth he's got, he had a little more taste.

MUSIC MASTER: So do I and that's exactly what we're both trying to give him – so far as we can. But in any case, he's giving us a chance to make our names. He'll make up for the others by paying while they do the praising.

DANCING MASTER: He's coming!

Scene ii:

MONSIEUR JOURDAIN *in dressing-gown and*
night-cap, two footmen, MUSIC MASTER, DANCING
MASTER, *violinists, singers and dancers*

M. JOURDAIN: Well gentlemen, what's it to be today? Are you going to let me see your bit of tomfoolery?

DANCING MASTER: Tomfoolery? What bit of tomfoolery?

M. JOURDAIN: Your . . . er . . . What do you call it? Your prologue, or dialogue, you know, your singing and dancing.

DANCING MASTER: Oh! That's what you mean.

MUSIC MASTER: As you see, we're all ready.

M. JOURDAIN: I kept you waiting a bit because today I'm dressing like one of the quality and my tailor sent me a pair of silk stockings so tight I thought I'd never get into them.

MUSIC MASTER: We are here entirely at your disposal.

M. JOURDAIN: Oh please don't go, either of you, before they bring me my suit. I want you to see how I look in it.

DANCING MASTER: If that's what you want.

M. JOURDAIN: You'll see me turned out in style – head to foot, everything in the latest fashion.

MUSIC MASTER: We don't doubt it for a moment.

M. JOURDAIN (*showing his dressing-gown*): I had this Indian stuff specially made up for me.

DANCING MASTER: My tailor tells me the best people wear this sort of thing of a morning.

MUSIC MASTER: It suits you splendidly.

M. JOURDAIN: Footman! Hey! Both my footmen!

FIRST FOOTMAN: You wanted something sir?

M. JOURDAIN: No. Just checking to see if you're hearing me loud and clear. (*To both Masters:*) What do you reckon to my livery?

DANCING MASTER: Magnificent!

M. JOURDAIN (*opening his dressing-gown and displaying a pair of tight, red velvet breeches and a green velvet jacket which he is wearing underneath*): This is another little casual outfit for doing my morning exercises in.

MUSIC MASTER: Very elegant.

M. JOURDAIN: Footman!

FIRST FOOTMAN: Sir?

M. JOURDAIN: No, the other one.

SECOND FOOTMAN: Sir?

M. JOURDAIN (*taking off his dressing-gown*): Take my dressing-gown. (*To both Masters*:) Think I look all right like this?

DANCING MASTER: Excellent. Couldn't be better.

M. JOURDAIN: Right, let's have a look at this show of yours.

MUSIC MASTER: Very well, but first I'd like you to hear a composition which this young man (*pointing to the pupil*) has just written for the concert you asked me to stage. He is one of my pupils and has a remarkable gift for that sort of thing.

M. JOURDAIN: All right – but you shouldn't have had it written by some schoolboy. You shouldn't have been above doing the job yourself.

MUSIC MASTER: You mustn't be misled, sir, by my use of the word 'pupil'. Pupils like him know as much as the greatest masters and the piece itself could not be bettered. Just listen.

M. JOURDAIN (*to his footmen*): Give me my dressing-gown so I can listen properly. No wait – I think I'll be better without it. No, give it back to me. I'll be best with it on.

SINGER: 'I languish night and day and sad must be my lay,
Till consenting to their sway I give your eyes their way.
But if those who love you, Iris, are treated so
I ask with hope set low: how will you treat a foe?'

M. JOURDAIN: That song sounds a bit dismal to me. It makes me want to nod off. Can't you cheer it up here and there?

MUSIC MASTER: But the tune must suit the words sir.

M. JOURDAIN: I learned a song once. Very pretty it was too. Half a mo' . . . Tum-te-tum-te . . . how does it go?

DANCING MASTER: Gracious, I haven't the faintest idea.

M. JOURDAIN: It had something about sheep in it.

DANCING MASTER: Sheep?

M. JOURDAIN: Yes – or lambs. Ah! I've got it! (*Sings*:)

'Jenny was methought
As sweet as she was fair
Jenny was methought
As gentle as a lamb
Alas, alack! No lamb she!

> Jenny was more cruel far
> Than a tiger up a tree.'

Isn't that nice?

MUSIC MASTER: Never heard anything nicer.

DANCING MASTER: And you sing it very well.

M. JOURDAIN: And yet I never learned music.

MUSIC MASTER: You should learn sir, just as you're learning to dance. The two arts are very closely linked together.

DANCING MASTER: And they develop one's appreciation of beauty.

M. JOURDAIN: Do the quality learn music as well?

MUSIC MASTER: They do sir.

M. JOURDAIN: Then I'll learn it. But I don't know how I'll find the time. I already have a fencing master who gives me lessons and I've just taken on a philosophy teacher who's supposed to be making a start this morning.

MUSIC MASTER: There's something in philosophy, of course, but music, sir, music . . .

DANCING MASTER: And dancing. Music and dancing – what more does anyone need?

MUSIC MASTER: There's nothing so valuable in the life of a nation as music.

DANCING MASTER: And nothing more necessary to mankind than dancing.

MUSIC MASTER: Without music, the country wouldn't survive.

DANCING MASTER: Without dancing, a man would never achieve anything.

MUSIC MASTER: All the unrest and all the wars we see in the world today come from not learning music.

DANCING MASTER: All the troubles of mankind, all the calamities which fill the annals of history, the blunders of the politicians, the failures of great leaders – it all comes from not learning to dance.

M. JOURDAIN: How do you work that out?

MUSIC MASTER: What is war but discord among nations?

M. JOURDAIN: True.

MUSIC MASTER: If all men learned music, wouldn't that be the way to bring about harmony and create universal peace throughout the world?

M. JOURDAIN: You're right.

DANCING MASTER: When a man makes a mistake in his private affairs or in governing the country, don't we always say: 'So-and-so has tripped up in this or that business?'

M. JOURDAIN: We do indeed.

DANCING MASTER: And if a man trips, doesn't that come from not knowing how to dance?

M. JOURDAIN: That's very true. You're both right.

DANCING MASTER: We wanted to make you realize the importance, the usefulness of music and dancing.

M. JOURDAIN: I quite see it now.

MUSIC MASTER: Would you like to see both our performances?

M. JOURDAIN: Yes.

MUSIC MASTER: As I've said already, the first is a little exercise I devised some time ago in the expression of various emotions through music.

M. JOURDAIN: Very good.

MUSIC MASTER (*to the singers*): Come, step forward. (*To M. Jourdain:*) You must imagine that they're dressed as shepherds.

M. JOURDAIN: Why are there always shepherds? Wherever you go, it's always shepherds.

DANCING MASTER: When you wish to have people discourse in song, verisimilitude requires the use of the pastoral. Singing has always been associated with shepherds. It would not seem natural in a vocal composition if princes or ordinary persons expressed their passions in song.

M. JOURDAIN: All right, all right. Let's hear them.

Composition for two male and one female voice

FIRST SINGER (*female*): Who gives her heart in loving
        To a thousand cares is bound;
        Men speak of joyous wooing
        Though it's bitter-sweet, they've found.
        Yet say what you will
        There is no other thrill
        Like being free and willing.

SECOND SINGER (*male*): There is no joy like love's sweet kiss
        That joins two hearts in loving bliss

And makes them beat as one.
There is no joy where love is spurned:
Take love from life and there's no sun,
For all life's charm to sand is turned.

THIRD SINGER (*male*): There'd be great joy in love to find
One heart, just one, was good and kind.
But no man e're saw shepherdess
Who was not false and faithless,
For woman's made in cruel fashion:
Her fickle ways drive out all passion.

SECOND SINGER: Oh rarest rapture!

FIRST SINGER: Would I could capture!

THIRD SINGER: Deceivers ever.

SECOND SINGER: Love, leave me never.

FIRST SINGER: Happy surrender!

THIRD SINGER: Faithless pretender!

SECOND SINGER: Change that heart from hate to tenderness.

FIRST SINGER: Would you find your shepherdess?

THIRD SINGER: But how shall I earn her caress?

FIRST SINGER: To redeem my sex's part
I hereby offer you my heart.

THIRD SINGER: O shepherdess, dare I conceive
A hope that you will not deceive?

FIRST SINGER: Time will test and time will prove
Which heart feels the truest love.

THIRD SINGER: And which of us inconstant be
The gods shall punish cruelly.

ALL THREE SINGERS: To love's most tender might
Our loving hearts we bind.
Oh loving's such sweet delight
When two true hearts are fast entwined.

M. JOURDAIN: Is that it?

MUSIC MASTER: Yes.

M. JOURDAIN: I thought it turned out very nicely. There were some quite neat little sayings in it.

DANCING MASTER: And now for my show, a modest demonstration of the most beautiful movements and poses which dance can exemplify.

M. JOURDAIN: There aren't going to be more shepherds?

DANCING MASTER: They can be whatever you please. (*To the dancers*:) Positions!

Four dancers perform all the varied movements and different kinds of steps as the Dancing Master directs. The dance forms the first interlude.

Act II

Scene i:

MONSIEUR JOURDAIN, MUSIC MASTER, DANCING
MASTER, *footmen*

M. JOURDAIN: Well, that wasn't too bad at all. Those boys and girls certainly know how to shake a leg.

MUSIC MASTER: When the dancing and the music are put together, it will be even more effective, and you'll find that the little ballet we've devised for you is a very pretty thing.

M. JOURDAIN: Yes, but that's for later don't forget, for when the lady I'm going to all this bother for will be doing me the honour of dining here.

DANCING MASTER: Everything is arranged.

MUSIC MASTER: There's just one other thing sir. A gentleman such as yourself, living in style, with a taste for fine things, ought really to be holding musical at-homes every Wednesday or Thursday.

M. JOURDAIN: Is that what the quality do?

MUSIC MASTER: Yes sir.

M. JOURDAIN: Then I'll do it too. Will they be really grand?

MUSIC MASTER: Exquisite. You'll need three voices, treble, counter-tenor and bass, and to accompany them a bass viol, theorbo,[1] harpsichord for the continuo and over it two fiddles for the ritornellos.

M. JOURDAIN: I'd like a sea-trumpet[2] as well. The sea-trumpet's an instrument I'm fond of. Very dulcet.

MUSIC MASTER: Leave it all to us.

M. JOURDAIN: Remember, don't forget to send in singers later on so they can warble during dinner.

MUSIC MASTER: You shall have everything as it should be.

M. JOURDAIN: And above all, make sure the ballet's a treat.

MUSIC MASTER: You'll be pleased with it, and most particularly with some of the minuets.

M. JOURDAIN: Ah! Minuets! Minuets are my dance. You must see me dance a minuet. Come along, Mr Dancing Master.

DANCING MASTER: A hat, sir, if you please. (*Monsieur Jourdain takes the footman's hat and puts it on over his night-cap. The Dancing Master takes him by both hands and makes him dance to the tune of a minuet which he sings.*) One two three . . . la la la, one two three . . . la la la, and again . . . la la la . . . keep time if you please . . . la la la . . . now the right leg . . . la la la . . . don't move your shoulders so much . . . la la la . . . your arms are limp . . . la la la . . . head up, point your toes outward . . . la la la . . . keep your body erect.

M. JOURDAIN: Phew!

MUSIC MASTER: Splendid, quite splendid!

M. JOURDAIN: By the way, just show me how to bow when you meet a countess. I'll need to know a bit later on.

DANCING MASTER: How to make a bow to a countess?

M. JOURDAIN: Yes, a countess called Dorimène.

DANCING MASTER: Give me your hand.

M. JOURDAIN: No, you do it. I'll remember.

DANCING MASTER: If you wish to show great respect, you make your bow first stepping backwards and then advance towards her bowing three times, the third time going right down to the level of her knee.

M. JOURDAIN: Let's see you try it. (*The Dancing Master bows three times.*) Good!

FOOTMAN: Sir, your fencing master is here.

M. JOURDAIN: Tell him to come in. He can give me my lesson here. (*To both Masters:*) Stay, I'd like you to see me perform.

Scene ii:

FENCING MASTER, MUSIC MASTER, DANCING
MASTER, MONSIEUR JOURDAIN, *footman carrying*
two foils

FENCING MASTER (*taking both foils from the footman and presenting one to Monsieur Jourdain*): Come sir, your salute. Hold yourself erect.

Take the weight of your body more on your left thigh. Legs not spread so wide. Feet parallel. Wrist level with your hip. Point of the foil level with your shoulder. Arm not quite so extended. Left hand level with your eye. Left shoulder squarer on. Head up. Look confident. Advance. Keep your body steady. Engage my point in quart and lunge. One, two! As you were. Again, and keep steady on your feet. One, two, and recover. When you make a pass, sir, it is essential that the foil be advanced before you lunge, keeping your body well covered. One, two. Come, engage my foil in tierce and hold it. Advance. Keep your body steady. Advance and lunge from there. One, two. As you were. And again. One, two. Take one step back. On guard sir, on guard! (*The Fencing Master scores two or three hits crying out as he does so*:) 'Parry!'

M. JOURDAIN: Phew!

MUSIC MASTER: You're doing splendidly!

FENCING MASTER: I've told you already, the whole art of fencing consists of just two things: hitting and not being hit. And as I proved to you the other day by demonstrative logic,[3] it is impossible for you to be hit if you know how to turn your opponent's blade from the line of your body. All it takes is a slight movement of the wrist, inward or outward.

M. JOURDAIN: At that rate, a man who is not particularly brave can be sure of killing his man and not being killed himself?

FENCING MASTER: Of course! Didn't you follow my demonstration?

M. JOURDAIN: Oh yes.

FENCING MASTER: And that is precisely why you can see what respect men of my calling should be given by the nation and how very much more important skill at arms is than other futile pursuits, such as dancing and music.

DANCING MASTER: Now just a minute, Mr Parry-and-Thrust. Mind what you say about dancing.

MUSIC MASTER: And try to treat music with a little more respect, if you don't mind.

FENCING MASTER: You're a couple of comedians, trying to compare your skills with mine!

DANCING MASTER: Did you ever see such arrogance?

MUSIC MASTER: Such a ridiculous brute, with that leather chest-protector of his.

FENCING MASTER: Listen, you silly Prancing Master, I'd make you hop and skip if I had a mind to, and as for you, you musical moron, I could make you sing a different tune.

DANCING MASTER: I shall have to teach you your trade, you metal-beater.

M. JOURDAIN (*to the Dancing Master*): You must be mad to want to pick a quarrel with a man who knows all about tierce and quart and can kill a man by demonstrative logic!

DANCING MASTER: I don't give a damn for his demonstrative logic, nor his tierce, nor his quart.

M. JOURDAIN (*to the Dancing Master*): I say, don't be hasty!

FENCING MASTER: What did you say, you impertinent jackanapes?

M. JOURDAIN: Oh, Fencing Master!

DANCING MASTER (*to the Fencing Master*): You great cart horse!

M. JOURDAIN: Oh, Dancing Master!

FENCING MASTER: If I start on you . . .

M. JOURDAIN (*to the Fencing Master*): Easy now.

DANCING MASTER: If I get my hands on you . . .

M. JOURDAIN (*to the Dancing Master*): Steady on.

FENCING MASTER: I'll tan your hide till you're . . .

M. JOURDAIN (*to the Fencing Master*): Oh, please . . .

DANCING MASTER: I'll give you such a hiding . . .

M. JOURDAIN (*to the Dancing Master*): I beg you . . .

MUSIC MASTER: Just give us a chance and we'll teach him to keep a civil tongue in his head.

M. JOURDAIN (*to the Music Master*): For goodness' sake, stop this!

Scene iii:

PHILOSOPHY MASTER, MUSIC MASTER, DANCING
MASTER, FENCING MASTER, MONSIEUR JOURDAIN,
two footmen

M. JOURDAIN: Ah! It's my Philosophy Master. You've arrived just in time with your philosophy. Come and make peace between this lot.

PHILOSOPHY MASTER: What is it? What's this all about gentlemen?

M. JOURDAIN: They've got so worked up about which of their professions is the most important that they've started a slanging match and very nearly came to blows.

PHILOSOPHY MASTER: Come come, gentlemen! You mustn't let yourselves be carried away like this. Haven't you read Seneca's learned disquisition on anger?[4] Is there anything more base and contemptible than a passion which turns a man into a ravening beast? Surely you would agree that reason should direct all our actions?

DANCING MASTER: But my good sir, he has just insulted both of us, by disparaging both music, which is this gentleman's profession, and dance, which is mine.

PHILOSOPHY MASTER: A wise man is above all the insults which may be put upon him, and the best reply to any affront is moderation and patience.

FENCING MASTER: Both had the impudence to compare their professions with mine.

PHILOSOPHY MASTER: And why should that upset you? One should never compete in matters of mere reputation and precedence. What truly distinguishes men one from another is wisdom and virtue.

DANCING MASTER: I maintain that dance is a science to which sufficient honour can never be paid.

MUSIC MASTER: And I that music is a science which has been revered down all the centuries.

FENCING MASTER: And I continue to maintain against the pair of them that mastery of arms is the finest and the most indispensable of all the sciences.

PHILOSOPHY MASTER: If that's so, what is philosophy? I consider all three of you most presumptuous to speak in my presence with such assurance and to have the impudence to grace with the name of science mere accomplishments which do not even rate the title of art and can only be adequately described under the tiresome trades of bruiser, warbler and foot tapper!

FENCING MASTER: Get out, you philosophic cur!

MUSIC MASTER: Get out, you miserable pedant!

DANCING MASTER: Get out, you pettifogging book-worm!

PHILOSOPHY MASTER: Now look here! You swine, you . . . (*He hurls himself at them and all three set about him.*)

M. JOURDAIN: Oh, Mr Philosophy Master!

PHILOSOPHY MASTER: Ruffians! Villains! Jumped-up nobodies!

M. JOURDAIN: Oh, Mr Philosophy Master!

FENCING MASTER: Confound the brute!

M. JOURDAIN: Gentlemen!

PHILOSOPHY MASTER: Of all the insulting . . . !

M. JOURDAIN: Oh, Mr Philosophy Master!

DANCING MASTER: The devil take the stupid clod!

M. JOURDAIN: Gentlemen!

PHILOSOPHY MASTER: Villains!

M. JOURDAIN: Oh, Mr Philosophy Master!

MUSIC MASTER: Damned impertinence!

M. JOURDAIN: Gentlemen!

PHILOSOPHY MASTER: Good-for-nothings! Vagabonds! Back-stabbers! Mountebanks!

M. JOURDAIN: Oh, Mr Philosophy Master! Gentlemen! Oh, Mr Philosophy Master! Gentlemen! Oh Mr Philosophy Master! (*They go out, still fighting.*) Go on, beat each other up as much as you like. I can't do anything about it and I don't intend to mess up my dressing-gown trying to separate you. I'd be mad pushing in between them and getting myself seriously injured.

Scene iv:

PHILOSOPHY MASTER, MONSIEUR JOURDAIN,
two footmen

PHILOSOPHY MASTER (*straightening his neck-band*): It's time for our lesson.

M. JOURDAIN: I'm sorry, sir, that they knocked you about like that.

PHILOSOPHY MASTER: It's nothing. A philosopher knows how to take things as they come. I shall attack them in a satire I shall compose in the manner of Juvenal in which they shall be torn into very small pieces. Let's leave that now. What do you want to learn?

M. JOURDAIN: Whatever I can, for if there's one thing I want more than anything else, it's to be a man of learning. I'm extremely cross with my father and mother who never made me study everything when I was young.

PHILOSOPHY MASTER: A most proper sentiment! *Nam sine doctrina vita est quasi mortis imago.* Did you understand that? You know Latin of course?

M. JOURDAIN: Of course, but just carry on as if I didn't. Tell me what it means.

PHILOSOPHY MASTER: It means 'Without knowledge life is no more than the foreshadow of death'.

M. JOURDAIN: Your Latin has hit the nail bang on the head.

PHILOSOPHY MASTER: Have you not mastered a few of the first principles, the rudiments of the sciences?

M. JOURDAIN: Oh yes! I can read and write.

PHILOSOPHY MASTER: Where would you like us to start? Shall I teach you logic?

M. JOURDAIN: What do you mean when you say logic?

PHILOSOPHY MASTER: Logic teaches us the three processes of reasoning.

M. JOURDAIN: And what are these three processes of reasoning?

PHILOSOPHY MASTER: The first, the second and the third. The first consists of apprehending the world by means of universals, the second, of forming judgements by means of categories, and the third, of drawing rigorous conclusions by the use of syllogisms – Barbara, Celarent, Darii, Ferio, Baralipton and so on and so forth.[5]

M. JOURDAIN: Ugh! those are very off-putting words. No, logic doesn't appeal to me. Let me learn something jollier.

PHILOSOPHY MASTER: Would you like to study moral philosophy?

M. JOURDAIN: Moral philosophy?

PHILOSOPHY MASTER: Yes.

M. JOURDAIN: What's this moral philosophy about?

PHILOSOPHY MASTER: It's to do with the nature of happiness, teaches men how to moderate their passions and –

M. JOURDAIN: No, let's not. I'm as hot-tempered as the next man. Moral philosophy or no moral philosophy, I'll get as carried away as I want whenever I feel like it.

PHILOSOPHY MASTER: Then is it the natural sciences you want to learn about?

M. JOURDAIN: Natural sciences? And what have they got to say for themselves?

PHILOSOPHY MASTER: Natural science explains the principles of natural phenomena and the properties of matter. It is concerned with the nature of the elements, metals, minerals, stones, plants and animals and it tells us the causes of meteors, rainbows, will-o'-the-wisps, comets, lightning, thunder and thunderbolts, rain, snow, hail, wind and vortices.[6]

M. JOURDAIN: That all sounds very loud, it's much too noisy.

PHILOSOPHY MASTER: Well what do you want me to teach you then?

M. JOURDAIN: Teach me how to spell.

PHILOSOPHY MASTER: Willingly.

M. JOURDAIN: And then you can teach me the calendar, so I'll know when there's a moon and when there isn't.

PHILOSOPHY MASTER: Very well. Now, to follow your wishes and at the same time to treat the subject philosophically, we must begin, according to the proper order of these things, by having a sound grounding in the nature of the letters of the alphabet and of the different ways they are all pronounced. At this point, I must explain that the letters are divided into vowels, so called because they are vocal, and consonants, so named because they are 'sounded with' the vowels, and serve only to differentiate the various articulations of the voice. There are five vowels: A, E, I, O, U.

M. JOURDAIN: I've got all that.

PHILOSOPHY MASTER: The vowel A is produced by opening the mouth wide: A.[7]

M. JOURDAIN: A. A. Right.

PHILOSOPHY MASTER: The vowel E is produced by bringing the lower jaw up until it almost meets the upper jaw: E.

M. JOURDAIN: A, E. A, E. My word, yes! Oh, this is marvellous!

PHILOSOPHY MASTER: For the vowel I, bring the jaws even closer together and stretch the corners of the mouth towards the ears: A, E, I.

M. JOURDAIN: A, E, I, I, I, I. Quite right. Isn't knowledge wonderful!

PHILOSOPHY MASTER: The vowel O is produced by opening the jaws and rounding the lips top and bottom and at each side: O.

M. JOURDAIN: O, O. That's absolutely right. A, E, I, O, I, O. This is splendid! I, O, I, O.

PHILOSOPHY MASTER: The opening of the mouth forms a small circle which mimics exactly the shape of the letter O.

M. JOURDAIN: O, O, O. You're right again. Ah, it's really tremendous when you know stuff like this.

PHILOSOPHY MASTER: The vowel U is produced by bringing the teeth close together but without quite meeting, and pushing the lips out and bringing them close together too but not letting them touch: U.

M. JOURDAIN: U, U. It's as true as I'm sitting here.

PHILOSOPHY MASTER: Both your lips are pushed out, as if you were pulling a face, so that if you want to let someone know you don't think much of him, you only need say: U!

M. JOURDAIN: U, U. That's absolutely right. Oh, why didn't I study when I was younger so I'd have known all this earlier!

PHILOSOPHY MASTER: Tomorrow we'll look at the other letters, the consonants.

M. JOURDAIN: And are they as interesting as those we've done?

PHILOSOPHY MASTER: No doubt about it. For instance, the consonant D is pronounced by putting the tip of the tongue against the upper teeth: Duh.

M. JOURDAIN: Duh, Duh. That's it! Splendid! Splendid!

PHILOSOPHY MASTER: F by resting the upper teeth on the lower lip: Fuh.

M. JOURDAIN: Fuh, Fuh. Quite true. Oh, father and mother, I'll never forgive you . . .

PHILOSOPHY MASTER: And R by placing the tip of the tongue against the highest part of the palate, so that the force of the air coming out flows all round it, making it lift and then return to the same spot, which produces a sort of trilling sound: Rrr, Rrruh.

M. JOURDAIN: Rrr, Rrruh, Rrruh. Rrr, Rrruh, Rrr, Rrruh. That's it again! Ah, what a clever man you are! When I think of all the time I've been wasting! Rrr, Rrruh. Rrr, Rrruh.

PHILOSOPHY MASTER: I'll explain all these fascinating things to you in detail.

M. JOURDAIN: Please do. But now I must let you into a secret. I'm in love with a lady of the highest quality and I'd like you to help me to write her a little note that I can drop at her feet.

PHILOSOPHY MASTER: Very well.

M. JOURDAIN: That's the proper way I believe?

PHILOSOPHY MASTER: Absolutely. You want to write to her in verse?

M. JOURDAIN: No, no. Not verse.

PHILOSOPHY MASTER: You want it in prose, then?

M. JOURDAIN: No. I don't want prose and I don't want verse.

PHILOSOPHY MASTER: But it must be one or the other.

M. JOURDAIN: Why?

PHILOSOPHY MASTER: For the very good reason, sir, that if you want to say anything at all there's only prose or verse.

M. JOURDAIN: Only prose or verse?

PHILOSOPHY MASTER: There's nothing else. If it's not prose, it's verse. If it's not verse, it's prose.

M. JOURDAIN: And when you talk, what is that?

PHILOSOPHY MASTER: Prose.

M. JOURDAIN: You mean that when I say: 'Nicole, fetch me my slippers' and 'Give me my night-cap', that's prose?

PHILOSOPHY MASTER: Yes sir.

M. JOURDAIN: Gracious me! Here I've been, talking prose for more than forty years and never knew it! I'm ever so grateful to you for teaching me that. Now, what I want to put in the letter is: 'Fair Countess, I am dying for love of your beautiful eyes', but I want it said elegantly, so it sounds genteel.

PHILOSOPHY MASTER: Then say that the fire of her glance reduces your heart to ashes and that night and day you suffer on her account the pain –

M. JOURDAIN: No, no, no. I don't want anything like that. All I want is what I told you: 'Fair Countess, I am dying for love of your beautiful eyes.'

PHILOSOPHY MASTER: But surely it needs a little elaboration.

M. JOURDAIN: No, I tell you, I don't want anything in the letter except those words, but they've got to be said stylishly and properly set out. Would you please give me an idea of the different ways they can be put, just so I can see.

PHILOSOPHY MASTER: To start with, you can put them they way you've done it: 'Fair Countess, I am dying for love of your beautiful eyes.' Or you could say: 'For love, fair Countess, of your beautiful eyes I am dying.' Or: 'For love of your beautiful eyes, fair Countess, dying I am.' Or: 'Your beautiful eyes, fair Countess, for love of, dying am I.' Or even: 'Dying, fair Countess, for love of your beautiful eyes, I am.' Or maybe: 'Fair Countess, of your beautiful eyes, dying am I for love.'

M. JOURDAIN: But which of all these ways is the best?

PHILOSOPHY MASTER: The one you used yourself: 'Fair Countess, I am dying for love of your beautiful eyes.'

M. JOURDAIN: I've never done much studying and yet I get it right first time! I can't say how grateful I am. Please come in good time tomorrow.

PHILOSOPHY MASTER: You may rely on me sir. (*Exit.*)

M. JOURDAIN (*to Footman*): What? Hasn't my new suit come yet?

FOOTMAN: No sir.

M. JOURDAIN: That dratted tailor has kept me hanging about a whole day at a time when I'm very busy. It makes me very angry! I wish that damned tailor would catch something nasty! The hell with the tailor! A plague on the tailor! If I had that vile, odious, cheating tailor here, I'd . . . I'd . . .

Scene v:

MASTER TAILOR, *a tailor's assistant who carries*
Monsieur Jourdain's suit, MONSIEUR JOURDAIN,
two footmen

M. JOURDAIN: Ah, there you are! I was just beginning to get cross with you.

TAILOR: I couldn't get here any earlier. I've had a score of my men working on your suit.

M. JOURDAIN: Those silk stockings you sent me were so tight I've had the very devil of a job getting them on. I've already torn two holes in them.

TAILOR: They'll work slack.

M. JOURDAIN: Yes, if I go on making holes in them. You also made me a pair of shoes which pinch like blazes.

TAILOR: Not at all sir.

M. JOURDAIN: How d'you mean, 'not at all'?

TAILOR: They don't pinch at all.

M. JOURDAIN: And I tell you they do!

TAILOR: You're just imagining it.

M. JOURDAIN: I imagine it because I can feel it. Isn't that a good enough reason?

TAILOR: Look at this. The coat I have here is as fine as any at Court and the most beautifully designed. It is a miracle of art to have made a suit that is sober without using black. I'd wager anything that the most skilful tailor couldn't have brought it off as I have.

M. JOURDAIN: What's this? You've put the florals upside-down!

TAILOR: You didn't say you wanted them the other way up.

M. JOURDAIN: Should I have said so?

TAILOR: Oh, yes. All the best gentlemen wear them like that.

M. JOURDAIN: Gentlemen of quality wear their florals upside-down?

TAILOR: Most certainly sir.

M. JOURDAIN: Well, that's all right then.

TAILOR: You can have them the other way up if you want.

M. JOURDAIN: No, no.

TAILOR: Just say the word.

M. JOURDAIN: No I said. You've done very well. Do you think the suit will fit?

TAILOR: What a question! I defy the brush of any artist to get nearer your fit. I have a man in my shop who's a genius at cutting out a pair of breeches, and another who has no equal at making a doublet.

M. JOURDAIN: Are my wig and these feathers all they should be?

TAILOR: Everything is perfect.

M. JOURDAIN (*looking at the tailor's own suit*): Hold on, Master Tailor, isn't that some of the material you used for the last suit you made me? I recognize it.

TAILOR: The fact is the cloth looked so uncommon handsome that I felt I just had to have a suit made up from it myself.

M. JOURDAIN: That's as maybe, but you shouldn't have had it made up out of my material.

TAILOR: Are you going to try on your suit?

M. JOURDAIN: Yes, hand it here.

TAILOR: One moment! That's not the way these things are done. I've brought my men with me to dress you to strict tempo. Suits like these must be put on with ceremony. You there, come in! Dress the gentleman in this suit in the manner you use when dealing with persons of quality.

Enter four tailor's assistants. Two remove the breeches in which Monsieur Jourdain did his exercises and the other two take off his jacket, after which they dress him in his new suit. He struts among them, showing off his suit to see if he looks well in it. All this is done in time to music played by the full orchestra.

TAILOR'S ASSISTANT: Please sir, won't a gentleman like yourself give these lads something to drink your honour's health with?

M. JOURDAIN: What did you call me?

TAILOR'S ASSISTANT: Your honour sir.

M. JOURDAIN: That's what getting togged up like the quality gets you!

Carry on dressing like a commoner and nobody will ever call you 'your honour'. (*Giving money*) Here you are. That's for 'your honour'.

TAILOR'S ASSISTANT: Oh my Lord, we are infinitely obliged to you.

M. JOURDAIN: 'My Lord!' Oh my goodness! 'My Lord!' Wait a minute lad. 'My Lord' deserves a reward. 'My Lord'! Now that's something like it! Here, that's what 'My Lord' gets you. (*He gives more money.*)

TAILOR'S ASSISTANT: My Lord, we'll all drink to your Grace's good health.

M. JOURDAIN: 'Your Grace!' Oh! Oh! Wait, don't go. Come to 'Your Grace'. (*Aside*) My stars, if he goes as far as 'Your Highness', he'll get the whole purse. (*To the lad*:) Here, that's for 'Your Grace'.

TAILOR'S ASSISTANT: My Lord, we humbly thank your Lordship for your Grace's liberality.

M. JOURDAIN: It's just as well he stopped. I'd have given him the lot.

The four Tailor's assistants show their appreciation by a dance which forms the second interlude.

Act III

Scene i:

MONSIEUR JOURDAIN, *two footmen*

M. JOURDAIN: Follow me. I'm going out to show off my new suit in town. Mind you both keep close behind me, so that people will know that you are mine.

FOOTMEN: Yes sir.

M. JOURDAIN: Call Nicole for me. I've got some instructions I want to give her. No, wait. She's coming.

Scene ii:

NICOLE, MONSIEUR JOURDAIN, *two footmen*

M. JOURDAIN: Nicole!

NICOLE: What is it?

M. JOURDAIN: Listen . . .

NICOLE: Ha! ha! ha! ha! ha!

M. JOURDAIN: What are you laughing at?

NICOLE: Ha! ha! ha! ha! ha! ha!

M. JOURDAIN: What's wrong with the dratted girl?

NICOLE: Ha! ha! ha! Look at you, rigged out like that! Ha! ha! ha!

M. JOURDAIN: What are you talking about?

NICOLE: Oh Lord! Ha! ha! ha! ha!

M. JOURDAIN: Silly creature! Are you laughing at me?

NICOLE: Oh no sir, I wouldn't dream of it. Ha! ha! ha! ha! ha! ha!

M. JOURDAIN: I'll warm your ears for you if you don't stop laughing.

NICOLE: Sir, I can't help it. Ha! ha! ha! ha! ha! ha!

M. JOURDAIN: Stop, I tell you!

NICOLE: I'm ever so sorry sir, but you look so comical that I can't help laughing. Ha! ha! ha! ha!

M. JOURDAIN: Oh! the impudence!

NICOLE: You look so funny like that. Ha! ha!

M. JOURDAIN: I'll –

NICOLE: Please excuse me, I . . . ha! ha! ha! ha!

M. JOURDAIN: Listen, if you laugh any more, even smile, I swear I'll land you a smack across the face such as you never had in your life!

NICOLE: All right sir, it's all over, I shan't laugh any more.

M. JOURDAIN: Take care you don't. Now, I want you to clean the hall ready for . . .

NICOLE: Ha! ha!

M. JOURDAIN: . . . clean the hall ready for . . .

NICOLE: Ha! ha!

M. JOURDAIN: I'm telling you, you're to clean the hall and . . .

NICOLE: Ha! ha!

M. JOURDAIN: Not again!

NICOLE (*unable to stand for laughing*): Listen sir, you can wallop me after, but let me have my laugh out, it'll do me more good. Ha! ha! ha! ha!

M. JOURDAIN: I'm losing my temper . . .

NICOLE: Oh sir, please let me laugh. Ha! ha! ha!

M. JOURDAIN: If I start on you . . .

NICOLE: Oh sir . . . I'll burst . . . if you don't let me laugh. Ha! ha! ha!

M. JOURDAIN: Was there ever such a good-for-nothing, impertinent . . . She just laughs in my face instead of listening to my instructions!

NICOLE: What is it you want me to do sir?

M. JOURDAIN: To turn your mind, you hussy, to getting the house ready for the company I'm expecting here shortly.

NICOLE (*getting up*): Oh Lord, that's made me laugh on the other side of my face. Those visitors of yours make such a mess in the house that just hearing the word 'company' is enough to give me the grumps.

M. JOURDAIN: So am I to shut my door to everybody on your account?

NICOLE: You ought to shut it to some people.

Scene iii:

MADAME JOURDAIN, MONSIEUR JOURDAIN, NICOLE, *two footmen*

MME JOURDAIN: Oh! what new nonsense is it this time? Whatever are you doing in that get up, man? What do you think you're playing at, getting dressed up like a dog's dinner like that? Do you want to make yourself a laughing-stock?

M. JOURDAIN: Only the fools will laugh at me, woman.

MME JOURDAIN: Well, it isn't as if people haven't waited till now! The way you carry on has been a joke to everybody for ages.

M. JOURDAIN: Who do you mean by 'everybody', may I ask?

MME JOURDAIN: By 'everybody' I mean people who are right, people who've got more sense than you. I'm disgusted by the sort of life you lead. I've no idea what's happening in our house any more. Anybody'd think it was carnival time every day here. From first thing in the morning, as if you're afraid people might miss something, the place is full of scraping fiddles and screeching singers making enough din to rouse the whole neighbourhood.

NICOLE: The mistress is right. I can't keep the place clean because of all the rabble you bring into the house. They've got feet that go walking through every part of town looking for mud so that they can bring it in here. Poor Françoise is wearing herself out polishing the floors for your fine gentlemen to come along every day and muck them up again.

M. JOURDAIN: Now now, Nicole! For a country girl you've certainly got a tongue on you!

MME JOURDAIN: Nicole's quite right. She's got more sense than you have. I'd like to know what you think you want with a dancing master at your age.

NICOLE: Or with that great big fencing master who comes in with his clumping great boots making the house shake and loosening every tile on the floor.

M. JOURDAIN: Be quiet, both of you!

MME JOURDAIN: Are you wanting to learn dancing against the time when your legs have gone?

NICOLE: And are you wanting to run somebody through?

M. JOURDAIN: Be quiet I said. You're just ignorant, the pair of you. You don't understand the significance of these things.

MME JOURDAIN: You ought rather to be thinking of finding a husband for your daughter. She's of an age to be married.

M. JOURDAIN: I'll think of finding my daughter a husband when a suitable prospect turns up. But I also intend to give my mind to the study of fine things.

NICOLE: I also heard Madame, to cap it all, that he's gone and taken on a philosophy master today.

M. JOURDAIN: And why not? I want to improve my mind and be able to discuss things rationally with civilized people.

MME JOURDAIN: Then why not go back to school one of these days? Imagine getting the cane at your age!

M. JOURDAIN: And why not? I wish to God I could be caned this very minute, never mind who saw it, if it would help me to know the things they teach in school.

NICOLE: Yes, and a fat lot of good it would do you!

M. JOURDAIN: But it would.

MME JOURDAIN: And I suppose it would be a great help to you in running your household affairs.

M. JOURDAIN: Of course. You're both talking twaddle. I'm ashamed of your ignorance. (*To Madame Jourdain:*) For instance, do you know what it is you're talking at this very moment?

MME JOURDAIN: Yes, I know I'm talking plain common-sense. I also know that you should be thinking of mending your ways.

M. JOURDAIN: That's not what I mean. What I'm asking is what kind of words you're speaking.

MME JOURDAIN: They are very sensible words, which is more than can be said of your behaviour.

M. JOURDAIN: I'm not talking about that, I tell you. I ask you: what I'm talking to you, what I'm saying now, what is it?

MME JOURDAIN: It's rubbish!

M. JOURDAIN: Not at all. I mean what is it we're both talking, the language we're using at this minute?

MME JOURDAIN: I don't follow.

M. JOURDAIN: What's it called?

MME. JOURDAIN: Call it whatever you like.

M. JOURDAIN: It's prose, you ignoramus.

MME JOURDAIN: Prose?

M. JOURDAIN: Yes, prose. Everything that's prose isn't verse, and everything that isn't verse is prose. There! Now you see what studying does for you! (*To Nicole*:) Now you. Do you know what you have to do when you say U?

NICOLE: What?

M. JOURDAIN: That's right, what do you do when you say U?

NICOLE: How d'you mean?

M. JOURDAIN: Say U, just to see.

NICOLE: All right. U.

M. JOURDAIN: Well, what did you do?

NICOLE: I said U.

M. JOURDAIN: Yes, but when you said U, what did you do?

NICOLE: I did what you told me to.

M. JOURDAIN: Oh, what it is to have to deal with stupid people! You push your lips out and bring the upper jaw close to the lower jaw: U – see? I pull a face: U.

NICOLE: Very fine, I'm sure.

MME JOURDAIN: How wonderful.

M. JOURDAIN: It would have been even better if you'd seen O and Duh, Duh and Fuh, Fuh . . .

MME JOURDAIN: What's the meaning of all this rigmarole?

NICOLE: What good's it going to be to anybody?

M. JOURDAIN: It exasperates me to see how ignorant women can be.

MME JOURDAIN: Get away with you! You ought to send these people and their ridiculous tomfoolery packing.

NICOLE: And especially that tall streak of a fencing master who leaves everything covered with dust.

M. JOURDAIN: Not the fencing master again? You've got him on the brain! I see I'm going to have to teach you to mind your manners. (*He calls for the foils and gives one to Nicole.*) Take it. Now, demonstrative logic. The line of the body. When you lunge in quart, you do this. When you lunge in tierce, you do that. That's the way to ensure you never get killed. Isn't it grand to know the thing's in the bag when you go up against your man? Go on, have at me, just to see.

NICOLE: All right, how about this? (*She thrusts several times.*)

M. JOURDAIN: Steady on! Ow! Go easy! Confound the girl!

NICOLE: You told me to lunge.

M. JOURDAIN: Yes, but you led in tierce before you led in quart and you didn't wait for me to parry.

MME JOURDAIN: Husband, you're mad. All this nonsense has gone to your head. You've been like this ever since you started hob-nobbing with the gentry.

M. JOURDAIN: If I hob-nob with the gentry, at least I show good taste. It's better than hanging round your middle-class crowd.

MME JOURDAIN: Oh yes, to be sure. A fat lot of good hob-nobbing with the gentry will do you. You got yourself in a right old pickle with this count you're so daft about –

M. JOURDAIN: Quiet! Mind what you're saying. Do you know, my good woman, that you don't know who it is you're talking about when you're talking about him? He's a much more important person than you think – a lord, a big noise at Court. He talks to the king just like I'm talking to you now. Isn't that something to be proud of, that people should see a person of *his* quality coming round to my house so often and calling me his dear friend and treating me just like I was his equal? He's very good to me, though you wouldn't guess. I'm quite embarrassed by the kindness he shows me, and quite openly too.

MME JOURDAIN: Yes, he's very good to you and shows you such kindness – but he also borrows your money.

M. JOURDAIN: Well? Isn't it a privilege for me to lend money to a man of his standing? Can I do less for a noble who calls me his dear friend?

MME JOURDAIN: And what's this noble do for you?

M. JOURDAIN: Things that would surprise you if you only knew.

MME JOURDAIN: Such as?

M. JOURDAIN: Never you mind, I can't explain. It's enough to know that if I've lent him money, he'll pay it all back soon enough.

MME JOURDAIN: Yes, you can count on it.

M. JOURDAIN: I do. He's given me his word, hasn't he?

MME JOURDAIN: Yes, and he wont fail to break it.

M. JOURDAIN: He gave me his word as a gentleman.

MME JOURDAIN: Oh fiddlesticks!

M. JOURDAIN: Really! you are very obstinate, my dear. I tell you he'll keep his word. I'm sure of it.

MME JOURDAIN: And I'm sure he won't. All this kindness he shows you is just a way of getting round you.

M. JOURDAIN: Be quiet! Here he comes.

MME JOURDAIN: That's the last straw. He's probably come to borrow some more. I'm fed up with the sight of him.

M. JOURDAIN: Hold you tongue I tell you.

Scene iv:

DORANTE, MONSIEUR JOURDAIN, MADAME JOURDAIN, NICOLE

DORANTE: Monsieur Jourdain! My dear friend, how are you?

M. JOURDAIN: Very well sir, at your service.

DORANTE: And Madame Jourdain here, how is she?

MME JOURDAIN: Madame Jourdain is as well as can be expected.

DORANTE: I say, Monsieur Jourdain, you're looking very smart!

M. JOURDAIN: Do you think so?

DORANTE: You look very handsome in that suit. We've no young men at Court better dressed than you.

M. JOURDAIN: He! he!

MME JOURDAIN (*aside*): That's scratching him where it itches.

DORANTE: Turn round. Oh yes, very elegant!

MME JOURDAIN (*aside*): Yes, he looks as silly from the back as he does from the front.

DORANTE: Upon my faith Jourdain, I've been looking forward immensely to seeing you. There isn't a man alive for whom I have more regard. Why, only this morning I was talking about you in the Royal Presence.

M. JOURDAIN: You do me too much honour sir. (*To Madame Jourdain:*) In the Royal Presence!

DORANTE: Come, put your hat on.

M. JOURDAIN: Sir, I know my place.

DORANTE: No really, put your hat on. Please, let's have no ceremony between us.

M. JOURDAIN: Sir . . .

DORANTE: Do put on your hat Monsieur Jourdain. You're my friend.

M. JOURDAIN: Sir, I am your most humble servant.

DORANTE: I can't put my own hat on unless you put on yours.

M. JOURDAIN (*putting his hat on*): I'd rather forget my manners than cause any trouble.

DORANTE: As you are aware, I am in your debt.

MME JOURDAIN (*aside*): Aye, only too aware.

DORANTE: You have been generous enough to lend me money on several occasions, and shown yourself most obliging and gracious in so doing, of that there is no question.

M. JOURDAIN: Sir, you don't mean it!

DORANTE: But I make a point of repaying all loans and of acknowledging the kindnesses that are done to me.

M. JOURDAIN: Sir, I don't doubt it for one moment.

DORANTE: I would like to settle up with you. I came here today so that we can go over our accounts together.

M. JOURDAIN (*aside to Madame Jourdain*): Well woman? See how presumptuous you were?

DORANTE: I'm a man who likes to pay his debts as promptly as possible.

M. JOURDAIN (*aside to Madame Jourdain*): What did I tell you?

DORANTE: Let's see what I owe you.

M. JOURDAIN (*aside to Madame Jourdain*): You and your silly suspicions.

DORANTE: Can you remember exactly how much money you've lent me?

M. JOURDAIN: Yes, I think so. I've kept a note of the amounts. Here we are. The first time, I let you have two hundred louis.

DORANTE: Quite right.

M. JOURDAIN: The next time, a hundred and twenty.

DORANTE: Yes.

M. JOURDAIN: On a further occasion, a hundred and forty.

DORANTE: Correct.

M. JOURDAIN: These three items add up to four hundred and sixty louis, which makes five thousand and sixty livres.[8]

DORANTE: The amount's correct. Five thousand and sixty livres.

M. JOURDAIN: Then there was one thousand and thirty livres to the man who makes the plumes for your hats.

DORANTE: Right.

M. JOURDAIN: Two thousand seven hundred and eighty livres to your tailor.

DORANTE: True.

M. JOURDAIN: Four thousand three hundred and seventy-nine livres twelve sous and eight deniers to your haberdasher.

DORANTE: Excellent. Twelve sous and eight deniers. Absolutely right.

M. JOURDAIN: Plus one thousand seven hundred and forty-eight livres, seven sous and four deniers to your saddler.

DORANTE: That's all in order. Now, how much does that make?

M. JOURDAIN: Total – fifteen thousand eight hundred livres.

DORANTE: The total sum is correct: fifteen thousand eight hundred livres. Now add on the two hundred pistoles you're going to let me have and that will make it exactly eighteen thousand which I will repay at the earliest possible opportunity.

MME JOURDAIN (*aside to Monsieur Jourdain*): Aha! didn't I guess as much?

M. JOURDAIN (*aside to Madame Jourdain*): Be quiet!

DORANTE: Are you sure it's no trouble to let me have that amount?

M. JOURDAIN: Oh, no trouble at all.

MME JOURDAIN (*aside to Monsieur Jourdain*): That man is milking you like a cow.

M. JOURDAIN (*aside to Madame Jourdain*): Hold your tongue!

DORANTE: If it's inconvenient I can go somewhere else.

M. JOURDAIN: No no, sir.

MME JOURDAIN (*aside to Monsieur Jourdain*): He won't be satisfied until he's ruined you.

M. JOURDAIN (*aside to Madame Jourdain*): Shut up I tell you!

DORANTE: Just say if it's any trouble.

M. JOURDAIN No trouble at all sir.

MME JOURDAIN (*aside to Monsieur Jourdain*): He's a smooth talker!

M. JOURDAIN (*aside to Madame Jourdain*): Why don't you shut up!

MME JOURDAIN (*aside to Monsieur Jourdain*): He'll bleed you dry, down to your last penny.

M. JOURDAIN (*aside to Madame Jourdain*): Will you be quiet!

DORANTE: I know plenty of people who'd be only too delighted to lend me the cash. But since you are my dearest friend, I thought you would be offended if I asked somebody else.

M. JOURDAIN: I'm honoured to oblige you sir. I'll go and fetch what you want.

MME JOURDAIN (*aside to Monsieur Jourdain*): What! You're not going to let him have any more?

M. JOURDAIN (*aside to Madame Jourdain*): What else can I do? You don't want me to say no to a man of his standing who was talking about me only this morning in the Royal Presence?

MME JOURDAIN (*aside to Monsieur Jourdain*): Go on with you, you're such an easy target. (*Monsieur Jourdain leaves.*)

Scene v:

DORANTE, MADAME JOURDAIN, NICOLE

DORANTE: You look very down in the mouth Madame Jourdain. What's the matter?

MME JOURDAIN: I've got a head on my shoulders. I wasn't born yesterday.

DORANTE: And your daughter, where is she? I don't see her today.

MME JOURDAIN: My daughter's all right where she is.

DORANTE: How is she getting on?

MME JOURDAIN: On her two legs.

DORANTE: Would you care to bring her along one of these days to see the ballet and the comedy that are now being performed at Court?

MME JOURDAIN: Oh yes. We could do with a good laugh, a good laugh is exactly what we need.

DORANTE: I imagine, Madame Jourdain, you must have had many admirers in your younger days – beautiful and charming as you were then.

MME JOURDAIN: Lawks sir, is Madame Jourdain that decrepit? Has she gone all doddery already?

DORANTE: 'Pon my soul Madame Jourdain, please forgive me. I was forgetting how young you still are – I'm often very unobservant. Please excuse my rudeness.

Scene vi:
MONSIEUR JOURDAIN, MADAME JOURDAIN, DORANTE, NICOLE

M. JOURDAIN (*to Dorante*): Here we are. Two hundred louis exactly.

DORANTE: I do assure you, Monsieur Jourdain, that I am entirely at your disposal. If I can perform any service for you at Court, I should be only too pleased.

M. JOURDAIN: You are really too kind.

DORANTE: If Madame Jourdain would like to see the Royal Entertainment, I shall arrange for her to have one of the very best seats.

MME JOURDAIN: Madame Jourdain says no, thank you very much.

DORANTE (*aside to Monsieur Jourdain*): As I wrote you in my note, our fair countess will be arriving soon for the ballet and the banquet. I persuaded her in the end to say yes to the entertainment you wish to put on for her.

M. JOURDAIN (*aside to Dorante*): Let's move a little further away – you can appreciate why.

DORANTE: It's a week since I saw you, so I haven't given you any news of the diamond ring you entrusted to me to give her as a present from you. But the fact is I've had a devil of a job in overcoming her scruples and it was only today that she agreed to accept it.

M. JOURDAIN: And how did she like it?

DORANTE: She thought it was wonderful. Unless I'm very much mistaken, the beauty of the gem will work wonders for you in her way of thinking.

M. JOURDAIN: If only it would!

MME JOURDAIN (*to Nicole*): Once he's with that man, there's no getting him away.

DORANTE: I fully impressed on her the value of your gift and the depth of your love for her.

M. JOURDAIN: Sir, your kindness overwhelms me. I am embarrassed beyond words to think that a gentleman of your rank should lower himself to do what you are doing for me.

DORANTE: Don't mention it. Between friends, you don't worry about such scruples. Wouldn't you do as much for me if the occasion arose?

M. JOURDAIN: Oh, of course, and most willingly.

MME JOURDAIN (*to Nicole*): I can't stand seeing him here!

DORANTE: Personally, I never spare myself if I can be of service to a friend. When you confided to me the passion you felt for the charming countess, since I happened to know her, I offered at once to help, as you know.

M. JOURDAIN: Oh I do know and I can't thank you enough for your kindness.

MME JOURDAIN (*to Nicole*): Won't he ever go?

NICOLE (*to Madame Jourdain*): They get on like a house on fire.

DORANTE: You've gone about it the right way to win her heart. Women love nothing so much as having money spent on them. Your regular concerts, all the flowers you keep sending her, the superb firework display on the lake, the diamond ring she's got from you and the entertainment you're preparing for her now, these speak far more loudly in your favour than all the words you might have said for yourself.

M. JOURDAIN: I'd go to any expense if it would help me to find the way to her heart. To me there is something quite captivating about a lady of quality. To be honoured by her love is something I'd pay any price for.

MME JOURDAIN (*to Nicole*): What on earth can they be going on about for so long? Sneak up and have a listen.

DORANTE: You'll soon have plenty of opportunity to enjoy seeing her. You'll be able to feast your eyes on her for as long as you like.

M. JOURDAIN: So that I can be quite free I've arranged for my wife to go and have her dinner at my sister's and stay there all afternoon.

DORANTE: That was very sensible of you. Your wife might have got in our way. I've given the necessary instructions to the chef for you and I've also seen to all the arrangements for the ballet. I devised it myself and provided the performance lives up to what I had in mind, I'm sure it will be judged to be –

M. JOURDAIN (*noticing that Nicole is listening, slaps her*): Take that! The sauce! (*To Dorante:*) Let's go somewhere else, if you don't mind. (*They go out.*)

Scene vii:
MADAME JOURDAIN, NICOLE

NICOLE: Mercy Madame, that's what I get for being inquisitive! But I think there's something fishy going on. They were talking about some arrangement they don't want you to be part of.

MME JOURDAIN: This isn't the first time Nicole that I've had suspicions about my husband. Either I am very much mistaken, or he's got himself involved with a woman – and I'm going to find out who it is. But let's give some thought to my daughter. You know how much Cléonte loves her. He's a man after my own heart and I want to give him a helping hand and let him marry Lucile, if I can.

NICOLE: To tell the truth Madame, I'm really very pleased to know you feel that way. If you fancy the man for her, I fancy his manservant for myself and I'd like nothing better if we could get married at the same time as them.

MME JOURDAIN: Go and give him a message from me. Tell him he's to come and see me soon. Then we can tackle my husband together about asking for my daughter's hand.

NICOLE: I'll go this minute Madame, and very gladly. I can't imagine a pleasanter errand. (*Madame Jourdain goes out.*) I think I'm about to make a lot of people happy.

Scene viii:
CLÉONTE, COVIELLE, NICOLE

NICOLE (*to Cléonte*): Ah! there you are sir! Just at the right moment. I'm the bringer of good tidings and –

CLÉONTE: Go away, you deceitful hussy! Don't you try pulling the wool over my eyes with your lying talk!

NICOLE: Is that how you receive –

CLÉONTE: Go away, I tell you! You can go this minute and inform your faithless mistress that never again will she make a fool of the all too-trusting Cléonte!

NICOLE: Is this some sort of brainstorm? My dear Covielle, do tell me what's going on!

COVIELLE: Don't you 'dear Covielle' me, you little minx! Quick, get out of my sight you jade, and leave me alone.

NICOLE: What! You too . . .

COVIELLE: Out of my sight, I tell you! Never speak to me again!

NICOLE (*aside*): Heavens! What's bitten the pair of them? I'd better go and tell the mistress about this fine old mess. (*She goes out.*)

Scene ix:
CLÉONTE, COVIELLE

CLÉONTE: What a way to treat a man who's in love with you, the most faithful, the most passionate lover that ever breathed!

COVIELLE: It's appalling the way they've treated both of us.

CLÉONTE: I show a woman all the love and tenderness imaginable. She's the only thing in the world I love. I haven't a thought for anyone else. She is all I care about, all I want, all my delight. She's all I talk about, she fills my dreams, I only live for her, my heart beats only for her – and is this a proper reward for all my devotion? I don't see her for two days, two hideous days that seem like centuries. I meet her by accident. When I see her, my heart leaps up, I have happiness written all over my face. I run madly to her – and the faithless creature turns her face away and passes me by as if she'd never seen me before in this life!

COVIELLE: That all goes for me too.

CLÉONTE: Did you ever see, Covielle, the like of that faithless, unfeeling Lucile?

COVIELLE: Or you, sir, of Nicole, the baggage?

CLÉONTE: After all the burning sacrifices, sighs and vows I've offered to her beauty!

COVIELLE: After all the constant devotion, services and helping hands I've lavished on her in her kitchen!

CLÉONTE: After all the tears I've shed at her feet!

COVIELLE: After all the buckets of water I've drawn from the well for her!

CLÉONTE: After all the fervour I've shown, which made it obvious that I love her more than myself!

COVIELLE: After all the heat I've had to stand, turning the spit for her!

CLÉONTE: And now she walks past me in disdain!

COVIELLE: And now she brazenly turns her back on me!

CLÉONTE: It's a betrayal for which no punishment is good enough.

COVIELLE: It's treachery, and deserves a damn good hiding.

CLÉONTE: I advise you never to speak to me in her defence.

COVIELLE: Me sir? Heaven forbid!

CLÉONTE: Don't come to me and try to excuse her faithlessness.

COVIELLE: No fear!

CLÉONTE: Oh no! Nothing you can say in her defence will do any good.

COVIELLE: I wouldn't dream of trying.

CLÉONTE: I shall never cease to hate her and I'll have nothing more to do with her.

COVIELLE: I'm all for it.

CLÉONTE: Perhaps that count who comes calling at the house has taken her fancy. It's obvious to me she's let herself be dazzled by his rank. To protect my honour, I've got to prevent her unfaithfulness becoming public knowledge. I can see she's moving in the right direction and I intend to precede her down that self-same road step by step. I shall not give her the satisfaction of jilting me first.

COVIELLE: Well said. I'm with you all the way.

CLÉONTE: Hold me to my resentment. Back me in my determination to resist any lingering traces of love which might speak in her favour. I want you to tell me all the horrible things you can about her. Describe her in terms that will make me despise her. Point out all the faults you see in her so that I end up being sick of her.

COVIELLE: Of her sir? What did you want to go falling so madly in love with her for? She's a conceited little madam and a terrible tease. I look at her and don't see anything special. You could find any number of girls who'd be worthier of you. In the first place, her eyes are too small.

CLÉONTE: Yes. They are small – but as full of fire, as sparkling, as bright, as tender as you could possibly hope to see.

COVIELLE: She's got a large mouth.

CLÉONTE: True, but it has an attractiveness you don't find in ordinary mouths. Her mouth, when you see it, is so tempting. It's the most enticing mouth – just made for kissing.

COVIELLE: As far as her figure goes, she's not very tall.

CLÉONTE: No, but how slender and well-shaped.

COVIELLE: She's got a casual, affected manner in everything she says and does.

CLÉONTE: So she has, yet she carries it off very gracefully and the way she manages it is very engaging and has a certain charm that is quite irresistible.

COVIELLE: As for brains . . .

CLÉONTE: Oh come, Covielle! She's got a fine mind, so quick and subtle . . .

COVIELLE: Her conversation . . .

CLÉONTE: Her conversation is delightful.

COVIELLE: She's always serious.

CLÉONTE: Would you rather have a lot of loud, silly laughing and everlasting high spirits? Don't you find there's nothing more tiresome than women who giggle all the time?

COVIELLE: But, she's the most capricious woman alive.

CLÉONTE: Yes, she is capricious I agree. But a beautiful woman can get away with anything. We put up with anything from beautiful women.

COVIELLE: Well, if that's the way of it, I can see you are determined to love her for ever.

CLÉONTE: Me? I'd sooner die first! I intend to hate her as much as I used to love her.

COVIELLE: But how are you going to do that if you find her so perfect?

CLÉONTE: That's exactly where my revenge will be spectacular, that's how I'll show her clearly what stuff my heart is made of – by hating her and walking out on her, however beautiful and attractive and lovable I might find her. Here she is.

Scene x:

CLÉONTE, LUCILE, COVIELLE, NICOLE

NICOLE (*to Lucile*): Really shocking, I call it.

LUCILE: The only explanation, Nicole, is what I was telling you. But there he is.

CLÉONTE (*to Covielle*): I won't even speak to her.

COVIELLE: Neither will I.

LUCILE: What is it Cléonte? What's the matter?

NICOLE: What's got into you Covielle?

LUCILE: Is there something worrying you?

NICOLE: Did you get out of bed on the wrong side this morning?

LUCILE: Can't you speak Cléonte?

NICOLE: Cat got your tongue Covielle?

CLÉONTE (*to Covielle*): It's shameful!

COVIELLE (*to Cléonte*): Oh, the two-faced . . .

LUCILE: I can see our meeting just now has upset you.

CLÉONTE (*to Covielle*): Aha! She knows what she's done.

NICOLE: The way we walked straight past you this morning has got your goat, has it?

COVIELLE (*to Cléonte*): They've guessed where the shoe pinches.

LUCILE: Isn't that it Cléonte? Is that why you're cross?

CLÉONTE: Yes you faithless creature, since I have to speak out. Let me tell you that you shan't have the last laugh by being unfaithful to me, as you expect, because I intend to break it off first and you shan't have the satisfaction of jilting me. No doubt I shall find it hard to forget what I feel for you. I shall grieve, I shall suffer for a while. But I'll get over it in the end and I'd rather kill myself than be so weak as to return to you.

COVIELLE: Ditto for me.

LUCILE: This is a lot of fuss about nothing Cléonte. I want to tell you why I avoided you this morning.

CLÉONTE (*makes as if to go, to avoid her*): No, I won't listen.

NICOLE (*to Covielle*): I want to tell you why we were in such a hurry.

COVIELLE (*also turning to leave and avoid Nicole*): No, I won't hear a word.

LUCILE (*going after Cléonte*): When we met you this morning –

CLÉONTE (*walks on, refusing to look at Lucile*): No, I say!

NICOLE (*going after Covielle*): Let me tell you —

COVIELLE (*also walks on, refusing to look at Nicole*): No, you Jezebel!

LUCILE: Listen —

CLÉONTE: Shan't

NICOLE: Just let me say —

COVIELLE: Can't hear.

LUCILE: Cléonte!

CLÉONTE: No!

NICOLE: Covielle!

COVIELLE: Never!

LUCILE: Stop!

CLÉONTE: Fiddlesticks!

NICOLE: Listen to me —

COVIELLE: Rubbish!

LUCILE: Just a moment —

CLÉONTE: Not an instant!

NICOLE: Just be patient a minute.

COVIELLE: Not likely!

LUCILE: Just one word —

CLÉONTE: No, it's all over.

NICOLE: A word in your ear —

COVIELLE: We're finished.

LUCILE (*stopping*): Very well then, since you won't listen, you can think what you like and do as you please.

NICOLE (*also stopping*): Since that's how you want to act, take it any way you like.

CLÉONTE (*turning to Lucile*): All right then, we might as well know why you were so very, very glad to see me.

LUCILE (*it's her turn to walk away and avoid Cléonte*): I don't feel like telling you now.

COVIELLE (*turning to Nicole*): Go on then, tell us what happened.

NICOLE (*walking away to avoid Covielle*): I don't want to any more.

CLÉONTE (*following Lucile*): Won't you say —

LUCILE (*walks on, refusing to look at Cléonte*): No, I'm not saying anything.

COVIELLE (*following Nicole*): Tell me —

NICOLE (*walks on, refusing to look at Covielle*): No, I'm not telling you anything.

CLÉONTE: Please . . .

LUCILE: No I say.

COVIELLE: Have a heart!

NICOLE: Nothing doing.

CLÉONTE: I implore you . . .

LUCILE: Leave me alone.

COVIELLE: I'm begging you.

NICOLE: Get out of it!

CLÉONTE: Lucile!

LUCILE: No.

COVIELLE: Nicole!

NICOLE: Never!

CLÉONTE: For heaven's sake!

LUCILE: Don't want to.

COVIELLE: Speak to me!

NICOLE: I won't.

CLÉONTE: Clear up my doubts!

LUCILE: I'll do no such thing.

COVIELLE: Put my mind at rest!

NICOLE: Don't feel like it.

CLÉONTE: Very well then, since you care so little about putting me out of my misery or about justifying the heartless way you've trampled my feelings underfoot, you see me now, you ungrateful girl, for the last time! I'm going far away from you, to die of grief and love.

COVIELLE (*to Nicole*): And I'll be right behind him.

LUCILE (*to Cléonte who turns to leave*): Cléonte!

NICOLE (*to Covielle who turns to leave*): Covielle!

CLÉONTE (*stopping*): What?

COVIELLE (*stopping*): Did you say something?

LUCILE: Where are you going?

CLÉONTE: Where I told you.

COVIELLE: We're going away to die.

LUCILE: Are you really going to die Cléonte?

CLÉONTE: Yes, cruel beauty, since that is what you want.

LUCILE: Me? Want you to die?

CLÉONTE: Yes, that's what you want.

LUCILE: Who said so?

CLÉONTE (*turns to her*): It must be what you want if you refuse to clear up my suspicions.

LUCILE: Is that my fault? If you'd only been willing to listen, I'd have told you that this little episode you're making so much of only came about because an old aunt of mine was with us this morning. She's utterly convinced that a young girl is dishonoured if a man comes anywhere near her. She's always lecturing us on the subject and makes out that men are all devils to be avoided like the plague.

NICOLE: And that's all there is to it.

CLÉONTE: You're not deceiving me, Lucile?

COVIELLE: You're not leading me up the garden path?

LUCILE: It's the truth, the whole truth.

NICOLE: And nothing but the truth.

COVIELLE (*to Cléonte*): Is this where we surrender?

CLÉONTE: Oh Lucile! how many fears that trouble my heart you allay with one single word from your lips! How easily we let ourselves be convinced by the persons we love!

COVIELLE: How easily we let ourselves by led by the nose by them, confounded creatures!

Scene xi:
MADAME JOURDAIN, CLÉONTE, LUCILE,
COVIELLE, NICOLE

MME JOURDAIN: I'm delighted to see you Cléonte. You've come just at the right moment. My husband's on his way out, so grab the chance now to ask him to let you marry Lucile.

CLÉONTE: Oh Madame! how sweet your words are! How they encourage my desires! I could not receive a more delightful command nor value a favour more highly.

Scene xii:

MONSIEUR JOURDAIN, MADAME JOURDAIN,
CLÉONTE, LUCILE, COVIELLE, NICOLE

CLÉONTE: Sir, I did not wish to go through a third person to put to you a request I have been considering for some time. It is a matter so close to my heart that I have chosen to undertake it myself. So, without further preamble, I shall tell you that the honour of being your son-in-law would be a signal favour which I hereby ask you to grant me.

M. JOURDAIN: Before I give you my answer sir, I ask you to tell me if you are of noble birth.

CLÉONTE: Sir, most men do not hesitate long in answering that question. It is a matter that's very easily settled. People have no scruples about applying the word 'gentleman' to themselves and common usage today appears to sanction the appropriation. Myself, I will confess, I have rather more delicate sentiments on the subject. I take the view that any form of deception is unworthy of a man of honour and that it is an act of cowardice to conceal the estate to which it has pleased heaven to call us, to appear in the eyes of the world decked out in a borrowed title and pretend to be what we are not. I was born, to be sure, of a family which has held distinguished public office. I have had the honour of six years' army service and am the possessor of wealth sufficient to keep up a very fair position in society. Yet notwithstanding all that, I have no wish to give myself a title which others in my place might feel able to assume. I therefore tell you frankly that I am not nobly born.

M. JOURDAIN: Let's shake on it sir. My daughter's not for you.

CLÉONTE: What?

M. JOURDAIN: You're not a gentleman, so you can't have my daughter.

MME JOURDAIN: What do you mean with all this gentleman business? Do you reckon we're descended from the rib of Saint Louis?[9]

M. JOURDAIN: Hold your tongue woman. I can see what you're after.

MME JOURDAIN: What are we, either of us, but good, plain commoners?

M. JOURDAIN: That's slanderous!

MME JOURDAIN: Wasn't your father in business, same as mine?

M. JOURDAIN: Confound the woman! She's always bringing this up. If your father was in trade, that's his bad luck, but as for mine, it's only ignoramuses that say so. All I've got to say to you is that I insist on having a gentleman for a son-in-law.

MME JOURDAIN: What your daughter needs is a husband who suits her. She'll be much better off with a decent man who's good-looking and comfortably off than with some broken-down aristocrat without a penny to his name.

NICOLE: The mistress is right. In our village, the son of the hall is the biggest lout and the stupidest ninny I ever set eyes on.

M. JOURDAIN: Be quiet! you impudent prattlebox! You're always sticking your oar into the conversation. I've got more than enough money for my daughter. What I need is honour. I intend to make her a marquise.

MME JOURDAIN: A marquise!

M. JOURDAIN: Yes, a marquise.

MME JOURDAIN: Oh, God forbid!

M. JOURDAIN: It's something I've made my mind up about.

MME JOURDAIN: So have I, and it's something I'll never agree to. Marrying above your station is liable to end in tears. I don't want a son-in-law who'll look down on my daughter on account of her family, and I don't want my daughter to have children who'll be ashamed to call me their granny either. If it turned out she had to come and visit me in a grand carriage and was careless enough to forget to speak to one or other of the neighbours, people would be sure to say all sorts of nasty things. 'See her over there?' they'd say, 'that marquise, all hoity-toity? That's old Monsieur Jourdain's girl. She was happy enough to play being ladies with us when she was little. She's gone up in the world since then. Both her grandfathers sold cloth just by the gates of the Holy Innocents.[10] They made a pile and left it to their children and they must be paying pretty dear for it in the next world: you don't get to be that rich by being honest.' Well, I don't want that sort of talk going on. What I do want is a man who'll be grateful to me for my daughter, so I can say to him: 'Sit yourself down there, lad, and have your dinner with us.'

M. JOURDAIN: Those are sentiments that show what a small mind you have – not wanting to better yourself. Now, no more arguing. My daughter will be a marquise even if the whole world turns against me. And if you make me angry, I'll make her a duchess! (*He goes out.*)

Scene xiii:

MADAME JOURDAIN, CLÉONTE, LUCILE, NICOLE, COVIELLE

MME JOURDAIN: Cléonte, don't lose heart yet. Come with me, Lucile, and tell your father in no uncertain terms that if you can't have him, you won't marry anybody. (*They go out.*)

Scene xiv:

CLÉONTE, COVIELLE

COVIELLE: A fine mess you've got us into with all your noble sentiments.

CLÉONTE: What else could I do? To me it's a matter of principle that can't be overcome by the example other people set.

COVIELLE: You must be joking. How can you take a man like that seriously? Can't you see he's off his head? What would it have cost you to go along with his fancy notions?

CLÉONTE: You're right. But I never thought I'd have to furnish proofs of nobility to become Monsieur Jourdain's son-in-law.

COVIELLE: Ha ha ha!

CLÉONTE: What are you laughing at?

COVIELLE: Just an idea that's come to me. A way we could take the old boy in and get what you want.

CLÉONTE: How?

COVIELLE: It's a rather funny idea.

CLÉONTE: What is?

COVIELLE: There was this comic play recently that would fit the bill perfectly. I could work it up into a practical joke to play on the old fool. The whole thing's a bit of a farce, but with him we can try just about anything, so no need to be too fussy. He'd be perfect in the part. He'd swallow whatever we choose to tell him. I can get the actors, I've got the costumes all ready. Just let me look after it.

CLÉONTE: But tell me what —

COVIELLE: All in good time. Let's be off. He's coming back. (*They go out.*)

Scene xv:
MONSIEUR JOURDAIN

M. JOURDAIN: I can't see what the devil the fuss is about. The only thing they've got against me is that I hob-nob with the quality. But to me there's nothing to compare with hob-nobbing with the great and the good. It's only with them that you get honourable, civilized behaviour. I'd have given my right hand to have been born a count or a marquis.

Scene xvi:
MONSIEUR JOURDAIN, *a footman*

FOOTMAN: Sir, the count is here, and he's got a lady on his arm.

M. JOURDAIN: Oh my God! I've some instructions I must go and give. Tell them I'll be here right away.

Scene xvii:
DORIMÈNE, DORANTE, *a footman*

FOOTMAN: The master says he'll be with you in just a minute.

DORANTE: Very well. (*Exit Footman.*)

Scene xviii:

DORIMÈNE, DORANTE

DORIMÈNE: I don't know Dorante. At this moment I again have the feeling I'm doing something strange, letting you bring me into a house where I don't know anyone.

DORANTE: But where then, Madame, do you want me to entertain you since, to avoid gossip, you rule out both your own house and mine?

DORIMÈNE: But you ignore the fact that with each day that passes I'm gradually becoming more and more committed to receiving these extravagant tokens of your affection. Saying no to you doesn't do any good, you wear down my resistance and behave with such polite insistence that I am gently persuaded to do whatever you want. Your frequent visits started it. Then came the declarations of love which brought in their wake the concerts and the entertainments, and finally there were the presents. I set my face against it all, but you don't take no for an answer, and one by one you undermine all my good resolutions. I really don't know where I stand and I do believe that in the end you'll talk me into marriage, despite my distaste for it.

DORANTE: Upon my word Madame, married is exactly what you should already be. You are a widow and your own mistress. I am my own master and love you more than life itself. What's to prevent your making me happy this very day?

DORIMÈNE: Heavens Dorante! Many good qualities are needed, on both sides, if two people are to live happily together. Even the most reasonable couple often find it hard to form a union that fully satisfies them.

DORANTE: You are absurd, Madame, to imagine all these difficulties. Your experience of one marriage proves nothing about all the others.

DORIMÈNE: That's as may be, but I still return to my point. All this expense I see you incurring for me causes me concerns for two reasons: firstly, it commits me further than I wish, and secondly I am sure, if you will forgive me for saying so, that you are spending more than you can afford – and I don't want that.

DORANTE: But Madame, these things are trifles and that's not how –

DORIMÈNE: No, I know what I'm saying. For instance, the diamond you forced me to accept is so valuable that –

DORANTE: Oh Madame, please. You mustn't exaggerate the value of a bauble which I consider quite unworthy of you. Allow me to . . . ah, here comes the master of the house.

Scene xix:
MONSIEUR JOURDAIN, DORIMÈNE, DORANTE

M. JOURDAIN (*after bowing twice and finding himself too close to Dorimène*): Stand back a little, Madame.

DORIMÈNE: What on earth . . .

M. JOURDAIN: Just one step back please.

DORIMÈNE: What for?

M. JOURDAIN: Go back a bit, for the third one.

DORANTE: Madame, Monsieur Jourdain knows his etiquette.

M. JOURDAIN: Madame, it is for me a great honour to have the good fortune to be so happy as to have the happiness to know you have deigned to condescend to grant me the kindness of doing me the honour of honouring me with the favour of your presence. And if I had the merit of meriting merit such as yours, and if heaven . . . envious of my bliss . . . had granted me . . . er . . . the privilege of finding myself worthy . . . er . . .

DORANTE: That'll do, Monsieur Jourdain. Madame does not much care for formal compliments. She is quite aware that you are a man of the world. (*Aside to Dorimène:*) He's a decent enough man of business but, as you see, quite bizarre in the way he behaves.

DORIMÈNE (*aside to Dorante*): It's not difficult to see that!

DORANTE: Madame, Monsieur Jourdain is a very dear friend . . .

M. JOURDAIN: You do me too much honour.

DORANTE: A complete gentleman.

DORIMÈNE: I have formed an excellent opinion of him.

M. JOURDAIN: I haven't done anything yet, Madame, to deserve such kindness.

DORANTE (*aside to Monsieur Jourdain*): Whatever you do, take care not to mention the diamond you gave her.

M. JOURDAIN (*aside to Dorante*): Can't I even ask how she likes it?

DORANTE (*aside to Monsieur Jourdain*): Not on any account. It would be terribly vulgar. If you wish to behave like a gentleman, you must act as though it wasn't you who gave it to her as a present. (*To Dorimène*:) Madame, Monsieur Jourdain was just saying how delighted he is to see you in his house.

DORIMÈNE: I am greatly honoured.

M. JOURDAIN (*aside to Dorante*): I'm most grateful to you, sir, for putting in a word for me.

DORANTE (*aside to Monsieur Jourdain*): I had the devil's own job of it getting her to come.

M. JOURDAIN (*aside to Dorante*): I don't know how to thank you.

DORANTE: He is just saying, Madame, how utterly charming he finds you.

DORIMÈNE: That's extremely kind of him.

M. JOURDAIN: Ah Madame, it is you who are kind and . . . (*A footman comes in.*)

DORANTE: Let's think about supper.

Scene xx:

MONSIEUR JOURDAIN, DORIMÈNE, DORANTE, *a footman*

FOOTMAN (*to Monsieur Jourdain*): Everything is ready sir.

DORANTE: Then let's all sit down. Send in the musicians.

> *Six cooks who prepared the banquet dance together:*
> *this forms the Third Interlude. Then they bring in a*
> *table laden with various dishes.*

Act IV

Scene i:

DORANTE, DORIMÈNE, MONSIEUR JOURDAIN, *two male singers, a woman singer, footmen*

DORIMÈNE: Why Dorante, this is a magnificent banquet!

M. JOURDAIN: It's nothing of the sort Madame. I only wish it was more worthy of being offered to you. (*They all sit at the table.*)

DORANTE: Madame, Monsieur Jourdain is absolutely right in what he says. I am greatly indebted to him for receiving you so hospitably in his house, but I agree with him that the banquet is not worthy of you. I made the arrangements myself, but I do not have the flair of some of our friends in these matters. Consequently, what you have here is a repast which might be found wanting by exact critical standards. You may detect in it gastronomic incongruities, certain solecisms of taste. If an arbiter of taste like Damis had taken a hand in it, everything would have been according to the rules, all elegance and classic formalism. He would not have omitted to commend each dish of the meal he served you or left you with any choice but to applaud his superior gifts for the science of cookery. He would have held forth about his bread, baked in the bottom of the oven, golden brown, with an even crust all over, and delicately crumbly in the mouth; the wine, aromatic, silky, with a hint of youthful vigour which never becomes overpowering; a saddle of mutton garnished with parsley; a loin of Normandy veal, as long as my arm, white, tender, that melts like almond paste on the tongue; partridges cooked to preserve all the amazing flavour; and his crowning masterpiece, a plump young turkey flanked by pigeons and topped with white onions blended with endive, all swimming in a pearly broth. As far as I'm concerned, I must own up to complete ignorance and, as Monsieur Jourdain has put it so well, I only wish that the repast were more worthy of you.

DORIMÈNE: My reply to such a compliment is to eat as heartily as you see I am doing.

M. JOURDAIN: Ah! Such lovely hands!

DORIMÈNE: The hands are so-so Monsieur Jourdain, but I think you are referring to the diamond, which is magnificent.

M. JOURDAIN: I, Madame? Heaven forbid I should mention it. To do so would be very ungentlemanly – the gem is a trifling thing.

DORIMÈNE: You have very high standards.

M. JOURDAIN: You are too kind . . .

DORANTE (*with a warning gesture to Monsieur Jourdain*): Come, some wine for Monsieur Jourdain and for these gentlemen here who are about to give us the pleasure of singing a drinking song.

DORIMÈNE: There's no better seasoning for good food than music. Really, I'm being most admirably entertained.

M. JOURDAIN: Madame, it isn't —

DORANTE: Monsieur Jourdain, let's give silence for these gentlemen. What they will say in song will be much more entertaining than anything we could say ourselves. (*The singers, each taking a glass, sing two drinking songs, accompanied by full orchestra.*)

First drinking song

(*The two male singers together, glass in hand:*)

A health to you, Phyllis — thus we begin our round.
In a glass and your eyes our best pleasures are found:
You and wine, wine and you, combine in disarming
Our care — and we ne'er
Find you other than charming!
So we swear, yes we swear,
To love and to wine, ever faithful we'll be,
Ever faithful to wine, ever constant to thee!

Touch the glass with your lips and give wine a new relish,
The wine in its turn doth those bright eyes embellish.
You and wine, wine and you, together combining,
For a lass and a glass set us ever repining.
So let's clink, as we drink,
To love and to wine, ever faithful we'll be,
Ever faithful to wine, ever constant to thee!

Second drinking song

(*Second male singer and woman singer together:*)

Drink, let us drink, for time is fast fleeting!
Drink while we may, for brief is our meeting.
We must not be dull
But live to the full!
For time passes on and soon we are gone
And then there's no wine, no love and no song.
So drink up my friends
Before it all ends.

> Let's leave it to fools to think and surmise
> As they ponder upon where happiness lies.
> To find where it is, we drinkers needn't think hard:
> We drink and we drink — lo it's there in the tankard.
> Of wealth, wit and fame the world should beware,
> For none of these helps to chase away care.
> Only through wine as heady as this
> Can we boozers and tipplers ever find bliss!

(*The three singers together.*)

> So send the cup round, lads, in every glass pour
> As long as there's someone still asking for more.

DORIMÈNE: I don't think that could have been better sung. It was quite lovely.

M. JOURDAIN: But I spy with my little eye something, Madame, that's even lovelier.

DORIMÈNE: Oho, Monsieur Jourdain is more gallant than I thought.

DORANTE: Why, Madame, who do you take Monsieur Jourdain for?

M. JOURDAIN: I could tell you whom I'd like her to take me for.

DORIMÈNE: He's at it again!

DORANTE (*to Dorimène*): You don't know him.

M. JOURDAIN: She can get to know me better whenever she likes.

DORIMÈNE: Oh, I give up.

DORANTE: He's a gentleman who always has an answer ready. Haven't you noticed Madame how Monsieur Jourdain takes from the dish all the titbits your fork has touched?

DORIMÈNE: Monsieur Jourdain is a very delightful man.

M. JOURDAIN: If I could delight your heart, I . . .

Scene ii:

MADAME JOURDAIN, MONSIEUR JOURDAIN,
DORIMÈNE, DORANTE, *singers, footmen*

MME JOURDAIN: Aha! Here's a pretty gathering, I must say. I can see I was not expected. So, dear husband, it was for these shenanigans that you were so anxious to pack me off to have dinner at my sister-in-law's? I've just seen a stage downstairs and here I find a banquet that looks like a wedding breakfast. So this is how you spend your money, is it? Laying on a spread for your lady friends when my back's turned, putting on music and plays for them while I get sent away to amuse myself elsewhere!

DORANTE: What on earth are you talking about Madame Jourdain? Where did you get such fanciful notions, getting it into your head that your husband has been spending his own money and that he's the one footing the bill for this party? Allow me to inform you that I am entertaining the lady. All Monsieur Jourdain has done is to permit me the use of his house. You should be more careful what you say.

M. JOURDAIN: Quite right! The impertinence! His Lordship's the one who's providing all this for her Ladyship who is a person of quality. He has done me the honour of using my house and of inviting me to join him.

MME JOURDAIN: Fiddlesticks! I wasn't born yesterday!

DORANTE: Madame Jourdain, you're not wearing your spectacles.

MME JOURDAIN: I don't need spectacles sir. I can see perfectly well without them. I've known for ages that there was something going on. I'm not a fool. It is very wicked of you, a great lord, to encourage my husband's follies the way you do. And as for a grand lady like you, Madame, it's neither admirable nor decent to be causing trouble in a family and letting my husband think he's in love with you.

DORIMÈNE: Whatever is she talking about? Come Dorante, what were you thinking of, exposing me like this to the stupid suspicions of this raving madwoman!

DORANTE (*following Dorimène who turns to leave*): Madame, one moment . . . Madame, where are you going in such a hurry?

M. JOURDAIN: Madame! My Lord, give her my apologies and try to get her to come back! (*Dorante goes out.*)

Scene iii:
MADAME JOURDAIN, MONSIEUR JOURDAIN,
a footman

M. JOURDAIN: Oh you and your confounded meddling. Now see what you've done? You come here and insult me to my face in front of everybody, and you drive persons of quality out of the house!

MME JOURDAIN: I couldn't care less about their quality!

M. JOURDAIN: Damn you, I don't know what's keeping me from braining you with the crockery from the banquet you've ruined! (*Footmen remove the table.*)

MME JOURDAIN (*going*): Do whatever you want. I'm standing up for my rights and I'll have every wife behind me.

M. JOURDAIN: You would do well to stay out my way when I'm angry!

Scene iv:
MONSIEUR JOURDAIN

M. JOURDAIN: She couldn't have come at a worse time. I was in the mood for saying all sorts of witty things. I never felt wittier in all my life. But what's all this?

Scene v:
COVIELLE *in disguise*, MONSIEUR JOURDAIN, *footman*

COVIELLE: Sir, I don't think I have the honour of being known to you.

M. JOURDAIN: No sir.

COVIELLE: I haven't seen you since you were that high. (*He holds his hand a foot from the ground.*)

M. JOURDAIN: Me?

COVIELLE: Yes. You were the prettiest little boy that ever was. The ladies were forever picking you up and cuddling you.

M. JOURDAIN: Cuddling me?

COVIELLE: Yes. I was a close friend of your late father.

M. JOURDAIN: My late father?

COVIELLE: Yes, a most worthy gentleman.

M. JOURDAIN: What did you say?

COVIELLE: I said he was a most worthy gentleman.

M. JOURDAIN: My father?

COVIELLE: That's right.

M. JOURDAIN: You knew him well?

COVIELLE: I certainly did.

M. JOURDAIN: And you knew him to be a gentleman?

COVIELLE: Of course.

M. JOURDAIN: In that case, I don't understand what sort of world we live in.

COVIELLE: What do you mean?

M. JOURDAIN: There are some stupid people about who will have it that he was in trade.

COVIELLE: Him! In trade? That's pure slander. He never was! All he ever did was to be very obliging and helpful, and since he knew all about cloth, he'd go all over the place choosing samples, have them brought to his house and then give them away to his friends – for a consideration.

M. JOURDAIN: I'm delighted to make your acquaintance and have your testimony that my father was a gentleman.

COVIELLE: I'd testify to that to anybody.

M. JOURDAIN: I'd be eternally grateful. But what brings you here?

COVIELLE: Since the days when I used to know your father, who was an estimable gentleman, as I was saying, I have travelled the globe.

M. JOURDAIN: The globe!

COVIELLE: Yes.

M. JOURDAIN: I reckon that must be a fair way.

COVIELLE: That it is. I only got back from my travels four days ago and on account of the interest I take in everything that concerns you, I've come to give you the most exciting news.

M. JOURDAIN: News?

COVIELLE: Did you know that the son of the Grand Turk is here?

M. JOURDAIN: Me? No.

COVIELLE: Really? He's come with a magnificent retinue. Everybody's going along to a look at him. He's been given the sort of welcome that only the highest ranking lord usually gets.

M. JOURDAIN: Bless me! I didn't know.

COVIELLE: Now where you stand to gain in all this is that he's fallen in love with your daughter.

M. JOURDAIN: The son of the Grand Turk?

COVIELLE: Yes, and he won't be happy until he's your son-in-law.

M. JOURDAIN: My son-in-law, the son of the Grand Turk?

COVIELLE: The son of the Grand Turk, your son-in-law. I've been to see him and, since I speak his language fluently, we had quite a chat.

After discussing one or two other matters, he said to me: 'Acciam croc soler ouch alla moustaph gidelum amanahem varahini oussere carbulath.' That means, 'Have you come across a beautiful young lady, the daughter of Monsieur Jourdain, a gentleman of Paris?'

M. JOURDAIN: The son of the Grand Turk said that about me?

COVIELLE: Yes. And when I replied that I knew you personally and had met your daughter, he said: 'Ah! Marababa sahem', meaning: 'Oh! how I love her!'

M. JOURDAIN: 'Marababa sahem' means 'Oh! how I love her!'?

COVIELLE: That's right.

M. JOURDAIN: Good Lord, I'm glad you told me. Personally, I'd never have thought that 'marababa sahem' meant 'Oh! how I love her!'. What a marvellous language Turkish is!

COVIELLE: More marvellous than you'd think. Do you know what 'Cacaracamouchen' means?

M. JOURDAIN: 'Cacaracamouchen'? Not a clue.

COVIELLE: It means: 'My darling'.

M. JOURDAIN: 'Cacaracamouchen' means 'My darling'?

COVIELLE: Yes.

M. JOURDAIN: That's wonderful! 'Cacaracamouchen', 'My darling'! Who'd have thought it! It beats me.

COVIELLE: But to conclude my mission. He's on his way here to ask for your daughter's hand. And so that he has a father-in-law who's worthy of him, he wishes to make you a 'Mamamouchi', a title of high dignity in his country.

M. JOURDAIN: A Mamamouchi?

COVIELLE: Yes, a Mamamouchi, that is, in our language, a Paladin.[11] Paladins in ancient times were . . . er . . . Paladins. There's no higher rank anywhere in the world. You'll be on an equal footing with the noblest lords on earth.

M. JOURDAIN: The son of the Grand Turk does me a very great honour. Please take me to him so that I can thank him.

COVIELLE: But I told you – he's coming here.

M. JOURDAIN: Coming here?

COVIELLE: Yes, and he's bringing everything that's needed for the ceremony at which your new dignity is to be conferred on you.

M. JOURDAIN: It's all very sudden.

COVIELLE: His love won't wait.

M. JOURDAIN: The only thing that worries me is that my daughter is very stubborn. She's set her mind on somebody called Cléonte and swears she's won't marry anyone else.

COVIELLE: Oh, she'll have a change of heart when she sees the son of the Grand Turk. Anyway, by a very remarkable coincidence, the son of the Grand Turk is the spitting image of Cléonte, or near enough. I've just seen this Cléonte. He was pointed out to me. And the feelings she has for the one can easily be transferred to the other . . . But I can hear him coming. Yes, here he is.

Scene vi:
CLÉONTE *dressed as a Turk,* MONSIEUR JOURDAIN,
COVIELLE

CLÉONTE: Ambousahim oqui boraf, Jordina, salamelequi.

COVIELLE (*to Monsieur Jourdain*): Which is, interpreted: 'Monsieur Jourdain, may your heart be like a rose bush in bloom from one year's end to the other.' This is a customary courteous greeting in his country.

M. JOURDAIN: I am his Turkish Highness's most humble servant.

COVIELLE: Carigar comboto oustin moraf.

CLÉONTE: Oustin yoc catamalequi basum base alla moran.

COVIELLE: He says: 'May God give you the strength of the lion and the wisdom of the serpent.'

M. JOURDAIN: His Turkish Highness is too kind. Say I wish him every prosperity.

COVIELLE: Ossa binamen sadoc babally oracaf ouram.

CLÉONTE: Bel-men.

COVIELLE: He says you must go with him at once to prepare for the ceremony, so that he may then meet your daughter and conclude the marriage.

M. JOURDAIN: He said all that with two words?

COVIELLE: Yes. The Turkish language is like that. You can say a great deal in a few words. Now be quick, go where he wants you.

Scene vii:
COVIELLE

COVIELLE: Ha ha ha! My goodness, it's a hoot! What an idiot! He couldn't play the part better if he'd learned it by heart. Ha ha ha!

Scene viii:
DORANTE, COVIELLE

COVIELLE: Ah, sir! Would you lend a hand with a performance we're arranging here?

DORANTE: Why, Covielle! I'd never have recognized you. What sort of outfit is that you've got on?

COVIELLE: Take a look. Ha ha ha!

DORANTE: What are you laughing at?

COVIELLE: At something that deserves a good laugh sir.

DORANTE: What d'you mean?

COVIELLE: You'd never guess, sir, what joke we're playing on Monsieur Jourdain. It's intended to persuade him to agree to let his daughter marry my master.

DORANTE: I can't guess what the joke is, but I can guess it'll work out well if you've got a hand in it.

COVIELLE: I see you know me sir.

DORANTE: Put me in the picture.

COVIELLE: If you'd be good enough to step to one side and make room for what I see is about to come in. You can watch part of the plot unfolding while I tell you the rest.

The Turkish ceremony to ennoble Monsieur Jourdain is performed in music and dance and forms the Fourth Interlude

The Turkish Ceremony
MUFTI, TURKS, DERVISHES *who sing and dance,*
MONSIEUR JOURDAIN *in Turkish dress, but without
wig, turban or scimitar*

The FIRST BALLET is now danced

*Six Turks enter solemnly, two by two, while the orchestra plays. They
carry three carpets which they raise above their heads after dancing a
number of figures. The remaining Turks, singing the while, pass under
the carpets and then form up in rows on each side of the stage. The Mufti,
accompanied by the Dervishes, brings up the rear of the procession.*

*The Turks spread the carpets on the ground and kneel upon them. The
Mufti and the Dervishes remain standing in their midst. While the Mufti
invokes Mahomet, waving his arms about, pulling faces, raising his eyes
to heaven, wiggling his hands like wings at each side of his head but
without speaking a word, the Turks prostrate themselves on the ground,
chanting Alli, then resume the kneeling position, lift their arms to heaven
chanting Allah. This they continue until the end of the invocation. Then
they all stand up and chant Allah Eckbar! Two dervishes bring on
Monsieur Jourdain.*

MUFTI (*sings to Monsieur Jourdain*):

Se ti sabir,[12]	If you savvy,
Ti respondir.	Answer.
Se non sabir,	If you no savvy,
Tazir, tazir.	Keepee mum, keepee mum.
Mi star Mufti.	Me be Mufti.
Ti qui star, ti?	Who am you?
Non intendir?	No compree?
Tazir, tazir.	Keepee mum, keepee mum.

(*Two dervishes make Monsieur Jourdain step back.*)

MUFTI: Dice, Turque, qui star   Say, good Turks, what am he?
quista?

Anabatista? Anabatista?   Anabaptist? Anabaptist?[13]

TURKS: Ioc.   No.

MUFTI: Zuinglista?   Zwinglian?

TURKS Ioc.	No.
MUFTI: Coffita?	Copt?
TURKS: Ioc.	No.
MUFTI: Hussita? Morista? Fronista?	Hussite? Moor? Phronist?
TURKS: Ioc, ioc, ioc!	No, no, no!
MUFTI: Ioc, ioc, ioc! Star pagana?	No, no, no! Him be heathen?
TURKS: Ioc.	No.
MUFTI: Luterana?	Lutheran?
TURKS: Ioc.	No.
MUFTI: Puritana?	Puritan?
TURKS: Ioc.	No.
MUFTI: Bramina? Moffina? Zurina?	Brahmin? Moffino? Zurino?
TURKS: Ioc, ioc, ioc!	No, no, no!
MUFTI: Ioc, ioc, ioc! Mahametana? Mahametana?	No, no, no. Muslim? Muslim?
TURKS: Hi Valla. Hi Valla.	Yes, by Allah. Yes, by Allah.
MUFTI: Como chamara? Como chamara?	What him name? What him name?
TURKS: Giourdina, Giourdina.	Jourdain, Jourdain.
MUFTI: (*leaping high and staring all around him*): Giourdina? Giourdina? Giourdina?	Jourdain? Jourdain? Jourdain?
TURKS: Giourdina, Giourdina, Giourdina.	Jourdain, Jourdain, Jourdain.
MUFTI: Mahameta, per Giourdina Mi pregar sera e matina. Voler far un paladina De Giourdina, de Giourdina.	To Mahomet, for this Jourdain I pray both night and morning. I will make a Paladin Of Jourdain, of Jourdain.
Dar turbanta é dar scarcina,	Give him turban, give him scimitar,
Con galera é brigantina,	Give him galley, give him brigantine,
Per deffender Palestina.	To fight for Palestine.
Mahameta, per Giourdina	To Mahomet, for this Jourdain

Mi pregar sera e matina.
(*To the Turks:*) Star bon
Turca, Giourdina?

I pray both night and morning.
Him good Turk, Jourdain?

TURKS: Hi Valla! Hi Valla!

Yes, by Allah! Yes, by Allah!

MUFTI: (*sings and dances*): Ha, la,
ba, ba, chou, ba, la, ba, ba, la,
da!

Ah, li, ba, ba, oh, li, ma, krel!

TURKS: Ha, la, ba, ba, chou, ba,
la, ba, ba, la, da.

Ah, li, ba, ba, oh, li, ma, krel!

The SECOND BALLET is now danced

*The Mufti returns in his great ceremonial turban, which is absurdly large
and decorated with four or five rows of lighted candles. He is accompanied
by two dervishes who carry the Koran. They wear pointed hats which are
also decorated with blazing candles.*

*The two other dervishes bring forward Monsieur Jourdain who is
terrorized by the ceremony. They make him kneel on all fours so that his
back, upon which they place the Koran, makes a lectern for the Mufti.
The Mufti now makes a second burlesque invocation, scowling and opening
his mouth without saying a word. Then he speaks very forcefully, at
times lowering his voice and at others raising it to a fearsome bellow,
squeezing his rib-cage with both hands as if to force the words out,
thumping the Koran at intervals and turning the pages rapidly. Finally,
he lifts both arms heavenwards and cries in a loud voice:* Hou!!!

*All through this second invocation, the Turks who assist him bow three
times and straighten up three times, also singing* Hou, hou, hou!

M. JOURDAIN: (*when they take the Koran off his back*): Phew!

MUFTI: (*to Monsieur Jourdain*): Ti
non star furba?

Be you villain?

TURKS: No, no, no!

No, no, no!

MUFTI: Non star forfanta?

Be you braggart?

TURKS: No, no, no!

No, no, no!

MUFTI: Donar turbanta, donar
turbanta.

Give him turban, give him
turban.

TURKS: Ti non star furba?
No, no, no!
Non star forfanta?

Be you villain?
No, no, no!
Be you braggart?

No, no, no!	No, no, no!
Donar turbanta, donar turbanta.	Give him turban, give him turban.

The THIRD BALLET is now danced

The Turks, dancing and singing, place the turban upon Monsieur Jourdain's head while the music plays.

MUFTI (*presenting the scimitar to Monsieur Jourdain*): Ti star nobile, non star fabbola,	You am noble, this no lie,
Pigliar schiabbola.	You take scimitar.

(*The Turks all draw their scimitars and repeat his words.*)

The FOURTH BALLET is now danced

As they dance, the Turks tap Monsieur Jourdain with the flat of their scimitars in time to the music.

MUFTI: Dara, dara Bastonnara, bastonnara, bastonnara!	Give him, give him Beating, beating, beating!

(*The Turks repeat these words.*)

The FIFTH BALLET is now danced

As they dance, the Turks beat Monsieur Jourdain with sticks in strict tempo.

MUFTI: Non tener honte:	Feel no shame:
Questa star l'ultima affronta.	That be last indignity.

The Mufti now begins a third invocation. The Dervishes support him respectfully, holding his arms up. Then the Turks, singing, dancing and leaping around the Mufti, leave the stage with him and lead off Monsieur Jourdain.

Act V

Scene i:

MADAME JOURDAIN, MONSIEUR JOURDAIN

MME JOURDAIN: Lord have mercy on us! What on earth are you up to? You look a sight! Are you in fancy dress? It's the wrong time of year for carnivals. Tell me, what's going on? Who rigged you out like this?

M. JOURDAIN: The impertinence of the woman, talking like that to a Mamamouchi!

MME JOURDAIN: A what?

M. JOURDAIN: Oh yes, you're going to have to show me more respect now I've been made a Mamamouchi.

MME JOURDAIN: What on earth are you talking about, with your Mamamouchi?

M. JOURDAIN: Mamamouchi, I tell you, I'm a Mamamouchi!

MME JOURDAIN: And what's that when it's at home?

M. JOURDAIN: Mamamouchi, in our language, means Paladin.

MME JOURDAIN: Ballading! You should know better than go round ballading at your age.

M. JOURDAIN: The ignorance! I said Paladin! It's a title that's just been conferred on me in a ceremony.

MME JOURDAIN: What sort of ceremony?

M. JOURDAIN: Mahameta per Giourdina.

MME JOURDAIN: What's that mean?

M. JOURDAIN: Giourdina means Jourdain.

MME JOURDAIN: And what about Jourdain?

M. JOURDAIN: Voler far un Paladina de Giourdina.

MME JOURDAIN: What?

M. JOURDAIN: Dar turbanta con galera.

MME JOURDAIN: What d'you mean?

M. JOURDAIN: Per deffender Palestina.

MME JOURDAIN: What are you on about?

M. JOURDAIN: Dara, dara, bastonnara.

MME JOURDAIN: What's all this gibberish?

M. JOURDAIN: Non tener honta: questa star l'ultima affronta.

MME JOURDAIN: Where's the sense in all that?

M. JOURDAIN (*dancing and singing*): Hou la ba, ba la chou, ba la ba, ba la da. (*He falls over.*)

MME JOURDAIN: Oh my God! My husband's gone raving mad!

M. JOURDAIN (*as he picks himself up and goes out*): Silence, you insolent creature! Show some respect to a Mamamouchi.

MME JOURDAIN (*alone*): Where on earth did he manage to get his wits turned? I must go this minute and keep him from going out. (*Catching sight of Dorimène and Dorante*) Oh, that's all I need! I see nothing but trouble wherever I look. (*She goes out.*)

Scene ii:
DORANTE, DORIMÈNE

DORANTE: Yes, Madame, you're about to see the most amazingly funny thing imaginable. I don't think you could find a bigger fool than our man anywhere. Besides, we must do what we can to advance Cléonte's cause and keep the masquerade going. He's a very decent, honest sort and deserves our support.

DORIMÈNE: Yes, I think very highly of him. He deserves to have things to turn out well for him.

DORANTE: On top of that, Madame, we have a ballet owing us and we mustn't let it go to waste. And we've got to see if my idea will work.

DORIMÈNE: I saw some of the preparations back there: they are magnificent. Dorante, I can't permit this sort of thing any longer. Yes, I have finally made up my mind to put a stop to your extravagance, and to stem the flow of all the money you're spending on me. I have decided to marry you without more delay. It's the best solution. All that sort of thing comes to a stop with marriage.

DORANTE: Oh Madame, have you really made a decision in my favour, the one I have longed for?

DORIMÈNE: It's only to prevent you from ruining yourself. If I didn't, I can see you'd soon be without a penny to your name.

DORANTE: I am very grateful, Madame, for the concern you show for safeguarding my fortune. It is entirely yours, along with my heart, to dispose of as you will.

DORIMÈNE: I shall make good use of both. But here's our man — and what a wonderful sight he makes!

Scene iii:
MONSIEUR JOURDAIN, DORANTE, DORIMÈNE

DORANTE: Madame and I have come to pay our respects to your new dignity sir, and to rejoice with you on the occasion of the marriage you have arranged between your daughter and the son of the Grand Turk.

M. JOURDAIN (*bowing in the Turkish fashion*): Sir, I wish you the strength of the serpent and the wisdom of the lion.

DORIMÈNE: I am delighted to be among the first to congratulate you, sir, on the exalted degree of eminence that you have achieved.

M. JOURDAIN: Madame, may your rose-tree bloom all year long. I am infinitely obliged to you for coming here to share in the honours which have been done me, and I take great joy in seeing that you have come back, because it allows me to make my very humble apologies for my wife's atrocious behaviour.

DORIMÈNE: It was nothing. I have forgiven her outburst: she must value your affection highly, and it is not surprising that wanting to keep a man like you should make her apprehensive on occasions.

M. JOURDAIN: My affections are already entirely yours to have.

DORANTE: You see, Madame, Monsieur Jourdain is not one of those people who are dazzled by their wealth. Even in his hour of glory, he still remembers his friends.

DORIMÈNE: It is the mark of a truly great and noble spirit.

DORANTE: But where is his Turkish Highness? As your friends, we should like to pay him our respects.

M. JOURDAIN: He's coming now, and I've sent for my daughter so I can give him her hand.

Scene iv:

CLÉONTE *in Turkish dress*, COVIELLE, MONSIEUR
JOURDAIN, DORANTE, DORIMÈNE

DORANTE (*to Cléonte*): Sir, we have come, as friends of your father-in-law-to-be, to make obeisance to Your Highness and respectfully offer our most humble services.

M. JOURDAIN: Where's the interpreter so I can tell him who you are and make him understand what you're saying? You'll see, he'll answer you all right, he speaks perfect Turkish. Hello? Where the devil's he got to? (*To Cléonte*:) Strouf, strif, strof, straf. This gentleman is a grande segnore, grande segnore, grande segnore. Madame here is a granda dama, granda dama. (*Seeing that he is not making himself understood*) Ahi, this one (*to Cléonte, pointing to Dorante*), this Gentleman, him French Mamamouchi, and Lady, she French Mamamouchess. That's as plain as I can put it. Ah good! here's the interpreter.

Scene v:

MONSIEUR JOURDAIN, DORIMÈNE, DORANTE,
CLÉONTE *in Turkish dress*, COVIELLE, *in disguise*

M. JOURDAIN: Where did you get to? We can't say a thing without you. (*Pointing to Cléonte*) Just tell him this gentleman and this lady are persons of the highest quality who're here as my friends to make obeisance to him and offer their services. (*To Dorimène and Dorante*:) You'll see if he can talk!

COVIELLE: Alabala crociam acci boram alabamen.

CLÉONTE: Catalequi tubal ourin soter amalouchan.

M. JOURDAIN (*to Dorimène and Dorante*): See?

COVIELLE: He says may the rain of prosperity ever water the garden of your family.

M. JOURDAIN: Didn't I tell you he speaks Turkish?

DORANTE: It's amazing.

Scene vi:

LUCILE, MONSIEUR JOURDAIN, DORANTE,
DORIMÈNE, CLÉONTE, COVIELLE

M. JOURDAIN: Come my girl, come along and give your hand to this gentleman who has done you the honour of asking for your hand in marriage.

LUCILE: Gracious father, why on earth are you all dressed up like that? Are you in a play?

M. JOURDAIN: No no, it isn't a play, it's a very serious business — something that stands to confer greater honour on you than anybody could wish for. (*Pointing to Cléonte*) This is the man I want you to marry.

LUCILE: Me? Marry him father?

M. JOURDAIN: Yes, you. Come on, give him your hand and thank heaven for letting things turn out so well for you.

LUCILE: I don't want to get married.

M. JOURDAIN: But I want you to, and I'm your father.

LUCILE: Well, I shan't.

M. JOURDAIN: Oh, what a fuss. Come along I say, give him your hand.

LUCILE: No father, I've told you, there's no power on earth that can make me marry anyone except Cléonte. I'll go to any lengths rather than ... (*She recognizes Cléonte.*) But it's true, you're my father and it's my duty to obey you in everything. It's for you to decide my future as you think best.

M. JOURDAIN: Oh, I'm delighted to see you remember your duty so quickly. What a pleasure it is to have an obedient daughter!

Scene vii:

MADAME JOURDAIN, MONSIEUR JOURDAIN,
CLÉONTE, LUCILE, DORANTE, DORIMÈNE,
COVIELLE

MME JOURDAIN: Now then, what's all this? I hear you want to marry off your daughter to some clown in fancy dress.

M. JOURDAIN: Oh will you be quiet, you tiresome woman! You're

always sticking your blasted oar into everything with your silly ideas.
There's no way of making you see sense.

MME JOURDAIN: It's you who needs teaching sense. You go from one
mad idea to another. What's it now? What are you up to with this
tomfoolery?

M. JOURDAIN: I intend to marry my daughter to the son of the Grand
Turk.

MME JOURDAIN: The son of the Grand Turk?

M. JOURDAIN (*pointing to Covielle*): That's right. Pay your respects to
him through the interpreter here.

MME JOURDAIN: I don't need an interpreter. I'll tell him to his face
myself that he's not going to have my daughter.

M. JOURDAIN: I'm telling you once more, will you hold your tongue!

DORANTE: Come now Madame Jourdain, how can you refuse such an
honour? Surely you're not going to turn down His Turkish Highness
as your son-in-law?

MME JOURDAIN: My dear sir, why don't you mind your own business?

DORIMÈNE: It's a very great honour and can hardly be refused.

MME JOURDAIN: Madame, I also ask you not to meddle with things that
don't concern you.

DORANTE: It's because of the friendly regard we have for you that we
take a close interest in your welfare.

MME JOURDAIN: I can manage quite well without your friendly interest.

DORANTE: But your daughter is willing to fall in with her father's
wishes.

M. JOURDAIN: My daughter is willing to marry a Turk?

DORANTE: Certainly.

MME JOURDAIN: She can forget Cléonte?

DORANTE: What won't a woman do to become a great lady?

MME JOURDAIN: I'd strangle her with my bare hands if she ever pulled
a trick like that.

M. JOURDAIN: That's enough of your jabbering. I'm telling you, this
wedding will take place.

MME JOURDAIN: And I'm telling you it won't.

M. JOURDAIN: Jabber, jabber!

LUCILE: Mother!

MME JOURDAIN: Go on with you, you're a wicked girl.

M. JOURDAIN (*to Madame Jourdain*): What's this? You're telling her off because she's doing what I tell her?

MME JOURDAIN: Yes, she's as much my daughter as yours.

COVIELLE (*to Madame Jourdain*): Madame.

MME JOURDAIN: And what have you got to say for yourself?

COVIELLE: Just a word —

MME JOURDAIN: I won't have anything to do with any word from you.

COVIELLE (*to Monsieur Jourdain*): Sir, if she'll only listen to me for one moment in private, I can promise I'll get her to agree to what you want.

MME JOURDAIN: I'll never agree.

COVIELLE: Just listen to me.

MME JOURDAIN: No!

M. JOURDAIN (*to Madame Jourdain*): Listen to him.

MME JOURDAIN: I don't want to listen to him.

M. JOURDAIN: He'll tell you —

MME JOURDAIN: I don't want him to tell me anything.

M. JOURDAIN: Oh the obstinacy of the woman! What harm will it do to listen?

COVIELLE (*to Madame Jourdain*): Just listen to what I have to say. You can do as you please afterwards.

MME JOURDAIN: Go on then, what is it?

COVIELLE (*takes her aside*): We've been trying to tip you the wink for the last hour Madame. Can't you see that all this has been set up to hum along with the bee your husband's got in his bonnet? We've taken him in with all this dressing-up business. The son of the Grand Turk is none other than Cléonte himself!

MME JOURDAIN (*aside to Covielle*): Ah!

COVIELLE (*aside to Madame Jourdain*): And the interpreter is me, Covielle!

MME JOURDAIN (*to Covielle*): Well, if that's the way of it, I'm converted.

COVIELLE (*to Madame Jourdain*): Don't give the game away.

MME JOURDAIN: Well, that settles it. I consent to the marriage.

M. JOURDAIN: Ah, now everyone's seeing sense! (*To Madame Jourdain:*) You wouldn't listen, would you? I just knew he'd explain to you all about the son of the Grand Turk.

MME JOURDAIN: He explained it very clearly and I'm quite satisfied. Send for a notary.

DORANTE: That's very well said. And so that your mind may be set completely at ease Madame Jourdain, and to clear up any jealousy you might have felt about your husband, let me say that this lady and I intend to use the same notary to arrange our own marriage.

MME JOURDAIN: I consent to that too.

M. JOURDAIN (*aside to Dorante*): Is that to lead her up the garden path?

DORANTE: Yes, we've got to keep her amused with our subterfuge.

M. JOURDAIN (*aside*): Good! (*To the others:*) Someone go and fetch the notary.

DORANTE: While we are waiting for him to come and draw up the contracts, let's watch our ballet. It will keep His Turkish Highness entertained.

M. JOURDAIN: Excellent idea! Come, let's take our places.

MME JOURDAIN: What about Nicole?

M. JOURDAIN: I give her to the interpreter – and my wife to anyone who'll have her.

COVIELLE: Thank you sir. (*Aside*) If there's a bigger fool than him anywhere on earth, I'll shout it from the rooftops!

> *The comedy continues and concludes with a 'Ballet of*
> *the Nations' which has no relevance, except as a*
> *spectacle, to the play which ends here.*

Those Learned Ladies
A Comedy

Les Femmes savantes
Comédie

*First performed on 11 March 1672 at the Théâtre du
Palais Royal by the King's Players*

Conceived in 1668 and completed by December 1670, *Les Femmes savantes* was staged in March 1672. Audiences reacted positively at first but quickly lost interest, and after Easter, having been played nineteen times, it was withdrawn. Its modest success may perhaps be attributed to the fact that war was in the air (Louis XIV would invade Holland in June), but there was also a feeling that the subject – the follies of preciosity – was too slight for five acts and that Molière was too sweeping in his strictures on women.

His new play, which showed how intellectual ambitions ruin women, gave the opposite side of the argument put in *The School for Wives* (1662) which had shown the unwisdom of raising girls in ignorance. It also resumed the attack on the foolish *précieuses* he had satirized in 1659. Philaminte and Bélise seem to be Magdelon and Cathos a generation on. They know everything but have learned nothing: they have ideas but no judgement, taste but no discrimination, passion but no affection. They are silly, snobbish and pretentious. Bélise has had her wits turned by reading too many novels. Philaminte, who is more intelligent, nevertheless dotes on the nature of the universe and Armande, taking her lead from her assertive mother, is odious. But whereas Molière had let his *précieuses* down lightly in 1659, he now shows them little mercy, for he presents them as a threat to the family and to society at large.

He had regularly attacked the excesses of preciosity, often in similar terms: Trissotin reads his poems in 1672 as Mascarille had done in 1659, and with equally comic results. But the comedy now acquires a harder edge. The mood may be lightened by the satire of pedantry and by the character of Henriette, who is a sister to Elmire and Éliante and a splendid advertisement for the freedom Molière was prepared to allow 'natural' women. But he shows as little sympathy for his learned ladies as he does for learned men (the play was originally titled *Trissotin*). They neither understand science and philosophy nor do they show much sign of being capable of the mental effort required by serious study. Yet they are prepared to foist Trissotin on Henriette and propose to play an intellectual role in society by setting up an academy to police language and censor whatever offends them. Clearly, a little knowledge is dangerous and Molière treats them with a noticeable lack of charity.

Indeed, there is evidence to suggest that he had abandoned his usual practice of satirizing human types and was settling personal scores. His target was certain coteries dominated by women which had made his professional life difficult. But while there is no clear model for Philaminte, there was no doubt in the minds of his contemporaries that Trissotin (initially named Tricotin) was based on the caustic abbé Cotin who had achieved little success in the pulpit but had acquired great influence in fashionable literary circles. He had criticized *The School for Wives*, attacked Molière's friend Boileau (who had replied in his *Satires*) and spoken dismissively of the wretched farces staged by actors, a breed judged to be 'infamous' by any standards, Christian or pagan. Molière turns him into a ridiculous figure (his name suggests that he is 'three times a fool') who is also a repulsive dowry-chaser: unlike Tartuffe, who desires Elmire, his appetites are simply venal. Here, too, Molière is less than fair. Cotin was more pompous than vicious and the two poems which he attributes to Trissotin were in fact examples of how not to write gallant verse. His opponent, Vadius, shelters the Hellenist Gilles Ménage who, though clever in several languages, was reckoned to be dull in all of them.

But though the tone of the play is darkened by this strong element of personal satire, it nevertheless remains one of Molière's most sophisticated comedies of manners. His ladies are Célimène's inferiors. They belong in the ranks of the upper middle class and are as socially pretentious in their way as Monsieur Jourdain. Into this carefully observed setting Molière inserts a plot which is another version of the clash between young love and the selfishness of a parent. But he adds enough variations to keep the action moving: two clearly defined camps, an intruder (who, like Tartuffe, does not appear until Act III), an impertinent kitchen-maid and a difference of opinion between two sisters which mirrors the disagreement between their parents. And once again we are offered a gallery of individualized types: Philaminte, whose ideas have destroyed her femininity, has enough character to face the loss of her fortune with courage, Bélise is the poor relation who lives in a world of 'notions' and Armande has read too many books for her own good. Among the men Clitandre and Ariste are prepared to act in defence of common-sense, unlike Chrysale, the blustering husband who fears his wife, while Trissotin is both comic and odious.

Molière takes up positions on a number of issues. In addition to satirizing pedantry, he shows how it disrupts families, turns rational people into fools and allows rogues to prosper. He warns against intellectual pretentiousness in both sexes and demonstrates that ill-digested ideas disturb both judgement and the imagination. He explores relationships – of husband and wife, parents and children – and judges all his characters by the yardstick of vanity. For while Molière might express strong views on women and vent his spleen on personal enemies, his real target remains the cheats and dupes who through weakness, blindness or self-interest deny the natural principles of tolerance and love without which there is no happiness.

Characters

CHRYSALE, a good citizen
PHILAMINTE, his wife
ARMANDE ⎱
HENRIETTE ⎰ his daughters
ARISTE, brother of Chrysale
BÉLISE, sister of Chrysale
CLITANDRE, in love with
   Henriette
TRISSOTIN, a wit
VADIUS, a pedant
MARTINE, a kitchen-maid
LÉPINE, a footman
JULIEN, servant to Vadius
NOTARY

The scene is set in Paris

Act I

Scene i:
ARMANDE, HENRIETTE

ARMANDE: But surely sister, to be called a 'Woman' is distinction enough. Are you seriously thinking of abandoning its pleasant ring and revelling in the notion of marriage? How can you entertain such a vulgar prospect?

HENRIETTE: But I do sister.

ARMANDE: Oh! That 'I do'! I can't stand it. The very words make my stomach turn.

HENRIETTE: But sister, how does marriage itself in any way force you to —

ARMANDE: Ooh! shame on you!

HENRIETTE: What?

ARMANDE: Shame on you I say! Don't you have the most awful sinking feeling every time you hear the word? Aren't you offended by the disgusting picture it evokes? the repulsive turn it gives your thoughts? Don't you shudder at the very idea? Henriette, how can you reconcile your feelings with the implications of the word 'marriage'?

HENRIETTE: When I consider the implications of the word, I see a husband, children and a home. And if I may say so, I find nothing there to offend me or make me shudder.

ARMANDE: Heavens, don't tell me you would gladly allow yourself to be shackled?

HENRIETTE: What better could a girl of my age do than bind herself to a husband, a man who loves her and is loved by her? And then in a marriage based on affection, surrender to the charm of a blameless life? Surely marriage, provided both partners are compatible, has much to recommend it?

ARMANDE: Oh really! What elementary lines your mind runs on! Can't you see how small you make yourself look in everybody's eyes by shutting yourself up in domestic bliss and seeing nothing more exciting than an adoring husband and a string of snivelling children? You ought to leave whatever simple amusements can be derived from that sort of thing to people who have neither minds nor taste.

You, Henriette, should set your sights higher. You must acquire a taste for the nobler things, learn to treat the senses and base matter with contempt, and give yourself completely, as we do, to the things of the mind. You have our mother as a living example. She is honoured everywhere, acknowledged as an intellectual. Try to be a true daughter to her as I do. Try to live up to the intelligence that runs in our family, and learn to appreciate the fascination and joy which the love of study brings to our hearts. Far from becoming the slave of one man, sister, marry Philosophy which raises us above the rest of humanity and recognizes reason as its sovereign lord by the power it exercises over our animal natures whose gross appetites reduce us to the level of beasts. These are burning passions, tender attachments worthy of filling every waking moment of our lives! And all the worry which makes life miserable for so many suggestible women I see, appears quite degrading and horrible to me.

HENRIETTE: When we are born, Heaven, which is only too visibly all-powerful in its workings, intends us all for different purposes. Not every mind is made of such stuff as can be moulded to produce a philosopher. Yours may be naturally suited to rarefied heights occupied by the speculations of scholars. But mine, Armande, was meant to be pedestrian and remain within its limitations by keeping to the practical side of things. Let's not disturb the proper dictates of Heaven. Let us each follow the direction of our instincts. You, borne along by a fine and clever mind, can dwell on the lofty mountain-tops of philosophy, whereas I, with both feet on the ground, shall taste the earthly delights of matrimony. That way, though our points of view are opposite, we shall both follow in our mother's footsteps. You will imitate her soul and noble aspirations, and I her senses and earthy pleasures; you shall emulate the products of her mind and intelligence, and I, sister, those which are made of base matter.

ARMANDE: When you claim to take your lead from other people, you should try to reflect their noblest qualities. Modelling yourself on them, sister, doesn't mean you should go around coughing and spluttering just because they do it.

HENRIETTE: But you would hardly be what you are so proud of being today, sister, if our mother had possessed only the noblest qualities: it's as well for you that her fine intellect did not always bury itself in philosophy. Please, can't you find it in your heart to allow me a little of those same lapses to which you owe your very existence? And in your determination to win me round to your way of thinking, don't snuff out some budding little intellectual who is waiting to be born.

ARMANDE: I can see there's no curing your mind of this crazy idea that you must have a husband. But tell me, who do you have in mind? I hope at least that you're not setting your sights on Clitandre?

HENRIETTE: And why should they not be set on him? Is he so lacking in merit? Would he really be an unsuitable choice?

ARMANDE: No. But it would be quite dishonest to run off with what belongs to someone else. For it is no secret to anybody that Clitandre has expressed the deepest regard for me.

HENRIETTE: Yes, but his regard hasn't got him very far, for you refuse to descend to such low human weakness. In your mind, you have given up all thought of marriage for ever and settled all your love on philosophy. So, since you have no sentimental plans for Clitandre yourself, how can it matter to you if someone else sets her cap at him?

ARMANDE: The control which reason exerts over the senses does not mean we have to give up the delightful experience of being loved. The qualities one would not wish for in a husband may be very desirable in one's retinue of admirers.

HENRIETTE: I have never tried to stop him worshipping your beauty. All I did was to take what his heart offered me, after you'd turned him down.

ARMANDE: But I ask you, how can you trust what the heart of a man on the rebound offers? Do you believe he really loves you and that his feelings for me are dead?

HENRIETTE: He tells me so Armande, and I believe him.

ARMANDE: Don't be so naïve Henriette. The truth is that when he says he has deserted me and loves you, he doesn't really mean it and is deceiving himself.

HENRIETTE: Perhaps. But if you like, we can easily find out. I see him coming and on this point he'll be able to tell us exactly how matters stand.

Scene ii:

CLITANDRE, ARMANDE, HENRIETTE

HENRIETTE: Ah Clitandre! To clear up a doubt my sister has just put into my mind, do tell us which of us you are in love with. Leave no corner of your heart unexplored and, please, let us know which of us has the better claim on your feelings.

ARMANDE: No, no. I have no wish to subject what you feel to rigorous analysis. I take an easier line with people. I know what a trial the strain of talking about these things face to face can be.

CLITANDRE (*to Armande*): Not at all Madame. I have nothing to hide and do not feel the least awkward about speaking freely. It is not something that embarrasses me at all and (*gazing at Henriette*) I don't mind saying out loud, frankly and unambiguously, that the tender coils in which I have been caught, that is my love and my dearest wishes, lie entirely with your sister. You shouldn't be upset by this admission: it's what you wanted. Your beauty captivated me at first, and my tender sighs gave you ample proof of the strength of my feelings. I was ready to give you my undying love. But you did not think that what you saw was a conquest worthy of you. The way you looked at me inflicted endless slights: your eyes ruled my heart like two proud tyrants. Tiring of being so consistently scorned, I looked for a less inhuman conqueror and softer chains. I found both in your sister's eyes: I shall always treasure the way she looked at me. With one gentle glance she dried my tears and did not despise what your beauty had rejected. Such rare kindness touched me so deeply that nothing now can ever loosen the ties that bind me. Which is why I dare ask you now, Madame, to do nothing to undermine my feelings or attempt to win back my heart, for it is filled with gentle love and will remain so until the day I die.

ARMANDE: And who says anyone wants to Monsieur? Who is so concerned about you to try? I find it amusing that you should imagine any such thing and consider you impertinent for telling me.

HENRIETTE: Not so hasty Armande. Aren't you forgetting your philosophy which governs our animal parts so easily and keeps such a tight rein on anger?

ARMANDE: And, since you've brought it up, aren't you forgetting your duty by listening to what is dressed up as a protestation of love without first obtaining the permission of our parents? Remember that duty makes you dependent on their authority, that you are not permitted to fall in love except with the man they choose, that they have absolute power over your feelings and that to decide these matters for yourself is a crime.

HENRIETTE: I am most grateful for the thoughtfulness you display in reminding me where my duty lies. I shall model my conduct on your lessons, and to show you just how much I take them to heart I ask you, Clitandre, to place what you feel for me on a proper footing by obtaining the approval of my parents. Obtain this legal sanction over my sentiments and give me the right to love you without committing a crime.

CLITANDRE: I shall set to work at once and spare no effort. I was only waiting for your consent.

ARMANDE: So you win, Henriette! And, judging by the look on your face, you seem to think I am upset by it.

HENRIETTE: I think that? Not at all! I know you believe that the requirements of reason are invariably more powerful than the call of the senses, and that by following the lessons learned from tranquil reflection you are above such weakness. Far from imagining that you are upset in any way, I feel sure you will now do everything you can to help me by supporting Clitandre when he asks for my hand and, by giving us your backing, hasten the happy day of our wedding. I implore you, and as a first step –

ARMANDE: Don't be sillier than you are by trying to be sarcastic with me! Anyone can see that the cast-off love I've tossed to you has gone to your head.

HENRIETTE: Cast-off it may be, but you wouldn't be altogether unhappy to catch it on the rebound. If you could get it off me again by looks and glances, you would soon learn modesty and lower your eyes accordingly.

ARMANDE: I shan't demean myself by replying to that. I refuse to listen to such nonsense.

HENRIETTE: That's very good of you. Thank you for showing such restraint. It's more than anything we could have imagined. (*Exit Armande.*)

Scene iii:

CLITANDRE, HENRIETTE

HENRIETTE: Your frankness rather took her by surprise.

CLITANDRE: She needed to be spoken to frankly. The airs her foolish pride give her deserved at the very least plain speaking. But now that I'm free to do so, Henriette, I shall go and speak to your father . . .

HENRIETTE: It would be best to start with my mother. Father will agree to anything but he never follows through the things he has decided. He was born with a very easy-going nature, which means he goes along with whatever his wife wants. She rules the whole house and is so categorical that whatever she decides is law. I'd prefer it if, in your dealings with her and my aunt too, you could go out of your way to be, frankly, a little more amenable and react in an enthusiastic way to their notions, for that would earn their respect and approval.

CLITANDRE: I am sincere by nature and could never bring myself to flatter those aspects of their character which have survived in your sister. Intellectual women are not to my taste. I grant you, a woman should know all sorts of things. But I cannot abide a woman who feels the deplorable urge to learn simply to become learned. When such matters crop up in conversation, I'd rather she knew enough not to know what she knows. I mean I would prefer her to wear her learning lightly, be content to have knowledge without wanting other people to be aware of how much she knows, and not go round quoting authors, using long words and adding clever comments to the most prosaic observations. I have a great deal of respect for your mother. But I don't approve of this mania she has. I refuse to be a sounding-box for whatever she says, nor can I understand why she idolizes her hero of wit, her Monsieur Trissotin. I find the man irritating, and boring beyond words. It makes me furious to see her showing someone like him such respect and raising him to the ranks of the greatest and finest minds, whereas he is a ninny whose books are laughed at, a pedant whose free-flowing pen supplies grocers with endless wrapping-paper.

HENRIETTE: Yes, to me everything he writes and says is tiresome, and my opinion of him more or less coincides with your tastes and views.

But since he has great influence over my mother you must make an effort to be agreeable to him. A man pays his court to a woman who possesses his heart. He'll try to win over everyone to his side and, to make sure that nobody opposes him, he will even be nice to the family dog.

CLITANDRE: You're right of course. But Monsieur Trissotin fills me with unutterable contempt, to the bottom of my soul. I could never agree to surrender my self-respect by praising his books, simply to get his backing. It was through his writings that I first became aware of him. I knew the man before ever I set eyes on him. In the drivelling books he foists on us, I saw the effects of the pedantic self-regard which he spreads far and wide: the constant arrogance of his presumption, the unflinchingly good opinion he has of himself, his lazy assumption of superiority, all these make him endlessly self-satisfied and enable him to smile unceasingly at his own brilliance, with the result that he congratulates himself on everything he publishes and would not exchange his fame for all the battle honours of a general.

HENRIETTE: How very clever you are to see all that!

CLITANDRE: It even worked for his appearance, for in the poems he inflicts on us I could see his face, even what the poet must look like. I guessed how he would look with such accuracy that one day I ran across a man in the Palais de Justice and bet that it was Trissotin himself – and I won my bet.

HENRIETTE: You're making it up!

CLITANDRE: No, it happened just as I said. But here's your aunt. Please, won't you let me reveal our secret to her? With her on our side, we'll have an ally close to your mother. (*Exit Henriette.*)

Scene iv:
CLITANDRE, BÉLISE

CLITANDRE: A word Madame, if you permit? Will you allow a man in love to take advantage of this fortunate moment to reveal to you the sincere feelings which –

BÉLISE: Oh, soft! Take care you do not speak to me too frankly of your passion. I have added you to my list of admirers, but you must make do with saying what you have to say with your eyes only, and refrain from using any other kind of language to express desires which, to my way of thinking, are an outrage. Love me, long for me, pine for my beauty, but oblige me by keeping it all to yourself. I can turn a blind eye to your secret yearnings as long as you don't go beyond the unspoken glance. But the moment you give them speech and utterance, I shall be forced to banish you from my sight for ever.

CLITANDRE: Don't be alarmed by what I feel in my heart Madame. Henriette is the one I love and I have come to beg you most earnestly to use your good offices to further the feelings I have for her.

BÉLISE: Ah! the approach is original I must confess! A clever subterfuge which deserves congratulations. In all the novels I have read I've yet to come across anything so ingenious.

CLITANDRE: I am not trying to be clever Madame, it's the straightforward truth about how I feel. With chains of everlasting love, Heaven has bound me to Henriette's beauty. She holds me entirely in her gentle power and to be married to Henriette is the only thing I aspire to. You can help a great deal and all I ask is that you should be good enough to support my efforts to win her.

BÉLISE: I see through what you're asking in your roundabout way. I know exactly what you mean when you say the name 'Henriette'. It is a pretty conceit and I'll continue it in stating what my heart prompts me to say in reply. I tell you 'Henriette' is not interested in marrying anybody and you must languish for her cherishing no hope.

CLITANDRE: Madame, what is the use of complicating matters in this way? Why do you insist on believing what is not the case?

BÉLISE: Oh please, no more protestations. Stop denying what your eyes have told me so often. It should be enough that the flight of fancy your love has so prettily devised has found favour in my sight. I am pleased to suffer your homage beneath this figure of speech which is a proper expression of respect – but on condition that its rapture, guided by honour, makes oblation upon my altar of only the purest of vows.

CLITANDRE: But –

BÉLISE: Farewell! For now, you must be satisfied with this, for I have said more than I intended.

CLITANDRE: But you are wrong to –

BÉLISE: Enough! I am blushing now. My modesty has been sorely tested.

CLITANDRE: I'm hanged if I love you and if –

BÉLISE: No no! I'll not hear another word! (*Exit Bélise.*)

CLITANDRE: The devil take the crazy woman and her idiotic notions! Did anyone ever see such bone-headedness? I'd better involve some-one else in this business which I must settle. I'll try and get help from someone wiser.

Act II

Scene i:
ARISTE

ARISTE (*to Clitandre who hurries off*): Yes, I'll bring you the answer the moment I have it. I'll back you up, I'll hurry things along, I'll do the necessary. (*To himself:*) What a lot of things a man in love says when all he wants is to hear just one word. And so impatient to have what he wants. Never . . .

Scene ii:
ARISTE, CHRYSALE

ARISTE: Ah, good day to you, brother!

CHRYSALE: And good day to you, brother.

ARISTE: Do you know why I'm here?

CHRYSALE: No, but I'm willing to listen if you are prepared to tell me.

ARISTE: Have you known Clitandre long?

CHRYSALE: Why yes. I often see him around the house.

ARISTE: And what do you make of him?

CHRYSALE: He's an honourable fellow, clever, heart's in the right place, very sound. There aren't many who have his qualities.

ARISTE: I've come here because there's something he wants. I'm delighted you think so well of him.

CHRYSALE: I met his late father when I was in Rome.

ARISTE: Good!

CHRYSALE: He was, brother, a most respectable gentleman.

ARISTE: So I've heard.

CHRYSALE: We were both only twenty-eight at the time and, if I say so myself, a fine couple of sparks!

ARISTE: I can well believe it!

CHRYSALE: We were most attentive to those Roman ladies. Everyone talked about the things we got up to. We made lots of men jealous.

ARISTE: Excellent! But let me turn to the reason that's brought me here.

Scene iii:

CHRYSALE, ARISTE, BÉLISE (*who enters and listens*)

ARISTE: Clitandre has asked me to see you and speak for him. He has fallen in love with pretty Henriette.

CHRYSALE: You don't say! With my daughter?

ARISTE: Yes. Clitandre is mad about her. I never saw anyone so smitten.

BÉLISE (*to Ariste*): No no! I overheard what you were saying. You don't know the full story. Things aren't the way you think.

CHRYSALE: What do you mean sister?

BÉLISE: Clitandre isn't being honest with you. He is in love with another person altogether.

ARISTE: You must be joking. Are you saying it's not Henriette he loves?

BÉLISE: That's right. I'm certain.

ARISTE: But he told me himself.

BÉLISE: Quite!

ARISTE: And you see me here, sister, because he wanted me to ask her father for her hand.

BÉLISE: Of course!

ARISTE: And he was so in love that he said it was most urgent that I should press ahead with the marriage as quickly as possible.

BÉLISE: Better and better! He could not have managed the deception more gallantly! Between ourselves, Henriette is no more than a diversion, a clever decoy, a pretext for his real feelings to which I hold the key. I am most anxious that both of you should not labour under a misapprehension a moment longer.

ARISTE: But if you know so much about this, tell us, please, who is this other woman he's in love with?

BÉLISE: You really want to know?

ARISTE: Yes. Who is it?

BÉLISE: Me.

ARISTE: You?

BÉLISE: Yes, me.

ARISTE (*laughs*): Really, sister!

BÉLISE: Why are you laughing? What's so surprising about what I've just said? Someone as attractive as myself can, I think, be allowed to claim to have more than one suitor in her retinue of admirers. Dorante, Damis, Cléonte and Lycidas are living proof that one is not entirely without charms.

ARISTE: Are all those men in love with you?

BÉLISE: Yes, and with all their might.

ARISTE: Have they told you so?

BÉLISE: None has dared take such a liberty. Thus far, they have worshipped so reverently that they have never spoken a word of their feelings. But their eyes, those silent witnesses, have done the work of offering their hearts and service to their lady.

ARISTE: Damis is hardly ever seen in this house.

BÉLISE: That's to show how completely he respects me.

ARISTE: Dorante is always making cutting remarks about you.

BÉLISE: The uncontrolled outbursts of jealous rage.

ARISTE: Both Cléonte and Lycidas have got married.

BÉLISE: They did so out of desperation. I drove them to it.

ARISTE: Really sister, these are obviously delusions.

CHRYSALE: You must forget these fanciful notions.

BÉLISE: Ooh! Notions! Fanciful notions, you call them? Are you saying I have fanciful notions? Really, there's nothing wrong with fanciful notions! I am glad I've got notions. I had no idea that they were fanciful! (*She goes out.*)

Scene iv:
CHRYSALE, ARISTE

CHRYSALE: Clearly our sister is mad.

ARISTE: And getting worse by the day. But let's get back to what we were talking about. Clitandre is asking you for Henriette's hand in marriage. Tell me, what answer am I to give him?

CHRYSALE: Need you ask? I agree with all my heart. I'll be honoured to have him in the family.

ARISTE: You do know that he is not terribly well off and . . .

CHRYSALE: A consideration that isn't of prime importance: he is rich in virtue and that's worth more than money. Moreover, his father and I always saw eye to eye on everything.

ARISTE: We'd better speak to your wife and try to win her over to –

CHRYSALE: No need. I'll have him for a son-in-law.

ARISTE: Yes, but to confirm your consent brother it would do no harm to have her agreement. Come now . . .

CHRYSALE: You're not serious? It's not necessary. I'll answer for my wife. Leave the whole thing to me.

ARISTE: But –

CHRYSALE: Leave it to me I say. There's nothing to be afraid of. I shall go this very minute and tell her how things stand.

ARISTE: Oh, very well. And I'll go and ask Henriette what she thinks and then come back to find out if . . .

CHRYSALE: Consider it done. I shall go and speak to my wife without further ado.

Scene v:

MARTINE, CHRYSALE

MARTINE (*in tears*): Oh, what a pickle! It's true wot they say: 'give a dog a bad name, then hang him' and 'wearing liveries don't bring legacies'.

CHRYSALE: What's all this? What's the matter Martine?

MARTINE: Matter?

CHRYSALE: Yes.

MARTINE: The matter, sir, is that I've just been given me marchin' orders.

CHRYSALE: You've been dismissed?

MARTINE: Yes. Madame told me to get out.

CHRYSALE: I don't understand. Say that again.

MARTINE: She told me if I didn't get out, I'd get a good thrashin'.

CHRYSALE: No, you shall stay. I'm satisfied with you. My wife gets a little carried away at times but I don't want . . .

Scene vi:
PHILAMINTE, BÉLISE, CHRYSALE, MARTINE

PHILAMINTE (*seeing Martine*): What! Are you still here, hussy? Get out this minute, you baggage! Be off with you and never show your face here ever again!

CHRYSALE: Steady on!

PHILAMINTE: No, it's all settled.

CHRYSALE: What's all settled?

PHILAMINTE: I want her out of here.

CHRYSALE: But what has she done to make you –

PHILAMINTE: What? Are you siding with her?

CHRYSALE: Not at all.

PHILAMINTE: Are you taking her part against me?

CHRYSALE: Heavens, no! I'm simply asking what terrible thing she's done.

PHILAMINTE: Am I the sort who would dismiss her without good reason?

CHRYSALE: I'm not saying that. But in the matter of servants, we –

PHILAMINTE: No! She will leave this house I tell you.

CHRYSALE: Well yes, of course. Has anyone said anything to the contrary?

PHILAMINTE: I will not have obstacles put in my way when I say I want something.

CHRYSALE: I agree.

PHILAMINTE: And if you were a considerate husband, you would side with me against her and be as furious as I am.

CHRYSALE: And so I will. (*To Martine:*) Yes, my wife was right to tell you to go, you wretched girl. What you did was quite unforgivable.

MARTINE: What did I do then?

CHRYSALE (*to himself*): Blest if I know.

PHILAMINTE: She still won't see how serious it is.

CHRYSALE: Did she give you good cause to be angry by breaking a mirror or some china ornament?

PHILAMINTE: Now would I dismiss her – and do you think I'd lose my temper – for something so trivial?

CHRYSALE (*to Martine*): What can it be? (*To Philaminte:*) So it was something more serious?

PHILAMINTE: It certainly was. Do you think I am an unreasonable woman?

CHRYSALE: Has she been careless, and mislaid a jug or a silver platter?

PHILAMINTE: I wouldn't have minded that.

CHRYSALE (*to Martine*): Oh, wretched girl! (*To Philaminte:*) What then? Did you catch her being dishonest?

PHILAMINTE: It's worse than anything of that sort.

CHRYSALE: Worse than that?

PHILAMINTE: Far worse.

CHRYSALE: What the devil! The jade! Ah! did she (*whispers*) . . .

PHILAMINTE: With an impudence the like of which was never seen, and though she's had thirty lessons, she insulted my ears by making improper use of a low, common word which Vaugelas categorically outlaws.[1]

CHRYSALE: Is that all she –

PHILAMINTE: All? She's been told often enough and yet she still goes on mangling the foundation of all learning – grammar, which makes even monarchs come to heel and obey the rules!

CHRYSALE: I thought she must have done something quite appalling.

PHILAMINTE: What! You mean you don't find this outrage unforgivable?

CHRYSALE: Oh, but I do!

PHILAMINTE: I'd just like to see you try to let her off lightly!

CHRYSALE: Wouldn't dream of it!

BÉLISE: It's pitiful, it really is. She rides roughshod over every construction known to man, though we've drilled her in the rules of language over and over.

MARTINE: What you preach is all very genteel, I'm sure. But I'll never be able to talk that lingo of yours.

PHILAMINTE: The impudence! She calls the way we speak, which is rooted in reason and good usage, a lingo!

MARTINE: If others folks can understand what you're on about, then you're talkin' proper. All your fancy lessons don't do no good to man nor beast.

PHILAMINTE: Do you hear that? 'Don't do no good'! That's another example of her style.

BÉLISE: Such a recalcitrant brain! When I think of all the trouble we are always going to, and you still can't learn to speak correctly!

You've put a 'not' with a 'no' again, though you've been told it's one negative too many.

MARTINE: Lawks! I ain't one for book-learnin' like you. I just talks plain like wot folks down our way do.

PHILAMINTE: Oh, I can't bear it!

BÉLISE: Such ghastly syntax!

PHILAMINTE: It's death to a sensitive ear!

BÉLISE: Your mind is, I confess, utterly material. 'I' is first person and 'talks' is third person. Do you intend to spend the rest of your life abusing your grammar?

MARTINE: Who said anythin' about abusin' me grandma – or me grandpa neither?

PHILAMINTE: Heavens above!

BÉLISE: You've misunderstood the word 'grammar'. I've told you where it comes from.

MARTINE: Mercy, whether it comes from Chaillot, Auteuil or Pontoise, it don't make no odds to me.

BÉLISE: What a rustic simpleton! Grammar teaches us the rules of the agreement between subject and verb, adjective and noun.

MARTINE: I must say, Madame, as how I don't know any of them people.

PHILAMINTE: This is torture!

BÉLISE: They are the names of words and we must be careful to ensure that they agree with one another.

MARTINE: Wot's the difference if they agree with each other or knock each other's blocks off?

PHILAMINTE (*to her sister*): Oh what's the use. Don't go on with this. (*To her husband:*) Now don't you want to send her packing?

CHRYSALE (*to himself*): Indeed I do not, but I'd better go along with her whim. (*To Martine:*) Go, don't upset her further. You'd best leave.

PHILAMINTE: What! Are you frightened of offending her? You talk to her in a most civil tone.

CHRYSALE: Not at all. Come now, be off with you. (*To Martine who leaves:*) Just go, poor child.

Scene vii:

PHILAMINTE, CHRYSALE, BÉLISE

CHRYSALE: There, you're satisfied now. She's gone. But I don't approve of packing her off like that. She's a good girl, well suited to her duties, and you've turned her out of my house for a very trivial reason.

PHILAMINTE: Would you rather I kept her on in my service so that she could go on forever assaulting my ears and breaking every rule of usage and reason by coming out with her barbaric assortment of grammatical errors, mangled words only occasionally strung together to make sense, and proverbs she's dragged up out of the gutters of the fish-market?

BÉLISE: It's true. Putting up with the way she speaks makes a person break out in a cold sweat. She tears Vaugelas to tatters each day that passes. The least of the errors perpetrated by that crude intellect of hers are tautology and cacophony.

CHRYSALE: What does it matter if she neglects the rules of Vaugelas as long as she doesn't neglect her duties in the kitchen? Myself, I'd much prefer her, when she's peeling vegetables, to put her pronouns next to the wrong verb form and repeat some common or vulgar word as often as she likes, than burn my meat or put too much salt in my stew. I live on good dinners, not on refined speech. Vaugelas doesn't tell you how to make a good soup. And maybe Malherbe and Balzac,[2] though they could turn a fine phrase, would have been nincompoops in a kitchen.

PHILAMINTE: These coarse observations of yours are really too trying! It's so gross, when you speak of the human race, to be forever lowering yourself to these material considerations when you should be rising to the call of the spirit! Is the body, which is dross, so important that all you can think of is what profits it? Shouldn't such things be far beneath us?

CHRYSALE: But my body is me and I intend to take good care of it. Call it dross if you like, but I'm very partial to my dross.

BÉLISE: Body and spirit are one, brother. But, if you believe learned opinion, the spirit must lead the body and our prime concern, our paramount attention, should be to feed it with the milk of science.

CHRYSALE: Good God! If you think you can feed your spirit, it's on insubstantial fare, so everyone says. You don't care or show any concern for –

PHILAMINTE: Ah! How the term 'concern' grates on my ear! It has an odd reek of the old-fashioned about it.

BÉBELISE: True, the word is quite outdated.

CHRYSALE: Do you want me to speak plainly? I must, or I'll burst: I must lift my mask and get all this off my chest. Everyone thinks you are quite mad, and it grieves me to –

PHILAMINTE: What on earth are you talking about?

CHRYSALE (*to Bélise*): It's you I'm talking to, sister. Any improper use of words people make when they speak sets you off, though you permit yourself some strange lapses in the way you behave. I can't stand having all your everlasting books around the house. Apart from the large Plutarch I use to keep my neckbands flat in, you should burn the rest of the useless clutter and leave science to the scientists. It would be a good start to get rid of that long telescope in the attic, it frightens people, and all those odd bits and pieces that make the whole place look untidy. You should stop bothering about what's happening on the moon and take a closer look at what's going on in your own home where anyone can see everything is in a terrible mess. There are many reasons why it's not right for a woman to study and know so much. Teaching her children to be good and behave properly, running her house, keeping an eye on the servants, seeing that she gets value for money – that's what she should study, that's what her philosophy ought to be. Our forefathers had a very sensible attitude to these matters. They reckoned a woman was sufficiently learned if her mental capacities rose to the task of telling a doublet from a pair of breeches. Their wives never read but they lived full lives. Their home was the only topic of philosophical discussion they knew, and instead of books they had a thimble, thread and needles which they used to make their daughters' trousseaus. The outlook of you women is very different nowadays, for you want to write and become authors. No science is too deep for you and here under my own roof, much more so than anywhere else, the profoundest mysteries are accommodated – you know everything except what you ought to know. You know all about the movements of the moon, the North star, Venus, Saturn and Mars which are none of my business, but for all this useless knowledge which you go to such lengths to acquire, you've no idea how my dinner is coming on, which is something I do need. The servants have taken up science to make you happy and they do no work save what they absolutely have to. Everyone under my roof is fully employed having discussions, and all this discussing has driven out common-sense. One servant burns my roast because he's reading some story. Another is thinking about his poetry when I ask for a glass of wine. Which is to say I observe that they follow the example you set, with the result that I have servants but get no service. I did have one maid left, poor girl, who hadn't been contaminated by inhaling your noxious fumes, but now she's been sent packing after a tremendous scene because she didn't talk like Vaugelas. I find the whole business very irritating and I'm telling you all this, Bélise, because, as I said, these remarks are intended for you. I don't like all your Latin-speaking friends who come here, and particularly the great Monsieur Trissotin. It was he who turned your heads with his poems. Everything he comes out with is twaddle. You have to try to work out what he's said after he's said it. Personally, I reckon he's cracked.

PHILAMINTE: Heaven help us! Such baseness of spirit! And such gross language!

BÉLISE: Was there ever a more solid agglomeration of base matter? a mind composed of such crassly middle-class atoms? Is it possible that the same blood runs in my veins that runs in his? I refuse to believe I am of the same race. I am quite mortified and shall withdraw.

Scene viii:
PHILAMINTE, CHRYSALE

PHILAMINTE: Have you got any more criticisms to make?

CHRYSALE: Me? Why no. Let's not talk of quarrelling, it's over and done with. There's something else we need to discuss. It looks as if your oldest daughter is none too keen on matrimony. She's a bookish girl, and that's no odds to me. You keep a strict eye on her and rightly so. But the other one, Henriette, is a different character altogether and it seems to me it would be a good idea to be thinking of marriage for her, of finding her a husband . . .

PHILAMINTE: I've already given the matter some thought and I shall now inform you of what I have in mind. Monsieur Trissotin, who stands accused of turning our heads with poems and does not have the honour of being liked by you, is the man I have chosen to be the husband she needs. I am a better judge than you of his many qualities. It's no good arguing, for my mind is utterly set on this. I ask you most particularly not to mention this business of a husband. I wish to speak to my daughter before you do. I have my reasons and they will justify my actions. Remember, I shall know if you've said anything to her.

Scene ix:
ARISTE, CHRYSALE

ARISTE: Well? Your good lady has just sallied forth brother. I see that the two of you have been having a little talk.

CHRYSALE: Yes indeed.

ARISTE: How did it go? Do we get our way with Henriette? Did Philaminte agree? Is it all arranged?

CHRYSALE: Not quite yet.

ARISTE: Did she refuse?

CHRYSALE: No.

ARISTE: Is she hesitating?

CHRYSALE: Absolutely not.

ARISTE: Well what, then?

CHRYSALE: The fact is she already has someone in mind to be my son-in-law.

ARISTE: Someone else . . .

CHRYSALE: Another candidate.

ARISTE: What's his name?

CHRYSALE: Monsieur Trissotin.

ARISTE: What! Not the Trissotin who –

CHRYSALE: Yes, the one who's always going on about poetry and Latin.

ARISTE: Did you say yes?

CHRYSALE: Me? God forbid!

ARISTE: What did you say?

CHRYSALE: Nothing, and I'm very pleased I didn't. That way, I haven't committed myself.

ARISTE: I suppose so. It's a step in the right direction. But at least were you able to put Clitandre's name forward?

CHRYSALE: No. When I saw she was talking about another son-in-law, I thought it best not to show too much of my hand.

ARISTE: But isn't that carrying prudence rather too far? Aren't you ashamed of being so weak-kneed? How's it possible that a man can be so unassertive that he hands absolute power to his wife and doesn't dare challenge what she has decided?

CHRYSALE: By God, it's all very well for you to talk, brother, but you've no idea how much I loathe squabbling. I like a quiet life, I like peace and calm. My wife is terrifying when she loses her temper. She makes a great thing about being what she calls 'philosophical' but I haven't noticed that it's improved her character. Her moral beliefs, which take a dim view of money, are guaranteed to rouse her bile. If you try to oppose whatever she's set her mind on, you uncork a whirlwind which can last a whole week. She scares me so much when she goes on the rampage that I don't know where to put myself – she's a fire-breathing dragon. All the same, though she can be the very devil, I've still got to call her 'my sweet' and 'dear heart'.

ARISTE: That's rubbish. Between you and me, if your wife wears the trousers it's because you've been so lily-livered. She is only strong because you are weak and she only thinks she is in charge because you allow it. You surrender to her domineering manner and let yourself be led by the nose, like an ox. Look, given the way you're treated, can't you bring yourself for once to behave like a man, force a woman to do what you want and have the guts to say 'No, my mind's made up'? Would you, without another thought, let your daughter be sacrificed to your family's idiotic ideas and hand over your whole estate to some oaf who is the apple of their eye because he can mumble half a dozen words in Latin? A pedant on whom your wife unhesitatingly confers the title of Great Wit and Deep Philosopher? A man whose ability to spout courtly verses is second to none but who, as everybody knows, has nothing else to be said in his favour? I repeat: you're talking rot. You're a coward and deserve to be laughed at.

CHRYSALE: Yes, you're right and I see that I'm wrong. Well then, I'm going to have to learn to be more forceful, brother.

ARISTE: That's more like it.

CHRYSALE: Being under the thumb of a woman is degrading.

ARISTE: Well said.

CHRYSALE: She has taken far too much advantage of my mildness.

ARISTE: True.

CHRYSALE: And abused my easy-going nature.

ARISTE: That she has.

CHRYSALE: So no later than today I intend to let her know that my daughter is my daughter and that I'm entitled to choose whatever husband I like for her.

ARISTE: Now you're talking sense. That's how I like to see you.

CHRYSALE: You've given your backing to Clitandre. You know where he lives. Ask him to come here right away.

ARISTE: I'll go and get him now.

CHRYSALE: I've put up with it for far too long. I'm going to be a man, and to hell with the lot of them!

Act III

Scene i:
PHILAMINTE, ARMANDE, BÉLISE, TRISSOTIN,
LÉPINE

PHILAMINTE: Come, let us sit here where we shall not be disturbed and listen to the poem and weigh each and every word as they deserve.

ARMANDE: I can't wait.

BÉLISE: We're all dying to hear it.

PHILAMINTE (*to Trissotin*): Everything you say and write casts a spell on me.

ARMANDE: Your verse is sweeter than any I know.

BÉLISE: It is ambrosia to my ears.

PHILAMINTE: Do not let our lofty longings languish any longer.

ARMANDE: Do hurry!

BÉLISE: Please begin and let our joy commence.

PHILAMINTE: Nourish our impatience with your epigram.[3]

TRISSOTIN: Alas Madame, it is but a new-born babe. Yet there is a reason why his fate should touch you: I gave him birth only moments ago in your very own courtyard.

PHILAMINTE: To make him dear to my heart, it is enough for me to know that you are his father.

TRISSOTIN: And your applause shall be his mother.

BÉLISE: Ah! such wit!

Scene ii:

HENRIETTE, PHILAMINTE, ARMANDE, BÉLISE, TRISSOTIN, LÉPINE

PHILAMINTE (*to Henriette who enters and tries to leave*): Stop! Why are you going?

HENRIETTE: I was afraid I might be interrupting your pleasant proceedings.

PHILAMINTE: Come here. Open your ears and share our pleasure as we listen to these wonderful verses.

HENRIETTE: I know little of the beauty of what poets write. Things of the mind are not my strong suit.

PHILAMINTE: That doesn't signify. Anyway, when it's over, I've something to tell you, a secret you must know.

TRISSOTIN (*to Henriette*): So, you are not enthused by matters of the intellect. The only thing that interests you is how to be charming.

HENRIETTE: The one interests me as little as the other. I really have no wish to –

BÉLISE: Ah! please! Let us not forget the new-born babe!

PHILAMINTE (*to Lépine*): Come boy, a chair for the gentleman. (*The footman falls over the chair he's carrying.*) Ungrateful wretch! How can anyone possibly fall over when they've been told about the equilibrium that rules the natural world?

BÉLISE: You stupid boy, can't you see the reason why you fell? You fell because you allowed the fixed point to move out of alignment with what we call the centre of gravity.

LÉPINE: I saw it clearly Madame, being on the floor at the time.

PHILAMINTE (*to Lépine as he goes out*): Clumsy oaf!

TRISSOTIN: It's just as well for him he's not made of glass.

ARMANDE: Oh! The wit just flows out of him!

BÉLISE: It never dries up.

PHILAMINTE: Bring on your gracious feast this very minute.

TRISSOTIN: To satisfy the gnawing hunger I see in your faces, a single course of eight lines seems very little. I think it would do no harm were I to add to my epigram, or shall I say my madrigal,[4] by way of relish, a sonnet which, in the salon of a princess, was lately found to be not lacking in finesse. It is liberally sprinkled with Attic salt[5] and you will find it, I venture, in the very best of taste.

ARMANDE: I have no doubt of it.

PHILAMINTE: Let us compose ourselves to listen.

BÉLISE (*interrupting him each time he starts to speak*): I feel my heart's all a flutter with anticipation . . . I love poetry with a passion that simply will not be denied . . . Especially, when the verse has a gallant turn . . .

PHILAMINTE: If we talk all the time, he won't be able to get a word in edgeways.

TRISSOTIN: *A Sonn —*

BÉLISE (*to Henriette*): Hold your tongue niece!

ARMANDE: Oh, let him get on with it!

TRISSOTIN: *A Sonnet. To Princess Uranie, on her fever.*[6]

> Your prudence surely sleeps, I trow,
> That you should treat so royally
> And lodge so wondrous lavishly
> A guest who is your bitt'rest foe.

BÉLISE: It begins very prettily!

ARMANDE: Such a beguiling conceit!

PHILAMINTE: No one makes verse sing as sweet!

ARMANDE: 'Prudence sleeps' takes one's breath away.

BÉLISE: I find 'Lodge a guest' utterly charming.

PHILAMINTE: I like 'royally'. I like 'lavishly'. Those two adverbs go admirably together.

BÉLISE: Let's hear the rest.

TRISSOTIN: Your prudence surely sleeps, I trow,
> That you should treat so royally
> And lodge so wondrous lavishly
> A guest who is your bitt'rest foe.

ARMANDE: 'Prudence sleeps'!

BÉLISE: 'Lodge a guest'!

PHILAMINTE: 'Royally'! 'Lavishly'!!

TRISSOTIN: Evict him, brooking no delays,
        From your gorgeous premises
        Where the trait'rous tenant promises
        To end your dear, your precious days.

BÉLISE: Oh stop there! You must, I beg you, let me catch my breath.

ARMANDE: Please, give us a moment to marvel.

PHILAMINTE: Listening to these verses, one feels a certain je ne sais quoi which rushes to the depths of one's heart and makes one feel quite ill.

ARMANDE: 'Evict him, brooking no delays, From your gorgeous premises.' 'Gorgeous premises' is deliciously turned. How wittily the metaphor is exploited!

PHILAMINTE: 'Evict him, brooking no delays.' 'Brooking no delays' is in such wonderful taste! To my sense, it is incomparable.

ARMANDE: My heart too has surrendered utterly to 'brooking no delays'.

BÉLISE: I share your opinion. 'Brooking no delays' is a happy phrase.

ARMANDE: I wish I'd written it.

BÉLISE: It's a whole poem in itself.

PHILAMINTE: But do you feel all its subtleties the way I do?

ARMANDE *and* BÉLISE (*together*): Oh! Ah!

PHILAMINTE: 'Evict him, brooking no delays.' Here the poet speaks of the fever. Forget all else, pay no heed to what others might say. 'Evict him, brooking no delays.' Brooking no delays, brooking no delays! That 'brooking no delays' says far more than it seems to. I have no idea if everyone else feels as I do but, speaking for myself, I hear a million other words reverberate behind that one little phrase.

BÉLISE: That's very true – it speaks very loudly for its size.

PHILAMINTE (*to Trissotin*): But, as you penned your wonderful 'brooking no delay', did you yourself feel the full force of it? Were you aware of all the things it says to us? Were you conscious of putting quite so much wit into it?

TRISSOTIN: Well . . .

ARMANDE: I can't get over 'trait'rous tenant' either, the 'trait'rous tenant' being the fever, so unjust and unscrupulous, which turns so abominably on the hostess who gives it houseroom.

PHILAMINTE: Yes yes, both quatrains are quite admirable. Now please, let's move quickly on to the tercets.[7]

ARMANDE: But first, if you would, could we hear 'brooking no delays' just once more?

TRISSOTIN: 'Evict him now, brooking no delays . . .'

PHILAMINTE, ARMANDE *and* BÉLISE (*together*): 'Brooking no delays'.

TRISSOTIN: 'From your gorgeous premises . . .'

PHILAMINTE, ARMANDE *and* BÉLISE (*together*): 'Gorgeous premises.'

TRISSOTIN: 'Where the trait'rous tenant promises . . .'

PHILAMINTE, ARMANDE and BÉLISE (*together*): The fever is a 'trait'rous tenant'!

TRISSOTIN: 'To end your dear, your precious days.'

PHILAMINTE: 'Your precious days'!

ARMANDE *and* BÉLISE (*together*): Ah!

TRISSOTIN: Scorning your rank on which he wars,
Insolently upon your blood he draws . . .

PHILAMINTE, ARMANDE *and* BÉLISE (*together*): Ah!

TRISSOTIN: Defiling, tainting by night and day!
Should a spa now feature in your plans,
Take your fever there and, in the spray,
Drown him with your own fair hands!

PHILAMINTE: It's too thrilling!

BÉLISE: I feel faint.

ARMANDE: I shall die of bliss.

PHILAMINTE: One is seized with the endless reverberation of the words.

ARMANDE: 'Should a spa now feature in your plans . . .'

BÉLISE: 'Take your fever and, in the spray . . .'

PHILAMINTE: 'Drown him with your own fair hands!' With your own fair hands, there, at the spa which features in your plans!

ARMANDE: At every turn of the verse a new delight is revealed.

BÉLISE: It is like walking through an enchanted landscape.

PHILAMINTE: Where the strolling foot encounters only beauty.

ARMANDE: Winding lanes strewn with roses.

TRISSOTIN: So you think the sonnet –

PHILAMINTE: Astonishing! Original! Nothing finer was ever written.

BÉLISE (*to Henriette*): How could you hear the poem and show no emotion niece? Your reaction is quite unnatural.

HENRIETTE: Everyone here below reacts as best he or she can aunt. Not everyone can be clever and witty.

TRISSOTIN: Perhaps my verse bores Mademoiselle?

HENRIETTE: Not at all, I don't listen.

PHILAMINTE: Bah! Let's have the epigram.

TRISSOTIN: *On a Vermilion Carriage, Offered as a Gift by the Poet to a Lady of his Acquaintance.*

PHILAMINTE: All his titles have something novel about them.

ARMANDE: The novelty is invariably a promise of innumerable beauties to come.

TRISSOTIN: Love has sold me his chains so dear . . .

PHILAMINTE, ARMANDE *and* BÉLISE: (*together*): Ah!

TRISSOTIN: . . . That half my wealth is spent, I fear.
          Now, when you see her carriage pass
          So richly decked with gold and glass
          That as a marvel strikes all eyes
          A glorious triumph for my Lais . . .

PHILAMINTE: Ah! 'My Lais'! A learned reference . . .[8]

BÉLISE: Which is symbolic. And quite priceless!

TRISSOTIN: Now, when you see her carriage pass
          So richly decked with gold and glass
          That as a marvel strikes all eyes,
          A glorious triumph for my Lais,
          Say not this carriage is vermilion:
          Say it cost me . . . above a million.

ARMANDE: Oooh! Aaah! We weren't expecting that!

PHILAMINTE: Here is the only man who can write with such taste.

BÉLISE: 'Say not this carriage is vermilion: Say it cost me . . . above a million.' You see how cleverly it rhymes: 'million, vermilion, above a million'

PHILAMINTE: I don't know if the very first time I met you I was somehow drawn to your mind, but I admire all you write in prose and verse.

TRISSOTIN (*to Philaminte*): Won't you read us something of yours, so that we in turn might admire?

PHILAMINTE: I have penned no verse, but I make so bold as to entertain hopes that soon I might be able to show you, as a friend, eight chapters concerning a literary Academy we propose to found. Plato simply stopped at the idea when he outlined his plans in the Republic. It was with the intention of realizing his concept that I have framed it on paper in prose. For I feel most strongly the wrongs done to us in matters of the mind. I intend to avenge women, all women everywhere, for the inferior position to which men have reduced us, for having restricted our talents to trivial pursuits and for closing the doors of higher learning to us.

ARMANDE: It is an immense insult to our sex to know that the scope of our intelligence is limited to judging a skirt or the hang of a coat or the beauty of a piece of lace or a sample of new brocade.

BÉLISE: We must rise above this shameful segregation and emancipate our minds.

TRISSOTIN: My respect for women is known in all quarters. If I pay homage to their sparkling eyes, I also pay tribute to their enlightened minds.

PHILAMINTE: And our sex acknowledges your fairness in this matter. But we wish to demonstrate to certain men, whose pride in their knowledge leads them to treat us with scorn, that women too can have a scientific turn of mind, that like them we too can meet in learned assemblies run according to the best principles, that in them we intend to bring together what is kept apart elsewhere,[9] to marry fine language with the higher knowledge, to penetrate the secrets of nature by experiment and in all questions selected for study to ensure that every school of thought is admitted but that none is espoused exclusively.

TRISSOTIN: In the matter of Order, I myself incline to the peripateticism of Aristotle.[10]

PHILAMINTE: In the matter of abstract reasoning, I favour Platonism.

ARMANDE: I like Epicurus – such lusty doctrines.

BÉLISE: Personally, I am quite drawn to atoms and particles. But I do find it hard to accept the vacuum. I am much more drawn to the idea of subtle matter.

TRISSOTIN: Descartes proposes the principle of the magnet, which meets my way of thinking.

ARMANDE: I love his swirls and eddies.

PHILAMINTE: And I his falling worlds.

ARMANDE: I cannot wait for our very own Academy to open and make us famous with some new discovery.

TRISSOTIN: We are expecting great things from the light you will shed on Nature which has few secrets from you.

PHILAMINTE: I do not wish to flatter myself, but I have indeed already made a discovery: I have clearly observed men standing on the moon.

BÉLISE: I haven't seen men there, as far as I know. But I have made out church steeples there as plain as I see you.

ARMANDE: Along with physics, our studies will include grammar, history, poetry and both moral and political philosophy.

PHILAMINTE: There is in the study of morals something which my heart cannot resist. In times gone by, it was the first love of the greatest minds. But to my sense, the Stoics were nearest the mark and I cannot conceive anything finer than their idea of the wise man.[11]

ARMANDE: And in the area of language,[12] we shall make our own rules known soon – and we intend to cause a stir. Each one of us, impelled by an aversion rooted in either reason or taste, has conceived a mortal loathing for certain words, both verbs and nouns, which we no longer use to each other. We are preparing to pronounce sentence of death on them, and it has been decided that we shall inaugurate our scholarly debates by edicts condemning all these different words of which we are determined to rid both prose and verse.

PHILAMINTE: But our Academy's finest project, a noble enterprise which thrills me, an endeavour so glorious that it will be trumpeted loud by all the best minds that posterity will produce, is this: the amputation of suggestive syllables which start scandalous echoes in even the most beautiful words. Such sounds are the perennial playthings of imbeciles in every age, the unimaginative commonplaces of tasteless jokers and the source of a mountain of disgusting innuendoes which are used to insult the modesty of women.

TRISSOTIN: Clearly, these are quite admirable plans.

BÉLISE: You shall see our rulings when they are all ready.

TRISSOTIN: I don't see that they can be anything but judicious and wise.

ARMANDE: With our laws, we shall become the arbiters of all new works. By our laws, all that is written in prose or verse will be subject to our decision. No author shall be allowed to be considered clever except by us and our friends. We shall seek out infringements everywhere and we shall find that no one henceforth will write well if they are not with us.

Scene iii:

LÉPINE, TRISSOTIN, PHILAMINTE, BÉLISE, ARMANDE, HENRIETTE, VADIUS

LÉPINE (*to Trissotin*): Sir, there's a man outside who'd like a word with you. He's dressed all in black and talks very quiet.

TRISSOTIN: It's the scholarly friend who's been begging me to do him the honour of arranging for him to meet you.

PHILAMINTE: You were absolutely right to ask him to come. (*To Armande and Bélise:*) Let us at least do him the honours of our minds. (*To Henriette, who makes as if to leave:*) Stop! I told you in the plainest terms that I need you here.

HENRIETTE: But what for?

PHILAMINTE: Come here. You'll be told soon enough.

TRISSOTIN (*as Vadius enters*): This is the man who has been dying to meet you. In bringing him here, Madame, I have no fear that I shall be taken to task for introducing an uninitiate into your company. He is more than qualified to take his place among the finest minds of the age.

PHILAMINTE: The hand that has guided him here is sufficient guarantee of his standing.

TRISSOTIN: He is utterly steeped in the writings of the ancients and knows as much Greek, Madame, as any man in France.

PHILAMINTE: Greek! Oh my God, sister, he knows Greek!

BÉLISE: Did you hear that niece? Greek!

ARMANDE: Greek! What bliss!

PHILAMINTE: So, sir, you know Greek. I beg you, allow us to embrace you for the love of Greek. (*Vadius kisses the cheeks of all the ladies but when he gets to Henriette she turns away.*)

HENRIETTE: Pray excuse me sir. I do not understand Greek.

PHILAMINTE: I positively dote on books written in Greek.

VADIUS: I fear that I might be intruding, Madame, in my eagerness which impels me to choose this day to offer my respects. Perhaps I am interrupting some learned discussion?

PHILAMINTE: Sir, a man who knows Greek cannot interrupt anything.

TRISSOTIN: He also performs miracles in both verse and prose and, if he is agreeable, he might give you a sample.

VADIUS: A common fault with authors is that they dominate the conversation by always dragging their works into it and by being indefatigable readers of their own fatiguing verses – in the Palais de Justice, the fashionable walks, in salons, even at the dinner table. Personally, to my way of thinking, there is nothing more ridiculous than an author who goes round looking for praise, bending the ears of whoever comes along and making them suffer the torments of the damned for the midnight oil he has burned. No one has ever seen me behaving with such tiresome persistence, and in this matter I share the opinion of a Greek sage who issued a clear instruction requiring authors to curb their unworthy enthusiasm for reading their own works aloud in public. I have here some lines, intended for young lovers, on which I would very much like to have your views.

TRISSOTIN: Your verse has a beauty of which other poets are quite incapable.

VADIUS: Venus and all the Graces preside over yours.

TRISSOTIN: Your lines flow so freely and you choose your words so well.

VADIUS: In every corner of yours the *ithos* and the *pathos* are visible.[13]

TRISSOTIN: You have given us eclogues in a style which far outstrips the sweetest charms of Theocritus and Virgil.

VADIUS: Your odes strike notes of such nobility, delicacy and sweetness that they leave Horace[14] limping in your wake.

TRISSOTIN: Was ever love sung more sweetly than in your songs?

VADIUS: Was there ever anything to equal the sonnets you have penned?

TRISSOTIN: Or anything more delightful than your little rondeaux?

VADIUS: Or anything more full of wit than all your madrigals?

TRISSOTIN: Your ballads are admirable.

VADIUS: I think your gift for improvising is quite captivating.

TRISSOTIN: If France would only acknowledge your gifts . . .

VADIUS: If the age in which we lived really valued its writers . . .

TRISSOTIN: . . . you would ride through the streets in a golden coach.

VADIUS: . . . the public would raise statues to you. But I have a ballad here and I insist that you –

TRISSOTIN: Have you come across a certain little sonnet upon the subject of the fever with which Princess Uranie has been struck?

VADIUS: Why yes. It was read out to me yesterday in a salon.

TRISSOTIN: Do you know who wrote it?

VADIUS: No. But this much I do know: without wishing to flatter him, his sonnet is quite worthless.

TRISSOTIN: Yet many people have found it admirable.

VADIUS: That doesn't prevent it being twaddle. If you'd read it, you'd think as I do.

TRISSOTIN: But I think no such thing! Few men are capable of writing such a sonnet.

VADIUS: Well, God preserve me from perpetrating any like it!

TRISSOTIN: I maintain that no one could do better and my reason for saying so is that I myself am its author.

VADIUS: You are?

TRISSOTIN: Yes.

VADIUS: I can't think how such a misunderstanding could have arisen.

TRISSOTIN: The fact is that one was unfortunate enough not to please you.

VADIUS: My mind must have wandered as I listened, or perhaps whoever read it out ruined it for me. But let's say no more about it and come to my ballad.

TRISSOTIN: I have always thought the ballad as being rather insipid. It's quite out of fashion nowadays. It reeks of the past.

VADIUS: Yet many people find the ballad charming.

TRISSOTIN: That does not prevent my disliking it intensely.

VADIUS: It's none the worse for that.

TRISSOTIN: It has a special charm for pedants.

VADIUS: How odd then that you don't care for it yourself.

TRISSOTIN: You should not be so stupid as to attribute your own failings to other people.

VADIUS: But you throw yours in my face with rare impertinence.

TRISSOTIN: Ignoramus! Scribbler!

VADIUS: Hack! You're a disgrace to the profession!

TRISSOTIN: Purveyor of second-hand poems! Bare-faced plagiarist!

VADIUS: Pettifogging pedant!

PHILAMINTE: Please gentlemen! Whatever are you thinking of?

TRISSOTIN: Be off with you and restore what you have so shamelessly stolen from the Greek and Roman authors who demand the return of what is theirs!

VADIUS: Be off yourself and do the decent thing by the Muses for having murdered Horace in your poems!

TRISSOTIN: Have you forgotten your book and how little impact it made?

VADIUS: Have you forgotten your publisher whom you have reduced to bread and water?

TRISSOTIN: My reputation is assured. Nothing you can say will undermine it.

VADIUS: Really? Then let me refer you to the author of the *Satires*.[15]

TRISSOTIN: Allow me to do the same for you.

VADIUS: I can at least take satisfaction from the fact that people can see that he treats me more honourably. He directs a brief aside at me when speaking of a number of writers revered in the best-informed circles. But he simply cannot let you alone in his verse where you crop up everywhere as the butt of his venom.

TRISSOTIN: But for that very reason it is I who emerge the more honourably. He relegates you to the crowd, like some miserable hanger-on. He obviously thought one thrust was enough to see you off and never did you the honour of striking a second time. But he singles me out for personal attention as a worthy opponent for whom he must needs call upon all his resources. And the fact that his attacks are repeated here, there and everywhere only goes to prove that he does not believe that he has won.

VADIUS: My pen will teach you what kind of man I am.

TRISSOTIN: And mine will show you who your master is.

VADIUS: I challenge you in verse and prose, Greek and Latin.

TRISSOTIN: Well then, we shall meet again, face to face, at Barbin's.[16]
(*Exit Vadius.*)

Scene iv:

TRISSOTIN, PHILAMINTE, ARMANDE, BÉLISE, HENRIETTE

TRISSOTIN: Do not blame me for losing my temper Madame, for I was merely defending your opinion on my sonnet which he had the impertinence to attack.

PHILAMINTE: I shall do everything I can to patch things up between you. But now let's turn to something else. Come here Henriette. For some time now I have been uneasy that you show no sign of possessing any intellectual curiosity whatsoever. But I have found a way of making you take an interest.

HENRIETTE: You shouldn't concern yourself about me on that score. Debating learned topics doesn't appeal to me. I prefer the simple life, for it's obvious from your discussions that you have to work very hard to be brilliant. I have absolutely no ambitions in that direction. I am quite happy, mother, to settle for being dull. I'd much rather have only ordinary things to say than have to go through agonies to be able to make clever remarks.

PHILAMINTE: I see. I am hurt by what you say, but I have no intention of allowing myself to be shamed like this by my own daughter. A beautiful face is a fragile advantage, a transient flower, a passing glory, which is never more than skin deep. But a beautiful mind exists beneath the surface and is more durable. That is why I have long been trying to find a way of giving you the kind of beauty which time shall not harvest, of encouraging a taste for learning in you, of opening your mind to the higher knowledge. That thought, the fruit of my deepest wishes, has finally led me to decide to find you a husband, a man of intellect. That man is none other than this gentleman, and you will oblige me by regarding him as the husband I have chosen for you.

HENRIETTE: For me, mother?

PHILAMINTE: Yes, for you. Now don't be coy.

BÉLISE (*to Trissotin*): I understand. Your eyes implore me to consent if you now wish to bestow upon another a heart which I possess. Very well, I agree. I shall not stand in the way of a marriage which will be the making of you.

TRISSOTIN (*to Henriette*): Madame, I do not know what to say, I am quite overwhelmed . . . , for this marriage by which I see I am honoured, makes me –

HENRIETTE: Hold on sir! We are not married yet. You must not be so hasty.

PHILAMINTE: That's no way to answer. Don't you realize that if . . . But I'll say no more. I think you understand me. (*To Trissotin:*) She'll see reason. Come, we'll leave her to think about it. (*Philaminte, Bélise and Trissotin leave.*)

Scene v:

HENRIETTE, ARMANDE

ARMANDE: Mother has spared no effort on your behalf. A more distinguished husband she could not have found for –

HENRIETTE: If you think he's such a catch, why don't you marry him yourself?

ARMANDE: He's been picked out for you, not for me.

HENRIETTE: I'll stand down and let you have him – you are my older sister, after all.

ARMANDE: If I thought as well of marriage as you do, I would be delighted to accept your offer.

HENRIETTE: If I thought as well of pedants as you do, I should find him a very suitable match.

ARMANDE: Nevertheless, though our tastes might be quite different sister, we still have to obey our parents. A mother has total authority over us and you are wrong to think that resistance . . .

Scene vi:

CHRYSALE, ARISTE, CLITANDRE, HENRIETTE, ARMANDE

CHRYSALE (*presenting Clitandre to Henriette*): Come my girl, you must give your approval to what I propose. Remove your glove. Take this gentleman's hand and, from this moment on, think of him in your heart as the man whose wife I intend you to be.

ARMANDE: Sister, you seem rather more enthusiastic about this one.

HENRIETTE: We must always obey our parents, sister. A father has total authority over us.

ARMANDE: A mother has some claim on our obedience.

CHRYSALE: What does that mean?

ARMANDE: I mean that I am very much afraid that in this matter you and my mother do not see eye to eye, for she has in mind another husband –

CHRYSALE: Hold your tongue, you prattlebox. You can talk philosophy with her to your heart's content, but keep your nose out of what I do. Tell her what I've decided and warn her that she's not to come here and start arguing. Now, be off with you.

ARISTE: Bravo! You are doing marvellously!

CLITANDRE: Oh joy! Such bliss! How sweetly life has treated me!

CHRYSALE (*to Clitandre*): Come along, take her hand. You two go on ahead. (*To Ariste:*) Take her up to her room. Such a tender scene. You know I'm deeply touched to see such affection. It's a tonic for this old heart of mine. I can remember when I was young and in love.

Act IV

Scene i:
ARMANDE, PHILAMINTE

ARMANDE: Yes, she did not hesitate for an instant. She took such pride in obeying him. Though I was there, she hardly gave her feelings time to hear what he'd decided before surrendering. It looked as though she wasn't so much respecting the will of her father as letting everyone know that she was challenging the orders of her mother.

PHILAMINTE: I'll teach her by whose authority, his or mine, the laws of reason must direct her wishes, and which should govern her conduct, her mother or her father, mind or body, form or matter.

ARMANDE: The wretched man should at least have paid you his respects. He's going about things in a very odd way if he's intending to be your son-in-law against your wishes.

PHILAMINTE: He hasn't got where he would dearly like to be yet. I thought him rather handsome when he was paying his court to you. But I never liked his attitude. He knows that I write, heaven be praised, but he never asked me to read him anything.

Scene ii:

CLITANDRE (*enters quietly and listens*), ARMANDE,
PHILAMINTE

ARMANDE: If I were you, I should never allow him to be Henriette's husband. It would be quite wrong if anyone thought that I am in any way biased in this matter and that the cowardly way he has been seen to behave towards me has sown the seed of some secret resentment in my heart. The soul arms itself against such adversity with the stout buckler of Philosophy, and with its support a person may rise above anything. But by treating you like this, he leaves you no choice. Your honour requires you to oppose his wishes, for he's not really the sort of man you could ever like. I never felt, when we use to talk together, that he really had any respect for you.

PHILAMINTE: The poor fool!

ARMANDE: Whenever you added to your reputation, he always seemed cool in singing your praises.

PHILAMINTE: The brute!

ARMANDE: There were many occasions when I read him poems you had written, new works, but he never thought much of them.

PHILAMINTE: The nerve!

ARMANDE: We often used to have words about it. You'd never believe what stupid things he —

CLITANDRE (*revealing himself, to Armande*): Now just a minute, if you don't mind. Show a little charity, or failing that, a little honesty. What harm did I ever do you? What offence have I committed that you should want to direct the full force of your eloquence against me, blacken my good name and to go such lengths to ensure that I am hated by the very people I need? Tell me. Speak. Why are you so terribly angry? I am happy to let Madame here, who is fair-minded, be the judge.

ARMANDE: If I were really as angry as I am accused of being, I could produce plenty of reasons to justify my resentment and you'd deserve it all. For our first love establishes such sacred rights over our souls that we should rather sacrifice wealth and even life itself than fall in love with someone else. There is no horror to compare with fickleness: a faithless heart is a moral monster.

CLITANDRE: Madame, how can you call fickle what your proud heart itself ordered me to do? I have done no more than act upon what its dictates imposed on me, and if I have offended you, then your own pride is the cause of it. At first, your beauty possessed my heart which for two years burned with a constant flame. There were no eager attentions, duties, respects, services, no loving sacrifice which I did not offer you. But all my passion, all my thoughts, had no effect and I found you opposed to my tenderest wishes. What you have spurned I have offered another to choose. Consider, Madame: is the fault mine or yours? Did I seek change or did you urge me to it? Was it I who left you, or you who drove me away?

ARMANDE: Sir, how can you call being opposed to your tenderest wishes the desire I have to purge those wishes of their vulgarity, to distil them until they reach that state of purity which is the true beauty of perfect love? Why can't you, for my sake, keep your thoughts free and clear of any hint of crude sensuality? Why can't you savour the sweeter joy of a union of souls in which the body has no part to play? You are capable of loving only with a love that is coarse, with all the trappings of material ties. To keep alive the passion which another heart ignites in yours, you need marriage and all that goes with it. Ah! this is a strange kind of love! Great souls do not burn with such earthly flames. Their senses play no part in their yearnings and their noble passion seeks only the union of two hearts: it sets the rest to one side, as being unworthy. It is a passion as pure and clean as the love of God. It impels them to breathe virtuous sighs and does not incline them to base desires. There's nothing impure in the goal which hearts like those set for themselves – they love for love and for nothing else. It is to the mind alone that all their joys are directed and they are never aware that they even have a body.

CLITANDRE: Well I personally, Madame, am unfortunately aware, if you don't mind my saying so, that I have a body as well as a soul, and I feel the one is too closely linked to the other simply to be set aside. I do not possess the art of detaching the one from the other. Heaven has not imparted that philosophy to me and my body and my soul go hand in hand. There is nothing finer, as you say, than the pure love which directs itself to the spirit, the twinning of souls, the tender yearnings cleansed of all hint of sensuality. But love like that is far too refined for me: I am rather coarsely inclined, as you accuse me. I love with my whole being and the love that anyone offers me, I admit, has to include my whole person. It's not a matter which calls for harsh punishment, and, without wishing to cast doubt on your admirable sentiments, I merely remark that I observe that my approach is widespread among people in general. Furthermore, marriage has not gone out of fashion, and is considered a sufficiently honest, wholesome bond for me to have wanted to become your husband, without giving you cause to take offence at the liberty of such a thought.

ARMANDE: Very well sir, very well. Since, despite all I have said, your animal urges must be satisfied and because you need carnal bonds and corporeal chains before you can be induced to appreciate love that is less earthly, then, if my mother consents, I am ready to ignore my better judgement for your sake and accept what you propose.

CLITANDRE: It's too late, Madame. Another has taken your place. And I should be ungrateful indeed if I, by any such change of heart, were to abuse the welcome and not repay the kindness which were my refuge against your pride.

PHILAMINTE: But are you really counting on my support, sir, for this other marriage which you have in mind? And are you aware, pray, in these plans of yours, that I already have another husband for Henriette?

CLITANDRE: But Madame, please give a thought to the man you have chosen. I beg you, do not expose me to such embarrassment, do not condemn me to the ignominious fate of being regarded as Monsieur Trissotin's rival. The love which clever people have in mind has turned you against me, and that kind of love could not have given me a less noble opponent. There are those, and they are numerous, who have had their reputation for cleverness made for them by the bad taste of the present age. But Monsieur Trissotin has fooled nobody. Everywhere justice is done to the writings he thrusts upon us and, outside this house, they are everywhere judged for what they are worth. But I have been amazed on a score of occasions to hear you praise to the skies silly poetry which you'd disown if you'd written it yourself.

PHILAMINTE: If you judge him differently from the way we do it is because we do not see him through the same eyes as you.

Scene iii:

TRISSOTIN, ARMANDE, PHILAMINTE, CLITANDRE

TRISSOTIN: I've come to tell you the good news. We had a narrow escape, Madame, as we slept in our beds last night! A comet passed close to us, falling right through our vortex. Now, if it had collided with us as it went on its way, the earth would have been shattered into small pieces, just like glass.

PHILAMINTE: Perhaps we could discuss that on some other occasion. This gentleman here would not see the point of it. He professes to be fond of ignorance and in particular he hates wit and learning.

CLITANDRE: That statement calls for some qualification. Let me explain, Madame. What I hate is the kind of wit and learning which spoil people. Of themselves, these things are fine and good, but I'd rather be classed as an ignoramus than to be clever the way some people are.

TRISSOTIN: Personally, I don't believe, whatever its effects, that science can spoil anything.

CLITANDRE: And it's my contention that science can make fools of people in both what they say and do.

TRISSOTIN: That is a very paradoxical remark.

CLITANDRE: I'm not particularly clever myself, but I think I would be able to substantiate it without difficulty. If arguments weren't sufficient, then at all events there is no shortage of well-known examples that I could call upon.

TRISSOTIN: You could quote as many as you like but they would prove nothing.

CLITANDRE: I shouldn't have to look very far for what I needed.

TRISSOTIN: I myself don't see these well-known examples.

CLITANDRE: I see them as plain as a pikestaff.

TRISSOTIN: I have always believed that it was ignorance, not science, that made fools.

CLITANDRE: Then you believed wrong. I can assure you that a learned fool is a bigger fool than an ignorant fool.

TRISSOTIN: The common view is against your generalizations, since ignorant and foolish are synonyms.

CLITANDRE: If you want to move the discussion to the way words are used, the link between pedant and fool is even closer.

TRISSOTIN: Foolishness in the latter is present in its purest, literal form.

CLITANDRE: And in the former, study serves merely to reinforce nature.

TRISSOTIN: Knowledge has its own in-built justification.

CLITANDRE: Knowledge is out of place in a fool.

TRISSOTIN: Ignorance must have a very great attraction for you since you leap so readily to its defence.

CLITANDRE: If ignorance has charms for me, it is only since I have had dealings with certain clever persons.

TRISSOTIN: If we were acquainted with those certain clever persons, they might well compare favourably with certain other people who draw attention to themselves.

CLITANDRE: Yes, but only if we took those certain clever persons at their own estimation. There is less agreement among those certain other people.

PHILAMINTE (*to Clitandre*): Sir, it seems to me that –

CLITANDRE: Please Madame. This gentleman is quite capable of holding his own without other people rushing to his aid. I am already reeling under the savagery of his attack and if I fight back I am very much on the defensive.

ARMANDE: But the insulting venom of the answers which you –

CLITANDRE: Someone else who wants to help him! I lay down my weapons!

PHILAMINTE: One can tolerate the cut and thrust of intellectual debate, as long as the attacks do not become personal.

CLITANDRE: But good God, nothing's been said so far for him to take offence at. He can take a joke as well as any man in France. He's had a lot worse barbs directed at him and his self-confidence has merely shrugged it all off.

TRISSOTIN: In this battle I have been drawn into, I am not the least surprised to see you defend the position you have adopted. It has taken root at Court: need I say more? As is well known, the Court has little regard for cleverness, for it is in its interest to promote ignorance. It is as a courtier that you rush to its defence.

CLITANDRE: You have a very low opinion of the much-maligned Court which must be saddened to observe that not a day passes without clever people like you openly sneering at it. You take out all your bilious ill-humour on it and lay the sole blame for your lack of success on the bad taste you accuse it of having. Allow me, Monsieur Trissotin, with all the respect with which your name fills me, to tell you that you and your colleagues would be much better employed in speaking of the Court in more moderate terms. When viewed objectively, the Court is really not as stupid as you gentlemen have persuaded yourselves that it is. It has enough common-sense to be able to form a sensible view of all things, and is a venue where anyone can learn the elements of good taste. And, setting all flattery aside, courtly wit is as commendable as all the obscure erudition of the pedants.

TRISSOTIN: We see the results of its good taste all too clearly, sir.

CLITANDRE: In what respects, sir, do you observe its taste to be bad?

TRISSOTIN: What I observe, sir, is that in the area of science Rasius and Baldus do honour to France, yet their merit, though trumpeted abroad loud enough, does not attract the eye of the Court, nor its bounty.

CLITANDRE: I quite see why you are not pleased, and I also see, sir, that modesty forbids you to include yourself in their number. But, if I may also leave you out of the reckoning, what have these intellectual warriors done for the state? What services have their writings performed for the Court to be accused of such dreadful injustice and for complaints to be made on all sides that it has failed to honour their learned names with its favour and tangible rewards? So their learning is vital to France! And the books they write are of great value to the Court! A few miserable blockheads with tiny brains get it into their heads that they are important persons in the state simply because what they write is printed and bound in leather. They think that they decide the fate of thrones with their pen, that when the news breaks of their latest offerings they should see pensions fly in their direction, that the eyes of the whole universe are watching them all the time, that the glory of their name spreads everywhere, and that they are famed as prodigies of learning simply because they know what other men discovered before them, because they have had eyes and ears for thirty years, because they have spent nine or ten thousand nights dabbling in Greek and Latin and filling their heads with a dubious haul of all the old rubbish that litters the pages of books. They appear intoxicated by all the things they know. The only quality they have is a wealth of tiresome chatter. They are good at noting, have no common-sense and are full of an absurd, preposterous zeal for belittling true wit and science everywhere.

PHILAMINTE: You are very heated sir, and your anger reveals the way Nature moves in you – it was being called a rival that stirred you to . . .

Scene iv:
JULIEN, TRISSOTIN, PHILAMINTE, CLITANDRE, ARMANDE

JULIEN: The learned gentleman who called earlier and whose valet I have the honour of being, Madame, requests you to read this note.

PHILAMINTE: No matter how important it is that I should read this note, you must learn, my man, that it is most inept to come blundering into a conversation like this. When you call at a house, you should go first to the servants so that you may make your entrance like valet who knows his business.

JULIEN: I shall write that down in my notebook Madame.

PHILAMINTE (*reads*): 'Madame, Trissotin has been boasting that he will marry your daughter. I beg to inform you that his philosophy thinks no further than your money, and that you would be well advised not to finalize the marriage before reading the poem which I am presently writing against him. Until I am ready with my portrait of him, in which I intend to paint him in his true colours, I send you Horace, Virgil, Terence and Catullus, where you will see that I have marked in the margins all the passages he has pilfered.'

Really! On account of this wedding I have set my heart on, a man of merit is attacked by many enemies. Well, their fury only confirms my intention to do something which will confound their jealousy and make it quite plain that what they are doing will have the effect of hastening what they are trying to prevent. (*To Julien:*) Take the note back to your master at once and tell him, so that he may be apprised of the importance I attach to his noble-minded warnings and of how worthy I consider them of being followed, that this very evening I shall give my daughter in marriage to (*pointing to Trissotin*) this gentleman. (*To Clitandre:*) You sir, as a family friend, may be present at the signing of the marriage contract and, for my own part, I gladly invite you to come. Armande, make sure to send word to the notary and then go and tell your sister what is happening.

ARMANDE: There's no need for me to go and tell my sister. Monsieur Clitandre here will be sure to run along at once to give her the news and encourage her to rebel against your plans.

PHILAMINTE: We shall see which of us has more power over her and whether or not I make her do her duty. (*Exit.*)

ARMANDE: I very much regret, sir, that things have not turned out quite the way you had in mind.

CLITANDRE: I intend to work with all the zeal at my command, Madame, to relieve you of that regret.

ARMANDE: I fear that all your efforts will not meet with success.

CLITANDRE: Perhaps you will see that your fears were groundless.

ARMANDE: I hope I do.

CLITANDRE: I am certain you will – and I am sure I can count on your support.

ARMANDE: Yes, I shall give you all the help I can.

CLITANDRE: And for your help I shall be most grateful. (*Exit Armande.*)

Scene v:

CHRYSALE, ARISTE, HENRIETTE, CLITANDRE

CLITANDRE: Without your support, sir, I am lost. Your wife has rejected my proposal of marriage and has set her heart on having Trissotin as her son-in-law.

CHRYSALE: But what fanciful idea has she got into her head? Why the devil does she want Trissotin?

ARISTE: It's because of the name he has for writing poems in Latin that he's seen off his rival.

CLITANDRE: She wants the marriage to take place this evening.

CHRYSALE: This evening?

CLITANDRE: This evening.

CHRYSALE: And this evening I, to foil her, intend you and Henriette to be married.

CLITANDRE: She has sent someone round to the notary to draw up the contract.

CHRYSALE: I'll send for him to come and draw up the right one.

CLITANDRE: Henriette is going to be told by her sister about the wedding and must put her feelings in readiness.

CHRYSALE: And I shall use my full authority to command her to get ready to give her hand in a quite different marriage. Ah, I'll show them when it comes to laying down the law whether or not I'm master in my own house. (*To Henriette:*) We'll be back, so wait for us. Come brother, follow me. You too my boy.

HENRIETTE (*to Ariste*): Oh, do try and keep him in the mood he's in now.

ARISTE: I shall do all I can to back you up.

CLITANDRE: Despite all the powerful help that's been promised me, your heart, Madame, is still my greatest hope.

HENRIETTE: You can always be sure of my heart.

CLITANDRE: I can only be happy if I can count on it.

HENRIETTE: You know by what chains they intend to bind it.

CLITANDRE: As long as it beats for me, I can't see that there's anything to fear.

HENRIETTE: I shall do everything I can to advance our tender cause. But if all my efforts fail and I do not become your wife, there is a holy retreat to which our souls are drawn: it will prevent me becoming the wife of anyone else.

CLITANDRE: May heavenly justice grant this day that I shall not receive that particular proof of your love!

Act V

Scene i:

HENRIETTE, TRISSOTIN

HENRIETTE: It is about this marriage my mother is planning, sir, that I wanted to speak privately to you. I thought that in the midst of all the commotion I see in the house that I might be able to make you listen to reason. I know you think that in addition to my love you believe I shall bring you a large dowry. But money, though many set great store by it, can have only tawdry attractions for a true philosopher. You should not limit your scorn of wealth and contempt for meaningless rank merely to the words you say.

TRISSOTIN: And indeed it is not that which draws me to you. Your lustrous beauty, your shining, gentle eyes, your gracefulness, your whole being – these are the riches, the wealth which have attracted my love and my tenderness, they are the only treasures that have captivated my heart.

HENRIETTE: I am obliged to you for your unstinting feelings. Your fulsome love embarrasses me, for I regret, sir, that I cannot return it. I respect you as much as anyone could, but I see an obstacle which stands in the way of my loving you. As you know, a single heart cannot belong to two persons and I sense that Clitandre has made himself master of mine. I am aware he does not have your merits. I know that I do not have a good eye when it come to choosing a husband. I know that you have many fine talents which by rights should delight me. I know I am wrong but I cannot help it. The only effect my reason has on me is to reprove of my blindness.

TRISSOTIN: When you give me your hand, to which others have urged me to aspire, you will give me the heart of which Clitandre is master. I make so bold as to venture that I myself am master of enough gentle arts to allow me to find the secret of being loved.

HENRIETTE: No sir. My heart is bound by its first impressions and will remain untouched by your arts. I can speak freely to you here, and there is nothing in what I am about to say that should shock you. The loving feeling which stirs in our hearts has nothing to do with merit, as you know. Whim has a part in it and when we love someone, we may often be hard put to say why. If we fell in love by conscious choice and common-sense, then, sir, you should have my heart and all my affection. But we observe that love works in a different way. Please leave me in my blindness and reject the force which others would use on your behalf to make me obey. When a man is honourable, he has no wish to be indebted to the power parents have over us. He shrinks from the idea that the woman he loves must be sacrificed to him and will want none but a heart that is willing. Do not encourage my mother to insist on her choice by asserting the full rigour of her rights over my wishes. Stop loving me and offer someone else the homage of a heart as precious as yours.

TRISSOTIN: But how can my heart do what you ask? Order it to do something it can do, for how can this heart of mine be incapable of loving you? Unless, that is, you stop being lovable Madame, and no longer allow my eyes to feast upon such heavenly charms –

HENRIETTE: Ah! let's have no more of this foolishness sir! In your poems you talk of Iris and Phyllis and Lais whom you portray as charming and swear such passionate feelings for them that –

TRISSOTIN: That's my mind speaking, not my heart. What you see with them is merely the poet in love. But Henriette I worship with all my heart and soul.

HENRIETTE: Please sir!

TRISSOTIN: If this offends you, then I am far from done offending you yet. My passion, which thus far has been hidden from view, offers you a fire which shall burn everlastingly: nothing can put out its tender flames! Although your beauty rejects my advances, I cannot refuse the help of a mother who intends to crown my love with success. And as long as I achieve such bewitching happiness, provided I have you, I don't care how it's done.

HENRIETTE: But do you realize that you run much greater risks than you imagine by wanting to use force to win my affections? To be blunt, little good can ever come of marrying a girl against her wishes. When she sees that she is being coerced, she might well give way to resentments which should make a husband quake and tremble.

TRISSOTIN: There is nothing in what you say to give me cause for concern. A philosopher is prepared for any eventuality. Purged by reason of all vulgar weakness, he rises above such things and has learned not to let himself be discomfited in any way by matters which are beyond his control.

HENRIETTE: Really sir, I am delighted with you. I never knew philosophy was so wonderful that it can teach people to bear conjugal strife with equanimity. The strength of character which you possess so particularly deserves to be given a worthier opportunity of showing what it can do. It calls for a wife who with loving care would provide constant opportunities for you to exercise it. And since, to be frank, I would not dare claim for one moment to be the kind of person who could bring out its full glory, I leave that task to someone else and swear here and now that I abandon all hope of having you for a husband.

TRISSOTIN: We shall soon see how all this turns out. The notary has been sent for. He's here. (*Exit.*)

Scene ii:

CHRYSALE, CLITANDRE, MARTINE, HENRIETTE

CHRYSALE: There you are my girl, I'm glad you're here. Come now, do your duty by sacrificing your own wishes to the will of your father. I intend, oh yes, I fully intend to teach your mother to behave herself. And to show her I mean business here's Martine whom I've brought back and shall reinstate under my roof, no matter what Madame says.

HENRIETTE: Such determination is to be commended, but do try, father, not to let your resolve falter. Be firm in wanting your wishes to come about and don't let your kind heart get the better of you. Don't weaken and be sure not to let mother get the upper hand.

CHRYSALE: What do you mean? What do you think I am? A ninny?

HENRIETTE: Heaven forbid.

CHRYSALE: Am I stupid?

HENRIETTE: I didn't say that.

CHRYSALE: Do you think I'm incapable of being firm and behaving like a sensible man?

HENRIETTE: Not at all father.

CHRYSALE: Is it that I, at my age, haven't got wit enough to be master in my own house?

HENRIETTE: Of course you have.

CHRYSALE: Or that I'm such a weak character that I let my wife lead me by the nose?

HENRIETTE: Certainly not father.

CHRYSALE: Well then! What do you mean? I think it's a joke the way you're speaking to me.

HENRIETTE: If I shocked you, that was not what I intended.

CHRYSALE: My word must be law in my own house.

HENRIETTE: Of course father.

CHRYSALE: Under this roof, I am the only one who has the right to command.

HENRIETTE: Yes, you're right.

CHRYSALE: I am the head of the household.

HENRIETTE: I agree.

CHRYSALE: I'm the one who says what's to become of my daughter.

HENRIETTE: Oh yes!

CHRYSALE: I have the full authority of Heaven to decide your future.

HENRIETTE: Who's going to argue with that?

CHRYSALE: And as to the matter of taking a husband, I'll show you that it's your father you must obey, not your mother.

HENRIETTE: Ah, in saying that you flatter my dearest wishes. Insist on being obeyed, that's all I ask.

CHRYSALE: We shall see if my wife dares oppose my wishes . . .

CLITANDRE: Here she is and she's bringing the notary with her.

CHRYSALE: You must all give me your support.

MARTINE: Don't worry about me, I'll be sure to back you up, if needs be.

Scene iii:

PHILAMINTE, BÉLISE, ARMANDE, TRISSOTIN,
NOTARY, CHRYSALE, CLITANDRE, HENRIETTE,
MARTINE

PHILAMINTE (*to the Notary*): Couldn't you modify your boorish style and give us a contract written in more literary language?

NOTARY: The style is very good Madame, and I'd be a fool to want to change a word of it.

BÉLISE: Oooh! such philistinism here in the heart of France! But at the very least sir, couldn't you defer to learning by expressing the amount of the dowry not in crowns, livres and francs but in minas and talents, and by dating the document with Ides and Calends?[17]

NOTARY: Why Madame, if I were to agree to what you ask, I should be the laughing-stock of all my colleagues.

PHILAMINTE: We're not getting anywhere complaining to this barbarian, so come sir, you may use this table to write on. (*Seeing Martine*) Oh! so the impudent hussy dares to show her face here again! Would you mind telling me why you've brought her back?

CHRYSALE: I'll tell you why later, when we've time. We have something else to settle first.

NOTARY: Let's proceed with the contract. Where is the bride?

PHILAMINTE: The daughter I'm giving away in marriage is my youngest.

NOTARY: Good.

CHRYSALE: And here she is, sir. Her name is Henriette.

NOTARY: Very good. And the groom?

PHILAMINTE (*indicating Trissotin*): The husband I am giving her is this gentleman.

CHRYSALE (*indicating Clitandre*): And the man I, myself, in my personal capacity, intend her to marry is this gentleman.

NOTARY: Two husbands? By law, that's one too many.

PHILAMINTE: Why have you stopped writing? Put down, sir, put Trissotin as my son-in-law.

CHRYSALE: For my son-in-law, put down, sir, put Clitandre.

NOTARY: You must come to some agreement between yourselves and, after mature reflection, see eye to eye about who is to be the groom.

PHILAMINTE: Abide, sir, by the choice I have made.

CHRYSALE: Sir, do this my way.

NOTARY: Tell me which of you I'm supposed to listen to.

PHILAMINTE (*to Chrysale*): So! You are set on contesting my wishes?

CHRYSALE: I will not stand by and let any man ask for my daughter's hand merely for the money he sees in my family.

PHILAMINTE: So you think your money is at the back of this? Money is hardly a matter to concern a philosopher!

CHRYSALE: Well, I've chosen Clitandre to be her husband.

PHILAMINTE (*indicating Trissotin*): And here is the gentleman I have chosen to marry her. My choice shall be respected. It's all settled.

CHRYSALE: My word, you're being very high-handed about this!

MARTINE: It ain't for wives to give the orders. I'm all for lettin' the men have their say in everythin'.

CHRYSALE: Well said.

MARTINE: Even if it was sure as sure as how I'll get me marchin' orders again for sayin' so, the hen mustn't crow before the cock.

CHRYSALE: That's right.

MARTINE: Look round and you'll see people always have a good larf at a man when it's his wife wot wears the trousers in his house.

CHRYSALE: True.

MARTINE: I tell you straight, if I had a nusband I'd want him to rule the roost. I couldn't love him if he acted all hen-pecked, like. And if I had a fancy to answer back or talked too much, I'd think it was fair enough if he taught me to mind my lip with a damned good hidin'.

CHRYSALE: That's the way to talk.

MARTINE: The master's right to want a proper hubby for his daughter.

CHRYSALE: Yes.

MARTINE: What reason could he have for not letting her have Clitandre? He's young and he's handsome. And please tell me why she should get herself saddled with a pedant who goes on and on? What she needs is a nusband, not somebody who'll be forever lecturin' her. She don't want to learn all that there Greek and Latin, so what do she want with Monsieur Trissotin?

CHRYSALE: Exactly!

PHILAMINTE: Of course, we have to let her prattle on and on.

MARTINE: All your professors is good for is spouting in public. If I wanted a nusband, and I've said this ever so many times, I'd never pick one with brains. Brains ain't what you want in a house. Books and marriage don't go together. Now if I was to say yes to a man, the only book he'd get would be me. He wouldn't know A from B and, begging your pardon Madame, he wouldn't be a doctor of nothing except his wife.

PHILAMINTE (*to Chrysale*): Is that the end? Have I listened long enough – unmoved – to your eloquent mouthpiece?

CHRYSALE: What she says is true.

PHILAMINTE: And I tell you, to put an end to this discussion, that I am absolutely determined that my wishes shall be carried out. Henriette and Monsieur Trissotin will be married at once. I have spoken. I insist, so don't argue. If you've given your word to Clitandre, offer him the alternative of marrying Armande.

CHRYSALE: That might be a way of settling this matter. Look here, you two, would you agree to that?

HENRIETTE: Oh father!

CLITANDRE: But sir . . .

BÉLISE: It might be possible to make him another offer he might prefer, but in that case I should insist on a kind of love which would be as pure as the sun's rays. Thinking matter would be allowable, but we will not tolerate gross matter which has mere extension.[18]

Scene iv:

ARISTE, CHRYSALE, PHILAMINTE, BÉLISE,
HENRIETTE, ARMANDE, TRISSOTIN, NOTARY,
CLITANDRE, MARTINE

ARISTE: I regret having to disturb these joyful proceedings and be the cause of vexation. These two letters make me the bearer of bad tidings which I can see have very serious implications for you. (*To Philaminte:*) This one is for you. It was sent to me by your lawyer. (*To Chrysale:*) The other one is for you and was sent to me from Lyons.

PHILAMINTE: What worrying disaster can he be writing to me about now?

ARISTE: There's one in this letter. You can read what it is.

PHILAMINTE (*reads*): 'Madame, I have asked your brother to convey this letter to you. It will inform you of what I have not dared to say to you in person. The utter neglect with which you mismanage your affairs has meant that your barrister's clerk has not been in touch with me and, as a result, you have lost the lawsuit which you should have won.'

CHRYSALE (*to Philaminte*): You've lost the case!

PHILAMINTE: You seem very upset! I am not the least shaken by the news. Come now, try at least to show a less commonplace spirit and set your face, as I do, against the adversity of fortune. (*Reads*) 'Your negligence has cost you forty thousand crowns, and you have been sentenced by order of the court to pay this sum, together with costs.' Sentenced! What a shocking word. It should be used only for criminals.

ARISTE: He's wrong of course and you are right to protest. He should have written that you are requested by order of the court to pay forty thousands crowns, plus costs, at your earliest convenience.

PHILAMINTE: What's in the other letter?

CHRYSALE (*reads*): 'Sir, The friendship which I have for your brother leads me to take an interest in everything that concerns you. I am aware that you placed your entire fortune in the hands of Argante and Damon, and beg to inform you that this day they have both been declared bankrupt.' Oh my God! I've lost all my money in one fell swoop!

PHILAMINTE: Your reaction is quite disgraceful. Fie, this is nothing. For the sage, there are no unconquerable reversals of fortune, for even if he loses everything, he still has himself. Let us finish what we began. Put all your worries to one side. (*Indicating Trissotin*) This gentleman's fortune is large enough for both him and us.

TRISSOTIN: No Madame, press this matter no further. I can see that everyone is opposed to this marriage and it is not my purpose to force people against their will.

PHILAMINTE: This observation is very sudden! And it follows hard on the heels, sir, of our misfortune.

TRISSOTIN: I have finally grow weary of all the opposition. I'd prefer to have nothing more to do with this whole vexatious business. I do not want a wife who is unwilling.

PHILAMINTE: I detect, yes, I detect something in you which I have refused to believe until now, and it reflects no credit on you.

TRISSOTIN: You may detect in me whatever you like and I couldn't care less about what you make of it. But I'm not the sort of man who is prepared to be placed in the ignominious position of being rejected in the insulting manner I have had to suffer. I deserve to be treated with greater consideration and when I am not wanted I take my leave. (*Exit.*)

PHILAMINTE: He could not have bared his mercenary soul more clearly! The way he has behaved is thoroughly unphilosophical!

CLITANDRE: I do not pretend to be a philosopher, but I can say that I shall remain devoted to you, Madame, whatever your destiny may hold. I venture to offer you, together with my loyalty, whatever money Fate has allotted me.

PHILAMINTE: I am touched, sir, by your generous gesture and am minded to reward your amorous passion – yes, I shall bestow Henriette upon your impatient ardour –

HENRIETTE: No mother, I have changed my mind. You must allow me to oppose your wishes.

CLITANDRE: What! You oppose my happiness? And, just when I see everyone accepting my love . . .

HENRIETTE: I know that you do not have very much money Clitandre. I always wanted you for my husband in the knowledge that, as well as satisfying my own dearest wishes, marrying me meant settling your affairs. But now that our destinies have turned out to be so different, I love you enough at this fateful moment not to want to burden you with our misfortune.

CLITANDRE: Any destiny shared with you would be precious to me. Any destiny without you would be unbearable.

HENRIETTE: We always say such things in the heat of passion. Let us avoid the embarrassment of future regrets. Nothing weakens the tie that binds us more than the tedious demands of daily living, and since often as not each partner accuses the other of being the cause of the black misery that ordinarily follows such ardent love . . .

ARISTE (*to Henriette*): Is the reason we have heard you give your only motive for refusing to marry Clitandre?

HENRIETTE: Yes, otherwise you would see how my heart would jump at the prospect. I reject his hand only because I love him too much.

ARISTE: Then let yourself be bound by such loving chains. The news I brought was false! It was a ruse, a sudden stratagem which I wished to try as a way of serving your love, opening my sister's eyes and making her see how her philosopher would turn out when faced with a real test.

CHRYSALE: God be praised!

PHILAMINTE: It does my heart good to think how furious that coward who ran away will feel. He will be punished for his despicable avarice when he sees how brilliantly we shall celebrate this wedding.

CHRYSALE (*to Clitandre*): I knew all along that you'd end up marrying her.

ARMANDE (*to Philaminte*): So, you intend to sacrifice me to their happiness!

PHILAMINTE: No, it is not you who has been sacrificing to them,[19] and you can call upon philosophy to help you to look smilingly on the consummation of their love.

BÉLISE: But he'd better make good and sure that no trace of me lingers on in his heart. People, you know, often get married on impulse because they are unhappy, with the result that they spend the rest of their life regretting it.

CHRYSALE (*to the Notary*): Come sir, enter the names as I told you and draw up the contract according to my instructions.

EXPLANATORY NOTES

Such Foolish Affected Ladies

1. LA GRANGE, DU CROISY: both offended lovers are given the names of the actors who played them. Du Croisy was the stage name of Philbert Gassot (c. 1626–?), and La Grange was born Charles Varlet (1639–92). A recent recruit to the company, he remained one of its leading members until Molière's death, after which he became its administrator. He kept a detailed record of its activities between 1659 and 1685.

2. *Cyrus ... Clélie*: characters in two novels by Mademoiselle de Scudéry: *Artamène, ou le Grand Cyrus* (1649–53, 10 vols.) and *Clélie* (1654–60, 10 vols.) which defined the ethic and rules of 'precious' love.

3. *Map of Love ... heard of*: the 'Carte de Tendre' was an allegorical map which appeared in the first volume of *Clélie*. Intended as a guide to winning the female heart, it showed by which ill-advised routes lovers might reach the 'Lake of Indifference', or, by following Cathos's directions (which are towns on the River of Inclination), find their heart's content.

4. *Polixène ... Aminte*: Polixène was the heroine of a novel by Molière d'Essertines published in 1632, while Aminte (like Magdelon's page, Almanzor) was a character in *Polexandre* (1619–37), a romance by Gomberville (1600–1674).

5. *gross matter*: that is, in the pseudo-philosophical jargon Molière attributes to his *précieuses*, his soul has a regrettably high animal content.

6. *king's retirement*: the last formal act of the monarch's day. After the public 'Grand Coucher', the king was ceremonially undressed for bed in his private apartments, in the presence of a small and select company of privileged courtiers.

7. *Amilcar*: a playful, witty character in *Clélie*.

8. *Miscellany of Collected Pieces*: the *Recueil des Pièces choisies* published prose and verse by writers associated with Preciosity: Corneille, Benserade, Georges de Scudéry, Cotin, Desmarets de Saint-Sorlin and others.

9. *madrigal*: not a song as in English but a short poem on a topical subject in which the author was expected to be witty and original. Molière makes further fun of the genre in the third act of *Those Learned Ladies*.

10. *beneath my rank*: after the civil wars of the Fronde (1648–52), the political power of the aristocracy was broken and their ambitions were contained by a complex system of Court etiquette which dispensed honour and pensions to those who observed the code. It required nobles to desist from activities which did not reflect honour on their rank, such as trade or industry. Thus a gentleman

might count occasional writing as an accomplishment, but not as a vocation or, worse still, as a profession.

11. *Hôtel de Bourgogne*: the best of the Paris playhouses and Molière's principal rival. The following passage is an ironic comment on Molière's own company which played tragedy in a manner considered too simple and unstylized.

12. *Perdrigeon*: the most fashionable haberdasher of the time.

13. *Jodelet*: another character named after the actor who played him. Julien Bedeau (*c.* 1595–1660), one of the most popular *farceurs* of his day, joined the company in April 1659 from the Hôtel de Bourgogne. He took his stage-name from a farce by Scarron, *Jodelet, ou le Maître valet* (*Jodelet, or the Master Servant*) in which he had played the lead in 1645.

14. *a very pale face*: as Jodelet, Bedeau always appeared on stage with his face whitened with flour.

15. *Knights Templar*: based at Malta, they were engaged on a protracted war against the Turks in the Mediterranean. Of course, a regiment of horse on a galley is as useful as a handle on a cabbage.

16. *Arras*: Arras was taken from the besieging Spanish in 1654. A half-moon was a crescent-shaped fortification built in front of a bastion. There was, of course, no such thing as a full moon.

17. *Gravelines*: Gravelines, between Calais and Dunkirk, had been besieged twice by French troops, in 1640 and 1658.

18. *coranto*: a lively dance, originally from Italy.

Tartuffe

1. *the late troubles*: that is, the Fronde, see note 10 to *Such Foolish Affected Ladies*. Molière makes a point of showing that Orgon is foolish only in his infatuation with Tartuffe. The implication is that even men of courage and principle are not immune to the Tartuffes of this world.

2. Molière's note: 'A servant is speaking.'

3. Molière's note: 'It is a scoundrel speaking.'

4. *purity of our intentions*: while the Jansenists argued that God sees into our hearts and judges us by His own inscrutable law, the laxer Molinists and Jesuits were prepared to admit that our responsibility may be modified. If we intend no harm, then our actions may in certain circumstances be viewed as lesser sins. Tartuffe perverts the latter argument for his own shabby ends.

5. *the free-thinkers*: that is, the radical, sceptical and often atheistical philosophers who argued that the world is best understood through reason, not faith.

6. *cabals . . . before now*: as Molière, twice prevented from staging *Tartuffe* by the cabal of the Compagnie du Saint Sacrement, knew to his cost.

The Misanthrope

1. *The School for Husbands*: by Molière (1661), in which the tolerant Ariste opposes the domineering, ill-tempered Sganarelle.

2. *king's levée*: the ceremonial rising of the king, attended each morning by a select group of privileged nobility. The counterpart to the royal 'coucher', see note 6 to *Such Foolish Affected Ladies*.

3. *woman he loves*: the speech is borrowed from Lucretius, *De natura rerum*, IV. 1149–65.

4. *Marshals of France*: a court, first established in 1566, which dealt with affairs of honour as an alternative to the duel.

5. *green ribbons*: for the role of Alceste, Molière wore a waistcoat of gold and grey stripes enlivened by ribbons. He usually included green in his costume: it was the traditional colour of the buffoon.

The Doctor Despite Himself

1. *bark of a tree ... your finger*: Sganarelle muddles an old proverb which recommends that the finger should never come between the trunk and the bark, where it will surely be squeezed.

2. *Cabricias ... et casus*: the first four words, which are gibberish, are followed by oddments of church Latin and rudimentary Latin grammar. From 'Deus sanctus', the text means: 'God is holy, is this good Latin? Yes. Why? Because the adjective and the noun agree in gender, number and case'. The supposedly medical terms Sganarelle uses in the following exchanges are nearly all invented and mean nothing.

3. *full weight*: that is, the coins have not been clipped. The value of coins reflected that of the metal of which they were made. By removing slivers from the rim, criminals could pocket small amounts of gold and silver and thus devalue the king's money. The practice was punishable by death.

4. *comic business*: the 1734 edition of Molière's works gives a fuller stage direction: 'At the moment when Sganarelle holds out his arms to kiss Jacqueline, Lucas ducks underneath and pokes his head up between them. Sganarelle and Jacqueline look at Lucas and then leave the stage in opposite directions, the doctor with comic business.'

The Would-Be Gentleman

1. *theorbo*: a lute with two necks. One set of strings carried the melody and the other the lower-pitched 'diapason' or unstopped accompaniment.

2. *sea-trumpet*: not a trumpet at all but a single-stringed, medieval instrument

also known as a marine trumpet or nun's fiddle. It was tuned to the same pitch as a trumpet, whence, perhaps, its name.

3. *demonstrative logic*: by arguing from the most basic premises: part of the traditional discipline of Rhetoric.

4. *on anger*: *De Ira*, in three books, by Seneca (*c*. 4 BC–AD 65 .

5. *Barbara . . . and so forth*: mnemonics which, since the Middle Ages, had been used to help pupils memorize the nineteen forms of regular syllogisms.

6. *vortices*: a reference to the *tourbillons*, the swirls of matter moving around stars and planets, which Descartes had identified in *Le Discours de la méthode* (1637) to explain why heavenly bodies maintain their stations in space. The theory was eventually replaced by Newton's theory of gravity. Natural science was a fashionable subject in polite society.

7. *wide: A*: this description of how vowels are formed applies to French, not English, though R here is defined as trilled. The modern French R, pronounced in the back of the throat, dates from around the time of the French Revolution.

8. *five thousand and sixty livres*: at the rate of 11 livres to the louis. See Note on Money.

9. *the rib of Saint-Louis*: all humankind, according to Genesis, sprang from Adam's rib. But according to a popular expression, those who laid claim to the blue blood of the ancient aristocracy were said to be descended from that of Saint Louis (Louis IX, 1215–70).

10. *Holy Innocents*: a church with a famous cemetery in the Halles district of Paris where Molière was born.

11. *a Paladin*: a noble at the court of Charlemagne and therefore as inappropriate a title as the 'Turkish' Covielle speaks, which – though it does contain occasional Turkish words – is meaningless.

12. *ti sabir*: the language if the ceremony is no longer the vague 'Turkish' of previous scenes but a form of the pidgin used in the Mediterranean by sailors and traders from different parts of the Mediterranean basin. It is a mix of Arabic, Turkish, Maltese, French, Italian and Spanish.

13. *Anabaptist*: among the faiths named in the comic ceremony which follows are sects which grew out of the Reformation (Anabaptists, Zwinglians, Hussites and Lutherans), the Puritans of contemporary England, an assortment of 'oriental' faiths (the Christian Copts, the presumably Muslim 'Moors' and the Hindu Brahmins), and the fanciful Phronists, Moffinos and Zurinos. Though not too much should be made of this comic scene, Molière may have meant his catalogue as a comment on the unecumenical spirit of the Catholic establishment which had made life so complicated for him over *Tartuffe* and *Don Juan*.

Those Learned Ladies

1. *Vaugelas categorically outlaws*: in 1647, the grammarian Claude Favre de Vaugelas (1585–1650) had published *Remarques sur la langue française*, which ruled on niceties of the language used by 'the best part' of the Court and the most 'best' authors. It became the standard reference work of French linguistic usage in the classical age.

2. *Malherbe and Balzac*: the poet François de Malherbe (1555–1628) was considered by 1660 as the major precursor of classical taste. Guez de Balzac (1594–1654) was instrumental in shaping the refined, elegant literary prose so admired by supporters of Preciosity.

3. *epigram*: a short, eight-lined poem which concludes with a maxim, often satirical.

4. *my madrigal*: see note 9 to *Such Foolish Affected Ladies*.

5. *Attic salt*: refined, delicate (Athenian) wit.

6. *on her fever*: the sonnet 'To Mademoiselle de Longueville, now Madame de Nemours, on her fever' by the abbé Cotin (1604–82), was first published in 1659. Molière changed the title presumably because he did not wish to offend Madame de Nemours. Trissotin's epigram, which follows, is also by Cotin who, however, described it as a madrigal and intended it as an example of how such verses should not be written.

7. *tercets*: the fourteen lines of a sonnet are divided into two quatrains and two tercets.

8. *a learned reference*: Lais, famed for her beauty, lived in the fifth century BC at Corinth.

9. *what is kept apart elsewhere*: the Academy of Science, set up in 1666 by Colbert, admitted only scientists while the French Academy, founded by Cardinal Richelieu in 1635, had only literary members. Neither admitted women.

10. *Aristotle*: these exchanges make free with catchwords of science ancient and modern. Aristotle defined order as an essential characteristic of the created world. Plato interpreted creation as concrete reflections of abstract, ideal forms. Epicurus argued that all existence is determined by the atomic structures of matter. René Descartes (1596–1650) argued that nature abhors a vacuum and concluded that 'subtle matter' fills the spaces between planets which are formed by the swirls and eddies ('the vortices') of the ambient ether and have the sun as their centre. He identified comets and shooting stars as distant worlds which drop out of their station (i.e., fall), and defined magnetism as a property of the created universe.

11. *Stoics . . . wise man*: four hundred years before Christ the Greek Stoics believed that the 'wise man' pursued not wealth or passion but austere virtue. Philaminte is doctrinally on safe ground and runs no risk of falling foul of seventeenth-century theological orthodoxy: the moral philosophy of Stoicism,

though 'pagan' by definition, had long been regarded as compatible with Christian teaching.

12. *in the area of language*: the purification of the French language remained high on the agenda of Preciosity. The defenders of 'refined' speech banned archaisms, provincialisms and popular expressions, and demanded that 'crudity' be abolished in favour of 'decency': thus 'heart' would replace 'breast'. Extremists, however, went further and waged war on certain prefixes and suffixes, numerous in French, which, when detached from their stem, were vulgar, rather as in English 'titillate', say, might offend those who are expecting to be offended.

13. *ithos . . . pathos*: both terms derive from the principles of Greek rhetoric, the first dealing with manners, the second with the passions.

14. *Theocritus . . . Virgil . . . Horace*: for contemporary literary theorists, the pastoral poems of Theocritus (born *c.* 300 BC) and the *Bucolics* of Virgil (70–19 BC) were models of the genre, while Horace was master of the ode. All three authors were associated with the poet Gilles Ménage (1613–92), poet, Hellenist, lexicographer and linguistic purist who was the original of Molière's Vadius. Ménage had quarrelled with Cotin in about 1659 in circumstances which, as we shall see, Molière turns into farce.

15. *author of the Satires*: in the ninth of his *Satires* (1667–8), Nicolas Boileau (1636–1711) had consistently attacked the abbé Cotin, author of the poems attributed to Trissotin: see note 6 above. Boileau also lampooned Ménage, though less often and more indirectly.

16. *at Barbin's*: Barbin was also Molière's publisher.

17. *minas . . . Calends*: minas and talents were ancient Greek coins, while in the Roman calendar, the Ides was the thirteenth or fifteenth day in the month and the Calends was the first.

18. *Thinking matter . . . extension*: Bélise refers to Descartes's distinction between thinking and extended substances. The first give mind and spirit, and the second the physical. Bélise repeats the distinction between mind and body, form and matter made by Philaminte at the start of Act IV.

19. *sacrificed to them*: the French is unclear here and the line has been read in other ways. The 'sacrifice' may be Philaminthe's who must resign herself to not having a clever son-in-law; or the loss (in her view) may be Henriette's, for she will not marry a wit; or it may even be Clitandre's, for his wife will never be learned.